PERFECT
LIES

DOUBLEDAY

NEW YORK   LONDON   TORONTO   SYDNEY   AUCKLAND

PERFECT LIES

A CENTURY OF GREAT
GOLF STORIES

EDITED AND WITH AN
INTRODUCTION BY

WILLIAM HALLBERG

PUBLISHED BY DOUBLEDAY

A division of Bantam Doubleday Dell Publishing Group, Inc.,
666 Fifth Avenue, New York, New York 10103

DOUBLEDAY and the portrayal of an anchor
with a dolphin are trademarks of
Doubleday, a division of Bantam Doubleday
Dell Publishing Group, Inc.

Acknowledgments for permission to reprint the stories in this volume
appear on pages 365–67.

Library of Congress Cataloging-in-Publication Data

ISBN 0-385-24738-9
Copyright © 1989 by William Hallberg

DESIGNED BY • DIANE STEVENSON/SNAP·HAUS GRAPHICS

This book is dedicated to all my golf heroes:
Donald Ross
Bernard Darwin
Bobby Jones
Herbert Warren Wind
Jack Nicklaus
Arnold Palmer
Tom Watson
Ben Crenshaw
Chip Beck
. . . and of course, my dad.

ACKNOWLEDGMENTS

I would like to thank East Carolina University for providing me with a summer research grant, without which this book would have been all but impossible.

Herbert Warren Wind and Robert MacDonald also deserve my deepest thanks for their help in identifying and tracking down many of the stories collected here.

Lastly, I extend my gratitude to Richard Donovan, whose wonderful book *The Game of Golf and the Printed Word 1566–1985* was an invaluable resource.

CONTENTS

x i

CONTENTS

INTRODUCTION

Scratch your head and try to think of one, just one, golf novel that measures up to any of several dozen truly fine baseball books.

The fact is, this green sport, unlike baseball, thrives in a smaller literary arena. And well it should. After all, golf is a very personal game in which each player is hostage to his own incompetence. Sure, a golfer may strive toward conviviality as he and his comrades scour ankle-deep rough for the orphaned golf ball or wait at the tee for a sluggish foursome to clear the fairway. Even the professional may share a clubhouse beer with his fellow members of the touring circuit. But when it comes down to actually striking the ball and living with the consequences, golf provides a private metaphor. The transient exhilaration of a cleanly hit four iron, or the profound misery of a shanked wedge shot (resulting in a pitiful, squealy little embarrassment that ricochets off your CPA's garage door) is ultimately unshared. Rarely is golf a team sport, except on Saturdays when you're partnered with old Bernie or Irene for a skins game, and they never hold up their end of the bet anyway. Unless you're a Jack Nicklaus or a Nancy Lopez there are no cheering crowds to sustain you or urge you toward even mere competence. Likewise, the intricate topography of the sport, the inherent sensory beauties of its landscapes are imbibed subjectively by each golfer as he weaves his way around the course.

Without apology, the game of golf concedes the novel to writers who celebrate baseball for its undeniable poetry and larger-than-life pathos.

As its proper turf, golf claims the short story, a narrative form that allows more personal conflicts to play themselves out. Between the covers of this book you will find the very best golf short stories ever written; they span the ocean and the century. They are about love, death, disillusionment, triumph, aesthetics, sex, mathematics and even pure sport. Whatever their thematic goal, these stories have one thing in common: they are splendid examples of a genre that continues to flourish, and small portraits of a beautiful and complex sport as it comes to bear on our lives. You need not know a baffling spoon from a spike wrench to enjoy great short fiction by some of the finest writers of this century.

—*William Hallberg*
January 1989

PERFECT LIES

EVEN
THREES

·

OWEN JOHNSON

I

Ever since the historic day when a visiting clergyman
accomplished the feat of pulling a ball from the tenth
tee at an angle of two hundred and twenty-five degrees
into the river that is the rightful receptacle for the
eighth tee, the Stockbridge golf course has had seventeen out
of eighteen holes that are punctuated with water hazards. The
charming course itself lies in the flat of the sunken meadows
which the Housatonic, in the few thousand years which are
necessary for the proper preparation of a golf course, has obligingly eaten out of the high accompanying bluffs. The river,

1

which goes wriggling on its way as though convulsed with merriment, is garnished with luxurious elms and willows, which occasionally deflect to the difficult putting greens the random slices of certain notorious amateurs.

From the spectacular bluffs of the educated village of Stockbridge nothing can be imagined more charming than the panorama that the course presents on a busy day. Across the soft green stretches, diminutive caddies may be seen scampering with long buckling nets, while from the riverbanks numerous recklessly exposed legs wave in the air as the more socially presentable portions hang frantically over the swirling current. Occasionally an enthusiastic golfer, driving from the eighth or ninth tees, may be seen to start immediately in headlong pursuit of a diverted ball, the swing of the club and the intuitive leap of the legs forward forming so continuous a movement that the main purpose of the game often becomes obscured to the mere spectator. Nearer, in the numerous languid swales that nature has generously provided to protect the interests of the manufacturers, or in the rippling patches of unmown grass, that in the later hours will be populated by enthusiastic caddies, desperate groups linger in botanizing attitudes.

Every morning lawyers who are neglecting their clients, doctors who have forgotten their patients, businessmen who have sacrificed their affairs, even ministers of the gospel who have forsaken their churches gather in the noisy dressing room and listen with servile attention while some unscrubbed boy who goes around under eighty imparts a little of his miraculous knowledge.

Two hours later, for every ten that have gone out so blithely, two return crushed and despondent, denouncing and renouncing the game, once and for all, absolutely and finally, until the afternoon, when they return like thieves in the night and venture out in a desperate hope; two more come stamping back in even more offensive enthusiasm; and the remainder straggle home moody and disillusioned, reviving their sunken spirits by impossible tales of past accomplishments.

There is something about these twilight gatherings that suggests the degeneracy of a rugged race; nor is the contamination of merely local significance. There are those who lie consciously, with a certain frank, commendable, wholehearted plunge into iniquity. Such men return to their worldly callings with intellectual vigor unimpaired and a natural reaction toward the decalogue. Others of more casuistical temperament, unable all at once to throw over the traditions of a New England conscience to the exigencies of the game, do not at once burst into falsehood, but by a confusing process weaken their memories and corrupt their imaginations. They never lie of the events of the day. Rather they return to some jumbled happening of the week before and delude themselves with only a lingering qualm, until from habit they can create what is really a form of paranoia, the delusion of greatness, or the exaggerated ego. Such men, inoculated with self-deception, return to the outer world to deceive others, lower the standards of business morality, contaminate politics, and threaten the vigor of the republic.

R. N. Booverman, the treasurer, and Theobald Pickings, the unenvied secretary of an unenvied board, arrived at the first tee at precisely ten o'clock on a certain favorable morning in early August to begin the thirty-six holes which six times a week, six months of the year, they played together as sympathetic and well-matched adversaries. Their intimacy had arisen primarily from the fact that Pickings was the only man willing to listen to Booverman's restless dissertations on the malignant fates which seemed to pursue him even to the neglect of their international duties, while Booverman, in fair exchange, suffered Pickings to enlarge *ad libitum* on his theory of the rolling versus the flat putting greens.

Pickings was one of those correctly fashioned and punctilious golfers whose stance was modeled on classic lines, whose drive, though it averaged only twenty-five yards over the hundred, was always a well-oiled and graceful exhibition of the Royal St. Andrew's swing, the left sole thrown up, the eyeballs bulging with the last muscular tension, the club carried back until the whole body was contorted into the first position of the traditional hoop snake preparing to descend a hill. He used the interlocking grip, carried a bag with a spoon driver, an aluminum cleek, had three abnormal putters, and wore one chamois glove with air holes on the back. He never accomplished the course in less than eighty-five and never exceeded ninety-four, but, having aimed to set a correct example rather than to strive vulgarly for professional records, was always in a state of offensive optimism due to a complete sartorial satisfaction.

Booverman, on the contrary, had been hailed in his first years as a coming champion. With three holes eliminated, he could turn in a card distinguished for its fours and threes; but unfortunately these sad lapses inevitably occurred. As Booverman himself admitted, his appearance on the golf links was the signal for the capricious imps of chance who stir up politicians to indiscreet truths and keep the Balkan pot of discord bubbling, to forsake immediately these prime duties, and enjoy a little relaxation at his expense.

Now, for the first three years Booverman responded in a manner to delight imp and devil. When, standing thirty-four for the first six holes, he sliced into the jungle, and, after twenty minutes of frantic beating of the bush, was forced to acknowledge a lost ball and no score, he promptly sat down, tore large clutches of grass from the sod, and expressed himself to the admiring delight of the caddies, who favorably compared his flow of impulsive expletives to the choice moments of their own home life. At other times he would take an offending club firmly in his big hands and break it into four pieces, which he would drive into the ground, hurling the head itself, with a last diabolical gesture, into the Housatonic River, which, as may be repeated, wriggled its way through the course as though convulsed with merriment.

There were certain trees into which he inevitably drove, certain waggish bends of the river where, no matter how he might face, he was sure to arrive. There was a space of exactly ten inches under the clubhouse where his balls alone could disappear. He never ran down a long putt, but always hung on the rim of the cup. It was his adversary who executed phenomenal shots, approaches of eighty yards that dribbled home, sliced drives that hit a fence and bounded back to the course. Nothing of this agreeable sort had ever happened or could ever happen to him. Finally the conviction of a certain predestined damnation settled upon him. He no longer struggled; his once rollicking spirits settled into a moody despair. Nothing encouraged him or could trick him into a display of hope. If he achieved a four and two twos on the first holes, he would say vindictively:

"What's the use? I'll lose my ball on the fifth."

And when this happened, he no longer swore, but said gloomily with even a sense of satisfaction: "You can't get me excited. Didn't I know it would happen?"

Once in a while he had broken out,

"If ever my luck changes, if it comes all at once—"

But he never ended the sentence, ashamed, as it were, to have indulged in such a childish fancy. Yet, as Providence moves in a mysterious way its wonders to perform, it was just this invincible pessimism that alone could have permitted Booverman to accomplish the incredible experience that befell him.

II

Topics of engrossing mental interest are bad form on the golf links, since they leave a disturbing memory in the mind to divert it from that absolute intellectual concentration which the game demands. Therefore Pickings and Booverman, as they started toward the crowded first tee, remarked *de rigueur:*

"Good weather."

"A bit of a breeze."

"Not strong enough to affect the drives."

"The greens have baked out."

"Fast as I've seen them."

"Well, it won't help me."

"How do you know?" said Pickings politely, for the hundredth time. "Perhaps this is the day you'll get your score."

Booverman ignored the remark, laying his ball on the rack, where two predecessors were waiting, and settled beside Pickings at the foot of the elm which later, he knew, would rob him of a four on the home green.

Wessels and Pollock, literary representatives, were preparing to drive. They were converts of the summer, each sacrificing their season's output in a frantic effort to surpass the other. Pickings, the purist, did not approve of them in the least. They brought to the royal and ancient game a spirit of Bohemian irreverence and banter that offended his serious enthusiasm.

When Wessels made a convulsive stab at his ball and luckily achieved good distance, Pollock remarked behind his hand, "A good shot, damn it!"

Wessels stationed himself in a hopefully deprecatory attitude and watched Pollock build a monument of sand, balance his ball, and whistling nervously through his teeth, lunge successfully down. Whereupon, in defiance of etiquette, he swore with equal fervor, and they started off.

Pickings glanced at Booverman in a superior and critical way, but at this moment a thin dyspeptic man with undisciplined whiskers broke in serenely without waiting for the answers to the questions he propounded:

"Ideal weather, eh? Came over from Norfolk this morning; ran over at fifty miles an hour. Some going, eh? They tell me you've quite a course here; record around seventy-one, isn't it?

Good deal of water to keep out of? You gentlemen some of the cracks? Course pretty fast with all this dry weather? What do you think of the one-piece driver? My friend, Judge Weatherup. My name's Yancy—Cyrus P.''

A ponderous person who looked as though he had been pumped up for the journey gravely saluted, while his feverish companion rolled on:

"Your course's rather short, isn't it? Imagine it's rather easy for a straight driver. What's your record? Seventy-one amateur? Rather high, isn't it? Do you get many cracks around here? Caddies seem scarce. Did either of you gentlemen ever reflect how surprising it is that better scores aren't made at this game? Now, take seventy-one; that's only one under fours, and I venture to say at least six of your holes are possible twos, and all the rest, sometime or other, have been made in three. Yet you never hear of phenomenal scores, do you, like a run of luck at roulette or poker? You get my idea?"

"I believe it is your turn, sir," said Pickings, both crushing and parliamentary. "There are several waiting."

Judge Weatherup drove a perfect ball into the long grass, where successful searches averaged ten minutes, while his voluble companion, with an immense expenditure of force, foozled into the swale to the left, which was both damp and retentive.

"Shall we play through?" said Pickings with formal preciseness. He teed his ball, took exactly eight full practice swings, and drove one hundred and fifty yards as usual directly in the middle of the course.

"Well, it's straight; that's all can be said for it," he said, as he would say at the next seventeen tees.

Booverman rarely employed that slogan. That straight and narrow path was not in his religious practice. He drove a long ball, and he drove a great many that did not return in his bag. He glanced resentfully to the right, where Judge Weatherup was straddling the fence, and to the left, where Yancy was annoying the bullfrogs.

"Darn them!" he said to himself. "Of course now I'll follow suit."

But whether or not the malignant force of suggestion was neutralized by the attraction in opposition directions, his drive went straight and far, a beautiful two hundred and forty yards.

"Fine shot, Mr. Booverman," said Frank, the professional, nodding his head, "free and easy, plenty of follow-through."

"You're on your drive today," said Pickings, cheerfully.

"Sure! When I get a good drive off the first tee," said Booverman, discouraged, "I mess up all the rest. You'll see."

"Oh, come now," said Pickings, as a matter of form. He played his shot, which came methodically to the edge of the green.

Booverman took his mashy for the short running-up stroke to the pin, which seemed so near.

"I suppose I've tried this shot a thousand times," he said savagely. "Anyone else would get a three once in five times—anyone but Jonah's favorite brother."

He swung carelessly, and watched with a tolerant interest the white ball roll on to the green straight for the flag. All at once Wessels and Pollock, who were ahead, sprang into the air and began agitating their hats.

"By George! It's in!" said Pickings. "You've run it down. First hole in two! Well, what do you think of that?"

Booverman, unconvinced, approached the hole with suspicion, gingerly removing the pin. At the bottom, sure enough, lay his ball for a phenomenal two.

"That's the first bit of luck that has ever happened to me," he said furiously, "absolutely the first time in my whole career."

"I say, old man," said Pickings in remonstrance, "you're not angry about it, are you?"

"Well, I don't know whether I am or not," said Booverman

8

obstinately. In fact, he felt rather defrauded. The integrity of his record was attacked. "See here, I play thirty-six holes a day, two hundred and sixteen a week, a thousand a month, six thousand a year; ten years, sixty thousand holes; and this is the first time a bit of luck has ever happened to me—once in sixty thousand times."

Pickings drew out a handkerchief and wiped his forehead.

"It may come all at once," he said faintly.

This mild hope only infuriated Booverman. He had already teed his ball for the second hole, which was poised on a rolling hill one hundred and thirty-five yards away. It is considered rather easy as golf holes go. The only dangers are a matted wilderness of long grass in front of the tee, the certainty of landing out of bounds on the slightest slice, and of rolling down hill into a soggy substance on a pull. Also there is a tree to be hit and a sand pit to be sampled.

"Now watch my little friend the apple tree," said Booverman. "I'm going to play for it, because, if I slice, I lose my ball, and that knocks my whole game higher than a kite." He added between his teeth: "All I ask is to get around to the eighth hole before I lose my ball. I know I'll lose it there."

Due to the fact that his two on the first brought him not the slightest thrill of nervous joy, he made a perfect shot, the ball carrying the green straight and true.

"This is your day, all right," said Pickings, stepping to the tee.

"Oh, there's never been anything the matter with my irons," said Booverman darkly. "Just wait till we strike the fourth and fifth holes."

When they climbed the hill, Booverman's ball lay within three feet of the cup, which he easily putted out.

"Two down," said Pickings inaudibly. "By George! What a glorious start!"

"Once in sixty thousand times," said Booverman to himself. The third hole lay two hundred and five yards below, backed by the road and trapped by ditches, where at that moment Pollock, true to his traditions as a war correspondent, was laboring in the trenches, to the unrestrained delight of Wessels, who had passed beyond.

"Theobald," said Booverman, selecting his cleek and speaking with inspired conviction, "I will tell you exactly what is going to happen. I will smite this little homeopathic pill, and it will land just where I want it. I will probably put out for another two. Three holes in twos would probably excite any other human being on the face of this globe. It doesn't excite me. I know too well what will follow on the fourth or fifth watch."

"Straight to the pin," said Pickings in a loud whisper. "You've got a dead line on every shot today. Marvelous! When you get one of your streaks, there's certainly no use in my playing."

"Streak's the word," said Booverman, with a short, barking laugh. "Thank heaven, though, Pickings, I know it! Five years ago I'd have been shaking like a leaf. Now it only disgusts me. I've been fooled too often; I don't bite again."

In this same profoundly melancholy mood he approached his ball, which lay on the green, hole high, and put down a difficult putt, a good three yards for his third two.

Pickings, despite all his classic conservatism, was so overcome with excitement that he twice putted over the hole for a shameful five.

Booverman's face as he walked to the fourth tee was as joyless as a London fog. He placed his ball carelessly, selected his driver, and turned on the fidgety Pickings with the gloomy solemnity of a father about to indulge in corporal punishment.

"Once in sixty thousand times, Picky. Do you realize what a start like this—three twos—would mean to a professional like Frank or even an amateur that hadn't offended every busy little fate and fury in the whole hoodooing business? Why, the blooming record would be knocked into the middle of next week."

"You'll do it," said Pickings in a loud whisper. "Play carefully."

Booverman glanced down the four-hundred-yard straightaway and murmured to himself:

> *"I wonder, little ball, whither will you fly?*
> *I wonder, little ball, have I bid you good-by?*
> *Will it be 'mid the prairies in the regions to the west?*
> *Will it be in the marshes where the pollywogs nest?*
> *Oh, tell me, little ball, is it ta-ta or good-by?"*

He pronounced the last word with a settled conviction, and drove another long, straight drive. Pickings, thrilled at the possibility of another miracle, sliced badly.

"This is one of the most truly delightful holes of a picturesque course," said Booverman, taking out an approaching cleek for his second shot. "Nothing is more artistic than the tiny little patch of putting green under the shaggy branches of the willows. The receptive graveyard to the right gives a certain pathos to it, a splendid, quiet note in contrast to the feeling of the swift, hungry river to the left, which will now receive and carry from my outstretched hand this little white floater that will float away from me. No matter; I say again the fourth green is a thing of ravishing beauty."

His second shot, low and long, rolled up in the same unvarying line.

"On the green," said Pickings.

"Short," said Booverman, who found to his satisfaction that he was right by a yard.

"Take your time," said Pickings, biting his nails.

"Rats! I'll play it for a five," said Booverman.

His approach ran up on the line, caught the rim of the cup, hesitated, and passed on a couple of feet.

"A four, anyway," said Pickings with relief.

"I should have had a three," said Booverman doggedly. "Any one else would have had a three, straight on the cup. You'd have had a three, Picky; you know you would."

Pickings did not answer. He was slowly going to pieces, forgetting the invincible stoicism that is the pride of the true golfer.

"I say, take your time, old chap," he said, his voice no longer under control. "Go slow! Go slow!"

"Picky, for the first four years I played this course," said Booverman angrily, "I never got better than a six on this simple three-hundred-and-fifty-yard hole. I lost my ball five times out of seven. There is something irresistibly alluring to me in the mosquito patches to my right. I think it is the fond hope that when I lose this nice new ball I may step inadvertently on one of its hundred brothers, which I may then bring home and give decent burial."

Pickings, who felt a mad and ungolfish desire to entreat him to caution, walked away to fight down his emotion.

"Well?" he said, after the click of the club had sounded.

"Well," said Booverman without joy, "that ball is lying about two hundred and forty yards straight up the course, and by this time it has come quietly to a little cozy home in a nice, deep hoof track, just as I found it yesterday afternoon. Then I will have the exquisite pleasure of taking my niblick, and whanging it out for the loss of a stroke. That'll infuriate me, and I'll slice or pull. The best thing to do, I suppose, would be to play for a conservative six."

When, after four butchered shots, Pickings had advanced to where Booverman had driven, the ball lay in clear position just beyond the bumps and rills that ordinarily welcome a long shot. Booverman played a perfect mashy, which dropped clear on the green, and ran down a moderate putt for a three.

They then crossed the road and arrived by a planked walk at a dirt mound in the midst of a swamp. Before them the oozy marsh lay stagnant ahead and then sloped to the right in the figure of a boomerang, making for those who fancied a slice a delightful little carry of one hundred and fifty yards. To the left was a procession of trees, while beyond, on the course, for those who drove a long ball, a giant willow had fallen the year before in order to add a new perplexity and foster the enthusiasm for luxury that was beginning among the caddies.

"I have a feeling," said Booverman, as though puzzled but not duped by what had happened—"I have a strange feeling that I'm not going to get into trouble here. That would be too obvious. It's at the seventh or eighth holes that something is lurking around for me. Well, I won't waste time."

He slapped down his ball, took a full swing, and carried the far-off bank with a low, shooting drive that continued bounding on.

"That ought to roll forever," said Pickings, red with excitement.

"The course is fast—dry as a rock," said Booverman deprecatingly.

Pickings put three balls precisely into the bubbling water, and drew alongside on his eighth shot. Booverman's drive had skimmed over the dried plain for a fair two hundred and seventy-five yards. His second shot, a full brassy, rolled directly on the green.

"If he makes a four here," said Pickings to himself, "he'll be playing five under four—no, by thunder! Seven under four!" Suddenly he stopped, overwhelmed. "Why, he's actually around threes—two under three now. Heavens! if he ever suspects it, he'll go into a thousand pieces."

As a result, he missed his own ball completely, and then topped it for a bare fifty yards.

"I've never seen you play so badly," said Booverman in a grumbling tone. "You'll end up by throwing me off."

When they arrived at the green, Booverman's ball lay about thirty feet from the flag.

1 3

"It's a four, a sure four," said Pickings under his breath.
Suddenly Booverman burst into an exclamation,

"Picky, come here. Look—look at that!"

The tone was furious. Pickings approached.

"Do you see that?" said Booverman, pointing to a freshly laid circle of sod ten inches from his ball. "That, my boy, was where the cup was yesterday. If they hadn't moved the flag two hours ago, I'd have had a three. Now, what do you think of that for rotten luck?"

"Lay it dead," said Pickings anxiously, shaking his head sympathetically. "The green's a bit fast."

The putt ran slowly up to the hole, and stopped four inches short.

"By heavens! Why didn't I putt over it!" said Booverman, brandishing his putter. "A thirty-foot putt that stops an inch short—did you ever see anything like it? By everything that's just and fair I should have had a three. You'd have had it, Picky. Lord! If I only could putt!"

"One under three," said Pickings to his fluttering inner self. "He can't realize it. If I can only keep his mind off the score!"

The seventh tee is reached by a carefully planned, fatiguing flight of steps to the top of a bluff, where three churches at the back beckon so many recording angels to swell the purgatory lists. As you advance to the abrupt edge, everything is spread before you; nothing is concealed. In the first plane, the entangling branches of a score of apple-trees are ready to trap a topped ball and bury it under impossible piles of dry leaves. Beyond, the wired tennis courts give forth a musical, tinny note when attacked. In the middle distance a glorious sycamore draws you to the left, and a file of elms beckon the sliced way to a marsh, a wilderness of grass and an overgrown gully whence no balls return. In front, one hundred and twenty yards away, is a formidable bunker, running up to which is a tract of long grass, which two or three times a year is barbered by charitable enterprise. The seventh hole itself lies two hundred and sixty yards away in a hollow guarded by a sunken ditch, a sure three or—a sure six.

Booverman was still too indignant at the trick fate had played him on the last green to yield to any other emotion. He forgot that a dozen good scores had ended abruptly in the swale to the right. He was only irritated. He plumped down his ball, dug his toes in the ground, and sent off another long, satisfactory drive, which added more fuel to his anger.

"Anyone else would have had a three on the sixth," he muttered as he left the tee. "It's too ridiculous."

He had a short approach and an easy putt, plucked his ball from the cup, and said in an injured tone:

"Picky, I feel bad about that sixth hole, and the fourth, too. I've lost a stroke on each of them. I'm playing two strokes more than I ought to be. Hang it all! That sixth wasn't right! You told me the green was fast."

"I'm sorry," said Pickings, feeling his fingers grow cold and clammy on the grip.

The eighth hole has many easy opportunities. It is five hundred and twenty yards long, and things may happen at every stroke. You may begin in front of the tee by burying your ball in the waving grass, which is always permitted a sort of poetical license. There are the traps to the seventh hole to be crossed, and to the right the paralleling river can be reached by a short stab or a long curling slice, which the prevailing wind obligingly assists to a splashing descent.

"And now we have come to the eighth hole," said Booverman, raising his hat in profound salutation. "Whenever I arrive here with a good score I take from eight to eighteen, I lose one to three balls. On the contrary, when I have an average of six, I always get a five and often a four. How this hole has changed my entire life!" He raised his ball and addressed it tenderly: "And now, little ball, we must part, you and I. It seems a shame; you're the nicest little ball I ever have known. You've stuck to me an awful long while. It's a shame."

He teed up, and drove his best drive, and followed it with a brassy that laid him twenty yards off the green, where a good approach brought the desired four.

"Even threes," said Pickings to himself, as though he had seen a ghost. Now he was only a golfer of one generation; there was nothing in his inheritance to steady him in such a crisis. He began slowly to disintegrate morally, to revert to type. He contained himself until Booverman had driven free of the river, which flanks the entire green passage to the ninth hole, and then barely controlling the impulse to catch Booverman by the knees and implore him to discretion, he burst out:

"I say, dear boy, do you know what your score is?"

"Something well under four," said Booverman, scratching his head.

"Under four, nothing; even threes!"

"What?"

"Even threes."

They stopped, and tabulated the holes.

"So it is," said Booverman, amazed. "What an infernal pity!"

"Pity?"

"Yes, pity. If only someone else could play it out!"

He studied the hundred and fifty yards that were needed to reach the green that was set in the crescent of surrounding trees, changed his brassy for his cleek, and his cleek for his midiron.

"I wish you hadn't told me," he said nervously.

Pickings on the instant comprehended his blunder. For the first time Booverman's shot went wide of the mark, straight into the trees that bordered the river to the left.

"I'm sorry," said Pickings with a feeble groan.

"My dear Picky, it had to come," said Booverman, with a shrug of his shoulders. "The ball is now lost, and all the score

1 6

goes into the air, the most miraculous score anyone ever heard of is nothing but a crushed egg!"

"It may have bounded back on the course," said Pickings desperately.

"No no, Picky; not that. In all the sixty thousand times I have hit trees, barns, car tracks, caddies, fences—"

"There it is!" cried Pickings with a shout of joy.

Fair on the course at the edge of the green itself lay the ball, which soon was sunk for a four. Pickings felt a strange, unaccountable desire to leap upon Booverman like a fluffy, enthusiastic dog; but he fought it back with the new sense of responsibility that came to him. So he said artfully:

"By George! Old man, if you hadn't missed on the fourth or the sixth, you'd have done even threes!"

"You know what I ought to do now—I ought to stop," said Booverman in profound despair—"quit golf and never lift another club. It's a crime to go on; it's a crime to spoil such a record. Twenty-eight for nine holes, only forty-two needed for the next nine to break the record, and I have done it in thirty-three—and in fifty-three! I ought not to try; it's wrong."

He teed his ball for the two-hundred-yard flight to the easy tenth, and took his cleek.

"I know just what'll happen now; I know it well."

But this time there was no varying in the flight; the drive went true to the green, straight on the flag, where a good but not difficult putt brought a two.

"Even threes again," said Pickings, but to himself. "It can't go on. It must turn."

"Now, Pickings, this is going to stop," said Booverman angrily. "I'm not going to make a fool of myself. I'm going right up to the tee, and I'm going to drive my ball right smack into the woods and end it. And I don't care."

"What!"

"No, I don't care. Here goes."

Again his drive continued true, the mashy pitch for the second was accurate, and his putt, after circling the rim of the cup, went down for a three.

The twelfth hole is another dip into the long grass that might serve as an elephant's bed, and then across the Housatonic River, a carry of one hundred and twenty yards to the green at the foot of an intruding tree.

"Oh, I suppose I'll make another three here, too," said Booverman moodily. "That'll only make it worse."

He drove with his midiron high in the air and full on the flag.

"I'll play my putt carefully for a three," he said, nodding his head. Instead, it ran straight and down for a two.

He walked silently to the dreaded thirteenth tee, which, with the returning fourteenth, forms the malignant Scylla and Charybdis of the course. There is nothing to describe the thirteenth hole. It is not really a golf hole; it is a long, narrow breathing spot, squeezed by the railroad tracks on one side and by the river on the other. Resolute and fearless golfers often cut them out entirely, nor are ashamed to acknowledge their terror. As you stand at the thirteenth tee, everything is blurred to the eye. Nearby are rushes and water, woods to the left and right; the river and the railroad and the dry land a hundred yards away look tiny and distant, like a rock amid floods.

A long drive that varies a degree is doomed to go out of bounds or to take the penalty of the river.

"Don't risk it. Take an iron—play it carefully," said Pickings in a voice that sounded to his own ears unrecognizable.

Booverman followed his advice and landed by the fence to the left, almost off the fair. A midiron for his second put him in position for another four, and again brought his score to even threes.

When the daring golfer has passed quaking up the narrow way and still survives, he immediately falls a victim to the fourteenth, which is a bend hole, with all the agonies of the preceding thirteenth, augmented by a second shot over a long, mushy pond. If you play a careful iron to keep from the railroad, now on the right, or to dodge the river on your left, you are forced to approach the edge of the swamp with a cautious fifty-yard-running-up stroke before facing the terrors of the carry. A drive with a wooden club is almost sure to carry into the swamp, and only a careful cleek shot is safe.

"I wish I were playing this for the first time," said Booverman, blackly. "I wish I could forget—rid myself of memories. I have seen class A amateurs take twelve, and professionals eight. This is the end of all things, Picky, the saddest spot on earth. I won't waste time. Here goes."

To Pickings's horror, the drive began slowly to slice out of bounds, toward the railroad tracks.

"I knew it," said Booverman calmly, "and the next will go there, too; then I'll put one in the river, two in the swamp, slice into—"

All at once he stopped, thunderstruck. The ball, hitting tie or rail, bounded high in the air, forward, back upon the course, lying in perfect position.

Pickings said something in a purely reverent spirit.

"Twice in sixty thousand times," said Booverman, unrelenting. "That only evens up the sixth hole. Twice in sixty thousand times!"

From where the ball lay an easy brassy brought it near enough to the green to negotiate another four. Pickings, trembling like a toy dog in zero weather, reached the green in ten strokes, and took three more putts.

The fifteenth, a short pitch over the river, eighty yards to a slanting green entirely surrounded by more long grass, which gave it the appearance of a chin spot on a full face of whiskers, was Booverman's favorite hole. While Pickings held his eyes to the ground and tried to breathe in regular breaths, Booverman placed his ball, drove with the requisite backspin, and landed dead to the hole. Another two resulted.

"Even threes—fifteen holes in even threes," said Pickings to himself, his head beginning to throb. He wanted to sit down and take his temples in his hands, but for the sake of history he struggled on.

"Damn it!" said Booverman all at once.

"What's the matter?" said Pickings, observing his face black with fury.

"Do you realize, Pickings, what it means to me to have lost those two strokes on the fourth and sixth greens, and through no fault of mine, either? Even threes for the whole course— that's what I could do if I had those two strokes—the greatest thing that's ever been seen on a golf course. It may be a hundred years before any human being on the face of this earth will get such a chance. And to think I might have done it with a little luck!"

Pickings felt his heart begin to pump, but he was able to say with some degree of calm:

"You may get a three here."

"Never. Four, three and four is what I'll end."

"Well, good heavens! What do you want?"

"There's no joy in it, though," said Booverman gloomily. "If I had those two strokes back, I'd go down in history, I'd be immortal. And you, too, Picky, because you went around with me. The fourth hole was bad enough, but the sixth was heart-breaking."

His drive cleared another swamp and rolled well down the farther plateau. A long cleek laid his ball off the green, a good approach stopped a little short of the hole, and the putt went down.

"Well, that ends it," said Booverman, gloomily. "I've got to make a two or three to do it. The two is quite possible; the three absurd."

The seventeenth hole returns to the swamp that enlivens the sixth. It is a full cleek, with about six mental hazards distributed in Indian ambush, and in five of them a ball may lie until the day of judgment before rising again.

20

Pickings turned his back, unable to endure the agony of watching. The click of the club was sharp and true. He turned to see the ball in full flight arrive unerringly hole high on the green.

"A chance for a two," he said under his breath. He sent two balls into the lost land to the left and one into the rough to the right.

"Never mind me," he said, slashing away in reckless fashion.

Booverman, with a little care, studied the ten-foot route to the hole and putted down.

"Even threes!" said Pickings, leaning against a tree.

"Blast that sixth hole!" said Booverman, exploding. "Think of what it might be, Picky—what it ought to be!"

Pickings retired hurriedly before the shaking approach of Booverman's frantic club. Incapable of speech, he waved him feebly to drive. He began incredulously to count up again, as though doubting his senses.

"One under three, even threes, one over, even, one under—"

"What the deuce are you doing?" said Booverman angrily. "Trying to throw me off?"

"I didn't say anything," said Pickings.

"You didn't—muttering to yourself."

"I must make him angry, keep his mind off the score," said Pickings feebly to himself. He added aloud, "Stop kicking about your old sixth hole! You've had the darndest luck I ever saw, and yet you grumble."

Booverman swore under his breath, hastily approached his ball, drove perfectly, and turned in a rage.

"Luck?" he cried furiously. "Pickings, I've a mind to wring your neck. Every shot I've played has been dead on the pin, now, hasn't it?"

"How about the ninth hole—hitting a tree?"

"Whose fault was that? You had no right to tell me my score, and, besides, I only got an ordinary four there, anyway."

"How about the railroad track?"

"One shot out of bounds. Yes, I'll admit that. That evens up for the fourth."

"How about your first hole in two?"

"Perfectly played; no fluke about it at all—once in sixty thousand times. Well, any more sneers? Anything else to criticize?"

"Let it go at that."

Booverman, in this heckled mood, turned irritably to his ball, played a long midiron, just cleared the crescent bank of the last swale, and ran up on the green.

"Damn that sixth hole!" said Booverman, flinging down his club and glaring at Pickings. "One stroke back, and I could have done it."

Pickings tried to address his ball, but the moment he swung his club his legs began to tremble. He shook his head, took a long breath, and picked up his ball.

They approached the green on a drunken run in the wild hope that a short putt was possible. Unfortunately the ball lay thirty feet away, and the path to the hole was bumpy and riddled with worm casts. Still, there was a chance, desperate as it was.

Pickings let his bag slip to the ground and sat down, covering his eyes while Booverman with his putter tried to brush away the ridges.

"Stand up!"

Pickings rose convulsively.

"For heaven's sake, Picky, stand up! Try to be a man!" said Booverman hoarsely. "Do you think I've any nerve when I see you with chills and fever? Brace up!"

"All right."

Booverman sighted the hole, and then took his stance; but the cleek in his hand shook like an aspen. He straightened up and walked away.

"Picky," he said, mopping his face, "I can't do it. I can't putt it."

"You must."

"I've got buck fever. I'll never be able to putt it—never."

At the last, no longer calmed by an invincible pessimism, Booverman had gone to pieces. He stood shaking from head to foot.

"Look at that," he said, extending a fluttering hand. "I can't do it; I can never do it."

"Old fellow, you must," said Pickings. "You've got to. Bring yourself together. Here!"

He slapped him on the back, pinched his arms, and chafed his fingers. Then he led him back to the ball, braced him into position, and put the putter in his hands.

"Buck fever," said Booverman in a whisper. "Can't see a thing."

Pickings, holding the flag in the cup, said savagely:

"Shoot!"

The ball advanced in a zigzag path, running from worm cast to worm cast, wobbling and rocking, and at the last, as though preordained, fell plump into the cup!

At the same moment, Pickings and Booverman, as though carried off by the same cannonball, flattened on the green.

III

Five minutes later, wild-eyed and hilarious, they descended on the clubhouse with the miraculous news. For an hour the assembled golfers roared with laughter as the two stormed, expostulated, and swore to the truth of the tale.

They journeyed from house to house in a vain attempt to find some convert to their claim. For a day they passed as consummate comedians, and the more they yielded to their rage, the more consummate was their art declared. Then a change took place. From laughing the educated town of Stockbridge turned to resentment, then to irritation, and finally to suspicion. Booverman and Pickings began to lose caste, to be regarded as unbalanced, if not positively dangerous. Unknown to them, a committee carefully examined the books of the club. At the next election another treasurer and another secretary were elected.

Since then, month in and month out, day after day, in patient hope, the two discredited members of the educated community of Stockbridge may be seen, *accompanied by caddies,* toiling around the links in a desperate belief that the miracle that would restore them to standing may be repeated. Each time as they arrive nervously at the first tee and prepare to swing, something between a chuckle and a grin runs through the assemblage, while the left eyes contract waggishly, and a murmuring may be heard:

"Even threes."

The Stockbridge golf links is a course of ravishing beauty and the Housatonic River, as has been said, goes wriggling around it as though convulsed with merriment.

THE MAN
WHO QUIT

·

CHARLES VAN LOAN

I

Mr. Ingram Tecumseh Parkes squinted along the line of his short putt, breathed hard through his prominent and highly decorative nose, concentrated his mighty intellect upon the task before him, and tapped the small white ball ever so lightly. It rolled toward the cup, wavered from the line, returned to it again, seemed about to stop short of its destination, hovered for one breathless instant on the very lip, and at last fell into the hole.

Mr. Parkes, who had been hopping up and down on one leg, urging the ball forward with inarticulate commands and violent contortions of his body, and behaving generally in the manner of a baseball fan or a financially interested spectator at a horse race, suddenly relaxed with a deep grunt of relief. He glanced at his opponent—a tall, solemn-looking gentleman—who was regarding Mr. Parkes with an unblinking stare in which disgust, chagrin and fathomless melancholy were mingled.

"Well, that'll be about all for you, Mister Good Player!" announced Parkes with rather more gusto than is considered tactful at such a time. "Yes; that cooks your goose, I guess! Three down and two to go, and I licked you"—here his voice broke and became shrill with triumph. "I licked you on an even game! An even game—d'you get that, Bob? Didn't have to use my handicap at all! Ho ho! Licked a six-handicap man on an even game! That's pretty good shooting, I guess! You didn't think I had it in me, did you?"

The other man did not reply, but continued to stare moodily at Mr. Parkes. He did not even seem to be listening. After a time the victor became aware of a certain tenseness in the situation. His stream of self-congratulation checked to a thin trickle and at last ran dry. There was a short, painful silence.

"I don't want to rub it in, or anything," said Parkes apologetically, "but I've got a right to swell up a little. You'll admit that. I didn't think I had a chance when we started, and I never trimmed a six-handicap man before—"

"Oh, that's all right!" said the other with the nervous gesture of one who brushes away an unpleasant subject. "Holler your fat head off—I don't care. Give yourself a *loud* cheer while you're at it. I'm not paying any attention to you."

Mr. Parkes was not exactly pleased with the permission thus handsomely granted.

"No need for you to get sore about it" was the sulky comment.

The vanquished golfer cackled long and loud, but there was a bitter undertone in his mirth.

"Sore? Who, me? Just because a lopsided, left-handed freak like you handed me a licking? Where do you get that stuff?"

"Well," said Mr. Parkes, still aggrieved, "if you're not sore you'd better haul in the signs. Your lower lip is sticking out a foot and you look as if you'd lost your last friend."

"I've lost every shot in my bag" was the solemn reply. "I've lost my game. You don't know what that means, because you've never had any game to lose. It's awful—awful!"

"Forget it!" advised Parkes. "Everybody has a bad day once in a while."

"You don't understand," persisted the other earnestly. "A month ago I was breaking eighties as regular as clockwork, and every club I had was working fine. Then, all at once, something went wrong—my shots left me. I couldn't drive any more; couldn't keep my irons on the course—couldn't do anything. I kept plugging away, thinking my game would come back to me, hoping every shot I made that there would be some improvement; but I'm getting worse instead of better! Nobody knows any more about the theory of golf than I do, but I can't seem to make myself do the right thing at the right time. I've changed my stance; I've changed my grip; I've changed my swing; I've never tried harder in my life—and look at me! I can't even give an eighteen-handicap man a battle!"

"Forget it!" repeated Parkes. "The trouble with you is that you worry too much about your golf. It isn't a business, you poor fish! It's a sport—a recreation. I get off my game every once in a while, but I never worry. It always comes back to me. Last Sunday I was rotten; today—"

"Today you shot three sevens and a whole flock of sixes! Bah! I suppose you call that good—eh?"

"Never you mind!" barked the indignant Mr. Parkes. "Never you mind! Those sevens and sixes were plenty good enough to lick you! Come on, take a reef in your underlip and we'll play the last two holes. The match is over, so you won't have that to worry about."

"You don't get me at all," protested the loser. "Not being a golfer yourself, you can't understand a golfer's feelings. It's not being beaten that troubles me. It's knowing just how to make a shot and then falling down on the execution—that's what breaks my heart! If ever you get so good that you can shoot a seventy-eight on this course, and your game leaves you over-night—steps right out from under you and leaves you flat— then you'll know how I feel."

"There you go!" complained Parkes. "Knocking my game again! I'm a bad player—oh, a rotten player! I admit it; but I can lick you today. And just to prove it I'll bet you a ball a hole from here in—no handicap—not even a bisque. What say?"

"Got you!" was the grim response. "Maybe if I hit one of my old-time tee shots again it'll put some heart in me. Shoot!"

Twenty minutes later the two men walked across the broad lawn toward the clubhouse. Mr. Ingram Tecumseh Parkes was in a hilarious mood. He grinned from ear to ear and illustrated an animated discourse with sweeping gestures. His late opponent shuffled slowly along beside him, kicking the inoffending daisies out of his way. His shoulders sagged listlessly, his hands hung open at his sides, and his eyes were fixed on the ground. Utter dejection was written in every line and angle of his drooping form. When he entered the lounging room he threw himself heavily into the nearest chair and remained motionless, staring out of the window but seeing nothing.

"What's the matter, Bob? You sick?" The query was twice repeated before the stricken man lifted his head slightly and turned his lackluster eyes upon a group of friends seated at a table close at hand.

"Eh? What's that? . . . Yes; I'm sick. Sick and disgusted with this double-dash-blanked game."

Now there comes to every experienced golfer a time when from a full heart he curses the Royal and Ancient Pastime. Mr. Robert Coyne's friends were experienced golfers; consequently his statement was received with calmness—not to say a certain amount of levity.

"We've all been there!" chuckled one of the listeners.

"Many's the time!" supplemented another.

"Last week," admitted a third, "I broke a driver over a tee box. I'd been slicing with it for a month, so I smashed the damned shaft. Did me a lot of good. Of course, Bob, you're a quiet, even-tempered individual, and you can't understand what a relief it is to break a club that has been annoying you. Try it sometime."

"Humph!" grunted Mr. Coyne. "I'd have to break 'em all!"

"Maybe you don't drink enough," hazarded another.

"Cheer up!" said the first speaker. "You'll be all right this afternoon."

The afflicted one lifted his head again and gazed mournfully at his friends.

"No," said he. "I won't be all right this afternoon. I'll be all wrong. I haven't hit a single decent shot in three weeks—not one. I—I don't know what's the matter with me. I'm sick of it, I tell you."

"Yep, he's sick," chirped the cheerful Mr. Parkes, coming in like an April zephyr. "He's sick, and I made him sicker. I'm a rotten-bad golfer—ask Bob if I ain't. I'm left-handed; I stand too close to my ball; I hook every tee shot; I top my irons; I can't hole a ten-foot putt in a washtub; but, even so, I handed this six man a fine trimming this morning. Hung it all over him like a blanket. Beat him three and two without any handicap. Licked him on an even game; but I couldn't make him like it. What do you think of that, eh?"

"How about it, Bob?" asked one of the listeners. "Is this a true bill?" Mr. Coyne groaned and continued to stare out of the window.

"Oh, he won't deny it!" grinned Parkes. "I'm giving it to you straight. Then, at number seventeen I offered to bet him a ball a hole, just to put some life into him and stir up his—er—

cupidity. I guess that's the word. No handicap, you understand. Not even a bisque. What did he do? Why, he speared a nice juicy nine on seventeen; and he picked up his ball on eighteen, after slicing one square into the middle of Hell's Half Acre. Yes, he's sick all right enough!"

"He has cause—if you beat him," said one of the older members.

"I wish I could win from a *well* man once in a while," complained Parkes. "Everytime I lick somebody I find I've been picking on an invalid."

"Oh, shut up and let Bob alone!"

"Yes, quit riding him."

"Don't rub it in!"

Mr. Coyne mumbled something to the effect that talk never bothered him, and the general conversation languished until the devil himself prompted one of the veteran golfers to offer advice:

"I'll tell you what's wrong with you, Bob. You're overgolfed. You've been playing too much lately."

"You've gone stale," said another.

"Nonsense!" argued a third. "You don't go stale at golf; you simply get off your game. Now what Bob ought to do is to take one club and a dozen balls and stay with that club until he gets his shots back."

"That's no good," said a fourth. "If his wood has gone bad on him he ought to leave his driver in his bag and use an iron off the tee. Chick Evans does that."

"An iron off the tee," said the veteran, "is a confession of weakness."

"Bob, why don't you get the 'pro' to give you a lesson or two? He might be able to straighten you out."

"Oh, what does a professional know about the theory of golf? All he can do is to tell you to watch him and do the way he does. Now what Bob needs—"

Every man who plays golf, no matter how badly, feels himself competent to offer advice. For a long ten minutes the air was heavy with well-meant suggestions. Coming at the wrong time, nothing is more galling than sympathetic counsel. Bob Coyne, six-handicap man and expert in the theory of golf, hunched his shoulders and endured it all without comment or protest. Somewhere in his head an idea was taking definite shape. Slowly but surely he was being urged to the point where decision merges into action.

"I tell you," said the veteran with the calm insistence of age, "Bob ought to take a layoff. He ought to forget golf for a while."

Coyne rose and moved toward the door. As his hand touched the knob the irrepressible Parkes hurled the last straw athwart a heavy burden.

"If ever I get so that I can't enjoy this game any more," said he, "I hope I'll have strength of character enough to quit playing it."

"Oh, you do, do you?" demanded Coyne with the cold rage of a quiet man, goaded beyond the limit of his endurance. "Well, don't flatter yourself. You haven't—and you won't!"

The door closed behind this rather cryptic remark, and the listeners looked at each other and shook their heads.

"Never knew Bob to act like this before," said one.

"Anything can happen when a man's game is in a slump," said the veteran. "Take a steady, brainy player—a first-class golfer; let him lose his shots for a week and there's no telling what he'll do. Nothing to it—this is the most interesting and the most exasperating outdoor sport in the world.

"Just when you think you've learned all there is to learn about it—bang! And there you are, flat!"

"He's been wolfing at me all morning," said Parkes. "Kind of silly to let a game get on your nerves, eh?"

"You'll never know how a real golfer feels when his shots go bad on him," was the consoling response. "There he goes with his bag of clubs. Practice won't help him any. What he needs is a layoff."

"He's headed for the caddie shed," said Parkes. "I'd hate to carry his bag this afternoon. Be afraid he'd bite me, or something. . . . Say, have you fellows heard about the two Scotchmen, playing in the finals for a cup? It seems that MacNabb lost his ball on the last hole, and MacGregor was helping him look for it—"

"I always did like that yarn," interrupted the veteran. "It's just as good now as it was twenty years ago. Shoot!"

A dozen caddies were resting in the shed, and as they rested they listened to the lively comment of the dean of the bag-carrying profession, a sixteen-year-old golfing Solomon who answered to the name of Butch:

"And you oughta seen him at the finish—all he needed was an undertaker! You know how good he used to be. Straight down the middle all the time. The poor sucker has blowed every shot in his bag—darned if it wasn't pitiful to watch him. He ain't even got his chip shot left. And on the last hole—"

"S-s-s-t!" whispered a youngster, glancing in the direction of the clubhouse. "Here he comes now!"

Because Mr. Coyne's game had been the subject of full and free discussion, and because they did not wish him to know it, every trace of expression vanished instantly from the twelve youthful faces. The first thing a good caddie learns is repression. Twelve wooden countenances turned to greet the visitor. His presence in the caddie shed was unusual, but even this fact failed to kindle the light of interest in the eye of the youngest boy. Coyne gave them small time to wonder what brought him into their midst.

"Butch," said he, speaking briskly and with an air of forced cheerfulness, "if you had a chance to pick a club out of this bag, which one would you take?"

"If I had a *what?*" asked Butch, pop-eyed with amazement.

"Which one of these clubs do you like the best?"

"Why, the light midiron, sir," answered the boy without an instant's hesitation. "The light midiron, sure!"

Mr. Coyne drew the club from the bag.

"It's yours," said he briefly.

"Mine!" ejaculated Butch. "You—you ain't *giving* it to me, are you?" Coyne nodded. "But—but what's the idea? You can't get along without that iron, sir. You use it more than any other club in your bag!"

"Take it if you want it, Butch. I'm going to quit playing golf."

"Yes, you are!" exclaimed the caddie, availing himself of one of the privileges of long acquaintance. "Nobody ever quits unless they get so old they can't walk!"

"Very well," said Coyne. "If you don't want this club, maybe some of these other boys—"

"Not a chance!" cried Butch, seizing the midiron. "I didn't think you meant it at first. I—"

"Now then, Frenchy," said Coyne, "which club will you have?"

"This is on the square, is it?" demanded Frenchy suspiciously. "This ain't Injun givin'? Because—me, I had my eye on that brassy for some time now. Weighted just right. Got a swell shaft in it. . . . Thank you, mister! Gee! What do you think of that—hey? Some club!"

At this point the mad philanthropist was mobbed by a group of eager youngsters, each one clamoring to share in his reckless generosity. So far as the boys knew, the situation was without parallel in golfing history; but this was a phase of the matter that could come up later for discussion. The main thing was to get one of those clubs while the getting was good.

"Please, can I have that driver?"

"Aw, mister, you know me!"

"The mashie would be my pick!"

"Who ast *you* to pick anything, dago? You ain't got an old

33

brass putter there, have you, sir? All my life I been wantin' a brass putter.''

"Gimme the one that's left over?" "Quitcha shovin', there! That's a mighty fine cleek. Wish I had it!"

In less time than it takes to tell it the bag was empty. The entire collection of golfing instruments, representing the careful and discriminating accumulation of years, passed into new hands. Everybody knows that no two golf clubs are exactly alike, and that a favorite, once lost or broken, can never be replaced. A perfect club possesses something more than proper weight and balance; it has personality and is, therefore, not to be picked up every day in the week. The driver, the spoon, the cleek, the heavy midiron, the jigger, the mashie, the scarred old niblick, the two putters—everything was swept away in one wild spasm of renunciation; and if it hurt Coyne to part with these old friends he bore the pain like a Spartan. "Well, I guess that'll be all," said he at length.

"Mr. Coyne," said Butch, who had been practicing imaginary approach shots with the light midiron, "you wouldn't care if I had about an inch taken off this shaft, would you? It's a little too long for me."

"Cut a foot off it if you like."

"I just wanted to know," said Butch apologetically. "Lots of people say they're going to quit, but—"

"It isn't a case of going to quit with me," said Coyne. "I *have* quit! You can make kindling wood out of that shaft if you like."

Then, with the empty bag under his arm, and his bridges aflame behind him, he marched back to the clubhouse, his chin a bit higher in the air than was absolutely necessary.

Later his voice was heard in the shower room, loud and clear above the sound of running water. It suited him to sing and the ditty of his choice was a cheerful one; but the rollicking words failed to carry conviction. An expert listener might have detected a tone smacking strongly of defiance and suspected that Mr. Coyne was singing to keep up his courage.

When next seen he was clothed, presumably in his right mind, and rummaging deep in his locker. On the floor was a pile of miscellaneous garments—underwear, sweaters, shirts, jackets, knickerbockers and stockings. To his assistance came Jasper, for twenty years a fixture in the locker room and as much a part of the club as the sun porch or the front door.

"Gettin' yo' laundry out, suh? Lemme give you a hand."

Now Jasper was what is known as a character; and, moreover, he was a privileged one. He was on intimate terms with every member of the country club and entitled to speak his mind at all times. He had made a close study of the male golfing animal in all his varying moods; he knew when to sympathize with a loser, when to congratulate a winner, and when to remain silent. Jasper was that rare thing known as the perfect locker room servant.

"This isn't laundry," explained Coyne. "I'm just cleaning house—that's all. . . . Think you can use these rubber-soled golf shoes?"

"Misteh Coyne, suh," said Jasper, "them shoes is as good as new. Whut you want to give 'em away faw?"

"Because I won't be wearing 'em any more."

"H-m-m! Too small, maybe?"

"No; they fit all right. Fact of the matter is, Jasper, I'm sick of this game and I'm going to quit it."

Jasper's eyes oscillated rapidly.

"Aw, no, Misteh Coyne!" said he in the tone one uses when soothing a peevish child. "You jus' *think* you goin' to quit— tha's all!"

"You never heard me say I was going to quit before, did you?" demanded Coyne.

"No, suh. No."

"Well, when I say I'm going to quit, you can bet I mean it!" Jasper reflected on this statement.

"Yes, suh," said he gently. "Betteh let me put them things back, Misteh Coyne. They in the way here."

"What's the use of putting 'em back in the locker? They're no good to me. Make a bundle of 'em and give 'em to the poor."

"Mph! Po' folks ain't wearin' them shawt pants much—not this season, nohow!"

"I don't care what you do with 'em! Throw 'em away—burn 'em up—pitch 'em out. I don't care!"

"Yes, suh. All right, suh. Jus' as you say." Jasper rolled the heap into a bundle and began tying it with the sleeves of a shirt. "I'll look afteh 'em, suh."

"Never mind looking after 'em. Get rid of the stuff. I'm through, I tell you—done—finished—quit!"

"Yes, suh. I heard you the firs' time you said it."

The Negro was on his knees fumbling with the knot. Something in his tone irritated Coyne—caused him to feel that he was not being taken seriously.

"I suppose a lot of members quit—eh?" said he.

"Yes, suh," replied Jasper with a flash of ivory. "Some of 'em quits oncet a month, reg'leh."

"But you never heard of a case where a player gave all his clubs away, did you?" demanded Coyne.

"Some of 'em *breaks* clubs," said Jasper; "but they always gits new shafts put in. Some of 'em th'ow 'em in the lake; but they fish 'em out ag'in. But—give 'em away? No, suh! They don' neveh do that."

"Well," said Coyne, "when I make up my mind to do a thing I do it right. I've given away every club I owned."

Jasper lifted his head and stared upward, mouth open and eyelids fluttering rapidly.

"You—you given yo' clubs away!" he ejaculated. "Who'd you give 'em to, suh?"

"Oh, to the caddies," was the airy response. "Made a sort of general distribution. One club to each kid."

"Misteh Coyne," said Jasper earnestly, "tha's foolishness—jus' plain foolishness. S'pose you ain' been playin' yo' reg'leh game lately—s'pose you had a lot o' bad luck—that ain' no reason faw you to do a thing like that. Givin' all them expensible clubs to them pin-headed li'l' boys! Lawd! Lawd! They don't know how to treat 'em! They'll be splittin' the shafts, an' crackin' the heads, an' nickin' up the irons, an'—"

"Well," interrupted Coyne, "what of it? I hope they do break 'em!"

Jasper shook his head sorrowfully and returned to the bundle. While studying golfers he had come to know the value placed on golfing tools.

"O' course," said he slowly, "yo' own business is yo' own business, Misteh Coyne. Only, suh, it seem like a awful shame to me. Seem like bustin' up housekeepin' afteh you been married a long time. . . . Why not wait a few days an' see how you feel then?"

"No! I'm through."

Jasper jerked his head in the direction of the lounging room.

"You tol' the otheh gen'lemen whut you goin' to do?" he asked.

"What's the use? They'd only laugh. They wouldn't believe me. Let 'em find it out for themselves. And, by the way—there's my empty bag in the corner. Dispose of it somehow. Give it away—sell it. You can have whatever you get for it."

"Thank you, suh. You comin' back to see us once in a while?"

"Oh, I suppose so. With the wife and the kids. Well, take care of yourself."

Jasper followed him to the door and watched until the little runabout disappeared down the driveway.

"All foolishness—tha's whut it is!" soliloquized the Negro.

"This golf game—she's sutny a goat getteh when she ain' goin' right. Me, I ratheh play this Af'ican golf with two dice. That's some goat getteh, too, an' lots of people quits it; but I notice they always comes back. Yes, suh. They always comes back."

3 7

II

As the runabout coughed and sputtered along the county road the man at the wheel had time to think over the whole matter. Everything considered, he decided that he had acted wisely.

"Been playing too much golf, anyway," he told himself. "Wednesday and Saturday afternoons, Sundays and holidays— too much! . . . And then worrying about my game in between. It'll be off my mind now. . . . One thing sure— Mary'll be glad to hear the news. That old joke of hers about being a golf widow won't go any more. Yes, she'll have to dig up a new one. . . . Maybe I have been a little selfish and neglectful. I'll make up for it now, though. Sundays we can take the big car and go on picnics. The kids'll like that."

He pursued this train of thought until he felt almost virtuous. He could see himself entering the house; he could picture his wife's amazement and pleasure; he could hear himself saying something like this:

"Well, my dear, you've got your wish at last. After thinking it all over I've decided to cut out the golf and devote myself to the family. Yes, I'm through!"

In this highly commendable spirit he arrived at home, only to find the shades drawn and the front door locked. As Coyne felt for his key ring he remembered that his wife had said something about taking the children to spend the day with her mother. It was also the servant's afternoon off and the house was empty. Coyne was conscious of a slight disappointment; he was the bearer of glad tidings, but he had no audience.

"Oh, well," he thought; "it's been a long time since I had a quiet Sunday afternoon at home. Do me good. Guess I'll read a while and then run over to Mother's for supper. I don't read as much as I used to. Man ought to keep up-to-date."

Then, because he was a creature of habit and the most

methodical of men, he must have his pipe and slippers before sitting down with his book. Mary Coyne was a good wife and a faithful mother, but she abominated a pipe in the living room; and she tolerated slippers only when they were of her own choosing.

Now there are things which every woman knows; but there is one thing which no woman has ever known and no woman will ever know—namely, that she is not competent to select slippers for her lord and master. Bob Coyne was a patient man, but he loathed slippers his wife picked out for him. He was pledged to a worn and disreputable pair of the pattern known as Romeos—relics of his bachelor days. They were run down at the heel and thin of sole; but they were dear to his heart and he clung to them obstinately in spite of their shabby appearance. After the honeymoon it had been necessary to speak sternly with his wife on the subject of the Romeos, else she would have thrown them on the ash heap. Since that interview Mrs. Coyne—obedient soul!—had spent a great portion of her married life in finding safe hiding places for those wretched slippers; but no matter where she put them, they seemed certain of a triumphant resurrection.

Coyne went on a still hunt for the Romeos, and found them at last, tucked away in the clothes closet of the spare room upstairs. This closet was a sort of catchall, as the closets of spare rooms are apt to be; and as Coyne stooped to pick up the slippers he knocked down something which had been standing in a dark corner. It fell with a heavy thump, and there on the floor at his feet was a rusty old midiron—the first golf club Coyne had ever owned.

He had not seen that midiron in years, but he remembered it well. He picked it up, sighted along the shaft, found it still reasonably straight and unwarped, balanced the club in his hands, waggled it once as if to make a shot; then he replaced it hastily, seized the slippers, and hurried downstairs.

The book of his selection was one highly recommended by

press and pulpit, hence an ideal tale for a Sunday afternoon; so he dragged an easy chair to the front window, lighted his pipe, put his worn Romeos on a taboret, and settled down to solid comfort. In spite of the fact that the book was said to be gripping, and entertaining from cover to cover, Coyne encountered some difficulty in getting into the thing. He skimmed through the first chapter, yawned and looked at his watch.

"They're just getting away for the afternoon round," said he; and then, with the air of one who has caught himself in a fault, he attacked chapter two. It proved even worse than the first. He told himself that the characters were out of drawing, the situations impossible, and the humor strained or stale.

At the end of chapter three he pitched the book across the room and closed his eyes. Five minutes later he rose, knocked the ashes from his pipe, and went slowly upstairs. He assured himself he was not in search of anything; but his aimless wanderings brought him at last to the spare room, where he seated himself on the edge of the bed. He remained there for twenty minutes, motionless, staring into space. Then he rose, crossed the room and disappeared in the clothes closet. When he came out the rusty midiron came with him. Was this a sign of weakness, of deterioration in the moral fiber, an indication of regret? Perish the thought! The explanation Mr. Coyne offered himself was perfectly satisfactory. He merely wished to examine the ten-year-old shaft and ascertain whether it was cracked or not. He carried the venerable souvenir to the window and scrutinized it closely; the shaft was sound.

"A good club yet," he muttered.

As he stood there, holding the old midiron in his hands, ten years slipped away from him. He remembered that club very well—almost as well as a man remembers his first sweetheart. He remembered other things too—remembered that, as a youth, he had never had the time or the inclination to play at games of any sort. He had been too busy getting his start, as the saying goes. Then, at thirty, married and well on his way to business success, he had felt the need of open air and exercise. He had mentioned this to a friend and the friend had suggested golf.

"But that's an old man's game!" Yes, he had said that very thing. His ears burned at the recollection of his folly.

"Think so? Tackle it and see."

He had been persuaded to spend one afternoon at the country club. Is there a golfer in all the world who needs to be told what happened to Mr. Robert Coyne? He had hit one long, straight tee shot; he had holed one difficult putt; and the whole course of his serious, methodical existence had been changed. The man who does not learn to play any game until he is thirty years of age is quite capable of going daft over tiddledywinks or dominoes. If he takes up the best and most interesting of all outdoor sports his family may count itself fortunate if he does not become violent.

Never the sort of person who could be content to do anything badly, Bob Coyne had applied himself to the Royal and Ancient Pastime with all the simple earnestness and dogged determination of a silent, self-centered man. He had taken lessons from the professional. He had brought his driver home and practiced with it in the backyard. He had read books on the subject. He had studied the methods and styles of the best players. He had formed theories of his own as to stance and swing. He had even talked golf to his wife—which is the last stage of incurable golfitis.

As he stood at the window, turning the rusty midiron in his hands, he recalled the first compliment ever paid him by a good player—the more pleasing because he had not been intended to hear it. It came after he had fought himself out of the duffer class and had reached the point where he was too good for the bad ones, but not considered good enough for the topnotchers.

One day Corkrane had invited him into a foursome—Coyne had been the only man in sight—and Corkrane had taken him as a partner against such redoubtable opponents as Millar and Duffy. Coyne had halved four holes and won two, defeating Millar and Duffy on the home green. Nothing had been said at the time; but later on, while polishing himself with a towel in the shower room, Coyne had heard Corkrane's voice:

"Hey, Millar!"

"Well?"

"That fellow Coyne—he's not so bad."

"I believe you, Corky. He won the match for you."

"Thought I'd have to carry him on my back, but he was right there all the way round. Yep, Coyne's a comer, sure as you live!"

And the subject of this kindly comment had blushed pink out of sheer gratification.

A pretty good bunch, those fellows out at the club! If it had done nothing else for him, Coyne reflected, golf had widened his circle of friends. Suddenly there came to him the realization that he would have a great deal of spare time on his hands in the future. Wednesdays and Saturdays would be long days now; and Sundays— Coyne sighed deeply and swung the rusty midiron back and forth as if in the act of studying a difficult approach.

"But what's the use?" he asked himself. "I haven't got a shot left—not a single shot!"

He sat down on the edge of the bed, the midiron between his knees and his head in his hands. At the end of twenty minutes he rose and began to prowl about the house, looking into corners, behind doors, and underneath beds and bureaus.

"Seems to me I saw it only the other day," said he. "Of course Bobby might have been playing with it and lost it."

It was in the children's playroom that he came upon the thing, which he told himself he found by accident. It was much the worse for wear; nearly all the paint had been worn off it and its surface was covered with tiny dents. Bob Junior had been teaching his dog to fetch and carry and the dents were the prints of sharp puppy teeth.

"Well, what do you think of that!" ejaculated Mr. Coyne, pretending to be surprised. "As I live—a golf ball! Yes; a golf ball!"

He stood looking at it for some time; but at last he picked it up. With the rusty midiron in one hand and the ball in the other, he went downstairs, passed through the house, unlocked the back door, and went into the yard. Behind the garage was a smooth stretch of lawn, fifty feet in diameter, carefully mowed and rolled. In the center of this emerald carpet was a hole, and in the hole was a flag. This was Mr. Coyne's private putting green.

"Haven't made a decent chip shot in a month. . . . No use trying now. All confounded foolishness!"

So saying, the man who had renounced Colonel Bogey and all his works dropped the ball twenty feet from the edge of the putting green. The lie did not suit him; so he altered it slightly. Then he planted his disreputable Romeos firmly on the turf, waggled the rusty midiron a few times, pressed the blade lightly behind the ball, and attempted that most difficult of all performances—the chip shot. The ball hopped across the lawn to the smooth surface of the putting green and rolled straight for the cup, struck the flag and stopped two inches from the hole.

"Heavens above!" gasped Mr. Coyne, rubbing his eyes. "Look at that, will you? I hit the pin, by golly—*hit the pin!*"

At dusk Mrs. Coyne returned. The first thing she noticed was that a large rug was missing from the dining room. Having had experience, she knew exactly where to look for it. On the back porch she paused, her hands on her hips. The missing rug was hanging over the clothesline, and her lord and master, in shirtsleeves and the unspeakable Romeos, was driving a single golf ball against it.

Whish-h-h! Click! Thud!

"And I guess that's getting my weight into the swing!" babbled Mr. Coyne. "I've found out what I've been doing that was wrong. Watch me hit this one, Mary."

Mrs. Coyne was everything that a good wife should be, but she sniffed audibly.

"I've told you a dozen times that I didn't want you knocking holes in that rug!" said she.

"Why, there isn't a hole in it, my dear."

"Well, there will be if you keep on. It seems to me, Bob, that you might get enough golf out at the club. Then you won't scandalize the neighbors by practicing in the backyard on Sunday afternoons. What do you suppose they'll think of you?"

"They'll think I'm crazy" was the cheerful response. "But, just between you and me, my dear, I'm not near so crazy right now as I have been!"

III

Jasper was cleaning up the locker room—his regular Monday morning job. As he worked he crooned the words of an old Negro melody:

> *"Ole bline hawss, come outen the wilderness,*
> *Outen the wilderness, outen the wilderness;*
> *Ole bline hawss—"*

The side door opened and Jasper dropped his mop.

"Who's that?" he asked. "This early in the mawnin'?" But when he recognized the caller he did not show the faintest symptoms of surprise. Jasper was more than a perfect servant; he was also a diplomat. "Good mawnin', Misteh Coyne."

The caller seemed embarrassed. He attempted to assume a cheerful expression, but succeeded in producing a silly grin.

"Jasper," said he, "I was a little bit sore yesterday—"

44

"Yes, suh; an' nobody could blame you," said the Negro, coming gallantly to the rescue.

"And you know how it is with a man when he's sore."

"Yes, suh. Man don' always mean whut he say—that is, he mean it all right at the *time*. Yes, suh. At—the—time. 'N'en ag'in, he might *change*."

"That's it exactly!" said Coyne, and floundered to a full stop.

Jasper's face was grave, but he found it necessary to fix his eyes on the opposite wall.

"Yes, suh," said he. "Las' month I swo' off too."

"Swore off on what?"

"Craps, Misteh Coyne. Whut Bu't Williams calls Af'ican golf. Yes, suh, I swo' off; but las' night—well, I kind o' fell f'um grace. I fell, suh; but I wasn't damaged so much as some o' them boys in the game." Jasper chuckled to himself. "Yes, suh; I sutny sewed 'em up propeh! Look like I come back in my ole-time fawm!"

"That's it!" Coyne agreed eagerly. "I've got my chip shot back, Jasper. Last night, at home, I was hitting 'em as clean as a whistle. I—I ran out here this morning to have a little talk with you. You remember about those clubs?" Jasper nodded. "That was a foolish thing to do—" began Coyne.

"No, suh!" interrupted Jasper positively. "No, suh! When a man git good an' sore he do a lot o' things whut awdinarily he wouldn't think o' doin'! Las' month I th'owed away the best paih o' crap dice you eveh saw. You givin' away yo' clubs is exackly the same thing."

"That was what I wanted to see you about," said Coyne with a shamefaced grin. "I was wondering if there wouldn't be some way to get those clubs back—buying 'em from the boys. You could explain—"

Jasper cackled and slapped his knees.

"Same thing all oveh ag'in!" said he. "I th'owed them dice away, Misteh Coyne; but I th'owed 'em kind o' *easy*, an' I knowed where to look. So, when you tol' me 'bout them clubs

4 5

I—well, suh, I ain' been c'nected with this club twenty yeahs faw nothin'. If I was you, suh, I think I'd look in my lockeh."

Coyne drew the bolt and opened the door. His clothes were hanging on the hooks; his shoes were resting on the steel floor; his golf bag was leaning in the corner, and it was full of clubs— the clubs he had given away the day before! Coyne tried to speak, but the words would not come.

"You see, Misteh Coyne," explained Jasper, "I knowed them fool boys would bust them clubs or somethin', an' I kind of s'pected you'd be wantin' 'em back ag'in; so I didn't take no chances. Afteh you left yestiddy I kind o' took mattehs in my own hands. I tol' them caddies you was only foolin'. The younges' ones, they was open to conviction; but them oldeh boys—they had to be showed. Now that light midiron—I had to give Butch a dollah an' twenty cents faw it. That brassy was a dollah an' a half—"

Ten minutes later the incomparable Jasper was alone in the locker room, examining a very fine sample of the work turned out by the Bureau of Engraving and Printing at Washington, D.C. Across the bottom of this specimen were two words in large black type: TWENTY DOLLARS.

"Haw!" chuckled Jasper. "I wisht some mo' of these membehs would quit playin' golf!"

THE WOODEN
PUTTER

·

BERNARD DARWIN

It was not for want of clubs that Mr. Polwinkle's handicap obstinately refused to fall below sixteen. His rack full of them extended round three sides of the smoking room. In addition, there was an enormous box resembling a sarcophagus on the floor, and in one corner was a large loose heap of clubs. To get one out of the heap without sending the others crashing to the ground was as delicate and difficult as a game of spillikins, and the housemaid had bestowed on it many an early morning malediction.

The rack along one side of the wall was clearly of a peculiarly sacred character. The clips holding the clubs were of plush, and behind each clip there was pasted on the wall an inscription in Mr. Polwinkle's meticulously neat handwriting. There was a driver stated to have belonged to the great James Braid; a mashie of J. H. Taylor's; a spoon of Herd's.

Nor were illustrious amateurs unrepresented. Indeed, these were the greatest treasures in Mr. Polwinkle's collection, because they had been harder to come by. The midiron had quite a long pedigree, passing through a number of obscure and intermediate stages, and ending in a blaze of glory with the awful name of Mr. John Ball, who was alleged once to have played a shot with it at the request of an admirer. A putting cleek with a rather long, old-fashioned head and a battered grip bore the scrupulous inscription: ATTRIBUTED TO THE LATE MR. F. G. TAIT.

Mr. Polwinkle always sighed when he came to that cleek. Its authenticity was, he had to admit, doubtful. There were so many Freddie Tait putters. Half the clubhouses in England seemed to possess one; they could hardly all be genuine. His Hilton he no longer even pretended to believe in.

"I bought that," he would say, "when I was a very young collector, and I'm afraid I was imposed upon." But, at any rate, there was no doubt about his latest acquisition, before which he now paused lovingly. Here was the whole story, written down by a man, who knew another man, who knew the people with whom Mr. Wethered had been staying. Mr. Wethered had overslept himself, packed up his clubs in a hurry, and left his iron behind; so he had borrowed this one, and had graciously remarked that it was a very nice one.

It must not be supposed that Mr. Polwinkle was ever so daring as to play with these sacred clubs. He contented himself with gazing and, on rare occasions, with a reverent waggle.

Mr. Polwinkle, as I have said, was not a good player. He was aware of not playing consistently up to his sixteen handicap. If he did not always insist on his rights of giving two strokes to his friend Buffery, he might, he was conscious, have suffered the indignity of being beaten level by an eighteen handicap player; and with all this nonsense about scratch scores and a raising of the standard, he saw before him the horrid certainty of soon being eighteen himself.

This evening he was feeling particularly depressed. It had been a bad day. Buffery had won by five and four without using either of his strokes, and had hinted pretty strongly that he did not propose to accept them any more. Confound the tactless creature!

Mr. Polwinkle tried to soothe himself by looking at his treasures. Ah! If only he could just for one day be endued with the slash and power of those who had played with them. If only something of their virtue could have passed into their clubs, what a splendid heritage! Such a miracle might even be possible if he had but faith enough. Coué-suggestion—better and better and better—how wonderful it would be!

Suddenly he felt a glow of new hope and inspiration. Greatly daring, he took from the rack the driver WITH WHICH as the inscription lyrically proclaimed JAMES BRAID WON THE CHAMPIONSHIP AT PRESTWICK IN 1908, WITH THE UNEXAMPLED SCORE OF 291; EIGHT STROKES BETTER THAN THE SECOND SCORE, AND PLAYING SUCH GOLF AS HAD NEVER BEEN SEEN BEFORE ON THAT CLASSIC COURSE.

He took one glance to see that his feet were in the right place—long practice enabled him to judge to an inch the position in which the furniture was safe—and then he swung.

Gracious goodness! What had happened? Back went the club, instinct with speed and power, and he felt a violent and unaccustomed wrenching round of his hips. Down it came more swiftly than ever, his knees seemed to crumple under him with the vehemence of the blow, and swish went the clubhead, right out and round in a glorious finish. A shower of glass fell all over him and he was left in darkness.

Never had he experienced anything before in the least like

that tremendous sensation; the electric light had always been perfectly safe. With trembling fingers he struck a match and groped his way, crunching glass as he walked, to the two candles on the chimney piece. Once more he swung the club up; then paused at the top of the swing, as he had done so many hundreds of times before, and gazed at himself in the glass. Could it really be?

He rushed to the bookshelf, tore down *Advanced Golf,* turned to the appropriate page, and again allowed the club to swing and wrench him in its grip. There could be no doubt about it. Allowing for differences of form and feature he was Braid to the very life—the poise, the turn of the body, the very knuckles—all were the same.

The miracle had happened with one club. Would it happen with all? Out came the Taylor mashie from the rack. As he picked it up his head seemed to shake formidably, his wrists felt suddenly as if they were made of whipcord, his boots seemed to swell and clutch the ground; another second—crash! —down came the club and out came a divot of carpet, hurtling across the room, while Mr. Polwinkle's eyes were fixed in a burning and furious gaze on the gaping rent that was left.

Then it really was all right. If he could swing the club like the great masters, he could surely hit the ball like them, and the next time he played Buffery, by Jove, it would not be only two strokes he could give him.

He was in the middle of being Mr. Wethered when the door opened and Buffery walked in. Mr. Polwinkle had got his feet so wide apart in his admirable impersonation that he could not move; for a perceptible moment he could only straddle and stare.

"They told me you were in, old chap," began Buffery, "so I just walked in. What on earth are you at? I always said that light would get it in the neck some day!" Buffery's heartiness, though well meant, was sometimes hard to bear. "However," he went on, while Mr. Polwinkle was still speechless, "what I came about was this. You remember you said you'd come down to Sandwich with me some day. Well, I suddenly find I can get off for three days. Will you come?"

Mr. Polwinkle hesitated a moment. He did not feel very kindly disposed toward Buffery. He should like to practice his new styles a little before crushing him; but still, Sandwich! And he had never seen it.

"All right," he said; "I'll come!"

"Topping!" cried Buffery. "We'll have some great matches, and I'm going to beat you level—you see if I don't!"

Mr. Polwinkle gathered himself together for an effort.

"I will give you," he said slowly and distinctly, "a stroke a hole, and I'll play you for"—and he hesitated on the brink of something still wilder—"five pounds!"

Buffery guffawed with laughter. He had never heard Mr. Polwinkle make so good a joke before.

The next evening saw them safely arrived and installed at the Bell.

The journey, though slow, had been for Mr. Polwinkle full of romance. When he changed at Minster he snuffed the air and thought that already he could smell the sea. His mind was a jumble of old championships and of the wondrous shots he was going to play on the morrow. At dinner he managed to make Buffery understand that he really did mean to give him a stroke a hole. And Buffery, when at last convinced that it was not a joke, merely observed that a fiver would be a pleasant little help toward his expenses.

After dinner he felt too restless and excited to sit still, and leaving Buffery to play bridge, wandered stealthily into the hall to see if his precious clubs were safe. He felt a momentary shiver of horror when he found someone examining his bag. Had news of the match been spread abroad? Was this a backer of Buffery's tampering with his clubs?

No; he appeared a harmless, friendly creature, and apologized very nicely. He was merely, he said, amusing himself by looking at the different sets of clubs.

"You've got some jolly good ones," he went on, making Mr. Polwinkle blush with pleasure. "And look here, your mashie and mine might be twins—they're as like as two peas!" And he produced his own from a neighboring bag. They certainly were exactly alike; both bore the signature of their great maker; in weight and balance they were identical.

"Taylor used to play with mine himself!" said Mr. Polwinkle in a voice of pride and awe. "And this is Herd's spoon, and here's a putter of—"

"I expect he'd have played just as well with mine," cut in the stranger—Jones was the unobtrusive name on his bag—with regrettable flippancy. "Anyhow, they're both good clubs. Wish I could play like Taylor with mine. Well, I'm going to turn in early—good night!"

Mr. Polwinkle, a little sad that Jones did not want to hear all about his collection, fastened up his bag, and thought he would go to bed, too. He lay awake for some time, for the cocks crow as persistently by night in the town of Sandwich as the larks sing by day upon the links; moreover, he was a little excited. Still, he slept at last, and dreamed of mashie shots with so much backspin on them that they pitched on Prince's and came back into the hole on St. George's.

"Well," said Buffery, as they stood next morning on the first tee at St. George's, "it's your honor—you're the giver of strokes," he added in a rather bitter tone.

Mr. Polwinkle took out the Braid driver with as nonchalant an air as he could muster. He could not help feeling horribly frightened, but no doubt the club would help him through. He gave one waggle with that menacing little shake of the club that Walton Heath knows so well, and then the ball sped away an incredible distance. It was far over the "kitchen," that grassy hollow that has caught and stopped so many hundreds of balls; but it had a decided hook on it, and ran on and on till it finished in the rough on the left.

One of the caddies gave a prolonged whistle of surprise and admiration. Who was this new, unknown, and infinitely mild-looking champion who made the club hum through the air like a hornet? Buffery, too, was palpably taken aback.

"I say, old chap," he remarked, "you seem to have been putting a lot on to your drive. Was that what you had up your sleeve?"

However, he managed to hit a very decent shot himself into the kitchen, and then, narrowly escaping that trappy little bunker on the right with his second, lay in a good strategic position in front of the big cross bunker.

Meanwhile, Mr. Polwinkle was following up his own vast tee shot in an agitated state of mind. Of course, he reflected, Braid *can* hook. It was, he had read, the one human weakness to which the great man was occasionally prone, but it seemed hard that this should be the occasion. The ball lay very heavy in the rough, and worse than all he had only his own niblick, with which he was singularly ineffective. He had once had the chance of acquiring a genuine Ray, but niblicks were clumsy, ugly things and did not interest him. Why had he been such a fool?

His first effort was a lamentable top, his second only just got the ball out of the rough, with a gaping wound in its vitals. Still, there was a hope if Herd's spoon would behave itself as it should, and he addressed himself to the shot with a desperate composure.

Heavens, what was the matter with him? Was he never going to hit the ball? He felt himself growing dizzy with all those waggles, a fierce little glance at the hole between each of them. There could be no possible doubt that this spoon was a genuine Herd. Just as he felt that he must scream if it went on much longer, up went the club, and away went the ball—the most divine spoon shot ever seen—cut up into the wind to perfection; the ball pitched over the bunker, gave a dying kick or two, and lay within a yard of the hole.

Even the ranks of Tuscany could scarce forbear to cheer. "Good shot!" growled Buffery grudgingly.

That was four—he would be down in five. The enemy with his stroke had three for the hole, but the big cross bunker yawned between him and the green. Drat the man, he had not topped it. He had pitched well over, and his approach putt lay so dead that Mr. Polwinkle, though in no generous mood, had to give it to him. One down.

At the second hole at Sandwich, as all the world knows, there is a long and joyous carry from the tee. A really fine shot will soar over the bunker and the hilltop beyond, and the ball will lie in a little green valley, to be pitched home on to the green; but the short driver must make a wide tack to the right and will have a more difficult second.

Buffery, inspired by his previous win, despite his opponent's mighty drive, decided to "go for it." And plump went his ball into the bunker.

The Braid driver was on its best behavior this time—a magnificent shot, straight as an arrow and far over the hill.

"H'm!" said Buffery, looking discontentedly at the face of his driver. "Is that any new patent kind of ball you are playing with?"

"No," returned Mr. Polwinkle frigidly. "You can weigh it after the round if you like." And they walked on in stony silence.

Buffery had to hack his ball out backward, and his third was away to the right of the green.

"Just a little flick with the mashie, sir," said Mr. Polwinkle's caddie, putting the club in his hand.

He took the mashie, but somehow he did not feel comfortable. He shifted and wriggled, and finally his eye was high in the heavens long before the ball was struck. When he looked down to earth again he found the ball had only moved about three yards forward—a total and ignominious fluff. He tried again; another fluff moved it forward but a few painful inches; again, and a third precisely similar shot deposited it in the bunker in front of his nose. Then he went berserk with his niblick, irretrievably ruined a second new ball, and gave up the hole.

"Let me look at that mashie!" he said to his caddie as he walked on toward the next tee. And, after microscopically examining its head, "I see what it is!" he exclaimed, in frantic accents. "It's that fellow—what's his damned name, who was looking at my clubs last night—he's mixed them up—he's got my mashie and I've got his! Do you know Mr. Jones by sight?" And he turned to his caddie.

"Yes, sir. I knows him. And that's a funny thing if you've got his mashie. I was just thinking to myself that them shots of yours was just like what he plays. 'Joneses,' his friends call them. He'll play like a blooming pro, for a bit, and then fluff two or three—"

"Where is he now? Is he in front of us?" Mr. Polwinkle interrupted. Yes, Jones had started some time ago.

"Then run as hard as you can and tell him I'm playing an important match and insist on having my mashie back. Quick now, run!"—as the caddie was going to say something. "I'll carry the clubs!" And the caddie disappeared reluctantly in the sandhills.

"Bad luck, old man!" said Buffery, his complacency restored by that wonderfully soothing medicine of two holes up, "But I'll tell you where to go. Now this is the Sahara. The hole's over there," pointing to the left, "but it's too long a carry for you and me—we must go round by the right."

"Which line would Braid take?" asked Mr. Polwinkle. "Straight at the flag, would he? Then I shall go straight for the flag!"

"Please yourself!" answered Buffery with a shrug, and

played away to the right—a mild little shot and rather sliced, but still clear of the sand. Mr. Polwinkle followed with another superb tee shot. Far over all that tumultuous mass of rolling sandhills the ball flew, and was last seen swooping down on to the green. Buffery's second was weak and caught in the hollow; his third was half topped and ran well past; his fourth put him within a yard or so of the hole.

The best he could do would be a five, and all the while there stood Mr. Polwinkle, calm, silent, and majestic, six yards from the flag in one. He had only to get down in two putts to win the hole; but he had not yet had a putt, and which putter was he to use—the Tait or the Harry Vardon? He decided on the Tait. A moment later he wished he had not, for his putt was the feeblest imaginable, and the ball finished a good five feet short. Still he persevered, and again was pitifully short.

"By Jove, that's a let-off, old chap!" said the tactless one, and popped his own ball into the hole.

"I'll give you that one!" he added magnanimously, and picked up Mr. Polwinkle's ball, which was reposing some three inches from the hole.

"I was always afraid it was a forgery!" murmured Mr. Polwinkle, mechanically accepting the ball. "Freddie Tait was never short with his putts—the books all say that!"

Buffery looked at him wonderingly, opened his mouth as if to make some jocular comment, then thought better of it and led the way to the tee.

Much the same thing happened at the fourth. Two magnificent shots by Braid and Herd respectively, right up to the edge of the little plateau, where it stands defiantly with the black railings in the background; a series of four scrambles and scuffles by Buffery, which just escaped perdition. Two for the hole again, and this time the Vardon putter was tried. The first putt was beautiful. How sweetly and smoothly and with what a free wrist it was taken back! The ball, perfectly struck, seemed in, then it just slipped past and lay two feet away.

"Ah!" he said to himself with a long sigh of satisfaction, "at any rate this is genuine!"

Alas! It was but too true, for when it came to the short putt, Mr. Polwinkle's wrist seemed suddenly to become locked, there was a quick little jerk of the club and—yes, somehow or other the ball had missed the hole. Buffery was down in his two putts again, and it was another half, this time in five to six.

"I ought to have been all square by now if I could have putted as well as an old lady with a broomstick!" said poor Mr. Polwinkle.

"Well, I like that!" answered the other truculently. "I ought to have been four up if I could have played a decent second either time!" And this time there was a lasting silence.

Mr. Polwinkle felt depressed and miserable. Still his heart rose a little when he contemplated the bunker that had to be carried from the tee at the fifth, and beyond it the formidable Maiden with its black terraces. And, sure enough, Buffery got into the bunker in three—not into the black terraces, because, sad to say, men do not now play over the Maiden's crown, but only over the lower spurs—touching, as it were, but the skirts of her sandy garment. Still, he was in the bunker, and Mr. Polwinkle had only a pitch to reach the green. Here it was that he wanted a good caddie to put an iron in his hand—to put anything there but the mashie that had played him false. But Mr. Polwinkle was flustered.

"After all," he thought, "a mashie is a mashie, even if it is not a genuine Taylor, and if I keep my eye on the ball—"

Clean off the socket this time the ball flew away toward cover point, and buried itself in a clump of bents. Why did he not "deem it unplayable"? I do not know. But since Mr. Horace Hutchinson once ruined a medal round and probably lost the St. George's Vase at the Maiden by forgetting that he could tee and lose two, Mr. Polwinkle may be forgiven. When his ball ultimately emerged from the bents he had played five; they holed out in nine apiece, for Buffery had also had his adventures and the stroke settled in. Three down.

Worse was to come, for at the sixth Buffery had the impudence to get a three—a perfect tee shot and two putts; no one could give a stroke to that. At the seventh Mr. Polwinkle, club in hand, walked forward with elaborate care to survey the ground, walked backward, his eye still fixed on the green—and heeled his ball smartly backward like a rugby forward. For a moment he was bewildered. Then he looked at his club. His Wethered iron! Of course. It was the tragedy of the Open Championship at St. Andrews over again!

At Hades his Vardon putter again misbehaved at short range, and Mr. Polwinkle looked at it reproachfully.

"I always thought it belonged to a bad period!" he groaned, remembering some of those tragic years in which the greatest of all golfers could do everything but hole a yard putt. He would use the Vardon no more. But, then, what on earth was he to putt with? He tried the pseudo-Tait again at the ninth, and by dint of taking only three putts got a half; but still he was six down.

There was one ray of comfort. There was his caddie waiting for him, having no doubt run the villain Jones to earth, and under his arm protruded the handle of a club.

"Well," he shouted, "have you got it?"

"No, sir," the caddie answered—and embarrassment and amusement seemed to struggle together in his voice. "Mr. Jones says he's playing an important match, too, and as you didn't send back his mashie he's going on with yours. Said they were just the same, he did, and he wouldn't know any difference between yours and his own."

"Then what's that club you've got there?" demanded Mr. Polwinkle.

"The gentleman lent you this to make up, so he said," the caddie replied, producing a wooden putter. "I was particularly

5 8

to tell you it belonged to someone who used it in a great match, and blessed if I haven't forgotten who it was."

Mr. Polwinkle took the putter in his hand and could not disguise from himself that it had no apparent merits of any description. The shaft was warped, not bent in an upward curve as a well-bred wooden putter should be, and decidedly springy; no name whatever was discernible on the head. Still, he badly needed a putter, and if it had been used by an eminent hand—

"Think, man, think!" he exclaimed vehemently. "You must remember!" But the caddie racked his brain in vain. And then—

"Really," said Buffery, "we can't wait all day while your caddie tries to remember ancient history. This is the match we're thinking about, and I'm six up!" And he drove off—a bad hook into the thick and benty rough on the left.

And now, thank goodness, I have reached the end of Mr. Polwinkle's misfortunes. The tide is about to turn. At the second shot Mr. Wethered's iron, I regret to have to say, made another error. It just pulled the ball into that horrid trappy bunker that waits voraciously at the left-hand corner of the plateau green—and that after Buffery had played three and was not on the green.

Mr. Polwinkle's temper had been badly shaken once or twice, and now it gave out entirely.

"Give me any dashed club you like!" he snarled, seized the first that came handy, and plunged into the bunker.

"Good sort of club to get out of a bunker with!" he said to himself, finding that he had a midiron in his hand, and then— out came the ball, as if it was the easiest thing in the world, and sat down within four yards of the hole.

How had it happened? Why, it was Mr. Ball's iron—and did not the hero of Hoylake habitually pitch out of bunkers with a straight-faced iron? Of course he did—and played his ordinary pitches with it as well. What a thing it was to know history!

Here at once was a magic niblick and a substitute for the mashie rolled into one. And just then his caddie smacked himself loudly and suddenly on the thigh.

"I've remembered it, sir. It was Tommy something—young Tommy, I think."

"Young Tommy Morris?" gasped Mr. Polwinkle breathlessly.

"Ah!" said the caddie. "Morris—that was it!"

"Give me the wooden putter!" said Mr. Polwinkle—and the ball rattled against the back of the tin. That was a four against Buffery's six. Down to five with eight to play.

It is a well-known fact that when golf is faultless there is next to nothing to write about it. The golfing reporter may say that So-and-So pushed his drive and pulled his second; but the real fact is that the great So-and-So was on the course with his tee shot, on the green with his second, and down in two putts— and kept on doing it. That is all the reporter need have said, but he says more because he has his living to earn. So have I; but, nevertheless, I shall not describe Mr. Polwinkle's homecoming at full length. More brilliantly faultless golf never was seen. Braid drove magnificently, Mr. Ball did all the pitching to perfection and even Mr. Wethered behaved impeccably. As for the wooden putter, most of the putts went in, and even those that did not gave Buffery a cold shiver down his spine. What could poor eighteen-handicap Buffery do against it? He must need wilt under such an onslaught. If he did a respectable five, Mr. Polwinkle did a "birdie" three. If he did a long hole in six, as he did at the Suez Canal, that wooden putter holed one for a four.

Here, for those who know the course, are the figures of Mr. Polwinkle's first eight holes coming home: four, three, three, four, four, four, two, four. That was enough. Buffery was a crushed man; hole after hole slipped away, and when he had reached the seventeenth green in eight, there was nothing for it but to give up the match. Six up at the turn and beaten by two and one!

As Mr. Polwinkle walked triumphantly into the clubhouse he met Jones, and almost fell on his neck.

"My dear fellow," he cried, "I can't thank you enough for that putter. I holed everything. Never saw anything like it! I suppose," he went on with a sudden desperate boldness, "there's no chance of your selling it me, is there?"

"Oh no, I won't sell it!" began Jones.

"I knew it was too much to ask!" said Mr. Polwinkle dejectedly.

"But I'll give it you with pleasure!"

"Oh, but I couldn't let you do that! Give me it for nothing—a putter that belonged to young Tommy—the greatest putter that ever—"

"Well, you see," said Jones, "I only told the caddie to tell you that because I thought it might put you on your putting. And, by George, it seems to have done it, too. Wonderful what a little confidence will do. You're perfectly welcome to the putter—I bought it in a toy shop for eighteen pence!"

Mr. Polwinkle fell swooning to the floor.

DORMIE
ONE

·

HOLWORTHY HALL

It was five o'clock and rapidly shading into dusk. The September sun, which earlier had set the air to simmering in tremulous heatwaves, now moved reluctant to ambush behind the hills, and, as though sullen at the exigency of its time, gave warning by its bloodshot eye of pitiless heat to be renewed with tomorrow's dawn. From the curving line of trees—thin elms and maples, bordering upon the hard-packed road—long, soothing shadows edged out into the fresh green of the fairway, measuring with their deeper green the flight of hours and the peaceful ebbing of the afternoon.

From the distant Sound, a transient breeze, shy as a maiden

in the manner of its coming, ventured out from the protection of the ridge, hesitated, wavered, and passed across the sward so fleetingly that almost before it seemed assured a fact, it was a memory.

Then, from the trees at the roadside, and from the trees beyond, and from the little brook dawdling along from east to west, and from the reeded lake far over to the right, a breath of evening crept out upon the lawns, and there was silence.

In a squared clearing at the southern end of the sinous line of maples there was a trim plateau, close-shorn of grass, and sharply defined by boundaries of sedge and stubble. From this spot forward an expansive belt of untrimmed land stretched northward for a hundred yards, to merge presently with the more aristocratic turf of the fairway. Thereafter, narrowing between the trees and a long alignment of arid pits, the trail of adventure ran through rolling country, skirted a grove of locusts, dipped down to ford the brook, climbed past a pair of shallow trenches which glistened with coarse sand, and finally found refuge on a terraced green protected by towering chestnuts and flanked by the arm of a colonial house which rested comfortably beneath the trees.

From clearing to terrace the crow, flying as crows are popularly supposed to fly, would have accomplished five hundred and twenty yards. It was the eighteenth hole at Kenilworth.

The trim plateau, which was the eighteenth tee, now marked the apex of a human letter, a V of which a thousand men and women formed each stroke. Converging sharply toward that rectangle in the sedge, two thousand men and women—twin lines of white slashed here and there with vivid, burning color—restrained and held in check by twisted ropes, leaned out and gaped and wondered, breathless; now standing hushed by things already seen, now vibrant to the future, uneasy, murmuring. And as in recompense for toiling through the humid afternoon, two thousand men and women held this privilege:

to stand, and wait, and watch until a boy—a sturdy, laughing boy—and then a man—a grayed and quiet man—played, stroke by stroke, the eighteenth hole at Kenilworth.

And silhouetted in the background, nervous on the tee, stood man and boy, paired finalists for the Amateur Championship; two wizards of the links whose faces had gone rigid, whose palms were suddenly wet and cold, whose souls were newly strung upon the natural laws which govern flying objects. Each of them had reason for his agitation; their mutual loss of equilibrium was mutual in its cause; for of these two, the man—Hargrave, the present champion—was dormie one.

He was fifty-five, this Hargrave; in commercial life he had known bankruptcy at forty. Golf, which had been heretofore diversion, he made the solace of his penury; it had then constituted itself his religion. Within a decade he had snatched the national title for his keepsake; subsequently he had lost it, struggled for it desperately, regained, and twice defended it. The gold medal meant infinitely more to him than a mere visible token of success at golf; it was suggestive of success elsewhere; it was the embodiment of conquests he had never made, of victories he never might accomplish. In other years wealth had eluded him, power had been alien to him, social distinction was to be classed among the impossibilities; but when he stepped morosely out upon the course, he vaunted in his heart that he was highborn to the purple.

Granted that he was poor indeed in purse, he knew no multimillionaire in all the world who could undertake to meet him on equal terms; he could concede six strokes, and still administer a beating, to the finest gentleman and the finest golfer in the Social Register. And so, while golf was his theology, and the arbitrary standard of par his creed, he played the Scottish game as though it symbolized the life he had proved incapable of mastering—and he mastered the game instead. It was his single virtue; it was the hyphen which allied him to the rest of civilization.

To win was the wine of his existence; to surmount obstacles was the evidence of his regeneration; to come from behind, to turn impending downfall into disconcerting triumph, was his acrid compensation for the days and months and years when the man in him had cried out for recognition, and the weakling in him had earned his failure. And he was dormie one—and it was Stoddard's honor at the last hole.

The man stiffened perceptibly as Stoddard, nodding to the referee, took a pinch of sand from the box, and teed for the final drive. Then, in accordance with the grimmest of his grim theories of golf, he abruptly turned his back on his opponent, and stared fixedly at the ground. He had trained himself to this practice for two unrelated reasons: the moral effect upon his adversary, and the opportunity to detach himself from the mechanics of his surroundings and to visualize himself in the act of playing his next stroke.

Habitually he conjured up a vision of the ball, the club, himself in the address, the swing, the attack, the aftermath. He compelled his faculties to rivet upon a superb ideal. And it was largely by virtue of this preliminary concentration that he was enabled to bring off his shots with such startling absence of delay: the orders were transmitted to his muscles in advance; his swing was often started when, to the openmouthed observer, he had hardly reached the ball. And it was by virtue of his utter disregard of his opponent that he was never discouraged, never unnerved, never disheartened. He was neither cheered by the disaster of the enemy, nor cast down by the enemy's good fortune. He was contemptuous not only of the personality of the opponent, but also of his entity. He played his own game, and his best game, ironically ignoring the fact that it was competitive. To all intents and purposes, Hargrave in contest was the only man on the course; he even disregarded his caddy, and expected the proper club, as he demanded it, to be placed in his hand extended backward.

But as now he formally prepared to shut Stoddard out of his consciousness, and as he exerted his stern determination to picture himself in yet another perfect illustration of golfing form, he discovered that his will, though resolute, was curiously languid. It missed of its usual persistence. The ideal came and went, as though reflected on a motion film at lowered speed. There was no continuity; there was no welding of motor impulses. According to his theory, Hargrave should have been purely mechanical. On the contrary, he was thinking.

He entertained no sense of actual antagonism toward Stoddard. Indeed, from the inception of the finals, at ten o'clock this morning, the boy had shown himself considerate and generous, quick of applause and slow of alibi, a dashing, brilliant, dangerous golfer with the fire of an adventurer and the grace of a cavalier. He was confident yet modest, and he had performed a score of feats for which his modesty was none of that inverted conceit of mediocrity in luck, but literal modesty, sheer lack of self-aggrandizement. He was dogged while he smiled; he was still smiling with his lips when his eyes betrayed his chastened mood; and the smile faded and vanished only when he saw that Hargrave was in difficulty. The gallery, nine tenths of it, was with him boisterously. The gallery was frankly on the side of youth and spontaneity. The mass, unresponsive to the neutral tints of Hargrave's character, thrilled to the juvenile star ascendant.

The gray-haired champion, introspective on the tee, frowned and grimaced, and toyed with his dread-naught driver. Early in the morning he had confessed guiltily to himself that Stoddard was the sort of lad he should have liked to call his son. And yet he knew that if he had ever married, if he had ever glowed to the possession of an heir, the boy couldn't conceivably have been in the least like Stoddard. Too many generations forbade the miracle. The mold of ancestry would have stamped out another failure, another charge upon the good opinion of the world. The child would have been the father of the man. And

Stoddard—witness his behavior and his generosity—was of no varnished metal. He was without alloy. He was a gentleman because his great-grandfathers had been gentlemen. He was rich because they had made him so. But Hargrave had allowed himself to experience an anomalous and paternal emotion toward Stoddard—Stoddard who at twenty was higher in rank, higher in quality, higher in the affection of the people than Hargrave at fifty-five. He had nourished this emotion by trying to imagine what he could have made of himself if, at his majority, he had been of the type of Stoddard.

And now, recalling this quondam sentiment, he shuddered in a spasm of self-pity; and simultaneously, in one of those racking bursts of humanity which come to men unloving and unloved, he longed to whirl about, to stride toward Stoddard, to grip his hand and say—well, one of the common platitudes. "May the best man win"—something of that sort; anything to show that he, too, was living rapidly in the crisis.

In another moment he might have yielded; he might have bridged the fearful chasm of self-imposed restraint. But he was slothful to the impulse. Behind him there was the sharp, pistol-like crack of a clean and powerful drive; and before him, brought clear by reflex and by the will that had been lagging, the ghostly mirage of a ball, and of himself swinging steadily and hard, and of the joy of impact, and a tremendous carry and run, true to the flag. The champion had remembered that he was dormie one. A voice, low but distinct, came to him through a volume of incoherent sound: "Mr. Hargrave!"

The man turned slowly. He saw neither the referee, who had spoken to him, nor Stoddard, who had stepped aside; he saw no caddies; he saw no fairway. Both lines of the V were weaving, undulating; on the faces of the men and women nearest him he perceived beatific, partizan delight. The thousand-tongued shout which had gone up in praise of Stoddard was dwindling by degrees to a pleasant hum, which throbbed mercilessly in Hargrave's ears and challenged him. He knew, as he had known for hours, how earnestly the public hoped for his defeat. He knew that if he bettered Stoddard's drive his sole reward would be a trifling ripple of applause, smirched by a universal prayer that ineptly he might spoil his second shot.

He grinned sardonically at the throng. He rubbed his palms together, drying them. He teed a ball, and took his stance; glanced down the course, took back the club a dozen inches, carried it ahead, and rested for the fraction of a second; then, accurate, machinelike to the tiniest detail, swung up, hit down, and felt his body carried forward in the full, strong finish of a master drive.

"Good ball!" said Stoddard in a voice that trembled slightly. From the V—sporadic hand clapping. Hargrave, the national champion, had driven two hundred and sixty yards.

Ahead of him, as he walked defiantly through the rough, the fairway bobbed with men and women who, as they chattered busily, stumbled over the irregularities of the turf. Now and then a straggler threw a look of admiration over his shoulder, and, meeting the expressionless mask of the amateur champion, insouciantly shrugged that shoulder and resumed his march.

Hargrave's caddy, dour and uncommunicative as the champion himself, stalked abreast, the clubs rattling synchronously to his stride. Hargrave was studying the contour of the land in front; he glowered at the marshals who had suffered the gallery to break formation and overflow the course; and he was tempted to ask his caddy how, when the entire middle distance was blocked by gabbling spectators, the Golf Association thought a finalist could judge the hole. But he denied himself the question; it was seven years since he had condescended to complain of, or to criticize, the conditions of any tournament. Nevertheless he was annoyed; he was certain that the ground sloped off just where his second shot should properly be placed; his memory was positive. Blindfold, he could have aimed correctly to a surveyor's minute.

Still, he was impatient, irritated. He wanted to verify his scheme of play. He wanted to do it instantly. The muscles of his neck twitched spasmodically; and without warning, even to himself, his canker flared into red hate. His eyes flashed venomously; and when it seemed that unless that crowd dispersed, and gave him room, his nerves would shatter in a burst of rage, he saw the marshals tautening their lines, the gallery billowing out into a wide and spacious funnel, and felt the caddy's timid touch upon his sleeve.

"Look out, Mr. Hargrave! Stoddard's away!"

The champion halted, and without a glance toward Stoddard, stared at his own ball. It was an excellent lie; he nodded imperceptibly and took a brassey which the caddy, without instructions, placed in his outstretched hand. His fingers closed around the smooth-worn grip; he tested the spring of the shaft, and focused his whole attention upon the ball. He strove to summon that mental cinema of Hargrave, cool, collected, playing a full brassey to the green. But Stoddard again intruded.

In the morning round, Hargrave had won the first three holes in a row, and he had held the advantage, and brought in his man three down. He had made a seventy-four, one over par, and Stoddard had scored a creditable seventy-eight—doubly creditable in view of his ragged getaway. And in the afternoon Hargrave had won the first two holes, and stood five up with sixteen more to play, when Stoddard had begun an unexpected spurt. Hargrave scowled at the toe of his brassey as he recounted errors which, if they could have been eliminated from his total, would have erased five needless strokes, and ended the match long since. Cruelly, three of those errors were on successive holes. On the fifteenth he had missed a simple putt for the win; on the sixteenth he had overapproached and thrown away a half; on the seventeenth he had topped an iron and still accomplished a par four—but Stoddard had made a three.

The champion felt his heart flutter and his knees yield a trifle as he reflected what havoc one more ineffectual shot would work upon his nerves. He was surely, steadily slipping, and he knew it. The bulk of his vitality was gone; and he was drawing heavily upon his light reserve. He realized, not in cowardice but in truth and in fact, that if the match should go to an extra hole, he, and not Stoddard, would be the loser. His customary command of his muscles was satisfactory, but his control of his nerves was waning. He was overgolfed; overstrained; stale. He could bear the strain of this hole, but that was all. His stamina had touched its limit; his fortitude could stand no more. He could gage it to a nicety; he had a debilitating intuition which told him that if he had to drive again from the first tee, he should founder wretchedly; and he believed this message from his soul, because he had never before received it.

If Stoddard won the eighteenth, it would be the fourth consecutive godsend for Stoddard, and Stoddard's game was improving, not deteriorating; he had moral courage behind him, he had the savage exhilaration of metamorphosing a forlorn chance into a delirious certainty, he had the stimulus and the impetus of his grand onrush, he had the responsive gallery to cheer him on. It was inevitable that Stoddard, if he won the eighteenth, would win the next; so that the champion, who was dormie one, must have a half—he must divide this hole with Stoddard. He *must!*

The champion grew restive. It needed the supreme effort of his career to force himself to inertia, to refrain from wheeling swiftly, and shrieking aloud to Stoddard, to demand why he didn't *play!* Was the boy asleep? Dead? Dreaming? Had he succumbed to paralysis? Was he gloating over his triumph? Hargrave wet his lips, and swallowed dustily.

A tremor ran through his limbs, and his wrists tightened in palsied fear. His eyes pained him; they reminded him of a doll's eyes, turning inward; he was aware that his face was drawn. He wondered stupidly whether the spoon would be safer than the brassey. He liked the spoon—but was the cleek surer yet? He caught his breath in a gasp, and at the same moment his spine was chilled in a paroxysm of futile terror. He essayed once more to swallow and thought he was strangling. His soul cried heartbreakingly out to Stoddard: "Shoot! For God's sake, *shoot!*"

The tension snapped. A roar of jubilance went up from twice a thousand throats, a roar which, dying momentarily, swelled up in glory, and hung, and splintered into a thousand reverberations against the hills. Hargrave shivered and cleared his throat. For the life of him he couldn't maintain his principles; his nature revolted; and jerking his head towards the north, he was gazing at a tiny fleck of white ten feet to the side of the terrace, which was the eighteenth green. Stoddard was hole high in two! A lucky ricochet from the stones of the brook! Five hundred and twenty yards in two! Hargrave went sickly white, and looked despairingly at his caddy.

He needed a half, and Stoddard was hole high. There was an outside possibility, then, that Stoddard could make a four—one under par. And Hargrave was nearly three hundred yards away. Could he, too, make a four—for the half?

The champion, with two alternatives looming bold before him, shuddered in exquisite incertitude. He could attempt a heroic stroke with the brassey, sacrificing accuracy for distance, or he could play his normal shot, which was practically sure to clear the brook, but still would leave him at a critical disadvantage. In the latter instance he could guarantee himself a five, but already Stoddard was assured of four. And that four, if he achieved it, meant a squared match for Stoddard, and a resultant victory. Hargrave would halve the hole only if Stoddard blundered; and for an hour and more Stoddard's golf had been flawless. There was no blunder in him.

7 1

But if Hargrave should risk his own crown on a mighty endeavor to equal Stoddard's titanic brassey shot, he would have the odds of war alarmingly against him. The trajectory must be perfect to a ruled, undeviating line. The ball must either fall short of the brook by ten yards, or clear it by ten, and bounding neither to the left, among the trees, nor to the right, among the sand pits, surmount the grade. An unfortunate angle of consequence, a mere rub of the green, would be doubly fatal. The ball might even be unplayable. There would yet be a hazardous last chance for a five; but again, there was no reason to expect that Stoddard would need so many. Stoddard had been deadly, uncannily deadly, on those short running approaches. Stoddard would make his four, and Hargrave knew it. He closed and unclosed his fingers around the grip of his brassey. A rim of ice, pressing inward, surrounded his heart. His brain was delicately clouded, as though he had just awakened out of the slumber of exhaustion, and looked upon the world without comprehending it, sensed it without perceiving its physiology. He passed a hand over his forehead, and found it damp with perspiration.

A year ago he had promised himself that, as champion, he would withdraw from competition. It was his dream to retire at the height of his prowess, to go down in the history of games as one of that rare company who have known when to file their resignations. Indeed, as late as February he had vowed not to defend his title this year. But when he had once sniffed the intoxicant atmosphere of a club grill, and after he had proved his strength in a practice round or two, he had diffidently entered for the Atlantic City tournament, and won it. Infectiously, the old ardor had throbbed in his veins. He was keenly alive to his dominant tenure; his nostrils dilated, his jaws set.

He would add one consummating honor to those that had gone before; he would take his third successive championship with him into exile. And so at Deal, at Apawamis, at Sleepy

Hollow and at Garden City, at Montclair and Wykagyl and Piping Rock, he had groomed himself, thoroughly and deliberately, for the fitting climax. The metropolitan supremacy was his for the fifth occasion; he had finished fourth in the Metropolitan Open, third in the National Open. In the handicap list of the great central association he stood proudly aloof at scratch. He was invincible.

And now, with six days of irreproachable golf behind him; with the greatest prize of a lifetime shining in his very eyes, he looked at a distant red flag, drooping on its staff, and looked at a ball lying in tempting prominence on the fairway, and felt his chin quiver in the excess of his passionate longing, and felt a white-hot band searing his forehead, and penetrating deep.

He kept the brassey. And as he took his stance, and struggled to centralize his wishes upon the problem of combining vast length with absolute precision, his mind became so acutely receptive to impression, so marvelously subjective, that he found himself repeating over and over to himself the series of simple maxims he had learned painfully by heart when he was a novice, striving to break through the dread barrier which divides those who play over and those who play under a hundred strokes for the single round.

He experienced, for the first time in years, a subtle premonition of ineptitude. He was again a tyro, whose margin of error was 95 percent. Where was the ball going? It was incredibly small, that sphere in the fairway; it was incredible that he should smite it so truly and so forcibly that it would fly even so far as a welcome furlong. Suppose he, a champion, with a champion's record, should slice, or pull, or top—or miss the ball completely?

Hargrave's teeth came grindingly together. His eyes dulled and contracted. He took the club back for a scant foot, raised it, took it forward, past the ball in the line of the hole, brought it to its original position, pressed it gently into the velvet turf with infinitesimal exertion of the left wrist, and swung. Wrists, forearms, shoulders and hips—his whole anatomy coordinated in that terrible assault. The click of the wood against the ball hadn't yet reached his ears when he knew, with exultation so stupendous that it nauseated him, that the shot had come off. His eager eyes picked up the ball in flight; and as he paused momentarily at the finish of his terrific drive, he was filled with a soft and yet an incongruously fierce content. Again he had foiled the gallery, and Stoddard! He saw the ball drop, across the brook; saw it leap prodigiously high in air, and fall again, and bound, and roll, slower and slower, and cease to roll—a good club's length from the lower pit, twenty yards from the green.

The champion and the challenger were on even terms.

Unlike the average man of gregarious instincts, Hargrave never sought proximity to his opponent during a match. His procedure was exactly as though, instead of playing against a flesh-and-blood antagonist, he were going around alone. He went his independent way, kept his peace, and entertained no thought of conversation or courtesy. If fortuitously he had to walk a course parallel to that of his opponent, and even if the interval between them were a matter of a scant rod or so, the champion was invariably thin-lipped, reflective, incommunicative.

He observed with a little flicker of amusement that Stoddard was eyeing him sidewise, and he felt that Stoddard was not a little affected by that enormous brassey, as well as by Hargrave's outward indifference toward it. Hargrave, however, appraised his own flinty exterior as one of his championship assets. He never praised the other man; and if the other man chose to burst into fervid eulogy, the champion's manner was so arctic, so repelling, that not infrequently he gained a point on the very next shot through the adversary's dazed inefficiency and even one stroke in match play is worth saving.

He knew that he was unpopular, he knew that he was affirmatively disliked; he knew that the public, the good-natured and friendly public, yearned for Stoddard's triumph rather as a vindication of gentility than as a proof of might. But as he observed that Stoddard showed premonitory symptoms of increased nervousness, and that Stoddard was impelled to speak, and yet held his tongue to save himself from sure rebuff, the champion's breast expanded with golden hope.

Stoddard, after all, was a mere boy: a veteran golfer—yes, but immature in the mentality of golf. And Hargrave sometimes won his matches, especially from younger men, in the locker room before he put on his shoes. If Stoddard congratulated him now, he could send Stoddard into catastrophe with one glowing sentence. But Stoddard didn't speak.

In addition to his other reasons, he was anxious to beat Stoddard because of his very youth. It had galled Hargrave to be called, by the luck of the draw, to meet five of the youngest experts of the country in this tournament; it had galled him, not because he was loath to win from younger men, but because the public naturally discounted his victories over them.

On Tuesday he had overwhelmed a Western prodigy, a freckled schoolboy who had blushingly donned full-length trousers for this great event. On Wednesday he had won, three up and two to go, from a Harvard freshman, a clubable youngster who had capitulated to Hargrave primarily because his optimism had slowly been destroyed by Hargrave's rude acerbity. On Thursday he had met, and easily defeated, the junior champion of Westchester—defeated him by the psychology of the locker room, by knocking him off-balance at the outset, much as the gladiator Corbett once shook the poise of the gladiator Sullivan. In the semifinals yesterday he had beaten his man—browbeaten him—by diligently creating an atmosphere of such electric stress that a too-little-hardened Southron, sensitive as a girl, had gone to pieces at the ninth, surrendered at the twenty-seventh hole.

And Hargrave, whose bitterness toward the golfing world

had progressed arithmetically through these earlier rounds, had come up to the finals in a mood of acid which, in the true analysis, was a form of specious envy and regret. He realized that in comparison with any of the men he had removed from brackets, he was unattractive, aged, cynical, repugnant. He envied youth—but how could he regain his own? How could he crystallize at fifty-five the secret ambitions of a boy too young to vote? He couldn't stand before this fashionable gallery and, indicating Stoddard, cry out to them: "But I *want* to be like him! I *want* to be! And it's too late! It's too late!"

A great wave of self-glorification swept over him, and left him calmer, more pragmatical. After all, he was Hargrave, phenomenon of the links, the man who, beginning serious golf at the age of forty, unaided by professional tutoring, unschooled by previous experience in the realm of sports, had wrenched three amateur championships and unnumbered lesser prizes from keen fields. He was the unconquerable Hargrave; the man who had victoriously invaded France, England, Austria, Canada, Scotland. He had averaged below seventy-five for the previous three years on all courses and at all seasons. He had been six down with nine to play in the finals of the English Amateur, and come romping home to triumph, four under par. It was said of him that he was never beaten until the last putt on the last hole. Better than that, it was true.

By this time the gallery was massed rows deep around the eighteenth green. Hargrave crossed the little footbridge over the brook and permitted the vestige of a smile to temper the severity of his face. They hoped to see him lose, did they? Well, he had often disappointed them in the past; he could disappoint them now! All he required was a half, and he was barely off the green in two.

But even in the vanity which somewhat relieved the strain upon him, he was conscious of a burdening weariness which wasn't solely physical. He was impatient, not only to end the hole, and the match, but also to end his tournament golf forever. He was sure now that, winner or loser, he should never enter an important contest again. His nerves were disintegrating. He was losing that essential balance without which no man, however skillful in the academics of the game, may be renowned for his examples.

Next year he should unquestionably play with less surety, less vigor. Some unknown duffer would catch him unawares and vanquish him; and after that the descent from scratch would be rapid—headlong. It had been so with the greatest golfers of old; it would be so with Hargrave. Great as he was, he wasn't immune to the calendar. But to retire as merely a runner-up—that was unthinkable! To retire in favor of a slim boy whose Bachelorhood of Arts was yet a fond delusion—that was impossible! He *must* win—and on the eighteenth green, after he had holed out, he would break his putter over his knee, and he would say to the gallery—and it ought to be dramatic . . .

He brought himself to a standstill. His heart pounded suffocatingly. A lump rose in his throat, and choked him, and his whole intellect seemed to melt into confusion and feeble horror; there was a crushing weight on his chest. A slow, insistent cacophony poured through his brain, and for an instant his universe went black. The ball, which had appeared to carry so magnificently, and roll so well, had found a bowl-shaped depression in the turf, a wicked concavity an inch and a half in depth, two in diameter; and there it lay, part in the sunlight, part nestling under the shelter of a dry leaf, a ball accursed and sinister.

Blindly, and apprehensive, the champion turned to look at Stoddard. The boy was struggling to conceal the manifestation of his hopes; the muscles of his lower face were flexed and unrelenting. Between him and the flag was level turf, untroubled by the slightest taint of trickery or unevenness. He knew, and Hargrave knew, that nothing short of superhuman skill could bring the like to Hargrave. He knew, and Hargrave knew, that at the playoff of a tie the champion was doomed. The champion had faltered on the last few holes; his game was destined to collapse as surely as Stoddard's game was destined to rise supreme. As Hargrave paused, aghast, there came a rustle and a murmur from the gallery. A clear voice—a woman's voice—said ecstatically, "Then Bobby'll *win*—won't he?"

Hargrave glared in the direction of that voice. The veil of horror had gradually dissolved, but Hargrave, as he weighed the enigma of the shot, was visited by a cold apathy which staggered him. It wasn't a phlegmatic calm which sat upon him; it was inappetency—as though he had just been roused to a sense of proportionate values.

The matter of coaxing a golf ball out of a casual depression —what significance had it? Tomorrow would yet be tomorrow; with breakfast, and the newspapers, and all the immaterial details of living and breathing. Why all this bother and heartache about it? What was golf, that it should stir a man to the otherwise unprobed depths of his soul? Why should he care, why should he squander so much mental torture as could be computed by one tick of a clock, why should he tremble at this ridiculous experiment with a little white ball and a bit of iron on the end of a shaft of hickory?

For one elemental moment he was almost irresistibly impelled to pick that ball out of its lie, and dash it in the face of the gallery, hurl his clubs after it, and empty himself of the accumulated passion of fifty-five years. Sulfurous phrases crowded to his lips. . . .

And then he realized that all this time he had been glaring in the direction of a woman's voice. He exhaled fully, and held his hand out backward to the caddy.

"Niblick!" said Hargrave thickly.

The distance to the hole was greater than he had fancied. The lie of the ball was worse than he had feared. His calculation intimated that he must strike hard, and stiffly, with a pronounced up-and-down swing to get at the back of the ball. The force of the extricating stroke must be considerable; the green, however, was too fast, too fine, to permit liberty in the manner of approaching it. The ball, if it were to carry the full thirty yards to the pin, couldn't possibly receive sufficient reverse power to fall dead. It must, therefore, be played to reach the nearer rim of the green, and to drift gently on to the hole.

Hargrave caught his breath. The knowledge that he distrusted himself was infinitely more demoralizing than any other factor in the personal equation; he was shocked and baffled by his own uncertainty. Through his brain ran unceasingly the first tenets of the kindergarten of golf. He didn't imagine himself playing this shot: he speculated as to how Braid, or Vardon, or Ray or Duncan would play it. He was strangely convinced that for anyone else on earth it would be the simplest of recoveries, the easiest of pitches to the green.

He glanced at his caddy, and in that glance there was hidden an appeal which bespoke genuine pathos. Hargrave wasn't merely disturbed and distressed: he was palpitatingly afraid. He was afraid to strike, and he was afraid not to strike. His mind had lost its jurisdictive functions; he felt that his thews and sinews were in process of revolt against his will. He was excruciatingly perceptive of people watching him; of Stoddard regarding him humorously.

The collective enmity of the gallery oppressed and befuddled him. He was crazily in dread that when he swung the niblick upright, someone would snatch at it and divert its orbit. His ears strained for a crashing sound from the void; his overloaded nerves expected thunder. He knew that the fall of an oak leaf would reverberate through his aching head like an explosion of maximite and make him strike awry. His vitals seemed suddenly to slip away from his body, leaving merely a febrile husk of clammy skin to hold his heartbeats. The throbbing of the veins in his wrists was agony.

The niblick turned in his perspiring hands. He gripped more

firmly, and as his wrists reacted to the weight of the club head, he was automatic. The niblick rose, and descended, smashing down the hinder edge of the bowl-like cavity, and tearing the ball free. A spray of dust sprang up, and bits of sod and dirt. The ball shot forward, overrunning the hole by a dozen feet. Almost before it came to rest, Stoddard played carefully with a jigger, and landed ten inches from the hole.

Hargrave's sensation was that he was encompassed with walls which were closing in to stifle and crush him. That they were living walls was evident by the continuous whisper of respiration, and by the cross-motion of the sides. He was buried under the tremendous weight of thousands of personalities in conflict with his own. He tottered on the verge of hysteria. He was nervously exhausted, and yet he was upheld, and compelled to go on, to play, to putt, by nervous energy which by its very goad was unendurable. Hargrave looked at the green under his feet, and fought back a mad impulse to throw himself prone upon it, to scream at the top of his lungs, and writhe, to curse and blaspheme, and claw the grass with his nails. Each breath he drew was cousin to a sob.

He stood behind the ball to trace the line, and recognized that he was seeing neither the ball nor the hole. He couldn't see clearly the grass itself. He was stricken, as far as his environment was concerned, with utter ophthalmia. And although the boy Stoddard was outside the scope of Hargrave's vision, the champion saw Stoddard's face, as he had seen it just now, before Stoddard turned away. He despised Stoddard; unreasonably but implacably he despised him, because of the light he had seen in Stoddard's eyes. The boy wasn't a philosopher, like Hargrave: he was a baby, a whining infant grasping for the moon. *He* had no sense of proportion. That expression in his eyes had convicted him. This tournament was to him the horizon of his life. It *was* his life!

Hargrave's mouth was parched and bitter. He tried to moisten his lips. Details of the green began to develop in his consciousness as in a photographic negative. He saw the zinc-lined hole twelve feet away. His eye traced an imaginary line, starting from his ball and leading, not straight to the cup, but perceptibly to the left, then curving in along the briefest of undulations, swerving past a tiny spot where the grass was sunscorched, and so to the haven of the hole.

If he could sink that curling putt, nothing could deprive him of his victory. He would be down in four, and Stoddard now lay three. He would have a half—and the match by one up in thirty-six holes. He would be the Amateur Champion of the United States—and he could quit! He could quit as the only man who ever won in three successive years. And if he missed, and Stoddard took the hole in four to five, Hargrave knew that even if his legs would support him to the first tee, his arms would fall at the next trial. He doubted if sanity itself would stay with him for another hole.

The murmur of the gallery appalled him with its vehemence. The noise was as the rushing of the falls of Niagara. Hargrave stood wearily erect, and eyed that section of the crowd which was before him. He was puzzled by the excitement, the anxiety of that crowd. He was violently angered that no smile of encouragement, of good-fellowship, met his inquiring gaze. The misanthrope in him surged to the surface, and he was supercilious—just for a second!—and then that sense of impotence, of futility, of shaken poise fell upon him once more, and his throat filled.

He needed the half. He must hole this putt. He was thinking now not so much of the result of holing it as of the result of missing it. He could fancy the wretched spectacle he would make of himself on the playoff; he could fancy the explosive, tumultuous joy of the gallery; he could picture the dumb, stunned radiance of Stoddard. And Stoddard was so young. Hargrave wouldn't have minded defeat at the hands of an older man, he told himself fiercely—but at the hands of a boy! Hargrave, the man who had made more whirlwind finishes than any other two players of the game, beaten by a stripling who had come from behind!

On the sixteenth and seventeenth holes the champion had reviled himself, scourged himself, between shots. He had clenched his teeth and sworn to achieve perfection. He had persuaded himself that each of his mishaps had been due to carelessness; and he had known in his heart that each of them was due to a fault, a palpable fault of execution. On the eighteenth hole he had reverted to sincerity with himself. He was harrowed and upset, and in confessing his culpability he had removed at least the crime of overconfidence. But this was far worse! He was doubting his own judgment now: he had determined upon the line of his putt, and he was reconsidering it.

He peered again and, blinking, discovered that there were tears in his eyes. The hole seemed farther away than ever, the green less true, the bare spot more prominent, the cup smaller. He wondered dully if he hadn't better putt straight for the hole. He braced himself, and tremblingly addressed the ball with his putter. This was the shot that would take stomach! This was the end!

He had a vision of tomorrow, and the day after, and the day after that. If he missed this putt, and lost the match, how could he exonerate himself? He had no other pleasure in life, he had no other recreation, no other balm for his wasted years. If he tried again next season, he would lose in the first round. He knew it. And he might live to be seventy—or eighty—always with this gloomy pall of failure hanging over him. Another failure—another Waterloo! And this time he would be to himself the apotheosis of failure! Why—Hargrave's heart stopped beating—*he wouldn't be champion!*

With a final hum, which was somehow different from those that had preceded it, the gallery faded from his consciousness.

Stoddard was as though he had never existed. Hargrave bent over the putter, and a curious echo rang not unpleasantly in his ears. He saw a white ball in the sunlight, a stretch of lawn, a zinc-lined hole in shadow. There was no longer an objective world in which he lived; there were no longer men and women. He himself was not corporeal. His brain, his rationality, were lost in the abysmal gulf of nothingness. He was merely a part of geometric space; he was an atom of that hypothetical line between two points. His whole being was, for the moment, the essence of the linear standard.

In a blank detachment—for he had no recollection of having putted—he saw the ball spinning on a course to the left of the hole. A terrible agony seized him, and for the second time a black curtain shut him off from actuality. It lifted, leaving him on the brink of apoplexy, and he saw that the ball had curved correctly to the fraction of an inch, and was just dropping solidly and unerringly into the cup.

And from the morning paper:

> *Hargrave was dormie one. Both men drove two hundred and fifty yards straight down the course. Stoddard banged away with his brassey, and nearly got home when the ball caromed off a stone in the brook. Hargrave, playing with that marvelous rapidity which characterizes his game, wouldn't be downed, and promptly sent off a screaming brassey which found a bad lie just off the green, but after studying it fully ten seconds—twice his usual allowance—he chipped out prettily with a niblick. Stoddard ran up, dead. Hardly glancing at the line of his fifteen-footer, Hargrave confidently ran down the putt for a birdie four, and the match. Probably no man living would have played the hole under similar conditions, with such absence of nerves and such abnormal assurance. From tee to green Hargrave barely addressed the ball at all. And certainly in the United States, if not in the world, there is*

no player who can compete with Hargrave when the champion happens to be in a fighting mood.

To our reporter Hargrave stated positively after the match that he will defend his title next year.

WINTER
DREAMS

·

F. SCOTT FITZGERALD

I

Some of the caddies were poor as sin and lived in one-room houses with a neurasthenic cow in the front yard, but Dexter Green's father owned the second best grocery store in Black Bear—the best one was "The Hub," patronized by the wealthy people from Sherry Island—and Dexter caddied only for pocket money.

In the fall when the days became crisp and gray, and the long Minnesota winter shut down like the white lid of a box, Dexter's skis moved over the snow that hid the fairways of the golf course. At these times the country gave him a feeling of profound melancholy—it offended him that the links should lie in enforced fallowness, haunted by ragged sparrows for the long season. It was dreary, too, that on the tees where the gay colors fluttered in summer there were now only the desolate sandboxes knee-deep in crusted ice. When he crossed the hills the wind blew cold as misery and if the sun was out he tramped with his eyes squinted up against the hard dimensionless glare.

In April the winter ceased abruptly. The snow ran down into Black Bear Lake scarcely tarrying for the early golfers to brave the season with red and black balls. Without elation, without an interval of moist glory, the cold was gone.

Dexter knew that there was something dismal about this Northern spring, just as he knew there was something gorgeous about the fall. Fall made him clinch his hands and tremble and repeat idiotic sentences to himself, and make brisk abrupt gestures of command to imaginary audiences and armies. October filled him with hope which November raised to a sort of ecstatic triumph, and in this mood the fleeting brilliant impressions of the summer at Sherry Island were ready grist to his mill. He became a golf champion and defeated Mr. T. A. Hedrick in a marvelous match played a hundred times over the fairways of his imagination, a match each detail of which he changed about untiringly—sometimes he won with almost laughable ease, sometimes he came up magnificently from behind. Again, stepping from a Pierce-Arrow automobile, like Mr. Mortimer Jones, he strolled frigidly into the lounge of the Sherry Island Golf Club—or perhaps, surrounded by an admiring crowd, he gave an exhibition of fancy diving from the springboard of the club raft. . . . Among those who watched him in open-mouthed wonder was Mr. Mortimer Jones.

And one day it came to pass that Mr. Jones—himself and not his ghost—came up to Dexter with tears in his eyes and said that Dexter was the damned best caddy in the club, and wouldn't he decide not to quit if Mr. Jones made it worth his while, because every other damn caddy in the club lost one ball a hole for him—regularly—

"No, sir," said Dexter decisively. "I don't want to caddie any more." Then, after a pause: "I'm too old."

"You're not more than fourteen. Why the devil did you decide just this morning that you wanted to quit? You promised that next week you'd go over to the state tournament with me."

"I decided I was too old."

Dexter handed in his "A Class" badge, collected what money was due him from the caddy master, and walked home to Black Bear Village.

"The best damned caddy I ever saw," shouted Mr. Mortimer Jones over a drink that afternoon. "Never lost a ball! Willing! Intelligent! Quiet! Honest! Grateful!"

The little girl who had done this was eleven—beautifully ugly as little girls are apt to be who are destined after a few years to be inexpressibly lovely and bring no end of misery to a great number of men. The spark, however, was perceptible. There was a general ungodliness in the way her lips twisted down at the corners when she smiled, and in the—Heaven help us!—in the almost passionate quality of her eyes. Vitality is born in such women. It was utterly in evidence now, shining through her thin frame in a sort of glow.

She had come eagerly out on to the course at nine o'clock with a white linen nurse and five small new golf-clubs in a white canvas bag which the nurse was carrying. When Dexter first saw her she was standing by the caddy house, rather ill at ease and trying to conceal the fact by engaging her nurse in an obviously unnatural conversation graced by startling and irrelevant grimaces from herself.

"Well, it's certainly a nice day, Hilda," Dexter heard her say. She drew down the corners of her mouth, smiled, and glanced furtively around, her eyes in transit falling for an instant on Dexter.

Then to the nurse:

"Well, I guess there aren't very many people out here this morning, are there?"

The smile again—radiant, blatantly artificial—convincing.

"I don't know what we're supposed to do now," said the nurse, looking nowhere in particular.

"Oh, that's all right. I'll fix it up."

Dexter stood perfectly still, his mouth slightly ajar. He knew that if he moved forward a step his stare would be in her line of vision—if he moved backward he would lose his full view of her face. For a moment he had not realized how young she was. Now he remembered having seen her several times the year before—in bloomers.

Suddenly, involuntarily, he laughed, a short abrupt laugh—then, startled by himself, he turned and began to walk quickly away.

"Boy!"

Dexter stopped.

"Boy—"

Beyond question he was addressed. Not only that, but he was treated to that absurd smile, that preposterous smile—the memory of which at least a dozen men were to carry into middle age.

"Boy, do you know where the golf teacher is?"

"He's giving a lesson."

"Well, do you know where the caddy master is?"

"He isn't here yet this morning."

"Oh." For a moment this baffled her. She stood alternately on her right and left foot.

"We'd like to get a caddy," said the nurse. "Mrs. Mortimer Jones sent us out to play golf, and we don't know how without we get a caddy."

Here she was stopped by an ominous glance from Miss Jones, followed immediately by the smile.

"There aren't any caddies here except me," said Dexter to

the nurse, "and I got to stay here in charge until the caddy master gets here."

"Oh."

Miss Jones and her retinue now withdrew, and at a proper distance from Dexter became involved in a heated conversation, which was concluded by Miss Jones taking one of the clubs and hitting it on the ground with violence. For further emphasis she raised it again and was about to bring it down smartly upon the nurse's bosom, when the nurse seized the club and twisted it from her hands.

"You damn little mean old *thing!*" cried Miss Jones wildly.

Another argument ensued. Realizing that the elements of the comedy were implied in the scene, Dexter several times began to laugh, but each time restrained the laugh before it reached audibility. He could not resist the monstrous conviction that the little girl was justified in beating the nurse.

The situation was resolved by the fortuitous appearance of the caddy master, who was appealed to immediately by the nurse.

"Miss Jones is to have a little caddy, and this one says he can't go."

"Mr. McKenna said I was to wait here till you came," said Dexter quickly.

"Well, he's here now." Miss Jones smiled cheerfully at the caddy master. Then she dropped her bag and set off at a haughty mince toward the first tee.

"Well?" The caddy master turned to Dexter. "What you standing there like a dummy for? Go pick up the young lady's clubs."

"I don't think I'll go out today," said Dexter.

"You don't—"

"I think I'll quit."

The enormity of his decision frightened him. He was a favorite caddy, and the thirty dollars a month he earned through the summer were not to be made elsewhere around the lake.

But he had received a strong emotional shock, and his perturbation required a violent and immediate outlet.

It is not so simple as that, either. As so frequently would be the case in the future, Dexter was unconsciously dictated to by his winter dreams.

II

Now, of course, the quality and the seasonability of these winter dreams varied, but the stuff of them remained. They persuaded Dexter several years later to pass up a business course at the state university—his father, prospering now, would have paid his way—for the precarious advantage of attending an older and more famous university in the East, where he was bothered by his scanty funds. But do not get the impression, because his winter dreams happened to be concerned at first with musings on the rich, that there was anything merely snobbish in the boy. He wanted not association with glittering things and glittering people—he wanted the glittering things themselves. Often he reached out for the best without knowing why he wanted it—and sometimes he ran up against the mysterious denials and prohibitions in which life indulges. It is with one of those denials and not with his career as a whole that this story deals.

He made money. It was rather amazing. After college he went to the city from which Black Bear Lake draws its wealthy patrons. When he was only twenty-three and had been there not quite two years, there were already people who liked to say: "Now *there's* a boy—" All about him rich men's sons were peddling bonds precariously, or investing patrimonies precariously, or plodding through the two dozen volumes of the "George Washington Commercial Course," but Dexter borrowed a thousand dollars on his college degree and his confident mouth, and bought a partnership in a laundry.

It was a small laundry when he went into it, but Dexter made a specialty of learning how the English washed fine woolen golf stockings without shrinking them, and within a year he was catering to the trade that wore knickerbockers. Men were insisting that their Shetland hose and sweaters go to his laundry, just as they had insisted on a caddy who could find golf balls. A little later he was doing their wives' lingerie as well— and running five branches in different parts of the city. Before he was twenty-seven he owned the largest string of laundries in his section of the country. It was then that he sold out and went to New York. But the part of his story that concerns us goes back to the days when he was making his first big success.

When he was twenty-three Mr. Hart—one of the gray-haired men who like to say, "Now there's a boy"—gave him a guest card to the Sherry Island Golf Club for a weekend. So he signed his name one day on the register, and that afternoon played golf in a foursome with Mr. Hart and Mr. Sandwood and Mr. T. A. Hedrick. He did not consider it necessary to remark that he had once carried Mr. Hart's bag over this same links, and that he knew every trap and gully with his eyes shut —but he found himself glancing at the four caddies who trailed them, trying to catch a gleam or gesture that would remind him of himself, that would lessen the gap which lay between his present and his past.

It was a curious day, slashed abruptly with fleeting, familiar impressions. One minute he had the sense of being a trespasser —in the next he was impressed by the tremendous superiority he felt toward Mr. T. A. Hedrick, who was a bore and not even a good golfer any more.

Then, because of a ball Mr. Hart lost near the fifteenth green, an enormous thing happened. While they were searching the stiff grasses of the rough there was a clear call of "Fore!" from behind a hill in their rear. And as they all turned abruptly from their search a bright new ball sliced abruptly over the hill and caught Mr. T. A. Hedrick in the abdomen.

"By Gad!" cried Mr. T. A. Hedrick, "they ought to put

PERFECT LIES

some of these crazy women off the course. It's getting to be outrageous."

A head and a voice came up together over the hill:

"Do you mind if we go through?"

"You hit me in the stomach!" declared Mr. Hedrick wildly.

"Did I?" The girl approached the group of men. "I'm sorry. I yelled, 'Fore!'"

Her glance fell casually on each of the men—then scanned the fairway for her ball.

"Did I bounce into the rough?"

It was impossible to determine whether this question was ingenuous or malicious. In a moment, however, she left no doubt, for as her partner came up over the hill she called cheerfully:

"Here I am! I'd have gone on the green except that I hit something."

As she took her stance for a short mashie shot, Dexter looked at her closely. She wore a blue gingham dress, rimmed at throat and shoulders with a white edging that accentuated her tan. The quality of exaggeration, of thinness, which had made her passionate eyes and down-turning mouth absurd at eleven, was gone now. She was arrestingly beautiful. The color in her cheeks was centered like the color in a picture—it was not a "high" color, but a sort of fluctuating and feverish warmth, so shaded that it seemed at any moment it would recede and disappear. This color and the mobility of her mouth gave a continual impression of flux, of intense life, of passionate vitality—balanced only partially by the sad luxury of her eyes.

She swung her mashie impatiently and without interest, pitching the ball into a sand pit on the other side of the green. With a quick, insincere smile and a careless "Thank you!" she went on after it.

"That Judy Jones!" remarked Mr. Hedrick on the next tee, as they waited—some moments—for her to play on ahead. "All

92

she needs is to be turned up and spanked for six months and then to be married off to an old-fashioned cavalry captain."

"My God, she's good-looking!" said Mr. Sandwood, who was just over thirty.

"Good-looking!" cried Mr. Hedrick contemptuously. "She always looks as if she wanted to be kissed! Turning those big cow eyes on every calf in town!"

It was doubtful if Mr. Hedrick intended a reference to the maternal instinct.

"She'd play pretty good golf if she'd try," said Mr. Sandwood.

"She has no form," said Mr. Hedrick solemnly.

"She has a nice figure," said Mr. Sandwood.

"Better thank the Lord she doesn't drive a swifter ball," said Mr. Hart, winking at Dexter.

Later in the afternoon the sun went down with a swirl of gold and varying blues and scarlets, and left the dry, rustling night of Western summer. Dexter watched from the veranda of the golf club, watched the even overlap of the waters in the little wind, silver molasses under the harvest moon. Then the moon held a finger to her lips and the lake became a clear pool, pale and quiet. Dexter put on his bathing suit and swam out to the farthest raft, where he stretched dripping on the wet canvas of the springboard.

There was a fish jumping and a star shining and the lights around the lake were gleaming. Over on a dark peninsula a piano was playing the songs of last summer and of summers before that—songs from "Chin-Chin" and "The Count of Lux-embourg" and "The Chocolate Soldier"*—and because the sound of a piano over a stretch of water had always seemed beautiful to Dexter he lay perfectly quiet and listened.

The tune the piano was playing at that moment had been gay

* Popular Broadway musicals of the day.

and new five years before when Dexter was a sophomore at college. They had played it at a prom once when he could not afford the luxury of proms, and he had stood outside the gymnasium and listened. The sound of the tune precipitated in him a sort of ecstasy and it was with that ecstasy he viewed what happened to him now. It was a mood of intense appreciation, a sense that, for once, he was magnificently attuned to life and that everything about him was radiating a brightness and a glamor he might never know again.

A low, pale oblong detached itself suddenly from the darkness of the island, spitting forth the reverberate sound of a racing motorboat. Two white streamers of cleft water rolled themselves out behind it and almost immediately the boat was beside him, drowning out the hot tinkle of the piano in the drone of its spray. Dexter raising himself on his arms was aware of a figure standing at the wheel, of two dark eyes regarding him over the lengthening space of water—then the boat had gone by and was sweeping in an immense and purposeless circle of spray round and round in the middle of the lake. With equal eccentricity one of the circles flattened out and headed back toward the raft.

"Who's that?" she called, shutting off her motor. She was so near now that Dexter could see her bathing suit, which consisted apparently of pink rompers.

The nose of the boat bumped the raft, and as the latter tilted rakishly he was precipitated toward her. With different degrees of interest they recognized each other.

"Aren't you one of those men we played through this afternoon?" she demanded.

He was.

"Well, do you know how to drive a motorboat? Because if you do I wish you'd drive this one so I can ride on the surfboard behind. My name is Judy Jones"—she favored him with an absurd smirk—rather, what tried to be a smirk, for, twist her mouth as she might, it was not grotesque, it was merely beautiful—"and I live in a house over there on the island, and in that house there is a man waiting for me. When he drove up at the door I drove out of the dock because he says I'm his ideal."

There was a fish jumping and a star shining and the lights around the lake were gleaming. Dexter sat beside Judy Jones and she explained how her boat was driven. Then she was in the water, swimming to the floating surfboard with a sinuous crawl. Watching her was without effort to the eye, watching a branch waving or a sea gull flying. Her arms, burned to butternut, moved sinuously among the dull platinum ripples, elbow appearing first, casting the forearm back with a cadence of falling water, then reaching out and down, stabbing a path ahead.

They moved out into the lake: turning, Dexter saw that she was kneeling on the low rear of the now uptilted surfboard.

"Go faster," she called, "fast as it'll go."

Obediently he jammed the lever forward and the white spray mounted at the bow. When he looked around again the girl was standing up on the rushing board, her arms spread wide, her eyes lifted toward the moon.

"It's awful cold," she shouted. "What's your name?"

He told her.

"Well, why don't you come to dinner tomorrow night?"

His heart turned over like the flywheel of the boat, and, for the second time, her casual whim gave a new direction to his life.

III

Next evening while he waited for her to come downstairs, Dexter peopled the soft deep summer room and the sun porch that opened from it with the men who had already loved Judy Jones. He knew the sort of men they were—the men who when he first went to college had entered from the great prep schools with graceful clothes and the deep tan of healthy summers. He had seen that, in one sense, he was better than these men. He was newer and stronger. Yet in acknowledging to himself that he wished his children to be like them he was admitting that he was but the rough, strong stuff from which they eternally sprang.

When the time had come for him to wear good clothes, he had known who were the best tailors in America, and the best tailors in America had made him the suit he wore this evening. He had acquired that particular reserve peculiar to his university, that set it off from other universities. He recognized the value to him of such a mannerism and he had adopted it; he knew that to be careless in dress and manner required more confidence than to be careful. But carelessness was for his children. His mother's name had been Krimplich. She was a Bohemian of the peasant class and she had talked broken English to the end of her days. Her son must keep to the set patterns.

At a little after seven Judy Jones came downstairs. She wore a blue silk afternoon dress, and he was disappointed at first that she had not put on something more elaborate. This feeling was accentuated when, after a brief greeting, she went to the door of a butler's pantry and pushing it open called: "You can serve dinner, Martha." He had rather expected that a butler would announce dinner, that there would be a cocktail. Then he put these thoughts behind him as they sat down side by side on a lounge and looked at each other.

"Father and mother won't be here," she said thoughtfully.

He remembered the last time he had seen her father, and he was glad the parents were not to be here tonight—they might wonder who he was. He had been born in Keeble, a Minnesota village fifty miles farther north, and he always gave Keeble as his home instead of Black Bear Village. Country towns were well enough to come from if they weren't inconveniently in sight and used as footstools by fashionable lakes.

They talked of his university, which she had visited frequently during the past two years, and of the nearby city which supplied Sherry Island with its patrons, and whither Dexter would return next day to his prospering laundries.

During dinner she slipped into a moody depression which gave Dexter a feeling of uneasiness. Whatever petulance she uttered in her throaty voice worried him. Whatever she smiled at—at him, at a chicken liver, at nothing—it disturbed him that her smile could have no root in mirth, or even in amusement. When the scarlet corners of her lips curved down, it was less a smile than an invitation to a kiss.

Then, after dinner, she led him out on the dark sun porch and deliberately changed the atmosphere.

"Do you mind if I weep a little?" she said.

"I'm afraid I'm boring you," he responded quickly.

"You're not. I like you. But I've just had a terrible afternoon. There was a man I cared about, and this afternoon he told me out of a clear sky that he was poor as a churchmouse. He'd never even hinted it before. Does this sound horribly mundane?"

"Perhaps he was afraid to tell you."

"Suppose he was," she answered. "He didn't start right. You see, if I'd thought of him as poor—well, I've been mad about loads of poor men, and fully intended to marry them all. But in this case, I hadn't thought of him that way, and my interest in him wasn't strong enough to survive the shock. As if a girl calmly informed her fiancé that she was a widow. He might not object to widows, but—

"Let's start right," she interrupted herself suddenly. "Who are you, anyhow?"

For a moment Dexter hesitated. Then: "I'm nobody," he announced. "My career is largely a matter of futures."

"Are you poor?"

"No," he said frankly, "I'm probably making more money than any man my age in the Northwest. I know that's an obnoxious remark, but you advised me to start right."

There was a pause. Then she smiled and the corners of her

mouth drooped and an almost imperceptible sway brought her closer to him, looking up into his eyes. A lump rose in Dexter's throat, and he waited breathless for the experiment, facing the unpredictable compound that would form mysteriously from the elements of their lips. Then he saw—she communicated her excitement to him, lavishly, deeply, with kisses that were not a promise but a fulfilment. They aroused in him not hunger demanding renewal but surfeit that would demand more surfeit . . . kisses that were like charity, creating want by holding back nothing at all.

It did not take him many hours to decide that he had wanted Judy Jones ever since he was a proud, desirous little boy.

IV

It began like that—and continued, with varying shades of intensity, on such a note right up to the dénouement. Dexter surrendered a part of himself to the most direct and unprincipled personality with which he had ever come in contact. Whatever Judy wanted, she went after with the full pressure of her charm. There was no divergence of method, no jockeying for position or premeditation of effects—there was a very little mental side to any of her affairs. She simply made men conscious to the highest degree of her physical loveliness. Dexter had no desire to change her. Her deficiencies were knit up with a passionate energy that transcended and justified them.

When, as Judy's head lay against his shoulder that first night, she whispered, "I don't know what's the matter with me. Last night I thought I was in love with a man and tonight I think I'm in love with you—" It seemed to him a beautiful and romantic thing to say. It was the exquisite excitability that for the moment he controlled and owned. But a week later he was compelled to view this same quality in a different light. She took him in her roadster to a picnic supper, and after supper she disappeared, likewise in her roadster, with another man. Dexter became enormously upset and was scarcely able to be decently civil to the other people present. When she assured him that she had not kissed the other man, he knew she was lying—yet he was glad that she had taken the trouble to lie to him.

He was, as he found before the summer ended, one of a varying dozen who circulated about her. Each of them had at one time been favored above all others—about half of them still basked in the solace of occasional sentimental revivals. Whenever one showed signs of dropping out through long neglect, she granted him a brief honeyed hour, which encouraged him to tag along for a year or so longer. Judy made these forays upon the helpless and defeated without malice, indeed half unconscious that there was anything mischievous in what she did.

When a new man came to town every one dropped out—dates were automatically canceled.

The helpless part of trying to do anything about it was that she did it all herself. She was not a girl who could be "won" in the kinetic sense—she was proof against cleverness, she was proof against charm: if any of these assailed her too strongly she would immediately resolve the affair to a physical basis, and under the magic of her physical splendor the strong as well as the brilliant played her game and not their own. She was entertained only by the gratification of her desires and by the direct exercise of her own charm. Perhaps from so much youthful love, so many youthful lovers, she had come, in self-defense, to nourish herself wholly from within.

Succeeding Dexter's first exhilaration came restlessness and dissatisfaction. The helpless ecstasy of losing himself in her was opiate rather than tonic. It was fortunate for his work during the winter that those moments of ecstasy came infrequently. Early in their acquaintance it had seemed for a while that there was a deep and spontaneous mutual attraction—that first August, for example—three days of long evenings on her dusky veranda, of strange wan kisses through the late afternoon, in

shadowy alcoves or behind the protecting trellises of the garden arbors, of mornings when she was fresh as a dream and
almost shy at meeting him in the clarity of the rising day. There
was all the ecstasy of an engagement about it, sharpened by his
realization that there was no engagement. It was during those
three days that, for the first time, he had asked her to marry
him. She said, "Maybe someday." She said, "Kiss me." She
said, "I'd like to marry you." She said, "I love you"—she said
—nothing.

The three days were interrupted by the arrival of a New
York man who visited at her house for half September. To
Dexter's agony, rumor engaged them. The man was the son of
the president of a great trust company. But at the end of a
month it was reported that Judy was yawning. At a dance one
night she sat all evening in a motorboat with a local beau, while
the New Yorker searched the club for her frantically. She told
the local beau that she was bored with her visitor, and two days
later he left. She was seen with him at the station, and it was
reported that he looked very mournful indeed.

On this note the summer ended. Dexter was twenty-four,
and he found himself increasingly in a position to do as he
wished. He joined two clubs in the city and lived at one of
them. Though he was by no means an integral part of the stag
lines at these clubs, he managed to be on hand at dances where
Judy Jones was likely to appear. He could have gone out socially as much as he liked—he was an eligible young man, now,
and popular with downtown fathers. His confessed devotion to
Judy Jones had rather solidified his position. But he had no
social aspirations and rather despised the dancing men who
were always on tap for the Thursday or Saturday parties and
who filled in at dinners with the younger married set. Already
he was playing with the idea of going East to New York. He
wanted to take Judy Jones with him. No disillusion as to the
world in which she had grown up could cure his illusion as to
her desirability.

Remember that—for only in the light of it can what he did for her be understood.

Eighteen months after he first met Judy Jones he became engaged to another girl. Her name was Irene Scheerer, and her father was one of the men who had always believed in Dexter. Irene was light-haired and sweet and honorable, and a little stout, and she had two suitors whom she pleasantly relinquished when Dexter formally asked her to marry him.

Summer, fall, winter, spring, another summer, another fall— so much he had given of his active life to the incorrigible lips of Judy Jones. She had treated him with interest, with encouragement, with malice, with indifference, with contempt. She had inflicted on him the innumerable little slights and indignities possible in such a case—as if in revenge for having ever cared for him at all. She had beckoned him and yawned at him and beckoned him again and he had responded often with bitterness and narrowed eyes. She had brought him ecstatic happiness and intolerable agony of spirit. She had caused him untold inconvenience and not a little trouble. She had insulted him, and she had ridden over him, and she had played his interest in her against his interest in his work—for fun. She had done everything to him except to criticize him—this she had not done—it seemed to him only because it might have sullied the utter indifference she manifested and sincerely felt toward him.

When autumn had come and gone again it occurred to him that he could not have Judy Jones. He had to beat this into his mind but he convinced himself at last. He lay awake at night for a while and argued it over. He told himself the trouble and the pain she had caused him, he enumerated her glaring deficiencies as a wife. Then he said to himself that he loved her, and after a while he fell asleep. For a week, lest he imagined her husky voice over the telephone or her eyes opposite him at lunch, he worked hard and late, and at night he went to his office and plotted out his years.

At the end of a week he went to a dance and cut in on her

once. For almost the first time since they had met he did not ask her to sit out with him or tell her that she was lovely. It hurt him that she did not miss these things—that was all. He was not jealous when he saw that there was a new man tonight. He had been hardened against jealousy long before.

He stayed late at the dance. He sat for an hour with Irene Scheerer and talked about books and about music. He knew very little about either. But he was beginning to be master of his own time now, and he had a rather priggish notion that he —the young and already fabulously successful Dexter Green— should know more about such things.

That was in October, when he was twenty-five. In January, Dexter and Irene became engaged. It was to be announced in June, and they were to be married three months later.

The Minnesota winter prolonged itself interminably, and it was almost May when the winds came soft and the snow ran down into Black Bear Lake at last. For the first time in over a year Dexter was enjoying a certain tranquillity of spirit. Judy Jones had been in Florida, and afterward in Hot Springs, and somewhere she had been engaged, and somewhere she had broken it off. At first, when Dexter had definitely given her up, it had made him sad that people still linked them together and asked for news of her, but when he began to be placed at dinner next to Irene Scheerer people didn't ask him about her any more—they told him about her. He ceased to be an authority on her.

May at last. Dexter walked the streets at night when the darkness was damp as rain, wondering that so soon, with so little done, so much of ecstasy had gone from him. May one year back had been marked by Judy's poignant, unforgivable, yet forgiven turbulence—it had been one of those rare times when he fancied she had grown to care for him. That old penny's worth of happiness he had spent for this bushel of content. He knew that Irene would be no more than a curtain spread behind him, a hand moving among gleaming teacups, a voice calling to children . . . fire and loveliness were gone, the magic of nights and the wonder of the varying hours and seasons . . . slender lips, downturning, dropping to his lips and bearing him up into a heaven of eyes. . . . The thing was deep in him. He was too strong and alive for it to die lightly.

In the middle of May when the weather balanced for a few days on the thin bridge that led to deep summer he turned in one night at Irene's house. Their engagement was to be announced in a week now—no one would be surprised at it. And tonight they would sit together on the lounge at the University Club and look on for an hour at the dancers. It gave him a sense of solidity to go with her—she was so sturdily popular, so intensely "great."

He mounted the steps of the brownstone house and stepped inside.

"Irene," he called.

Mrs. Scheerer came out of the living room to meet him.

"Dexter," she said. "Irene's gone upstairs with a splitting headache. She wanted to go with you, but I made her go to bed."

"Nothing serious, I—"

"Oh, no. She's going to play golf with you in the morning. You can spare her for just one night, can't you, Dexter?"

Her smile was kind. She and Dexter liked each other. In the living room he talked for a moment before he said good night.

Returning to the University Club, where he had rooms, he stood in the doorway for a moment and watched the dancers. He leaned against the door post, nodded at a man or two—yawned.

"Hello, darling."

The familiar voice at his elbow startled him. Judy Jones had left a man and crossed the room to him—Judy Jones, a slender enameled doll in cloth of gold: gold in a band at her head, gold in two slipper points at her dress's hem. The fragile glow of her face seemed to blossom as she smiled at him. A breeze of warmth and light blew through the room. His hands in the pockets of his dinner jacket tightened spasmodically. He was filled with a sudden excitement.

"When did you get back?" he asked casually.

"Come here and I'll tell you about it."

She turned and he followed her. She had been away—he could have wept at the wonder of her return. She had passed through enchanted streets, doing things that were like provocative music. All mysterious happenings, all fresh and quickening hopes, had gone away with her, come back with her now.

She turned in the doorway.

"Have you a car here? If you haven't, I have."

"I have a coupé."

In then, with a rustle of golden cloth. He slammed the door. Into so many cars she had stepped—like this—like that—her back against the leather, so—her elbow resting on the door—waiting. She would have been soiled long since had there been anything to soil her—except herself—but this was her own self outpouring.

With an effort he forced himself to start the car and back into the street. This was nothing, he must remember. She had done this before, and he had put her behind him, as he would have crossed a bad account from his books.

He drove slowly downtown and, affecting abstraction, traversed the deserted streets of the business section, peopled here and there where a movie was giving out its crowd or where consumptive or pugilistic youth lounged in front of pool halls. The clink of glasses and the slap of hands on the bars issued from saloons, cloisters of glazed glass and dirty yellow light.

She was watching him closely and the silence was embarrassing, yet in this crisis he could find no casual word with which to profane the hour. At a convenient turning he began to zigzag back toward the University Club.

"Have you missed me?" she asked suddenly.

1 0 4

"Everybody missed you."

He wondered if she knew of Irene Scheerer. She had been back only a day—her absence had been almost contemporaneous with his engagement.

"What a remark!" Judy laughed sadly—without sadness. She looked at him searchingly. He became absorbed in the dashboard.

"You're handsomer than you used to be," she said thoughtfully. "Dexter, you have the most rememberable eyes."

He could have laughed at this, but he did not laugh. It was the sort of thing that was said to sophomores. Yet it stabbed at him.

"I'm awfully tired of everything, darling." She called everyone darling, endowing the endearment with careless, individual camaraderie. "I wish you'd marry me."

The directness of this confused him. He should have told her now that he was going to marry another girl, but he could not tell her. He could as easily have sworn that he had never loved her.

"I think we'd get along," she continued on the same note, "unless probably you've forgotten me and fallen in love with another girl."

Her confidence was obviously enormous. She had said, in effect, that she found such a thing impossible to believe, that if it were true he had merely committed a childish indiscretion—and probably to show off. She would forgive him, because it was not a matter of any moment but rather something to be brushed aside lightly.

"Of course you could never love anybody but me," she continued. "I like the way you love me. Oh, Dexter, have you forgotten last year?"

"No, I haven't forgotten."

"Neither have I!"

Was she sincerely moved—or was she carried along by the wave of her own acting?

"I wish we could be like that again," she said, and he forced himself to answer:

"I don't think we can."

"I suppose not. . . . I hear you're giving Irene Scheerer a violent rush."

There was not the faintest emphasis on the name, yet Dexter was suddenly ashamed.

"Oh, take me home," cried Judy suddenly: "I don't want to go back to that idiotic dance—with those children."

Then, as he turned up the street that led to the residence district, Judy began to cry quietly to herself. He had never seen her cry before.

The dark street lightened, the dwellings of the rich loomed up around them, he stopped his coupé in front of the great white bulk of the Mortimer Joneses' house, somnolent, gorgeous, drenched with the splendor of the damp moonlight. Its solidity startled him. The strong walls, the steel of the girders, the breadth and beam and pomp of it were there only to bring out the contrast with the young beauty beside him. It was sturdy to accentuate her slightness—as if to show what a breeze could be generated by a butterfly's wing.

He sat perfectly quiet, his nerves in wild clamor, afraid that if he moved he would find her irresistibly in his arms. Two tears had rolled down her wet face and trembled on her upper lip.

"I'm more beautiful than anybody else," she said brokenly. "Why can't I be happy?" Her moist eyes tore at his stability—her mouth turned slowly downward with an exquisite sadness: "I'd like to marry you if you'll have me, Dexter. I suppose you think I'm not worth having, but I'll be so beautiful for you, Dexter."

A million phrases of anger, pride, passion, hatred, tenderness fought on his lips. Then a perfect wave of emotion washed over him, carrying off with it a sediment of wisdom, of convention, of doubt, of honor. This was his girl who was speaking, his own, his beautiful, his pride.

"Won't you come in?" He heard her draw in her breath sharply.

Waiting.

"All right," his voice was trembling. "I'll come in."

V

It was strange that neither when it was over nor a long time afterward did he regret that night. Looking at it from the perspective of ten years, the fact that Judy's flare for him endured just one month seemed of little importance. Nor did it matter that by his yielding he subjected himself to a deeper agony in the end and gave serious hurt to Irene Scheerer and to Irene's parents, who had befriended him. There was nothing sufficiently pictorial about Irene's grief to stamp itself on his mind.

Dexter was at bottom hard-minded. The attitude of the city on his action was of no importance to him, not because he was going to leave the city, but because any outside attitude on the situation seemed superficial. He was completely indifferent to popular opinion. Nor, when he had seen that it was no use, that he did not possess in himself the power to move fundamentally or to hold Judy Jones, did he bear any malice toward her. He loved her, and he would love her until the day he was too old for loving but he could not have her. So he tasted the deep pain that is reserved only for the strong, just as he had tasted for a little while the deep happiness.

Even the ultimate falsity of the grounds upon which Judy terminated the engagement that she did not want to "take him away" from Irene—Judy who had wanted nothing else—did not revolt him. He was beyond any revulsion or any amusement.

He went East in February with the intention of selling out his laundries and settling in New York—but the war came to

America in March and changed his plans. He returned to the West, handed over the management of the business to his partner, and went into the first officers' training camp in late April. He was one of those young thousands who greeted the war with a certain amount of relief, welcoming the liberation from webs of tangled emotion.

VI

This story is not his biography, remember, although things creep into it which have nothing to do with those dreams he had when he was young. We are almost done with them and with him now. There is only one more incident to be related here, and it happens seven years farther on.

It took place in New York, where he had done well—so well that there were no barriers too high for him. He was thirty-two years old, and, except for one flying trip immediately after the war, he had not been West in seven years. A man named Devlin from Detroit came into his office to see him in a business way, and then and there this incident occurred, and closed out, so to speak, this particular side of his life.

"So you're from the Middle West," said the man Devlin with careless curiosity. "That's funny—I thought men like you were probably born and raised on Wall Street. You know—wife of one of my best friends in Detroit came from your city. I was an usher at the wedding."

Dexter waited with no apprehension of what was coming.

"Judy Simms," said Devlin with no particular interest: "Judy Jones she was once."

"Yes, I knew her." A dull impatience spread over him. He had heard, of course, that she was married—perhaps deliberately he had heard no more.

"Awfully nice girl," brooded Devlin meaninglessly, "I'm sort of sorry for her."

"Why?" Something in Dexter was alert, receptive, at once.

"Oh, Lud Simms has gone to pieces in a way. I don't mean he ill-uses her, but he drinks and runs around—"

"Doesn't she run around?"

"No. Stays at home with her kids."

"Oh."

"She's a little too old for him," said Devlin.

"Too old!" cried Dexter. "Why, man, she's only twenty-seven."

He was possessed with a wild notion of rushing out into the streets and taking a train to Detroit. He rose to his feet spasmodically.

"I guess you're busy," Devlin apologized quickly. "I didn't realize—"

"No, I'm not busy," said Dexter, steadying his voice. "I'm not busy at all. Not busy at all. Did you say she was—twenty-seven? No, I said she was twenty-seven."

"Yes, you did," agreed Devlin dryly.

"Go on, then. Go on."

"What do you mean?"

"About Judy Jones."

Devlin looked at him helplessly.

"Well, that's—I told you all there is to it. He treats her like the devil. Oh, they're not going to get divorced or anything. When he's particularly outrageous she forgives him. In fact, I'm inclined to think she loves him. She was a pretty girl when she first came to Detroit."

A pretty girl! The phrase struck Dexter as ludicrous.

"Isn't she—a pretty girl, any more?"

"Oh, she's all right."

"Look here," said Dexter, sitting down suddenly. "I don't understand. You say she was a 'pretty girl' and now you say she's 'all right.' I don't understand what you mean—Judy Jones wasn't a pretty girl, at all. She was a great beauty. Why, I knew her. I knew her. She was—"

Devlin laughed pleasantly.

"I'm not trying to start a row," he said. "I think Judy's a nice girl and I like her. I can't understand how a man like Lud Simms could fall madly in love with her, but he did." Then he added: "Most of the women like her."

Dexter looked closely at Devlin, thinking wildly that there must be a reason for this, some insensitivity in the man or some private malice.

"Lots of women fade just like *that*," Devlin snapped his fingers. "You must have seen it happen. Perhaps I've forgotten how pretty she was at her wedding. I've seen her so much since then, you see. She has nice eyes."

A sort of dullness settled down upon Dexter. For the first time in his life he felt like getting very drunk. He knew that he was laughing loudly at something Devlin had said, but he did not know what it was or why it was funny. When, in a few minutes, Devlin went he lay down on his lounge and looked out the window at the New York skyline into which the sun was sinking in dull lovely shades of pink and gold.

He had thought that having nothing else to lose he was invulnerable at last—but he knew that he had just lost something more, as surely as if he had married Judy Jones and seen her fade away before his eyes.

The dream was gone. Something had been taken from him. In a sort of panic he pushed the palms of his hands into his eyes and tried to bring up a picture of the waters lapping on Sherry Island and the moonlit veranda, and gingham on the golf links and the dry sun and the gold color of her neck's soft down. And her mouth damp to his kisses and her eyes plaintive with melancholy and her freshness like new fine linen in the morning. Why, these things were no longer in the world! They had existed and they existed no longer.

For the first time in years the tears were streaming down his face. But they were for himself now. He did not care about mouth and eyes and moving hands. He wanted to care, and he could not care. For he had gone away and he could never go back any more. The gates were closed, the sun was gone down, and there was no beauty but the gray beauty of steel that withstands all time. Even the grief he could have borne was left behind in the country of illusion, of youth, of the richness of life, where his winter dreams had flourished.

"Long ago," he said, "long ago, there was something in me, but now that thing is gone. Now that thing is gone, that thing is gone. I cannot cry. I cannot care. That thing will come back no more."

A
CADDY'S
DIARY

·

RING LARDNER

I am 16 of age and am a caddy at the Pleasant View Golf Club but only temporary as I expect to soon land a job some wheres as asst pro as my game is good enough now to be a pro but to young looking. My pal Joe Bean also says I have not got enough swell head to make a good pro but suppose that will come in time. Joe is a wise cracker.

But first will put down how I come to be writeing this diary, we have got a member name Mr Colby who writes articles in the newspapers and I hope for his sakes that he is a better writer then he plays golf but any way I cadded for him a good many times last yr and today he was out for the first time this yr and I cadded for him and we got talking about this in that and something was mentioned in regards to the golf articles by Alex Laird that comes out every Sun in the paper Mr Colby writes his articles for so I asked Mr Colby did he know how much Laird got paid for the articles and he said he did not know but supposed that Laird had to split 50-50 with who ever wrote the articles for him. So I said don't he write the articles himself and Mr Colby said why no he guessed not. Laird may be a master mind in regards to golf he said, but this is no sign he can write about it as very few men can write decent let alone a pro. Writeing is a nag.

How do you learn it I asked him.

Well he said read what other people writes and study them and write things yourself, and maybe you will get on to the nag and maybe you wont.

Well Mr Colby I said do you think I could get on to it?

Why he said smileing I did not know that was your ambition to be a writer.

Not exactly was my reply, but I am going to be a golf pro myself and maybe some day I will get good enough so as the papers will want I should write them articles and if I can learn to write them myself why I will not have to hire another writer and split with them.

Well said Mr Colby smileing you have certainly got the right temperament for a pro, they are all big hearted fellows.

But listen Mr Colby I said if I want to learn it would not do me no good to copy down what other writers have wrote, what I would have to do would be write things out of my own head.

That is true said Mr. Colby.

Well I said what could I write about?

Well said Mr Colby why dont you keep a diary and every night after your supper set down and write what happened that day and write who you cadded for and what they done only leave me out of it. And you can write down what people say and what you think and etc., it will be the best kind of practice for you, and once in a wile you can bring me your writeings and I will tell you the truth if they are good or rotten.

So that is how I come to be writeing this diary is so as I can get some practice writeing and maybe if I keep at it long enough I can get on to the nag.

Friday, Apr. 14

We been haveing Apr. showers for a couple days and nobody out on the course so they has been nothing happen that I could write down in my diary but dont want to leave it go to long or will never learn the trick so will try and write a few lines about a caddys life and some of our members and etc.

Well I and Joe Bean is the 2 oldest caddys in the club and I been cadding now for 5 yrs and quit school 3 yrs ago tho my mother did not like it for me to quit but my father said he can read and write and figure so what is the use in keeping him there any longer as greek and latin dont get you no credit at the grocer, so they lied about my age to the trunce officer and I been cadding every yr from March till Nov and the rest of the winter I work around Heismans store in the village.

Dureing the time I am cadding I genally always manage to play at lease 9 holes a day myself on wk days and some times 18 and am never more then 2 or 3 over par figures on our course but it is a cinch.

I played the engineers course 1 day last summer in 75 which is some golf and some of our members who has been playing 20 yrs would give their right eye to play as good as myself.

I use to play around with our pro Jack Andrews till I got so as I could beat him pretty near every time we played and now he wont play with me no more, he is not a very good player for a pro but they claim he is a good teacher. Personly I think golf teachers is a joke tho I am glad people is suckers enough to fall for it as I expect to make my liveing that way. We have got a member Mr Dunham who must of took 500 lessons in the past

1 1 4

3 yrs and when he starts to shoot he trys to remember all the junk Andrews has learned him and he gets dizzy and they is no telling where the ball will go and about the safest place to stand when he is shooting is between he and the hole.

I dont beleive the club pays Andrews much salery but of course he makes pretty fair money giveing lessons but his best graft is a 3 some which he plays 2 and 3 times a wk with Mr Perdue and Mr Lewis and he gives Mr Lewis a stroke a hole and they genally break some wheres near even but Mr Perdue made a 83 one time so he thinks that is his game so he insists on playing Jack even, well they always play for $5.00 a hole and Andrews makes $20.00 to $30.00 per round and if he wanted to cut loose and play his best he could make $50.00 to $60.00 per round but a couple of wallops like that and Mr Perdue might get cured so Jack figures a small stedy income is safer.

I have got a pal name Joe Bean and we pal around together as he is about my age and he says some comical things and some times will wisper some thing comical to me wile we are cadding and it is all I can do to help from laughing out loud, that is one of the first things a caddy has got to learn is never laugh out loud only when a member makes a joke. How ever on the days when theys ladies on the course I dont get a chance to caddy with Joe because for some reason another the woman folks dont like Joe to caddy for them wile on the other hand they are always after me tho I am no Othello for looks or do I seek their flavors, in fact it is just the opp and I try to keep in the back ground when the fair sex appears on the seen as cadding for ladies means you will get just so much money and no more as theys no chance of them loosning up. As Joe says the rule against tipping is the only rule the woman folks keeps.

Theys one lady how ever who I like to caddy for as she looks like Lillian Gish and it is a pleasure to just look at her and I would caddy for her for nothing tho it is hard to keep your eye on the ball when you are cadding for this lady, her name is Mrs Doane.

Sat. Apr. 15

This was a long day and am pretty well wore out but must not get behind in my writeing practice. I and Joe carried all day for Mr Thomas and Mr Blake. Mr Thomas is the vice president of one of the big banks down town and he always slips you a $1.00 extra per round but beleive me you earn it cadding for Mr Thomas, there is just 16 clubs in his bag includeing 5 wood clubs tho he has not used the wood in 3 yrs but says he has got to have them along in case his irons goes wrong on him. I dont know how bad his irons will have to get before he will think they have went wrong on him but personly if I made some of the tee shots he made today I would certainly considder some kind of a change of weppons.

Mr Thomas is one of the kind of players that when it has took him more than 6 shots to get on the green he will turn to you and say how many have I had caddy and then you are suppose to pretend like you was thinking a minute and then say 4, then he will say to the man he is playing with well I did not know if I had shot 4 or 5 but the caddy says it is 4. You see in this way it is not him that is cheating but the caddy but he makes it up to the caddy afterwards with a $1.00 tip.

Mr Blake gives Mr Thomas a stroke a hole and they play a $10.00 nassua and niether one of them wins much money from the other one but even if they did why $10.00 is chickens food to men like they. But the way they crab and squak about different things you would think their last $1.00 was at stake. Mr Thomas started out this a.m. with a 8 and a 7 and of course that spoilt the day for him and me to. Theys lots of men that if they dont make a good score on the first 2 holes they will founder all the rest of the way around and raze H with their caddy and if I was laying out a golf course I would make the first 2 holes so darn easy that you could not help from getting a 4 or better

on them and in that way everybody would start off good na-
tured and it would be a few holes at lease before they begun to
turn sour.

Mr Thomas was beat both in the a.m. and p.m. in spite of my
help as Mr Blake is a pretty fair counter himself and I heard
him say he got a 88 in the p.m. which is about a 94 but any way
it was good enough to win. Mr Blakes regular game is about a
90 takeing his own figures and he is one of these cocky guys
that takes his own game serious and snears at men that cant
break 100 and if you was to ask him if he had ever been over
100 himself he would say not since the first yr he begun to
play. Well I have watched a lot of those guys like he and I will
tell you how they keep from going over 100 namely by doing
just what he done this a.m. when he come to the 13th hole.
Well he missed his tee shot and dubbed along and finely he got
in a trap on his 4th shot and I seen him take 6 wallops in the
trap and when he had took the 6th one his ball was worse off
then when he started so he picked it up and marked a X down
on his score card. Well if he had of played out the hole why the
best he could of got was a 11 by holeing his next niblick shot
but he would of probly got about a 20 which would of made
him around 108 as he admitted takeing a 88 for the other 17
holes. But I bet if you was to ask him what score he had made
he would say O I was terrible and I picked up on one hole but
if I had of played them all out I guess I would of had about a
92.

These is the kind of men that laughs themselfs horse when
they hear of some dub takeing 10 strokes for a hole but if they
was made to play out every hole and mark down their real
score their card would be decorated with many a big casino.

Well as I say I had a hard day and was pretty sore along
towards the finish but still I had to laugh at Joe Bean on the
15th hole which is a par 3 and you can get there with a fair
drive and personly I am genally hole high with a midiron, but
Mr Thomas topped his tee shot and dubbed a couple with his

mashie and was still quiet a ways off the green and he stood studing the situation a minute and said to Mr Blake well I wonder what I better take here. So Joe Bean was standing by me and he said under his breath take my advice and quit you old rascal.

Mon. Apr. 17

Yesterday was Sun and I was to wore out last night to write as I cadded 45 holes. I cadded for Mr Colby in the a.m. and Mr Langley in the p.m. Mr Thomas thinks golf is wrong on the sabath tho as Joe Bean says it is wrong any day the way he plays it.

This a.m. they was nobody on the course and I played 18 holes by myself and had a 5 for a 76 on the 18th hole but the wind got a hold of my drive and it went out of bounds. This p.m. they was 3 of us had a game of rummy started but Miss Rennie and Mrs Thomas come out to play and asked for me to caddy for them, they are both terrible.

Mrs Thomas is Mr Thomas wife and she is big and fat and shakes like jell and she always says she plays golf just to make her skinny and she dont care how rotten she plays as long as she is getting the exercise, well maybe so but when we find her ball in a bad lie she aint never sure it is hers till she picks it up and smells it and when she puts it back beleive me she don't cram it down no gopher hole.

Miss Rennie is a good looker and young and they say she is engaged to Chas Crane. He is one of our members and is the best player in the club and dont cheat hardly at all and he has got a job in the bank where Mr Thomas is the vice president. Well I have cadded for Miss Rennie when she was playing with Mr Crane and I have cadded for her when she was playing alone or with another lady and I often think if Mr Crane could hear her talk when he was not around he would not be so stuck on her. You would be surprised at some of the words that falls from those fare lips.

1 1 8

Well the 2 ladies played for 2 bits a hole and Miss Rennie was haveing a terrible time wile Mrs Thomas was shot with luck on the greens and sunk 3 or 4 putts that was murder. Well Miss Rennie used some expressions which was best not repeated but towards the last the luck changed around and it was Miss Rennie that was sinking the long ones and when they got to the 18th tee Mrs Thomas was only 1 up.

Well we had started pretty late and when we left the 17th green Miss Rennie made the remark that we would have to hurry to get the last hole played, well it was her honor and she got the best drive she made all day about 120 yds down the fair way. Well Mrs Thomas got nervous and looked up and missed her ball a ft and then done the same thing right over and when she finely hit it she only knocked it about 20 yds and this made her lay 3. Well her 4th went wild and lit over in the rough in the apple trees. It was a cinch Miss Rennie would win the hole unless she dropped dead.

Well we all went over to hunt for Mrs Thomas ball but we would of been lucky to find it even in day light but now you could not hardly see under the trees, so Miss Rennie said drop another ball and we will not count no penalty. Well it is some job any time to make a woman give up hunting for a lost ball and all the more so when it is going to cost her 2 bits to play the hole out so there we stayed for at lease 10 minutes till it was so dark we could not see each other let alone a lost ball and finely Mrs Thomas said well it looks like we could not finish, how do we stand? Just like she did not know how they stood.

You had me one down up to this hole said Miss Rennie.

Well that is finishing pretty close said Mrs Thomas.

I will have to give Miss Rennie credit that what ever word she thought of for this occasion she did not say it out loud but when she was paying me she said I might of give you a quarter tip only I have to give Mrs Thomas a quarter she dont deserve so you dont get it.

Fat chance I would of had any way.

Well we been haveing some more bad weather but today the weather was all right but that was the only thing that was all right. This p.m. I cadded double for Mr Thomas and Chas Crane the club champion who is stuck on Miss Rennie. It was a 4 some with he and Mr Thomas against Mr Blake and Jack Andrews the pro, they was only playing best ball so it was really just a match between Mr Crane and Jack Andrews and Mr Crane win by 1 up. Joe Bean cadded for Jack and Mr Blake. Mr Thomas was terrible and I put in a swell p.m. lugging that heavy bag of his besides Mr Cranes bag.

Mr Thomas did not go off of the course as much as usual but he kept hitting behind the ball and he run me ragged replaceing his divots but still I had to laugh when we was playing the 4th hole which you have to drive over a ravine and every time Mr Thomas misses his tee shot on this hole why he makes a squak about the ravine and says it ought not to be there and etc.

Today he had a terrible time getting over it and afterwards he said to Jack Andrews this is a joke hole and ought to be changed. So Joe Bean wispered to me that if Mr Thomas kept on playing like he was the whole course would be changed.

Then a little wile later when we come to the long 9th hole Mr Thomas got a fair tee shot but then he whiffed twice missing the ball by a ft and the 3rd time he hit it but it only went a little ways and Joe Bean said that is 3 trys and no gain, he will have to punt.

But I must write down about my tough luck, well we finely got through the 18 holes and Mr Thomas reached down in his pocket for the money to pay me and he genally pays for Mr Crane to when they play together as Mr Crane is just a employ in the bank and dont have much money but this time all Mr Thomas had was a $20.00 bill so he said to Mr Crane I guess you will have to pay the boy Charley so Charley dug down and got the money to pay me and he paid just what it was and not a dime over, where if Mr Thomas had of had the change I would of got a $1.00 extra at lease and maybe I was not sore and Joe Bean to because of course Andrews never gives you nothing and Mr Blake dont tip his caddy unless he wins.

They are a fine bunch of tight wads said Joe and I said well Crane is all right only he just has not got no money.

He aint all right no more than the rest of them said Joe.

Well at lease he dont cheat on his score I said.

And you know why that is said Joe, neither does Jack Andrews cheat on his score but that is because they play to good. Players like Crane and Andrews that goes around in 80 or better cant cheat on their score because they make the most of the holes in around 4 strokes and the 4 strokes includes their tee shot and a couple of putts which everybody is right there to watch them when they make them and count them right along with them. So if they make a 4 and claim a 3 why people would just laugh in their face and say how did the ball get from the fair way on to the green, did it fly? But the boys that takes 7 and 8 strokes to a hole can shave their score and you know they are shaveing it but you have to let them get away with it because you cant prove nothing. But that is one of the penaltys for being a good player, you cant cheat.

To hear Joe tell it pretty near everybody are born crooks, well maybe he is right.

Wed. Apr. 26

Today Mrs Doane was out for the first time this yr and asked for me to caddy for her and you bet I was on the job. Well how are you Dick she said, she always calls me by name. She asked me what had I been doing all winter and was I glad to see her and etc.

She said she had been down south all winter and played golf pretty near every day and would I watch her and notice how much she had improved.

Well to tell the truth she was no better than last yr and wont never be no better and I guess she is just to pretty to be a golf player but of course when she asked me did I think her game was improved I had to reply yes indeed as I would not hurt her feelings and she laughed like my reply pleased her. She played with Mr and Mrs Carter and I carried the 2 ladies bags wile Joe Bean cadded for Mr Carter. Mrs Carter is a ugly dame with things on her face and it must make Mr Carter feel sore when he looks at Mrs Doane to think he married Mrs Carter but I suppose they could not all marry the same one and besides Mrs Doane would not be a sucker enough to marry a man like he who drinks all the time and is pretty near always stood, tho Mr Doane who she did marry aint such a H of a man himself tho dirty with money.

They all gave me the laugh on the 3rd hole when Mrs Doane was makeing her 2d shot and the ball was in the fair way but laid kind of bad and she just ticked it and then she asked me if winter rules was in force and I said yes so we teed her ball up so as she could get a good shot at it and they gave me the laugh for saying winter rules was in force.

You have got the caddys bribed Mr Carter said to her.

But she just smiled and put her hand on my sholder and said Dick is my pal. That is enough of a bribe to just have her touch you and I would caddy all day for her and never ask for a cent only to have her smile at me and call me her pal.

Sat. Apr. 29

Today they had the first club tournament of the yr and they have a monthly tournament every month and today was the first one, it is a handicap tournament and everybody plays in it and they have prizes for low net score and low gross score and etc. I cadded for Mr Thomas today and will tell what happened.

They played a 4 some and besides Mr Thomas we had Mr Blake and Mr Carter and Mr Dunham. Mr Dunham is the worst man player in the club and the other men would not play with him a specialy on a Saturday only him and Mr Blake is partners together in business. Mr Dunham has got the highest handicap in the club which is 50 but it would have to be 150 for him to win a prize. Mr Blake and Mr Carter has got a handicap of about 15 a piece I think and Mr Thomas is 30, the first prize for the low net score for the day was a dozen golf balls and the second low score a 1/2 dozen golf balls and etc.

Well we had a great battle and Mr Colby ought to been along to write it up or some good writer. Mr Carter and Mr Dunham played partners against Mr Thomas and Mr Blake which ment that Mr Carter was playing Thomas and Blakes best ball, well Mr Dunham took the honor and the first ball he hit went strate off to the right and over the fence outside of the grounds, well he done the same thing 3 times. Well when he finely did hit one in the course why Mr Carter said why not let us not count them 3 first shots of Mr Dunham as they was just practice. Like H we wont count them said Mr Thomas we must count every shot and keep our scores correct for the tournament.

All right said Mr Carter.

Well we got down to the green and Mr Dunham had about 11 and Mr Carter sunk a long putt for a par 5. Mr Blake all ready had 5 strokes and so did Mr Thomas and when Mr Carter sunk his putt why Mr Thomas picked his ball up and said Carter wins the hole and I and Blake will take 6s. Like H you will said Mr Carter, this is a tournament and we must play every hole out and keep our scores correct. So Mr Dunham putted and went down in 13 and Mr Blake got a 6 and Mr Thomas missed 2 easy putts and took a 8 and maybe he was not boiling.

Well it was still their honor and Mr Dunham had one of his dizzy spells on the 2d tee and he missed the ball twice before he hit it and then Mr Carter drove the green which is only a midiron shot and then Mr Thomas stepped up and missed the ball just like Mr Dunham. He was wild and yelled at Mr Dunham no man could play golf playing with a man like you, you would spoil anybodys game.

Your game was all ready spoiled said Mr Dunham, it turned sour on the 1st green.

You would turn anybody sour said Mr Thomas.

Well Mr Thomas finely took a 8 for the hole which is a par 3 and it certainly looked bad for him winning a prize when he started out with 2 8s, and he and Mr Dunham had another terrible time on No 3 and wile they was messing things up a 2 some come up behind us and hollered fore and we left them go through tho it was Mr Clayton and Mr Joyce and as Joe Bean said they was probly dissapointed when we left them go through as they are the kind that feels like the day is lost if they cant write to some committee and preffer charges.

Well Mr Thomas got a 7 on the 3rd and he said well it is no wonder I am off of my game today as I was up 1/2 the night with my teeth.

Well said Mr Carter if I had your money why on the night before a big tournament like this I would hire somebody else to set up with my teeth.

Well I wished I could remember all that was said and done but any way Mr Thomas kept getting sore and sore and we got to the 7th tee and he had not made a decent tee shot all day so Mr Blake said to him why dont you try the wood as you cant do no worse?

By Geo I beleive I will said Mr Thomas and took his driver out of the bag which he had not used it for 3 yrs.

Well he swang and zowie away went the ball pretty near 8 inches distants wile the head of the club broke off clean and saled 50 yds down the course. Well I have got a hold on myself so as I dont never laugh out loud and I beleive the other men was scarred to laugh or he would of killed them so we all stood there in silents waiting for what would happen.

Well without saying a word he come to where I was standing

and took his other 4 wood clubs out of the bag and took them to a tree which stands a little ways from the tee box and one by one he swang them with all his strength against the trunk of the tree and smashed them to H and gone, all right gentlemen that is over he said.

Well to cut it short Mr Thomas score for the first 9 was a even 60 and then we started out on the 2d 9 and you would not think it was the same man playing, on the first 3 holes he made 2 4s and a 5 and beat Mr Carter even and followed up with a 6 and a 5 and that is how he kept going up to the 17th hole.

What has got in to you Thomas said Mr Carter.

Nothing said Mr Thomas only I broke my hoodoo when I broke them 5 wood clubs.

Yes I said to myself and if you had broke them 5 wood clubs 3 yrs ago I would not of broke my back lugging them around.

Well we come to the 18th tee and Mr Thomas had a 39 which give him a 99 for 17 holes, well everybody drove off and as we was following along why Mr Klabor come walking down the course from the club house on his way to the 17th green to join some friends and Mr Thomas asked him what had he made and he said he had turned in a 93 but his handicap is only 12 so that gave him a 81.

That wont get me no wheres he said as Charley Crane made a 75.

Well said Mr Thomas I can tie Crane for low net if I get a 6 on this hole.

Well it come his turn to make his 2d and zowie he hit the ball pretty good but they was a hook on it and away she went in to the woods on the left, the ball laid in behind a tree so as they was only one thing to do and that was waste a shot getting it back on the fair so that is what Mr Thomas done and it took him 2 more to reach the green.

How many have you had Thomas said Mr Carter when we was all on the green.

Let me see said Mr Thomas and then turned to me, how many have I had caddy?

I dont know I said.

Well it is either 4 or 5 said Mr Thomas.

I think it is 5 said Mr Carter.

I think it is 4 said Mr Thomas and turned to me again and said how many have I had caddy?

So I said 4.

Well said Mr Thomas personly I was not sure myself but my caddy says 4 and I guess he is right.

Well the other men looked at each other and I and Joe Bean looked at each other but Mr Thomas went ahead and putted and was down in 2 putts.

Well he said I certainly come to life on them last 9 holes.

So he turned in his score as 105 and with his handicap of 30 why that give him a net of 75 which was the same as Mr Crane so instead of Mr Crane getting 1 dozen golf balls and Mr Thomas getting 1/2 a dozen golf balls why they will split the 1st and 2nd prize makeing 9 golf balls a piece.

Tues. May 2

This was the first ladies day of the season and even Joe Bean had to carry for the fair sex. We cadded for a 4 some which was Miss Rennie and Mrs Thomas against Mrs Doane and Mrs Carter. I guess if they had of kept their score right the total for the 4 of them would of ran well over a 1000.

Our course has a great many trees and they seemed to have a traction for our 4 ladies today and we was in amongst the trees more then we was on the fair way.

Well said Joe Bean theys one thing about cadding for these dames, it keeps you out of the hot sun.

And another time he said he felt like a boy scout studing wood craft.

These dames is always up against a stump he said.

And another time he said that it was not fair to charge these dames regular ladies dues in the club as they hardly ever used the course.

Well it seems like they was a party in the village last night and of course the ladies was talking about it and Mrs Doane said what a lovely dress Miss Rennie wore to the party and Miss Rennie said she did not care for the dress herself.

Well said Mrs Doane if you want to get rid of it just hand it over to me.

I wont give it to you said Miss Rennie but I will sell it to you at 1/2 what it cost me and it was a bargain at that as it only cost me a $100.00 and I will sell it to you for $50.00.

I have not got $50.00 just now to spend said Mrs Doane and besides I dont know would it fit me.

Sure it would fit you said Miss Rennie, you and I are exactly the same size and figure, I tell you what I will do with you I will play you golf for it and if you beat me you can have the gown for nothing and if I beat you why you will give me $50.00 for it.

All right but if I loose you may have to wait for your money said Mrs Doane.

So this was on the 4th hole and they started from there to play for the dress and they was both terrible and worse then usual on acct of being nervous as this was the biggest stakes they had either of them ever played for tho the Doanes has got a bbl of money and $50.00 is chickens food.

Well we was on the 16th hole and Mrs Doane was 1 up and Miss Rennie sliced her tee shot off in the rough and Mrs Doane landed in some rough over on the left so they was clear across the course from each other. Well I and Mrs Doane went over to her ball and as luck would have it it had come to rest in a kind of a groove where a good player could not hardly make a good shot of it let alone Mrs Doane. Well Mrs Thomas was out in the middle of the course for once in her life and the other 2 ladies was over on the right side and Joe Bean with them so they was nobody near Mrs Doane and I.

Do I have to play it from there she said. I guess you do was my reply.

Why Dick have you went back on me she said and give me one of her looks.

Well I looked to see if the others was looking and then I kind of give the ball a shove with my toe and it come out of the groove and laid where she could get a swipe at it.

This was the 16th hole and Mrs Doane win it by 11 strokes to 10 and that made her 2 up and 2 to go. Miss Rennie win the 17th but they both took a 10 for the 18th and that give Mrs Doane the match.

Well I wont never have a chance to see her in Miss Rennies dress but if I did I aint sure that I would like it on her.

Fri. May 5

Well I never thought we would have so much excitement in the club and so much to write down in my diary but I guess I better get busy writeing it down as here it is Friday and it was Wed. a.m. when the excitement broke loose and I was getting ready to play around when Harry Lear the caddy master come running out with the paper in his hand and showed it to me on the first page.

It told how Chas Crane our club champion had went south with $8000 which he had stole out of Mr Thomas bank and a swell looking dame that was a stenographer in the bank had elloped with him and they had her picture in the paper and I will say she is a pip but who would of thought a nice quiet young man like Mr Crane was going to prove himself a gay Romeo and a specialy as he was engaged to Miss Rennie tho she now says she broke their engagement a month ago but any way the whole affair has certainly give everybody something to talk about and one of the caddys Lou Crowell busted Fat Brunner in the nose because Fat claimed to of been the last one that cadded for Crane. Lou was really the last one and cadded for him last Sunday which was the last time Crane was at the club.

Well everybody was thinking how sore Mr Thomas would be and they would better not mention the affair around him and etc. but who should show up to play yesterday but Mr Thomas himself and he played with Mr Blake and all they talked about the whole p.m. was Crane and what he had pulled.

Well Thomas said Mr Blake I am curious to know if the thing come as a suprise to you or if you ever had a hunch that he was libel to do a thing like this.

Well Blake said Mr Thomas I will admit that the whole thing come as a complete suprise to me as Crane was all most like my son you might say and I was going to see that he got along all right and that is what makes me sore is not only that he has proved himself dishonest but that he could be such a sucker as to give up a bright future for a sum of money like $8000 and a doll face girl that cant be no good or she would not of let him do it. When you think how young he was and the carreer he might of had why it certainly seems like he sold his soul pretty cheap.

That is what Mr Thomas had to say or at lease part of it as I cant remember a 1/2 of all he said but any way this p.m. I cadded for Mrs Thomas and Mrs Doane and that is all they talked about to, and Mrs Thomas talked along the same lines like her husband and said she had always thought Crane was to smart a young man to pull a thing like that and ruin his whole future.

He was geting $4000 a yr said Mrs Thomas and everybody liked him and said he was bound to get ahead so that is what makes it such a silly thing for him to of done, sell his soul for $8000 and a pretty face.

Yes indeed said Mrs Doane.

Well all the time I was listening to Mr Thomas and Mr Blake and Mrs Thomas and Mrs Doane why I was thinking about something which I wanted to say to them but it would of ment me looseing my job so I kept it to myself but I sprung it on my pal Joe Bean on the way home tonight.

1 2 9

Joe I said what do these people mean when they talk about Crane selling his soul?

Why you know what they mean said Joe, they mean that a person that does something dishonest for a bunch of money or a gal or any kind of a reward why the person that does it is selling his soul.

All right I said and it dont make no differents does it if the reward is big or little?

Why no said Joe only the bigger it is the less of a sucker the person is that goes after it.

Well I said here is Mr Thomas who is vice president of a big bank and worth a bbl of money and it is just a few days ago when he lied about his golf score in order so as he would win 9 golf balls instead of a 1/2 a dozen.

Sure said Joe.

And how about his wife Mrs Thomas I said, who plays for 2 bits a hole and when her ball dont lie good why she picks it up and pretends to look at it to see if it is hers and then puts it back in a good lie where she can sock it.

And how about my friend Mrs Doane that made me move her ball out of a rut to help her beat Miss Rennie out of a party dress.

Well said Joe what of it?

Well I said it seems to me like these people have got a lot of nerve to pan Mr Crane and call him a sucker for doing what he done, it seems to me like $8000 and a swell dame is a pretty fair reward compared with what some of these other people sells their soul for, and I would like to tell them about it.

Well said Joe go ahead and tell them but maybe they will tell you something right back.

What will they tell me?

Well said Joe they might tell you this, that when Mr Thomas asks you how many shots he has had and you say 4 when you know he has had 5, why you are selling your soul for a $1.00

tip. And when you move Mrs Doanes ball out of a rut and give it a good lie, what are you selling your soul for? Just a smile.

O keep your mouth shut I said to him.

I am going to said Joe and would advice you to do the same.

THE
HEART
OF A
GOOF

·

P. G. WODEHOUSE

It was a morning when all nature shouted "Fore!" The breeze, as it blew gently up from the valley, seemed to bring a message of hope and cheer, whispering of chip shots holed and brassies landing squarely on the meat. The fairway, as yet unscarred by the irons of a hundred dubs, smiled greenly up at the azure sky; and the sun, peeping above the trees, looked like a giant golf ball perfectly lofted by the mashie of some unseen god and about to drop dead by the pin of the eighteenth. It was the day of the opening of the course after the long winter, and a crowd of considerable dimensions had collected at the first tee. Plus fours gleamed in the sunshine, and the air was charged with happy anticipation.

In all that gay throng there was but one sad face. It belonged to the man who was waggling his driver over the new ball perched on its little hill of sand. This man seemed careworn, hopeless. He gazed down the fairway, shifted his feet, waggled, gazed down the fairway again, shifted the dogs once more, and waggled afresh. He waggled as Hamlet might have waggled, moodily, irresolutely. Then, at last, he swung, and, taking from his caddie the niblick which the intelligent lad had been holding in readiness from the moment when he had walked on to the tee, trudged wearily off to play his second.

The Oldest Member, who had been observing the scene with a benevolent eye from his favourite chair on the terrace, sighed.

"Poor Jenkinson," he said, "does not improve."

"No," agreed his companion, a young man with open features and a handicap of six. "And yet I happen to know that he has been taking lessons all the winter at one of those indoor places."

"Futile, quite futile," said the Sage with a shake of his snowy head. "There is no wizard living who could make that man go round in an average of sevens. I keep advising him to give up the game."

"You!" cried the young man, raising a shocked and startled face from the driver with which he was toying. *"You* told him to give up golf! Why, I thought—"

"I understand and approve of your horror," said the Oldest Member gently. "But you must bear in mind that Jenkinson's is not an ordinary case. You know and I know scores of men who have never broken a hundred and twenty in their lives, and yet contrive to be happy, useful members of society. However badly they may play, they are able to forget. But with Jenkinson it is different. He is not one of those who can take it or leave it alone. His only chance of happiness lies in complete abstinence. Jenkinson is a goof."

"A what?"

"A goof," repeated the Sage. "One of those unfortunate beings who have allowed this noblest of sports to get too great a grip upon them, who have permitted it to eat into their souls, like some malignant growth. The goof, you must understand, is not like you and me. He broods. He becomes morbid. His goofery unfits him for the battles of life. Jenkinson, for example, was once a man with a glowing future in the hay, corn, and feed business, but a constant stream of hooks, tops, and slices gradually made him so diffident and mistrustful of himself, that he let opportunity after opportunity slip, with the result that other, sterner, hay, corn, and feed merchants passed him in the race. Every time he had the chance to carry through some big deal in hay, or to execute some flashing *coup* in corn and feed, the fatal diffidence generated by a hundred rotten rounds would undo him. I understand his bankruptcy may be expected at any moment."

"My golly!" said the young man, deeply impressed. "I hope I never become a goof. Do you mean to say there is really no cure except giving up the game?"

The Oldest Member was silent for a while.

"It is curious that you should have asked that question," he said at last, "for only this morning I was thinking of the one case in my experience where a goof was enabled to overcome his deplorable malady. It was owing to a girl, of course. The longer I live, the more I come to see that most things are. But you will, no doubt, wish to hear the story from the beginning."

The young man rose with the startled haste of some wild creature, which, wandering through the undergrowth, perceives the trap in his path.

"I should love to," he mumbled, "only I shall be losing my place at the tee."

"The goof in question," said the Sage, attaching himself with quiet firmness to the youth's coat button, "was a man of about your age, by name Ferdinand Dibble. I knew him well. In fact, it was to me—"

"Some other time, eh?"

"It was to me," proceeded the Sage placidly, "that he came for sympathy in the great crisis of his life, and I am not ashamed to say that when he had finished laying bare his soul to me there were tears in my eyes. My heart bled for the boy."

"I bet it did. But—"

The Oldest Member pushed him gently back into his seat.

"Golf," he said, "is the Great Mystery. Like some capricious goddess—"

The young man, who had been exhibiting symptoms of feverishness, appeared to become resigned. He sighed softly.

"Did you ever read *The Ancient Mariner?*" he said.

"Many years ago," said the Oldest Member. "Why do you ask?"

"Oh, I don't know," said the young man. "It just occurred to me."

Golf (resumed the Oldest Member) is the Great Mystery. Like some capricious goddess, it bestows its favours with what would appear an almost fat-headed lack of method and discrimination. On every side we see big two-fisted he-men floundering round in three figures, stopping every few minutes to let through little shrimps with knock-knees and hollow cheeks, who are tearing off snappy seventy-fours. Giants of finance have to accept a stroke per from their junior clerks. Men capable of governing empires fail to control a small white ball, which presents no difficulties whatever to others with one ounce more brain than a cuckoo clock. Mysterious, but there it is. There was no apparent reason why Ferdinand Dibble should not have been a competent golfer. He had strong wrists and a good eye. Nevertheless, the fact remains that he was a dub. And on a certain evening in June I realized that he was also a goof. I found it out quite suddenly as the result of a conversation which we had on this very terrace.

I was sitting here that evening thinking of this and that, when by the corner of the clubhouse I observed young Dibble in conversation with a girl in white. I could not see who she was, for her back was turned. Presently they parted and Ferdinand came slowly across to where I sat. His air was dejected. He had had the boots licked off him earlier in the afternoon by Jimmy Fothergill, and it was to this that I attributed his gloom. I was to find out in a few moments that I was partly but not entirely correct in this surmise. He took the next chair to mine, and for several minutes sat staring moodily down into the valley.

"I've just been talking to Barbara Medway," he said, suddenly breaking the silence.

"Indeed?" I said. "A delightful girl."

"She's going away for the summer to Marvis Bay."

"She will take the sunshine with her."

"You bet she will!" said Ferdinand Dibble with extraordinary warmth, and there was another long silence.

Presently Ferdinand uttered a hollow groan.

"I love her, dammit!" he muttered brokenly. "Oh, golly, how I love her!"

I was not surprised at his making me the recipient of his confidences like this. Most of the young folk in the place brought their troubles to me sooner or later.

"And does she return your love?"

"I don't know. I haven't asked her."

"Why not? I should have thought the point not without its interest for you."

Ferdinand gnawed the handle of his putter distractedly.

"I haven't the nerve," he burst out at length. "I simply can't summon up the cold gall to ask a girl, least of all an angel like her, to marry me. You see, it's like this. Every time I work myself up to the point of having a dash at it, I go out and get trimmed by someone giving me a stroke a hole. Every time I feel I've mustered up enough pep to propose, I take on a bogey three. Every time I think I'm in good midseason form for putting my fate to the test, to win or lose it all, something goes all blooey with my swing, and I slice into the rough at every tee. And then my self-confidence leaves me. I become nervous, tongue-tied, diffident. I wish to goodness I knew the man who invented this infernal game. I'd strangle him. But I suppose he's been dead for ages. Still, I could go and jump on his grave."

It was at this point that I understood all, and the heart within me sank like lead. The truth was out. Ferdinand Dibble was a goof.

"Come, come, my boy," I said, though feeling the uselessness of any words. "Master this weakness."

"I can't."

"Try!"

"I have tried."

He gnawed his putter again.

"She was asking me just now if I couldn't manage to come to Marvis Bay, too," he said.

"That surely is encouraging? It suggests that she is not entirely indifferent to your society."

"Yes, but what's the use? Do you know"—a gleam coming into his eyes for a moment—"I have a feeling that if I could ever beat some really fairly good player—just once—I could bring the thing off." The gleam faded. "But what chance is there of that?"

It was a question which I did not care to answer. I merely patted his shoulder sympathetically, and after a little while he left me and walked away. I was still sitting there, thinking over his hard case, when Barbara Medway came out of the clubhouse.

She, too, seemed grave and preoccupied, as if there was

something on her mind. She took the chair which Ferdinand had vacated, and sighed wearily.

"Have you ever felt," she asked, "that you would like to bang a man on the head with something hard and heavy? With knobs on?"

I said I had sometimes experienced such a desire, and asked if she had any particular man in mind. She seemed to hesitate for a moment before replying, then, apparently, made up her mind to confide in me. My advanced years carry with them certain pleasant compensations, one of which is that nice girls often confide in me. I frequently find myself enrolled as a father confessor on the most intimate matters by beautiful creatures from whom many a younger man would give his eyeteeth to get a friendly word. Besides, I had known Barbara since she was a child. Frequently—though not recently—I had given her her evening bath. These things form a bond.

"Why are men such chumps?" she exclaimed.

"You still have not told me who it is that has caused these harsh words. Do I know him?"

"Of course you do. You've just been talking to him."

"Ferdinand Dibble? But why should you wish to bang Ferdinand Dibble on the head with something hard and heavy with knobs on?"

"Because he's such a goop."

"You mean a goof?" I queried, wondering how she could have penetrated the unhappy man's secret.

"No, a goop. A goop is a man who's in love with a girl and won't tell her so. I am as certain as I am of anything that Ferdinand is fond of me."

"Your instinct is unerring. He has just been confiding in me on that very point."

"Well, why doesn't he confide in *me,* the poor fish?" cried the high-spirited girl, petulantly flicking a pebble at a passing grasshopper. "I can't be expected to fling myself into his arms unless he gives some sort of a hint that he's ready to catch me."

"Would it help if I were to repeat to him the substance of this conversation of ours?"

"If you breathe a word of it, I'll never speak to you again," she cried. "I'd rather die an awful death than have any man think I wanted him so badly that I had to send relays of messengers begging him to marry me."

I saw her point.

"Then I fear," I said gravely, "that there is nothing to be done. One can only wait and hope. It may be that in the years to come Ferdinand Dibble will acquire a nice lissom, wristy swing, with the head kept rigid and the right leg firmly braced and—"

"What are you talking about?"

"I was toying with the hope that some sunny day Ferdinand Dibble would cease to be a goof."

"You mean a goop?"

"No, a goof. A goof is a man who—" And I went on to explain the peculiar psychological difficulties which lay in the way of any declaration of affection on Ferdinand's part.

"But I never heard of anything so ridiculous in my life," she ejaculated. "Do you mean to say that he is waiting till he is good at golf before he asks me to marry him?"

"It is not quite so simple as that," I said sadly. "Many bad golfers marry, feeling that a wife's loving solicitude may improve their game. But they are rugged, thick-skinned men, not sensitive and introspective, like Ferdinand. Ferdinand has allowed himself to become morbid. It is one of the chief merits of golf that nonsuccess at the game induces a certain amount of decent humility, which keeps a man from pluming himself too much on any petty triumphs he may achieve in other walks of life; but in all things there is a happy mean, and with Ferdinand this humility has gone too far. It has taken all the spirit out of him. He feels crushed and worthless. He is grateful to caddies when they accept a tip instead of drawing themselves up to their full height and flinging the money in his face."

"Then do you mean that things have got to go on like this for ever?"

I thought for a moment.

"It is a pity," I said, "that you could not have induced Ferdinand to go to Marvis Bay for a month or two."

"Why?"

"Because it seems to me, thinking the thing over, that it is just possible that Marvis Bay might cure him. At the hotel there he would find collected a mob of golfers—I used the term in its broadest sense, to embrace the paralytics and the men who play left-handed—whom even he would be able to beat. When I was last at Marvis Bay, the hotel links were a sort of Sargasso Sea into which had drifted all the pitiful flotsam and jetsam of golf. I have seen things done on that course at which I shuddered and averted my eyes—and I am not a weak man. If Ferdinand can polish up his game so as to go round in a fairly steady hundred and five, I fancy there is hope. But I understand he is not going to Marvis Bay."

"Oh yes he is," said the girl.

"Indeed! He did not tell me that when we were talking just now."

"He didn't know it then. He will when I have had a few words with him."

And she walked with firm steps back into the clubhouse.

It has been well said that there are many kinds of golf, beginning at the top with the golf of professionals and the best amateurs and working down through the golf of ossified men to that of Scotch University professors. Until recently this last was looked upon as the lowest possible depth; but nowadays, with the growing popularity of summer hotels, we are able to add a brand still lower, the golf you find at places like Marvis Bay.

To Ferdinand Dibble, coming from a club where the standard of play was rather unusually high, Marvis Bay was a revelation, and for some days after his arrival there he went about dazed, like a man who cannot believe it is really true. To go out on the links at this summer resort was like entering a new world. The hotel was full of stout, middle-aged men, who, after a misspent youth devoted to making money, had taken to a game at which real proficiency can only be acquired by those who start playing in their cradles and keep their weight down. Out on the course each morning you could see representatives of every nightmare style that was ever invented. There was the man who seemed to be attempting to deceive his ball and lull it into a false security by looking away from it and then making a lightning slash in the apparent hope of catching it off its guard. There was the man who wielded his midiron like one killing snakes. There was the man who addressed his ball as if he were stroking a cat, the man who drove as if he were cracking a whip, the man who brooded over each shot like one whose heart is bowed down by bad news from home, and the man who scooped with his mashie as if he were ladling soup. By the end of the first week Ferdinand Dibble was the acknowledged champion of the place. He had gone through the entire menagerie like a bullet through a cream puff.

First, scarcely daring to consider the possibility of success, he had taken on the man who tried to catch his ball off its guard and had beaten him five up and four to play. Then, with gradually growing confidence, he tackled in turn the Cat-Stroker, the Whip-Cracker, the Heart Bowed Down, and the Soup-Scooper, and walked all over their faces with spiked shoes. And as these were the leading local amateurs, whose prowess the octogenarians and the men who went round in bath chairs vainly strove to emulate, Ferdinand Dibble was faced on the eighth morning of his visit by the startling fact that he had no more worlds to conquer. He was monarch of all he surveyed, and, what is more, had won his first trophy, the prize in the great medal-play handicap tournament, in which he had nosed in ahead of the field by two strokes, edging out his nearest rival, a venerable old gentleman, by means of a brilliant and unexpected four on the last hole. The prize was a handsome pewter mug, about the size of the old oaken bucket, and Ferdinand used to go to his room immediately after dinner to croon over it like a mother over her child.

You are wondering, no doubt, why, in these circumstances, he did not take advantage of the new spirit of exhilarated pride which had replaced his old humility and instantly propose to Barbara Medway. I will tell you. He did not propose to Barbara because Barbara was not there. At the last moment she had been detained at home to nurse a sick parent and had been compelled to postpone her visit for a couple of weeks. He could, no doubt, have proposed in one of the daily letters which he wrote to her, but somehow, once he started writing, he found that he used up so much space describing his best shots on the links that day that it was difficult to squeeze in a declaration of undying passion. After all, you can hardly cram that sort of thing into a postscript.

He decided, therefore, to wait till she arrived, and meanwhile pursued his conquering course. The longer he waited, the better, in one way, for every morning and afternoon that passed was adding new layers to his self-esteem. Day by day in every way he grew chestier and chestier.

Meanwhile, however, dark clouds were gathering. Sullen mutterings were to be heard in corners of the hotel lounge, and the spirit of revolt was abroad. For Ferdinand's chestiness had not escaped the notice of his defeated rivals. There is nobody so chesty as a normally unchesty man who suddenly becomes chesty, and I am sorry to say that the chestiness which had come to Ferdinand was the aggressive type of chestiness which breeds enemies. He had developed a habit of holding the game up in order to give his opponent advice. The Whip-Cracker had not forgiven, and never would forgive, his well-meant but galling criticism of his backswing. The Scooper, who had always scooped since the day when, at the age of sixty-four, he subscribed to the correspondence course which was to teach him golf in twelve lessons by mail, resented being told by a snip of a boy that the mashie stroke should be a smooth, unhurried swing. The Snake-Killer— But I need not weary you with a detailed recital of these men's grievances; it is enough to say that they all had it in for Ferdinand, and one night, after dinner, they met in the lounge to decide what was to be done about it.

A nasty spirit was displayed by all.

"A mere lad telling me how to use my mashie!" growled the Scooper. "Smooth and unhurried, my left eyeball! I get it up, don't I? Well, what more do you want?"

"I keep telling him that mine is the old, full St. Andrew's swing," muttered the Whip-Cracker between set teeth, "but he won't listen to me."

"He ought to be taken down a peg or two," hissed the Snake-Killer. It is not easy to hiss a sentence without a single *s* in it, and the fact that he succeeded in doing so shows to what a pitch of emotion the man had been goaded by Ferdinand's maddening air of superiority.

"Yes, but what can we do?" queried an octogenarian, when this last remark had been passed on to him down his ear-trumpet.

"That's the trouble," sighed the Scooper. "What can we do?" And there was a sorrowful shaking of heads.

"I know!" exclaimed the Cat-Stroker, who had not hitherto spoken. He was a lawyer, and a man of subtle and sinister mind. "I have it! There's a boy in my office—young Parsloe— who could beat this man Dibble hollow. I'll wire him to come down here and we'll spring him on this fellow and knock some of the conceit out of him."

There was a chorus of approval.

"But are you sure he can beat him?" asked the Snake-Killer anxiously. "It would never do to make a mistake."

"Of course I'm sure," said the Cat-Stroker. "George Parsloe once went round in ninety-four."

1 4 3

"Many changes there have been since ninety-four," said the octogenarian, nodding sagely. "Ah, many, many changes. None of these motorcars then, tearing about and killing—"

Kindly hands led him off to have an egg-and-milk, and the remaining conspirators returned to the point at issue with bent brows.

"Ninety-four?" said the Scooper incredulously. "Do you mean counting every stroke?"

"Counting every stroke."

"Not conceding himself any putts?"

"Not one."

"Wire him to come at once," said the meeting with one voice.

That night the Cat-Stroker approached Ferdinand, smooth, subtle, lawyer-like.

"Oh, Dibble," he said, "just the man I wanted to see. Dibble, there's a young friend of mine coming down here who goes in for golf a little. George Parsloe is his name. I was wondering if you could spare time to give him a game. He is just a novice, you know."

"I shall be delighted to play a round with him," said Ferdinand kindly.

"He might pick up a pointer or two from watching you," said the Cat-Stroker.

"True, true," said Ferdinand.

"Then I'll introduce you when he shows up."

"Delighted," said Ferdinand.

He was in excellent humor that night, for he had had a letter from Barbara saying that she was arriving on the next day but one.

It was Ferdinand's healthy custom of a morning to get up in good time and take a dip in the sea before breakfast. On the morning of the day of Barbara's arrival, he arose as usual, donned his flannels, took a good look at the cup, and started

out. It was a fine, fresh morning, and he glowed both exter-
nally and internally. As he crossed the links, for the nearest
route to the water was through the fairway of the seventh, he
was whistling happily and rehearsing in his mind the opening
sentences of his proposal. For it was his firm resolve that night
after dinner to ask Barbara to marry him. He was proceeding
over the smooth turf without a care in the world, when there
was a sudden cry of "Fore!" and the next moment a golf ball,
missing him by inches, sailed up the fairway and came to a rest
fifty yards from where he stood. He looked round and observed a figure coming toward him from the tee.

The distance from the tee was fully a hundred and thirty
yards. Add fifty to that, and you have a hundred and eighty
yards. No such drive had been made on the Marvis Bay links
since their foundation, and such is the generous spirit of the
true golfer that Ferdinand's first emotion, after the not inexcus-
able spasm of panic caused by the hum of the ball past his ear,
was one of cordial admiration. By some kindly miracle, he
supposed, one of his hotel acquaintances had been permitted
for once in his life to time a drive right. It was only when the
other man came up that there began to steal over him a sickening apprehension. The faces of all those who hewed divots on
the hotel course were familiar to him, and the fact that this
fellow was a stranger seemed to point with dreadful certainty
to his being the man he had agreed to play.

"Sorry," said the man. He was a tall, strikingly handsome
youth, with brown eyes and a dark moustache.

"Oh, that's all right," said Ferdinand. "Er—do you always
drive like that?"

"Well, I generally get a bit longer ball, but I'm off my drive
this morning. It's lucky I came out and got this practice. I'm
playing a match tomorrow with a fellow named Dibble, who's
a local champion, or something."

"Me," said Ferdinand, humbly.

"Eh? Oh, you?" Mr. Parsloe eyed him appraisingly. "Well, may the best man win."

As this was precisely what Ferdinand was afraid was going to happen, he nodded in a sickly manner and tottered off to his bathe. The magic had gone out of the morning. The sun still shone, but in a silly, feeble way; and a cold and depressing wind had sprung up. For Ferdinand's inferiority complex, which had seemed cured for ever, was back again, doing business at the old stand.

How sad it is in this life that the moment to which we have looked forward with the most glowing anticipation so often turns out on arrival flat, cold, and disappointing. For ten days Barbara Medway had been living for that meeting with Ferdinand, when, getting out of the train, she would see him popping about on the horizon with the lovelight sparkling in his eyes and words of devotion trembling on his lips. The poor girl never doubted for an instant that he would unleash his pent-up emotions inside the first five minutes, and her only worry was lest he should give an embarrassing publicity to the sacred scene by falling on his knees on the station platform.

"Well, here I am at last," she cried gaily.

"Hullo!" said Ferdinand with a twisted smile.

The girl looked at him, chilled. How could she know that his peculiar manner was due entirely to the severe attack of cold feet resultant upon his meeting with George Parsloe that morning? The interpretation which she placed upon it was that he was not glad to see her. If he had behaved like this before, she would, of course, have put it down to ingrowing goofery, but now she had his written statements to prove that for the last ten days his golf had been one long series of triumphs.

"I got your letters," she said, persevering bravely.

"I thought you would," said Ferdinand, absently.

"You seem to have been doing wonders."

"Yes."

There was a silence.

"Have a nice journey?" said Ferdinand.

"Very," said Barbara.

She spoke coldly, for she was madder than a wet hen. She saw it all now. In the ten days since they had parted, his love, she realized, had waned. Some other girl, met in the romantic surroundings of this picturesque resort, had supplanted her in his affections. She knew how quickly Cupid gets off the mark at a summer hotel, and for an instant she blamed herself for ever having been so ivory-skulled as to let him come to this place alone. Then regret was swallowed up in wrath, and she became so glacial that Ferdinand, who had been on the point of telling her the secret of his gloom, retired into his shell and conversation during the drive to the hotel never soared above a certain level. Ferdinand said the sunshine was nice and Barbara said yes, it was nice, and Ferdinand said it looked pretty on the water, and Barbara said yes, it did look pretty on the water, and Ferdinand said he hoped it was not going to rain, and Barbara said yes, it would be a pity if it rained. And then there was another lengthy silence.

"How is my uncle?" asked Barbara at last.

I omitted to mention that the individual to whom I have referred as the Cat-Stroker was Barbara's mother's brother, and her host at Marvis Bay.

"Your uncle?"

"His name is Tuttle. Have you met him?"

"Oh yes. I've seen a good deal of him. He has got a friend staying with him," said Ferdinand, his mind returning to the matter nearest his heart. "A fellow named Parsloe."

"Oh, is George Parsloe here? How jolly!"

"Do you know him?" barked Ferdinand hollowly. He would not have supposed that anything could have added to his existing depression, but he was conscious now of having slipped a few rungs farther down the ladder of gloom. There had been a horribly joyful ring in her voice. Ah, well, he reflected morosely, how like life it all was! We never know what the morrow may bring forth. We strike a good patch and are beginning to think pretty well of ourselves, and along comes a George Parsloe.

"Of course I do," said Barbara. "Why, there he is."

The cab had drawn up at the door of the hotel, and on the porch George Parsloe was airing his graceful person. To Ferdinand's fevered eye he looked like a Greek god, and his inferiority complex began to exhibit symptoms of elephantiasis. How could he compete at love or golf with a fellow who looked as if he had stepped out of the movies and considered himself off his drive when he did a hundred and eighty yards?

"Geor-gee!" cried Barbara, blithely. "Hullo, George!"

"Why, hullo, Barbara!"

They fell into pleasant conversation, while Ferdinand hung miserably about in the offing. And presently, feeling that his society was not essential to their happiness, he slunk away.

George Parsloe dined at the Cat-Stroker's table that night, and it was with George Parsloe that Barbara roamed in the moonlight after dinner. Ferdinand, after a profitless hour at the billiard table, went early to his room. But not even the rays of the moon, glinting on his cup, could soothe the fever in his soul. He practiced putting somberly into his tooth glass for a while; then, going to bed, fell at last into a troubled sleep.

Barbara slept late the next morning and breakfasted in her room. Coming down toward noon, she found a strange emptiness in the hotel. It was her experience of summer hotels that a really fine day like this one was the cue for half the inhabitants to collect in the lounge, shut all the windows, and talk about conditions in the jute industry. To her surprise, though the sun was streaming down from a cloudless sky, the only occupant of the lounge was the octogenarian with the ear trumpet. She observed that he was chuckling to himself in a senile manner.

"Good morning," she said, politely, for she had made his acquaintance on the previous evening.

"Hey?" said the octogenarian, suspending his chuckling and getting his trumpet into position.

"I said, 'Good morning!' " roared Barbara into the receiver.

"Hey?"

"Good morning!"

"Ah! Yes, it's a very fine morning, a very fine morning. If it wasn't for missing my bun and glass of milk at twelve sharp," said the octogenarian, "I'd be down on the links. That's where I'd be, down on the links. If it wasn't for missing my bun and glass of milk."

This refreshment arriving at this moment, he dismantled the radio outfit and began to restore his tissues.

"Watching the match," he explained, pausing for a moment in his bun mangling.

"What match?"

The octogenarian sipped his milk.

"What match?" repeated Barbara.

"Hey?"

"What match?"

The octogenarian began to chuckle again and nearly swallowed a crumb the wrong way.

"Take some of the conceit out of him," he gurgled.

"Out of who?" asked Barbara, knowing perfectly well that she should have said "whom".

"Yes," said the octogenarian.

"Who is conceited?"

"Ah! This young fellow, Dibble. Very conceited. I saw it in his eye from the first, but nobody would listen to me. 'Mark my words,' I said, 'that boy needs taking down a peg or two.' Well, he's going to be this morning. Your uncle wired to young Parsloe to come down, and he's arranged a match between them. Dibble—" Here the octogenarian choked again and had to rinse himself out with milk. "Dibble doesn't know that Parsloe once went round in ninety-four!"

"What?"

Everything seemed to go black to Barbara. Through a murky mist she appeared to be looking at a Negro octogenarian, sipping ink. Then her eyes cleared, and she found herself clutching for support at the back of a chair. She understood now. She realized why Ferdinand had been so distrait, and her whole heart went out to him in a spasm of maternal pity. How she had wronged him!

"Take some of the conceit out of him," the octogenarian was mumbling, and Barbara felt a sudden sharp loathing for the old man. For two pins she could have dropped a beetle in his milk. Then the need for action roused her. What action? She did not know. All she knew was that she must act.

"Oh!" she cried.

"Hey?" said the octogenarian, bringing his trumpet to the ready.

But Barbara had gone.

It was not far to the links, and Barbara covered the distance on flying feet. She reached the clubhouse, but the course was empty except for the Scooper, who was preparing to drive off the first tee. In spite of the fact that something seemed to tell her subconsciously that this was one of the sights she ought not to miss, the girl did not wait to watch. Assuming that the match had started soon after breakfast, it must by now have reached one of the holes on the second nine. She ran down the hill, looking to left and right, and was presently aware of a group of spectators clustered about a green in the distance. As she hurried toward them they moved away, and now she could see Ferdinand advancing to the next tee. With a thrill that shook her whole body she realized that he had the honor. So he must have won one hole, at any rate. Then she saw her uncle.

"How are they?" she gasped.

Mr. Tuttle seemed moody. It was apparent that things were not going altogether to his liking.

"All square at the fifteenth," he replied, gloomily.

"All square!"

"Yes. Young Parsloe," said Mr. Tuttle with a sour look in the direction of that lissom athlete, "doesn't seem to be able to do a thing right on the greens. He has been putting like a sheep with the botts."

From the foregoing remark of Mr. Tuttle you will, no doubt, have gleaned at least a clue to the mystery of how Ferdinand Dibble had managed to hold his long-driving adversary up to the fifteenth green, but for all that you will probably consider that some further explanation of this amazing state of affairs is required. Mere bad putting on the part of George Parsloe is not, you feel, sufficient to cover the matter entirely. You are right. There was another very important factor in the situation —to wit, that by some extraordinary chance Ferdinand Dibble had started right off from the first tee, playing the game of a lifetime. Never had he made such drives, never chipped his chips so shrewdly.

About Ferdinand's driving there was as a general thing a fatal stiffness and overcaution which prevented success. And with his chip shots he rarely achieved accuracy owing to his habit of rearing his head like the lion of the jungle just before the club struck the ball. But today he had been swinging with a careless freedom, and his chips had been true and clean. The thing had puzzled him all the way round. It had not elated him, for, owing to Barbara's aloofness and the way in which she had gambolled about George Parsloe, like a young lamb in the springtime, he was in too deep a state of dejection to be elated by anything. And now, suddenly, in a flash of clear vision, he perceived the reason why he had been playing so well today. It was just because he was not elated. It was simply because he was so profoundly miserable.

That was what Ferdinand told himself as he stepped off the

sixteenth, after hitting a screamer down the center of the fairway, and I am convinced that he was right. Like so many indifferent golfers, Ferdinand Dibble had always made the game hard for himself by thinking too much. He was a deep student of the works of the masters, and whenever he prepared to play a stroke he had a complete mental list of all the mistakes which it was possible to make. He would remember how Taylor had warned against dipping the right shoulder, how Vardon had inveighed against any movement of the head; he would recall how Ray had mentioned the tendency to snatch back the club, how Braid had spoken sadly of those who sin against their better selves by stiffening the muscles and heaving.

The consequence was that when, after waggling in a frozen manner till mere shame urged him to take some definite course of action, he eventually swung, he invariably proceeded to dip his right shoulder, stiffen his muscles, heave, and snatch back the club, at the same time raising his head sharply as in the illustrated plate *(Some Frequent Faults of Beginners—No. 3—Lifting the Bean)* facing page thirty-four of James Braid's *Golf Without Tears.* Today, he had been so preoccupied with his broken heart that he had made his shots absently, almost carelessly, with the result that at least one in every three had been a lallapaloosa.

Meanwhile, George Parsloe had driven off and the match was progressing. George was feeling a little flustered by now. He had been given to understand that this bird Dibble was a hundred-at-his-best man, and all the way round the fellow had been reeling off fives in great profusion, and had once actually got a four. True, there had been an occasional six, and even a seven, but that did not alter the main fact that the man was making the dickens of a game of it. With the haughty spirit of one who had once done a ninety-four, George Parsloe had anticipated being at least three up at the turn. Instead of which he had been two down, and had had to fight strenuously to draw level.

Nevertheless, he drove steadily and well, and would certainly have won the hole had it not been for his weak and sinful putting. The same defect caused him to halve the seventeenth, after being on in two, with Ferdinand wandering in the desert and only reaching the green with his fourth. Then, however, Ferdinand holed out from a distance of seven yards, getting a five; which George's three putts just enabled him to equal.

Barbara had watched the proceedings with a beating heart. At first she had looked on from afar; but now, drawn as by a magnet, she approached the tee. Ferdinand was driving off. She held her breath. Ferdinand held his breath. And all around one could see their respective breaths being held by George Parsloe, Mr. Tuttle, and the enthralled crowd of spectators. It was a moment of the acutest tension, and it was broken by the crack of Ferdinand's driver as it met the ball and sent it hopping along the ground for a mere thirty yards. At this supreme crisis in the match Ferdinand Dibble had topped.

George Parsloe teed up his ball. There was a smile of quiet satisfaction on his face. He snuggled the driver in his hands, and gave it a preliminary swish. This, felt George Parsloe, was where the happy ending came. He could drive as he had never driven before. He would so drive that it would take his opponent at least three shots to catch up with him. He drew back his club with infinite caution, poised it at the top of the swing—

"I always wonder—" said a clear, girlish voice, ripping the silence like the explosion of a bomb.

George Parsloe started. His club wobbled. It descended. The ball trickled into the long grass in front of the tee. There was a grim pause.

"You were saying, Miss Medway—" said George Parsloe, in a small, flat voice.

"Oh, I'm so sorry," said Barbara. "I'm afraid I put you off."

"A little, perhaps. Possibly the merest trifle. But you were saying you wondered about something. Can I be of any assistance?"

"I was only saying," said Barbara, "that I always wonder why tees are called tees."

George Parsloe swallowed once or twice. He also blinked a little feverishly. His eyes had a dazed, staring expression.

"I am afraid I cannot tell you off-hand," he said, "but I will make a point of consulting some good encyclopaedia at the earliest opportunity."

"Thank you so much."

"Not at all. It will be a pleasure. In case you were thinking of inquiring at the moment when I am putting why greens are called greens, may I venture the suggestion now that it is because they are green?"

And, so saying, George Parsloe stalked to his ball and found it nestling in the heart of some shrub of which, not being a botanist, I cannot give you the name. It was a close-knit, adhesive shrub, and it twined its tentacles so lovingly around George Parsloe's niblick that he missed his first shot altogether. His second made the ball rock, and his third dislodged it. Playing a full swing with his brassie and being by now a mere caldron of seething emotions, he missed his fourth. His fifth came to within a few inches of Ferdinand's drive, and he picked it up and hurled it from him into the rough as if it had been something venomous.

"Your hole and match," said George Parsloe thinly.

Ferdinand Dibble sat beside the glittering ocean. He had hurried off the course with swift strides the moment George Parsloe had spoken those bitter words. He wanted to be alone with his thoughts.

They were mixed thoughts. For a moment joy at the reflection that he had won a tough match came irresistibly to the surface, only to sink again as he remembered that life, whatever its triumphs, could hold nothing for him now that Barbara Medway loved another.

"Mr. Dibble!"

He looked up. She was standing at his side. He gulped and rose to his feet.

"Yes?"

There was a silence.

"Doesn't the sun look pretty on the water?" said Barbara.

Ferdinand groaned. This was too much.

"Leave me," he said, hollowly. "Go back to your Parsloe, the man with whom you walked in the moonlight beside this same water."

"Well, why shouldn't I walk with Mr. Parsloe in the moonlight beside this same water?" demanded Barbara with spirit.

"I never said," replied Ferdinand, for he was a fair man at heart, "that you shouldn't walk with Mr. Parsloe beside this same water. I simply said you did walk with Mr. Parsloe beside this same water."

"I've a perfect right to walk with Mr. Parsloe beside this same water," persisted Barbara. "He and I are old friends."

Ferdinand groaned again.

"Exactly! There you are! As I suspected. Old friends. Played together as children, and what not, I shouldn't wonder."

"No, we didn't. I've only known him five years. But he is engaged to be married to my greatest chum, so that draws us together."

Ferdinand uttered a strangled cry.

"Parsloe engaged to be married!"

"Yes. The wedding takes place next month."

"But look here." Ferdinand's forehead was wrinkled. He was thinking tensely. "Look here," said Ferdinand, a close reasoner. "If Parsloe's engaged to your greatest chum, he can't be in love with *you*."

"No."

"And you aren't in love with him?"

"No."

"Then, by gad," said Ferdinand, "how about it?"

"What do you mean?"

"Will you marry me?" bellowed Ferdinand.

"Yes."

"You will?"

"Of course I will."

"Darling!" cried Ferdinand.

"There is only one thing that bothers me a bit," said Ferdinand thoughtfully, as they strolled together over the scented meadows, while in the trees above them a thousand birds trilled Mendelssohn's Wedding March.

"What is that?"

"Well, I'll tell you," said Ferdinand. "The fact is, I've just discovered the great secret of golf. You can't play a really hot game unless you're so miserable that you don't worry over your shots. Take the case of a chip shot, for instance. If you're really wretched, you don't care where the ball is going and so you don't raise your head to see. Grief automatically prevents pressing and over-swinging. Look at the topnotchers. Have you ever seen a happy pro?"

"No. I don't think I have."

"Well, then!"

"But pros are all Scotchmen," argued Barbara.

"It doesn't matter. I'm sure I'm right. And the darned thing is that I'm going to be so infernally happy all the rest of my life that I suppose my handicap will go up to thirty or something."

Barbara squeezed his hand lovingly.

"Don't worry, precious," she said soothingly. "It will be all right. I am a woman, and once we are married, I shall be able to think of at least a hundred ways of snootering you to such an extent that you'll be fit to win the Amateur Championship."

"You will?" said Ferdinand, anxiously. "You're sure?"

"Quite, quite sure, dearest," said Barbara.

"My angel!" said Ferdinand.

He folded her in his arms, using the interlocking grip.

THE
SWEET
SHOT

·

E. C. BENTLEY

"No; I happened to be abroad at the time," Philip
Trent said. "I wasn't in the way of seeing the English
papers, so until I came here this week I never heard
anything about your mystery."

Captain Royden, a small, spare, brown-faced man, was engaged in the delicate—and forbidden—task of taking his automatic telephone instrument to pieces. He now suspended his
labors and reached for the tobacco jar. The large window of his
office in the Kempshill clubhouse looked down upon the eighteenth green of that delectable golf course, and his eye roved

over the whin-clad slopes beyond as he called on his recollection.

"Well, if you call it a mystery," he said as he filled a pipe. "Some people do, because they like mysteries, I suppose. For instance, Colin Hunt, the man you're staying with, calls it that. Others won't have it, and say there was a perfectly natural explanation. I could tell you as much as anybody could about it, I dare say."

"As being secretary here, you mean?"

"Not only that. I was one of the two people who were in at the death, so to speak—or next door to it," Captain Royden said. He limped to the mantelshelf and took down a silver box embossed on the lid with the crest and mottoes of the Corps of Royal Engineers. "Try one of these cigarettes, Mr. Trent. If you'd like to hear the yarn, I'll give it you. You have heard something about Arthur Freer, I suppose?"

"Hardly anything," Trent said. "I just gathered that he wasn't a very popular character."

"No," Captain Royden said with reserve. "Did they tell you he was my brother-in-law? No? Well, now, it happened about four months ago, on a Monday—let me see—yes, the second Monday in May. Freer had a habit of playing nine holes before breakfast. Barring Sundays—he was strict about Sunday—he did it most days, even in the beastliest weather, going round all alone usually, carrying his own clubs, studying every shot as if his life depended on it. That helped to make him the very good player he was. His handicap here was two, and at Undershaw he used to be scratch, I believe.

"At a quarter to eight he'd be on the first tee, and by nine he'd be back at his house—it's only a few minutes from here. That Monday morning he started off as usual—"

"And at the usual time?"

"Just about. He had spent a few minutes in the clubhouse blowing up the steward about some trifle. And that was the last time he was seen alive by anybody—near enough to speak to, that is. No one else went off the first tee until a little after nine, when I started round with Browson—he's our local padre; I had been having breakfast with him at the Vicarage. He's got a game leg, like me, so we often play together when he can fit it in.

"We had holed out on the first green, and were walking on to the next tee, when Browson said, 'Great Scot! Look there. Something's happened.' He pointed down the fairway of the second hole; and there we could see a man lying sprawled on the turf, face down and motionless. Now there is this point about the second hole—the first half of it is in a dip in the land, just deep enough to be out of sight from any other point on the course, unless you're standing right above it—you'll see when you go round yourself. Well, on the tee, you *are* right above it; and we saw this man lying. We ran to the spot.

"It was Freer, as I had known it must be at that hour. He was dead, lying in a disjointed sort of way no live man could have lain in. His clothing was torn to ribbons, and it was singed too. So was his hair—he used to play bareheaded—and his face and hands. His bag of clubs was lying a few yards away, and the brassie, which he had just been using, was close by the body.

"There wasn't any wound showing, and I had seen far worse things often enough, but the padre was looking sickish, so I asked him to go back to the clubhouse and send for a doctor and the police while I mounted guard. They weren't long coming, and after they had done their job the body was taken away in an ambulance. Well, that's about all I can tell you at first hand, Mr. Trent. If you are staying with Hunt, you'll have heard about the inquest and all that probably."

Trent shook his head. "No," he said. "Colin was just beginning to tell me, after breakfast this morning, about Freer having been killed on the course in some incomprehensible way, when a man came to see him about something. So, as I was going to apply for a fortnight's run of the course, I thought I would ask you about the affair."

"All right," Captain Royden said. "I can tell you about the inquest anyhow—had to be there to speak my own little piece, about finding the body. As for what happened to Freer, the medical evidence was rather confusing. It was agreed that he had been killed by some tremendous shock, which had jolted his whole system to pieces and dislocated several joints, but had been not quite violent enough to cause any visible wound. Apart from that, there was a disagreement. Freer's own doctor, who saw the body first, declared he must have been struck by lightning. He said it was true there hadn't been a thunderstorm, but that there had been thunder about all that weekend, and that sometimes lightning did act in that way. But the police surgeon, Collins, said there would be no such displacement of the organs from a lightning stroke, even if it did ever happen that way in our climate, which he doubted. And he said that if it had been lightning, it would have struck the steel-headed clubs; but the clubs lay there in their bag quite undamaged. Collins thought there must have been some kind of explosion, though he couldn't suggest what kind."

Trent shook his head. "I don't suppose that impressed the court," he said. "All the same, it may have been all the honest opinion he could give." He smoked in silence a few moments, while Captain Royden attended to the troubles of his telephone instrument with a camel-hair brush. "But surely," Trent said at length, "if there had been such an explosion as that, somebody would have heard the sound of it."

"Lots of people would have heard it," Captain Royden answered. "But there you are, you see—nobody notices the sound of explosions just about here. There's the quarry on the other side of the road there, and anytime after 7 A.M. there's liable to be a noise of blasting."

"A dull, sickening thud?"

"Jolly sickening," Captain Royden said, "for all of us living nearby. And so that point wasn't raised. Well, Collins is a very sound man; but as you say, his evidence didn't really explain the thing, and the other fellow's did, whether it was right or wrong. Besides, the coroner and the jury had heard about a bolt from a clear sky, and the notion appealed to them. Anyhow, they brought it in death from misadventure."

"Which nobody could deny, as the song says," Trent remarked. "And was there no other evidence?"

"Yes, some. But Hunt can tell you about it as well as I can; he was there. I shall have to ask you to excuse me now," Captain Royden said. "I have an appointment in the town. The steward will sign you on for a fortnight, and probably get you a game too, if you want one today."

Colin Hunt and his wife, when Trent returned to their house for luncheon, were very willing to complete the tale. The verdict, they declared, was tripe. Dr. Collins knew his job, whereas Dr. Hoyle was an old footler, and Freer's death had never been reasonably explained.

As for the other evidence, it had, they agreed, been interesting, though it didn't help at all. Freer had been seen after he had played his tee shot at the second hole, when he was walking down to the bottom of the dip toward the spot where he met his death.

"But according to Royden," Trent said, "that was a place where he couldn't be seen, unless one was right above him."

"Well, this witness *was* right above him," Hunt rejoined. "Over one thousand feet above him, so he said. He was an RAF man, piloting a bomber from Bexford Camp, not far from here. He was up doing some sort of exercise, and passed over the course just at that time. He didn't know Freer, but he spotted a man walking down from the second tee, because he was the only living soul visible on the course. Gossett, the other man in the plane, is a temporary member here, and did know Freer quite well—or as well as anybody cared to know him—but he never saw him. However, the pilot was quite clear that he saw a man just at the time in question, and they took his evidence so as to prove that Freer was absolutely alone just before his death. The only other person who saw Freer was another man who knew him well; used to be a caddy here, and then got a job at the quarry. He was at work on the hillside, and he watched Freer play the first hole and go on to the second—nobody with him, of course."

"Well, that was pretty well-established then," Trent remarked. "He was about as alone as he could be, it seems. Yet something happened somehow."

Mrs. Hunt sniffed sceptically, and lighted a cigarette. "Yes, it did," she said. "However, I didn't worry much about it, for one. Edith—Mrs. Freer, that is: Royden's sister—must have had a terrible life of it with a man like that. Not that she ever said anything—she wouldn't. She is not that sort."

"She is a jolly good sort, anyhow," Hunt declared.

"Yes, she is: too good for most men. I can tell you." Mrs. Hunt added for the benefit of Trent, "if Colin ever took to cursing me and knocking me about, my well-known loyalty wouldn't stand the strain for very long."

"That's why I don't do it. It's the fear of exposure that makes me the perfect husband, Phil. She would tie a can to me before I knew what was happening. As for Edith, it's true she never said anything, but the change in her since it happened tells the story well enough. Since she's been living with her brother she has been looking far better and happier than she ever succeeded in doing while Freer was alive."

"She won't be living with him for very long, I dare say," Mrs. Hunt intimated darkly.

"No. I'd marry her myself if I had the chance," Hunt agreed cordially.

"Pooh! You wouldn't be in the first six," his wife said. "It will be Rennie, or Gossett, or possibly Sandy Butler—you'll see. But perhaps you've had enough of the local tittle-tattle, Phil. Did you fix up a game for this afternoon?"

"Yes—with the Jarman Professor of Chemistry in the University of Cambridge," Trent said. "He looked at me as if he thought a bath of vitriol would do me good, but he agreed to play me."

"You've got a tough job," Hunt observed. "I believe he is almost as old as he looks, but he is a devil at the short game, and he knows the course blindfold, which you don't. And he isn't so cantankerous as he pretends to be. By the way, he was the man who saw the finish of the last shot Freer ever played— a sweet shot if ever there was one. Get him to tell you."

"I shall try to," Trent said. "The steward told me about that, and that was why I asked the professor for a game."

Colin Hunt's prediction was fulfilled that afternoon. Professor Hyde, receiving five strokes, was one up at the seventeenth, and at the last hole sent down a four-foot putt to win the match. As they left the green he remarked, as if in answer to something Trent had that moment said, "Yes, I can tell you a curious circumstance about Freer's death."

Trent's eye brightened; for the professor had not said a dozen words during their game, and Trent's tentative allusion to the subject after the second hole had been met merely by an intimidating grunt.

"I saw the finish of the last shot he played," the old gentleman went on, "without seeing the man himself at all. A lovely brassie it was, too—though lucky. Rolled to within two feet of the pin."

Trent considered. "I see," he said, "what you mean. You were near the second green, and the ball came over the ridge and ran down to the hole."

"Just so," Professor Hyde said. "That's how you play it—if you can. You might have done it yourself today, if your second shot had been thirty yards longer. I've never done it; but Freer often did. After a really good drive, you play a long second, blind, over the ridge; and with a perfect shot, you may get the green. Well, my house is quite near that green. I was pottering about in the garden before breakfast, and just as I happened to be looking toward the green a ball came hopping down the slope and trickled right across to the hole. Of course, I knew whose it must be—Freer always came along about that time. If it had been anyone else, I'd have waited to see him get his three, and congratulate him. As it was, I went indoors, and didn't hear of his death until long afterward."

"And you never saw him play the shot?" Trent said thoughtfully.

The professor turned a choleric blue eye on him. "How the deuce could I?" he said huffily. "I can't see through a mass of solid earth."

"I know, I know," Trent said. "I was only trying to follow your mental process. Without seeing him play the shot, you knew it was his second—you say he would have been putting for a three. And you said too—didn't you?—that it was a brassie shot."

"Simply because, my young friend"—the professor was severe—"I happened to know the man's game. I had played that nine holes with him before breakfast often, until one day he lost his temper more than usual, and made himself impossible. I knew he practically always carried the ridge with his second —I won't say he always got the green—and his brassie was the only club that would do it. It is conceivable, I admit," Professor Hyde added a little stiffly, "that some mishap took place and that the shot in question was not actually Freer's second; but it did not occur to me to allow for that highly speculative contingency."

On the next day, after those playing a morning round were started on their perambulation, Trent indulged himself with an hour's practice, mainly on the unsurveyed stretch of the second hole. Afterward he had a word with the caddy master; then visited the professional's shop, and won the regard of that expert by furnishing himself with a new midiron. Soon he brought up the subject of the last shot played by Arthur Freer.

A dozen times that morning, he said, he had tried, after a satisfying drive, to reach the green with his second; but in vain. Fergus MacAdam shook his head. Not many, he said, could strike the ball with yon force. He could get there himself, whiles, but never for certainty. Mr. Freer had the strength, and he kenned how to use it forbye.

What sort of clubs, Trent asked, had Freer preferred? "Lang and heavy, like himsel'. Noo ye mention it," MacAdam said, "I hae them here. They were brocht here after the ahccident." He reached up to the top of a rack. "Ay, here they are. They shouldna be, of course; but naebody came to claim them, and it juist slippit ma mind."

Trent, extracting the brassie, looked thoughtfully at the heavy head with the strip of hard white material inlaid in the face. "It's a powerful weapon, sure enough," he remarked.

"Ay, for a man that could control it," MacAdam said. "I dinna care for yon ivorine face mysel'. Some fowk think it gies mair reseelience, ye ken; but there's naething in it."

"He didn't get it from you, then," Trent suggested, still closely examining the head.

"Ay, but he did. I had a lot down from Nelsons while the fashion for them was on. Ye'll find my name," MacAdam added, "stampit on the wood in the usual place, if yer een are seein' richt."

"Well, I don't—that's just it. The stamp is quite illegible."

"Tod! Let's see," the professional said, taking the club in hand. "Guid reason for its being illegible," he went on after a brief scrutiny. "It's been obleeterated—that's easy seen. Who ever saw sic a daft-like thing! The wood has juist been crushed some gait—in a vice, I wouldna wonder. Noo, why would onybody want to dae a thing like yon?"

"Unaccountable, isn't it?" Trent said. "Still, it doesn't matter, I suppose. And anyhow, we shall never know."

It was twelve days later that Trent, looking in at the open door of the secretary's office, saw Captain Royden happily engaged with the separated parts of some mechanism in which coils of wire appeared to be the leading motive.

"I see you're busy," Trent said.

"Come in! Come in!" Royden said heartily. "I can do this anytime—another hour's work will finish it." He laid down a pair of sharp-nosed pliers. "The electricity people have just changed us over to A.C., and I've got to rewind the motor of our vacuum cleaner. Beastly nuisance," he added, looking down affectionately at the bewildering jumble of disarticulated apparatus on his table.

"You bear your sorrow like a man," Trent remarked; and Royden laughed as he wiped his hands on a towel.

"Yes," he said, "I do love tinkering about with mechanical jobs, and if I do say it myself, I'd rather do a thing like this with my own hands than risk having it faultily done by a careless workman. Too many of them about. Why, about a year ago the company sent a man here to fit a new main fuse box, and he made a short-circuit with his screwdriver that knocked him right across the kitchen and might very well have killed him." He reached down his cigarette box and offered it to Trent, who helped himself; then looked down thoughtfully at the device on the lid.

"Thanks very much. When I saw this box before, I put you down for an R.E. man. *Ubique,* and *Quo fas et gloria ducunt.* H'm! I wonder why Engineers were given that motto in particular."

"Lord knows," the captain said. "In my experience, Sappers don't exactly go where right and glory lead. The dirtiest of all the jobs and precious little of the glory—that's what they get."

"Still, they have the consolation," Trent pointed out, "of feeling that they are at home in a scientific age, and that all the rest of the Army are amateurs compared with them. That's what one of them once told me, anyhow. Well now, Captain, I have to be off this evening. I've looked in just to say how much I've enjoyed myself here."

"Very glad you did," Captain Royden said. "You'll come again, I hope, now you know that the golf here is not so bad."

"I like it immensely. Also the members. And the secretary." Trent paused to light his cigarette. "I found the mystery rather interesting, too."

Captain Royden's eyebrows lifted slightly. "You mean about Freer's death? So you made up your mind it *was* a mystery."

"Why yes," Trent said. "Because I made up my mind he had been killed by somebody, and probably killed intentionally. Then, when I had looked into the thing a little, I washed out the 'probably.'"

Captain Royden took up a penknife from his desk and began mechanically to sharpen a pencil. "So you don't agree with the coroner's jury?"

"No, as the verdict seems to have been meant to rule out murder or any sort of human agency, I don't. The lightning idea, which apparently satisfied them, or some of them, was not a very bright one, I thought. I was told what Dr. Collins had said against it at the inquest; and it seemed to me he had disposed of it completely when he said that Freer's clubs, most of them steel ones, were quite undamaged. A man carrying his clubs puts them down, when he plays a shot, a few feet away at most; yet Freer was supposed to have been electrocuted without any notice having been taken of them, so to speak."

"H'm! No, it doesn't seem likely. I don't know that that quite decides the point, though," the captain said. "Lightning plays funny tricks, you know. I've seen a small tree struck when it was surrounded by trees twice the size. All the same, I quite agree there didn't seem to be any sense in the lightning notion. It was thundery weather, but there wasn't any storm that morning in this neighborhood."

"Just so. But when I considered what had been said about Freer's clubs, it suddenly occurred to me that nobody had said anything about *the* club, so far as my information about the inquest went. It seemed clear, from what you and the parson saw, that he had just played a shot with his brassie when he was struck down; it was lying near him, not in the bag. Besides, old Hyde actually saw the ball he had hit roll down the slope onto the green. Now, it's a good rule to study every little detail when you are on a problem of this kind. There weren't many left to study, of course, since the thing had happened four months before; but I knew Freer's clubs must be somewhere, and I thought of one or two places where they were likely to have been taken, in the circumstances, so I tried them. First, I reconnoitered the caddy master's shed, asking if I could leave my bag there for a day or two; but I was told that the regular place to leave them was the pro's shop. So I went and had a chat with MacAdam, and sure enough it soon came out that Freer's bag was still in his rack. I had a look at the clubs, too."

"And did you notice anything peculiar about them?" Captain Royden asked.

"Just one little thing. But it was enough to set me thinking, and next day I drove up to London, where I paid a visit to Nelsons, the sporting outfitters. You know the firm, of course."

Captain Royden, carefully fining down the point of his pencil, nodded. "Everybody knows Nelsons."

"Yes, and MacAdam, I knew, had an account there for his stocks. I wanted to look over some clubs of a particular make— a brassie, with a slip of ivorine let into the face, such as they had supplied to MacAdam. Freer had had one of them from him."

Again Royden nodded.

"I saw the man who shows clubs at Nelsons. We had a talk, and then—you know how little things come out in the course of conversation—"

"Especially," put in the captain with a cheerful grin, "when the conversation is being steered by an expert."

"You flatter me," Trent said. "Anyhow, it did transpire that a club of that particular make had been bought some months before by a customer whom the man was able to remember. Why he remembered him was because, in the first place, he insisted on a club of rather unusual length and weight—much too long and heavy for himself to use, as he was neither a tall man nor of powerful build. The salesman had suggested as much in a delicate way; but the customer said no, he knew exactly what suited him, and he bought the club and took it away with him."

"Rather an ass, I should say," Royden observed thoughtfully.

"I don't think he was an ass, really. He was capable of making a mistake, though, like the rest of us. There were some other things, by the way, that the salesman recalled about him. He had a slight limp, and he was, or had been, an Army officer. The salesman was an ex-Service man, and he couldn't be mistaken, he said, about that."

Captain Royden had drawn a sheet of paper toward him, and was slowly drawing little geometrical figures as he listened. "Go on, Mr. Trent," he said quietly.

"Well, to come back to the subject of Freer's death. I think he was killed by someone who knew Freer never played on Sunday, so that his clubs would be—or ought to be, shall we say?—in his locker all that day. All the following night, too, of course—in case the job took a long time. And I think this man was in a position to have access to the lockers in this clubhouse at any time he chose, and to possess a master key to those lockers. I think he was a skillful amateur craftsman. I think he had a good practical knowledge of high explosives. There is a branch of the Army"—Trent paused a moment and looked at the cigarette box on the table—"in which that sort of knowledge is specially necessary, I believe."

Hastily, as if just reminded of the duty of hospitality,

Royden lifted the lid of the box and pushed it toward Trent. "Do have another," he urged.

Trent did so with thanks. "They have to have it in the Royal Engineers," he went on, "because—so I'm told—demolition work is an important part of their job."

"Quite right," Captain Royden observed, delicately shading one side of a cube.

"Ubique!" Trent mused, staring at the box lid. "If you are 'everywhere,' I take it you can be in two places at the same time. You could kill a man in one place, and at the same time be having breakfast with a friend a mile away. Well, to return to our subject yet once more; you can see the kind of idea I was led to form about what happened to Freer. I believe that his brassie was taken from his locker on the Sunday before his death. I believe the ivorine face of it was taken off and a cavity hollowed out behind it; and in that cavity a charge of explosive was placed. Where it came from I don't know, for it isn't the sort of thing that is easy to come by, I imagine."

"Oh, there would be no difficulty about that," the captain remarked. "If this man you're speaking of knew all about H.E., as you say, he could have compounded the stuff himself from materials anybody can buy. For instance, he could easily make tetranitroaniline—that would be just the thing for him, I should say."

"I see. Then perhaps there would be a tiny detonator attached to the inner side of the ivorine face, so that a good smack with the brassie would set it off. Then the face would be fixed on again. It would be a delicate job, because the weight of the club head would have to be exactly right. The feel and balance of the club would have to be just the same as before the operation."

"A delicate job, yes," the captain agreed. "But not an impossible one. There would be rather more to it than you say, as a matter of fact; the face would have to be shaved down thin, for instance. Still, it could be done."

170

"Well, I imagine it done. Now, this man I have in mind knew there was no work for a brassie at the short first hole, and that the first time it would come out of the bag was at the second hole, down at the bottom of the dip, where no one could see what happened. What certainly did happen was that Freer played a sweet shot, slap on to the green. What else happened at the same moment we don't know for certain, but we can make a reasonable guess. And then, of course, there's the question what happened to the club—or what was left of it; the handle, say. But it isn't a difficult question, I think, if we remember how the body was found."

"How do you mean?" Royden asked.

"I mean, by whom it was found. One of the two players who found it was too much upset to notice very much. He hurried back to the clubhouse; and the other was left alone with the body for, as I estimate it, at least fifteen minutes. When the police came on the scene, they found lying near the body a perfectly good brassie, an unusually long and heavy club, exactly like Freer's brassie in every respect—except one. The name stamped on the wood of the club head had been obliterated by crushing. That name, I think, was not F. MacAdam, but W. J. Nelson; and the club had been taken out of a bag that was not Freer's—a bag which had the remains, if any, of Freer's brassie at the bottom of it. And I believe that's all." Trent got to his feet and stretched his arms. "You can see what I meant when I said I found the mystery interesting."

For some moments Captain Royden gazed thoughtfully out of the window; then he met Trent's inquiring eye. "If there was such a fellow as you imagine," he said coolly, "he seems to have been careful enough—lucky enough too, if you like—to leave nothing at all of what you could call proof against him. And probably he had personal and private reasons for what he did. Suppose that somebody whom he was much attached to was in the power of a foul-tempered, bullying brute; and suppose he found that the bullying had gone to the length of physical violence; and suppose that the situation was hell by day and by night to this man of yours; and suppose there was no way on earth of putting an end to it except the way he took. Yes, Mr. Trent, suppose all that!"

"I will—I do!" Trent said. "That man—if he exists at all—must have been driven pretty hard, and what he did is no business of mine anyway. And now—still in the conditional mood—suppose I take myself off."

THE
SATISFACTION

·

CAROLYN MCCORMICK

The country club in the Midwestern town where I grew up is exceptional in that a narrow road runs alongside every hole of the golf course, so you can follow a match without ever getting out of your automobile. My father used to play golf there with an elderly man who had a weak heart and who, for this reason, always had his automobile driven to the ninth green to pick him up and drive him back to the clubhouse. Sometimes my father rode back with him, but more often he finished the round alone. Now and then, I came out after school, changed my pumps for sneakers, which I kept in Father's golf bag, and walked around the last nine holes to keep him company.

One afternoon in July, I was waiting at the ninth green when he and his partner finished, and after the car drove off, my father and I crossed over to the tenth tee. Two men, acquaintances of my father's, were sitting on a bench waiting to tee off. They greeted him, and asked him to join their threesome. My father said that would be fine, and we sat down. The third man was on the tee taking a practice swing. This was Beckett Grotter, a man so ill-tempered that the local boys refused to caddy for him and he had to import caddies, at considerable expense, from out of town.

My father—a Virginian with a quiet manner, willing to put up with a good deal for the sake of peace and harmony—neither liked nor disliked Beckett Grotter, but he did dislike the feeling of being watched, and he attributed the same sensitivity to others; in his desire to be considerately unobservant he had developed an almost unlimited capacity for inattention. As he sat down, Beckett Grotter halted his swing in midair and glowered. My father, his elbows resting on his knees, gazed back mildly.

The game moved along uneventfully until the foursome reached the sixteenth hole—a very long par five with traps and hazards so cunningly placed that a par on this hole was more to be coveted than a birdie on most of the others. Beckett Grotter had reached the green in four—largely because of a shot colloquially termed at our club "rotten but good"; that is, playing a spoon shot, he had slightly topped the ball, and, the fairway being dry, it had rolled farther than it would have carried had it been properly hit. It stopped ten feet short of the cup. The other three balls lay several yards off the apron. My father chipped up, his ball rolling beyond the cup and coming to rest directly in line with, but on the opposite side of the cup from, Beckett Grotter's. The two other men shot, and then all four walked onto the green and stood beside their balls. My father saw that he was in Beckett Grotter's line and moved aside.

Everyone knew that Beckett Grotter was shooting for par. As he studied the roll of the green, and then carefully smoothed the turf along the curving path to the cup that he hoped the ball would take, the others, well aware of his instability of temperament, were held together by a common tension—all, that is, except for my father. While Beckett Grotter sank to one knee and, with his chin almost touching the ground, closed one eye and squinted down the imaginary line from ball to cup, my father stood contemplating the day.

It was a hot Midwestern afternoon, and the sky was bleached almost white by the sun. It had been a dry summer. The grass on the fairways was burnt up, and even a mediocre drive was good for two hundred and twenty-five yards. The sixteenth green had been trimmed and sprinkled the evening before, and a little mound of grass clipping lay nearby, still damp and sweet-smelling. With the first stirring of the evening's breeze, doves, red-winged blackbirds, and squirrels had suddenly become lively. The tree shadows on the green were so clearly etched that it was possible to pick out individual leaves.

Beckett Grotter would no doubt have been happy to become part of a frieze on an urn, forever shooting for a par. Several times he appeared on the verge of tapping the ball; then he stopped, seemingly powerless to deliver it to the uncertainties of the turf and the rotation of the earth upon its axis. His face grew red, and his breathing was audible even where I sat, well off the green with my back against a tree; out of everybody's way. The young caddie who held the flag at the edge of the green laid it down and moved off stealthily. My father's interest picked up slightly. He has a morbid dread of fits—that is, a morbid dread of being present when someone else has one. While this had never happened, it occurred to him now that Beckett Grotter looked very much as someone might look who was about to have a fit. My father raised his head and gazed intently at the sky, prepared to remove himself—in spirit, at least—from the scene of seizure, if such it should turn out to be. At that moment, Beckett Grotter finally struck the ball, which started up and around in a wide arc, performing, as it passed, a neat lobotomy on the shadow of my father's head. But the recently trimmed green was fast, and the ball sped up and over the top of the incline and down out of sight on the other side.

Beckett Grotter straightened and stood blinking at the green ridge behind which the sum of his aspirations had just sunk. From the direction of the clubhouse came the bray of an automobile horn. For what seemed like a very long time, no one moved or spoke. Then my father said, "I guess you're still away, Beckett."

Beckett Grotter swung around, planted his feet, and lowered his head at my father, who stood with his putter beside his ball, tentatively measuring the distance to the cup. Someone cleared his throat, and the caddie who had dropped the pin picked it up again.

"McCormick!" Beckett Grotter roared at my father. "It was you made me miss that putt! You moved your head! Where's your goddamn green etiquette!"

My father heard him, but that he should be accused of being responsible for anyone's missing a putt and par was so at variance with his conception of probability that at first the words held no meaning for him. When he did understand, the sensation came over him, at the same moment, that he was being watched. He drew himself up and saw that we were all looking at him. I dropped my eyes, because I knew how he felt about being looked at. One of the men said, "Forget it, Hub. You know how Beckett is."

My father turned toward Beckett Grotter and looked at him —really seeing him. Then, with the calm resolution of a man who has nothing further to lose, he putted out of turn, neatly sinking a six-footer.

After dinner that evening, my father went directly to his desk, sat down, and wrote something in pencil on a sheet of lined yellow paper. He erased and rewrote, deliberated and made additions, for nearly an hour. Finally, he crumpled the yellow sheet impatiently and pushed it aside. Then he took out a sheet of his writing paper, exchanged the pencil for a pen, and, in his neat hand, again began to write.

My mother, who was working a pair of Father's old trousers into a hooked rug, said, "Hub, what on earth are you writing?"

Never presuming to read the intent behind another's words, my father answered, "A letter."

I don't believe he ever did tell Mother what he had written, but a long time later he told me. The letter read:

> *Dear Sir:*
>
> *I cannot accept your insult. I request your immediate designation of a time and a suitable location for a meeting between us, so that I may obtain satisfaction for today's incident on the 16th green.*
>
> *Respectfully,*
> *H. McCormick*

When my father had finished this letter, he folded it without reading what he had written, and tucked it in an envelope, which he addressed, sealed, and stamped. Then he put on his hat, and carried the letter outside and down the block, and dropped it in a corner mailbox.

On a Saturday, about two weeks later, Father remarked at breakfast that he would not be home for lunch; he was having lunch at the club. Mother raised her eyebrows; Father always had lunch at the club on Saturday and it was not at all like him to announce this. Cautiously, like someone holding out a handful of crumbs to a wary squirrel, she murmured, "Really? With whom?"

"Beckett Grotter is having a luncheon," my father said.

"Beckett Grotter? Why on earth did he ask *you?*"

The hand snatched; the squirrel fled. "I expect," my father answered, "that he wants me to be there."

I happened to be upstairs just before my father left for the club, and, glancing through the open door of his room, I saw him take a nip from the bottle of bourbon he kept on his dresser. I had often seen him do this before he went down to dinner, but never before had I seen him take a nip before he went to lunch.

When he came home that evening, Mother asked him how the luncheon had been.

"Fine," my father answered. "He had pheasant and champagne."

Mother's eyebrows lifted. "And who all was there?" she asked.

"Different people. Twelve." My father puffed air gently through his nose, an indication that he was amused. "I sat on Grotter's right," he said.

This was too much for my mother. "Will you kindly tell me," she said, exploding, "why Beckett Grotter—and you hardly know the man—should give a luncheon with pheasant and champagne, invite twelve people, and put you on his right?"

"Well," my father said, "the right hand is the honor seat, and the luncheon was for me."

The reason for that luncheon never did leak out, but the luncheon itself was noted, of course, and from that time on, it was customary to invite my father into any foursome that included, for one reason or another, Beckett Grotter. It came to be generally believed that my father's gentle nature had a soothing effect upon him. As evidence, it was pointed out that Beckett Grotter watched his language and didn't throw things whenever my father was around.

1 7 8

OUR
GOLF
BALLS

·

JERRY BUMPUS

Imagine the spray of atoms jolted out of the golf ball's very being by the impact of the driver. In a close-up we see the ball's upper half spilling over the sharp edge of the club, while the lower half begins the incredible flight.

You believe the golf ball achieves maximum velocity at impact, but in fact this occurs several yards from the tee, and at the moment of greatest speed, when at its finest as a golf ball, it is flat, squashed against the air, an odd oblong resembling in my excellent photographs a forward-leaning ghost stumbling through space.

Exactly how fast is our golf ball traveling? We all would of course like to know, but even our most careful estimates smack of the wayward melancholy of oafs speculating in a pasture: Is there a face in the sun? Is a beautiful thing always beautiful or does it give over? In Heaven where will we pee—in the clouds? Science has turned its back on the question of the golf ball's speed, thick-headedly assuming accelerologists settled the matter in the days of the immortal Tommy Armour! But a safe and considered estimate of the golf ball's maximum velocity is six hundred and fifty miles per hour.

Carefully following its flight, we find it not only stumbles, it goes end over end: a ludicrous, not to say dizzying, moment unequaled in human experience—as far as we live to tell. During this moment the golf ball would, if it could, lose consciousness. I have paused to watch men and women in similar moments of excruciation; I'm sure you've watched too; we shall be watched when our time comes. Our shrinks slyly assure us we blot out the ultimately insufferable, but there are those who seem unfazed during great moments: our true heroes! They are capable of grandeur because they remain miraculously inviolate through those occasions when Heaven and Hell are one, when all things swirl off into light, and great Nothing roars like the sea. But they are shamming. They are no braver than our golf ball silently squealing its terror through space, and I have proof—a photo in which a racer is blurrily seen at the moment he gets a speed record: he hunkers in the cockpit of his jet-powered, fifty-thousand-pound, four-wheeled bullet, his face invisible beneath the black visor of his helmet. In this priceless photograph we penetrate distance, the blur of speed, the black visor, and see that our hero's moment of ultimate triumph is also his moment of ultimate shame: he's driving nine hundred miles per hour with his eyes shut!

We left our golf ball going through space end over end. Sun —earth—sun. . . . Then the silent descent, the deep breath of sanity.

The ball lands, hops along, stops, and can be seen, an object no bigger than the end of my thumb, from a distance of three hundred yards. How can this be?

After a tee shot the ball quite easily, though miraculously, sprawls! It is one of those ominous, necessarily shunned but daily miracles which crowd our days, making us yearn for boredom.

It's again itself—a tidy, round golf ball—when the player, clutching a club with a shiny steel head, comes tromping up. The player glances about, as if to see if anyone is watching, then drawing back, he begins viciously hacking the ball. The golf ball becomes an intimate of the two iron, the three, the inexorable five iron.

The golf ball lies on the green which is a sloping sky. Little taps send it rolling up and down—but in the wrong direction! It is being aimed toward a hole in the sky, and each time it passes it hears the cold suck of wind down the hole. Other balls slide up and down and our golf ball looks off, as only balls can, as one by one the others slip their grip and are gone.

We stand atop tall buildings and look at the cars and tiny people below. One hundred stories is as high as we dare go; higher, and we lose interest in looking down and, staring off, expect planes, birds and soon, vaguely, even things of miraculous bearing. We also stand, the tribe of Man, at great cracks and look at rivers writhing below. But always we stand firmly on the earth. We may throb with the bigness and looseness of things—"Ah! A wide vista!"—and we may suffer somewhat. But the earth is under our feet and we can always see the bottom of things.

Our golf ball, though, slides down a green sky that slants to a hole, and there's no wide vista: imagine looking into a hole, lit by tiny pinpoint light bulbs, four inches wide and a mile deep.

If you have succeeded in this, next imagine you are a golf ball. (Densely round. Squint. Clench your teeth.) Ready? Fall.

A golf ball loves a golf course without holes. Such courses exist, though golf as we know it is not played there.

One such course exists as vividly for me as it did in my student days when I played there between classes and on weekends, and I can see it even more distinctly than I could then, for the course was in a brick courtyard between the west stands of Stagg Field and an adjoining building, and the sky above, throughout my stay in Chicago, was dark and heavy with snow. Beyond was the football field where people ran up and down yelling. But on the strip behind the stands there was only our fraternity of special golfers. The course was roughly forty feet long by twenty wide; the walls rose one hundred feet. High in one wall was a window covered with a heavy screen in which many golf balls were stuck.

This area was a proper size for chip shots though there was no grass. I also took pleasure in raw Knock-O: I would wind up with my driver, hit the ball with all I had, and duck! The ball richocheted and the walls groaned in profound vibration. One Sunday morning six or seven of us were down there, all teeing off at the same time, when a man in a smock opened the window. He called down that we were disturbing him and his colleagues. We agreed to leave if he would free the balls stuck in the screen. He disappeared and in a moment returned with a little silver hammer with which he knocked the balls out. We caught them on the fly. Years later I recognized the fellow in photographs: he was none other than Enrico Fermi!

We should consider driving across creeks, ponds, lakes. But we go next directly to where all golf balls end. On the bottom of the little round lake that lies between every number seven tee and every number seven green, there's a veritable throng of golf balls, but they lie in isolation: the murk of the lake and the bleakness that inks their vision (had they eyes) from seeing their hand before their face (had they hands, faces) makes each wholly alone.

They lie there forever. Or it seems forever to them. But you and I know that boys and sometimes big golf ball-slugging men sneak out nights and, taking off their clothes, wade out to scavenge lost golf balls.

It is simple, it is fun.

He parks his wife's station wagon on the gravel parking lot and tiptoes down the fairway, gray under the moon. It is 2:30 A.M.; the clubhouse closed at midnight. Our golf ball poacher glances over his shoulder at a black line of trees under which he believes he sees movement—not the blur of a single person, but, impossibly, the surge of a gang—midnight loonies, experimental murderers! His heart pounding loudly, he stands frozen, hoping they can't see him. He strains to become invisible. . . .

But he would be plainly visible clear to the clubhouse.

In fact, let's go up to the clubhouse, dark and silent, smelling of cigarette smoke and booze. Look out the window across the pellucid fairway bordered with trees on the right, a creek down the left. That's him, there, at a hundred and fifty yards rather resembling a strayed shrub. Now he's moving on; bright fellow, he realized it wasn't a gang he saw, only shadows.

Before we go, I want to show you a picture.

On a long wall in the bar are at least a hundred photographs of professional golfers, politicians, movie actors, past club officers, and sundry local potentates whose identities have slipped. Those readily recognizable, the famous, were in all cases passing through en route to Chicago; they would stop long enough to hit a golf ball off that very tee outside our window, drink a gin rickey with the fellows, and have their picture taken. The photo in the corner is one of a kind, a true buried treasure: for over thirty years, incredibly, the bartenders, the club pros, the clubhouse presidents, and their underlings have had absolutely no awareness of the photo's rarity. Come here.

In the moonlight we see it clearly, not a large picture, five men standing shoulder to shoulder. They wear knickers, soft caps, sweaters, and the sloping background is the same fairway we see by turning slightly.

In the center is the immortal Tommy Armour! Because he is in this group, the picture will hang in the bar for as long as this clubhouse shall stand. The bar and the clubhouse are immortalized by this picture and the rather square-faced man in it. As for the rest, they are left to right: Russell Quinn, club pro; Henry Herring, club treasurer; Armour; Clarence "Fuzzy" Wooten, local banker and corn nabob; and Enrico Fermi!

Passing through en route to Chicago, Fermi stopped to hit a golf ball. He said hello to Tommy Armour, who also just happened to be passing through, and went into the bar with Armour and the others, had a gin rickey, then came out and stood . . . there.

He isn't smiling at the camera. "Fuzzy" Wooten appears to be laughing. At his own joke, likely. Armour is dour but alert; perhaps he is thinking of hitting another golf ball, or having another gin rickey. But Fermi is expressionless. *He* isn't thinking of golf balls or another drink. He must get on to Chicago. . . .

Our golf ball poacher has reached the lake and discovered it has shrunk. He whines softly.

Far enough at the back of his mind so he doesn't have to admit it, our poacher believes the world runs on magic. All day he's aware of the placid jury of clocks looking on, he feels the homage of desks and swivel chairs, and with acquaintances all day he gets and gives, and has careful conversations with strangers. Things usually stay put and when there's a slip he looks the other way. But nights in bed he closes his eyes and gives over—it all must end and begin again! Grinning, he skids down the long cloud hill and attacks the camps of friend and foe alike, ripping and tearing. Instantly the rampage widens, across the land people stagger forth in pajamas. The sky is burning, and all the streets and rooms and people, so laboriously put together, come undone. Every meaning and scrap of sense is scattered in trembling hunks. Poor fellow! Till dawn he tries to find his way home, stumbling through such debris it's as if the soup of the universe had sloshed out some of its logic for him to study. But wait! All is not lost. A bespectacled baboon in starred wizard robes and pointy hat is sifting through it. Tries to fit this to that—hipbone connected to the . . . telephone. Tosses the parts over its shoulder and, peering over the rims of its glasses, titters self-consciously. Can the baboon get the job done by morning? Indeed it does—and that, our poacher fellow is convinced, is the magic marvel of regeneration! For things work just as well as the day before— clocks tick tidily on, swivels swivel as sweetly as ever, and people will people with him again.

So when he sees the lake, black under the moon, is shrunken, he for a slow dismaying moment believes the magic has started at its usual time—and during that long moment it's a hard balance for him.

But it passes—he goes down the hill and in the high grass at the edge peels off his sweatshirt, kicks off his shoes, and takes off his socks and then his trousers.

Clutching his telescoping ball retriever in one hand and a pillowcase in the other, he grits his teeth and wades through the ankle-deep mud. He stops. He had no idea the lake was so muddy: he had pictured the golf balls in rows on a lake bottom as smooth as the blue concrete of the club swimming pool, and he had even seen himself, in goggles and snorkel (and once even in scuba gear) agilely upside-down plucking balls from the lake bottom.

He is sinking in the mud. He pushes on toward the water—and suddenly sinks clear to his knees. But it's only mud. He lurches on, and is at last in the water, splashing so loudly he's certain he can be heard up at the clubhouse, and the mud is even deeper than at the edge—he is sinking smoothly. But struggling farther out, he gains buoyancy.

All right, he whispers.

He feels along the bottom with his feet. But he can't tell when his feet are in the watery mud and when they're lifted out. And while feeling around with one foot, the other subtly sinks. He moves farther out.

As in his better fantasies, under the moon the lake is speckled with celestial golf balls. He'll dive for them!

First, get the face and head wet. He bobs. There. Not so bad, was it? Yes. The water smells yellow. He keeps his tongue inside the good cage of his teeth.

Under again. Lean out and stroke powerfully with both arms —let go the retriever; the cork handle will float it. . . .

He leans out.

He is under water.

From the high west bank we watch the ripples precisely radiating from the center of the lake. The final ring commemorates his head. Then a turbulence churns the water. That was his stroke pulling him down for his glide along the bottom!

He can't open his eyes. Fiercely holding his breath, he is suspended horizontally beneath the surface—hovering as in his imagination, but not deep enough. And he hasn't the nerve to go deeper!

He realizes that he is a great fool.

He is not out of air, but he heads for the surface, stroking powerfully toward air. . . .

He shoots waist-high from the water and when he sinks back he goes completely under!

There's no bottom! He's farther out than where he dived,

PERFECT LIES

and there's a drop in this lake, as there is in every lake and
pond in our land. These drop-offs remind the unwary that
small things hide whole mysteries. The drop-off is crude, but it
has the quality; we're reminded of endless lines, special yearn-
ings, tilted hills, knobless doors, immense cheeses, sudden circles, swastikas in a row, blue stones, giant mushrooms.

He thrashes. Swims wildly. Tries touching bottom—and
goes under again!

He earnestly strokes to the surface (he has let go the pillowcase), and gulps air.

His imagination snaps a side view of himself treading water
beyond the drop-off, the lake bottom far below.

He swims. Now put the feet down. . . . No. Not yet. They
might again touch nothing. He swims farther toward the black
shore. . . .

Now?

He lowers his feet—and his knees then his hips then his arms
sink in mud!

He yells. It carries across the fairways and in the distance
sounds like someone calling *Fore.*

He flops onto his back at the same time he kicks and strokes
hard with both arms. And he floats free, his feet dragging. (He
imagines, irresistibly, the two furrows his heels trace in the
mud, and he knows that if he tries now to get to his feet he will
drown in mud.)

Staring straight into the sky, he believes he is turning from
the shallows. Good. He must float to deeper water, then slowly
lower his legs, one at a time, and touch down. . . .

But he can't see the lake bank. Where is the deep water?

We know! He's again in safe water—is for the moment
spared! But he floats through safe waters and is again passing
over the drop-off. He's floating above two hundred and fifty
feet of water.

Have we forgotten our golf ball? It is at the bottom of this very lake, in the deepest part, enjoying a view of a man who appears to be floating in the sky. Our golf ball has been here a dozen years and is still intact. Science won't disclose how long a golf ball may lie at the bottom of a yellow lake before ceasing to be a golf ball.

The golf ball awaits forever, which is exactly what a golf ball, and everything else, is supposed to do. Twelve years ago a man in a green sweater and yellow slacks hit the golf ball into the lake. It sank like a pearl dreaming down into oil. Soon the man in the green sweater and yellow slacks came to the high west bank and looked down. The golf ball saw absolutely no expression on his face; he appeared not at all concerned that he had hit the ball into the lake, putting it there for all time. In fact, if there was anything in the man's face it was a certain smugness, as if he could see the golf ball—*There it is,* he perhaps said to himself, and actually smiled, as if from the beginning he intended to knock the ball into the lake. He turned and left.

Teeth chattering, our golf ball poacher is floating from the safety of the drop-off into the dangerous shallows, and as we might have expected, he again puts a leg down into mud.

More desperate thrashing. And this time he is truly almost done for. He is submerged in mud.

But he swims through it—literally through the mud!—and is again in deep water. He floats on his back, breathes. He ardently whispers, *Jesus,* as if He were passing by in the sky and could be hailed with a whisper.

Morning comes earlier on golf courses than anywhere else. Sportsmen love that indistinct period: hunters slip through the trees and pounce on creatures, finding in groves of gray nests so large the hunters are amazed they could walk right up and stand over the thing, straddle it even, before realizing it's there, glaring up with unblinking eyes.

1 8 8

Of course golfers love this hour, the still fairways emerging like immense women. The earliest golfers will sometimes fling their clubs aside, kick off their shoes, and run up and down the hills.

The old groundsman in bib overalls and gray shirt watches this and no amusement or disdain shapes his cracked face as he peers from the bushes. He goes from green to green in his silent cart, turning on the sprinklers.

The groundsman tops the hill above the seventh tee and is about to widely loop the lake when he sees a naked man floating on it. *Goddamn,* the groundsman whispers.

He steers the cart down the hill, weaving through the trees that last night a certain fellow thought concealed a gang of cutthroats. He stops well short of the mud and, stepping from the cart, climbs the high west bank.

As he tops the bank and looks down, there is a flash—dazzling and vast, a miraculous blast of light, and the old man lifts his arm to shield his eyes and his very being, and half-turns from this angelic, explosive light.

It is the sun, of course. The groundsman moves from the high bank, and when he can look on the water, the naked man isn't there.

He couldn't have slipped away without the groundsman seeing him. There is no place he could be hiding. . . .

A pillowcase floats on the lake. Could the old man have thought *that* was a naked man?

He turns. Doesn't try to rake the pillowcase from the lake with a branch. Doesn't snag it with the telescoping golf ball-retriever floating at the edge.

He drives his cart to the seventh green, turns on the sprinklers, and, listening to the spizz of water, the eager click of the nozzle heads, he gazes across the green through the sparkling diffusion of spray.

1 8 9

GOLF
DREAMS

·

JOHN UPDIKE

They steal upon the sleeping mind while winter steals upon the landscape, sealing the inviting cups beneath sheets of ice, cloaking the contours of the fairway in snow.

I am standing on a well-grassed tee with my customary summer foursome, whose visages yet have something shifting and elusive about them. I am getting set to drive; the fairway before me is a slight dogleg right, very tightly lined with trees, mostly conifers. As I waggle and lift my head to survey once more the intended line of flight, further complications have been imposed: the air above the fairway has been interwoven with the vines and wooden crosspieces of an arbor, presumably grape, and the land seems to drop away no longer with a natural slope but in nicely hedged terraces. Nevertheless, I accept the multiplying difficulties calmly, and try to allow for them in my swing, which is intently contemplated but never achieved, for I awake with the club at its apogee, waiting for my left side to pull it through and to send the ball toward that bluish speck of openness beyond the vines, between the all but merged forests.

It is a feature of dream golf that the shot never decreases in difficulty but instead from instant to instant melts, as it were, into deeper hardship. A ball, for instance, lying at what the dreaming golfer gauges to be a 7-iron distance from the green, has become, while he glanced away, cylindrical in shape—a roll of coins in a paper wrapper, or a plastic bottle of pills. Nevertheless, he swings, and as he swings he realizes that the club in his hands bears a rubber tip, a little red-rubber tab the color of a crutch tip, but limp. The rubber flips negligibly across the cylindrical "ball," which meanwhile appears to be sinking into a small trough having to do, no doubt, with the sprinkler system. Yet, most oddly, the dreamer surrenders not a particle of hope of making the shot. In this instance, indeed, I seem to recall, on my second or third swing, making crisp contact, and then striding in the direction of the presumed flight with a springy sensation of considerable expectancy.

After all, are these nightmares any worse than the "real" drive that skips off the toe of the club, strikes the prism-shaped tee marker, and is swallowed by weeds some twenty yards *behind* the horrified driver? Or the magical impotence of an utter whiff? Or the bizarre physical comedy of a soaring slice that strikes the one telephone wire strung across three hundred acres? The golfer is so habituated to humiliation that his dreaming mind never offers any protest of implausibility. Whereas dream life, we are told, is a therapeutic caricature, seamy side out, of real life, dream golf is simply golf played on another course. We chip from glass tables onto moving stairways; we swing in a straitjacket, through masses of cobweb, and awaken not with any sense of unjust hazard but only with a regret that the round can never be completed, and that one of our phantasmal companions has kept the scorecard.

Even the fair companion sleeping beside us has had a golf dream, with a feminist slant. An ardent beginner, she says, "I was playing with these men, I don't know who they were, and they kept using woods when we were on the green, so of course the balls would fly miles away, and then they had to hit all the way back! I thought to myself, They aren't using the right club, and I took my putter out and, of course, I kept beating them!"

"Didn't they see what you were doing, and adjust their strokes accordingly?"

"No, they didn't seem to get it, and I wasn't going to tell them. I kept *win*ning, and it was *won*derful," she insists.

We gaze at one another across the white pillows, in the morning light filtered through icicles, and realize we were only dreaming. Our common green hunger begins to gnaw afresh, insatiable.

THE PRO

·

JOHN UPDIKE

I am on my four-hundred-and-twelfth golf lesson, and my drives still have that pushed little tail, and my irons still take the divot on the wrong side of the ball. My pro is a big gloomy sun-browned man—age about thirty-eight, weight around a hundred and ninety-five. When he holds a club in his gloved hand and swishes it nervously (the nervousness comes over him after the first twenty minutes of our lesson), he makes it look light as a feather, a straw, a baton. Once I sneaked his three wood from his bag, and the head weighed more than a cannonball. "Easy does it, Mr. Wallace," he says to me. My name is not Wallace, but he smooths his clients toward one generic, acceptable name. I call him Dave.

"Easy does it, Mr. Wallace," he says. "That ball is not going anywhere by itself, so what's your hurry?"

"I want to clobber the bastard," I say. It took me two hundred lessons to attain this pitch of frankness.

"You dipped again," he tells me, without passion. "That right shoulder of yours dipped, and your knees locked, you were so anxious. Ride those knees, Mr. Wallace."

"I can't. I keep thinking about my wrists. I'm afraid I won't pronate them."

This is meant to be a joke, but he doesn't smile. "Ride those knees, Mr. Wallace. Forget your wrists. Look." He takes my five iron into his hands, a sight so thrilling it knocks the breath out of me. It is like, in the movies we all saw as children (oh, blessed childhood!), the instant when King Kong, or the gigantic Cyclops, lifts the beautiful blonde, who has blessedly fainted, over his head, and she becomes utterly weightless, a thing of sheer air and vision and pathos. I love it, I feel half sick with pleasure, when he lifts my club, and want to tell him so, but I can't. After four hundred and eleven lessons, I still repress.

"The hands can't *help* but be right," he says, "if the *knees* are right." He twitches the club, so casually I think he is brushing a bee from the ball's surface. There is an innocent click; the ball whizzes into the air and rises along a line as straight as the edge of a steel ruler, hangs at its remote apogee for a moment of meditation, and settles like a snowflake twenty yards beyond the shagging caddie.

"Gorgeous, Dave," I say with an affectation of camaraderie, though my stomach is a sour churning of adoration and dread.

He says, "A little fat, but that's the idea. Did you see me grunt and strain?"

"No, Dave." This is our litany.

"Did you see me jerk my head, or freeze at the top of the backswing, or rock forward on my toes?"

"No, Dave, no."

"Well then, what's the problem? Step up and show me how."

I assume my stance, and take back the club, low, slowly; at the top, my eyes fog over, and my joints dip and swirl like barn swallows. I swing. There is a fruitless commotion of dust and rubber at my feet. "Smothered it," I say promptly. After enough lessons, the terminology becomes second nature. The whole process, as I understand it, is essentially one of self-analysis. The pro is merely a catalyst, a random sample, I have read somewhere, from the grab bag of humanity.

He insists on wearing a droll porkpie hat from which his heavy brown figure somehow downflows; his sloping shoulders, his hanging arms, his faintly pendulous belly, and his bent knees all tend toward his shoes, which are ideally natty—solid as bricks, black and white, with baroque stitching, frilled kilties, and spikes as neat as alligator teeth. He looks at me almost with interest. His grass-green irises are tiny, whittled by years of concentrating on the ball. "Loosen up," he tells me. I love it, I clench with gratitude, when he deigns to be directive. "Take a few practice swings, Mr. Wallace. You looked like a rusty mechanical man on that one. Listen. Golf is an effortless game."

"Maybe I have no aptitude," I say, giggling, blushing, hoping to deflect him with the humility bit.

He is not deflected. Stolidly he says, "Your swing is sweet. When it's there." Thus he uplifts me and crushes me from phrase to phrase. "You're blocking yourself out," he goes on. "You're not open to your own potential. You're not, as we say, *free.*"

"I know, I know. That's why I'm taking all these expensive lessons."

"Swing, Mr. Wallace. Show me your swing."

195

I swing, and feel the impurities like bubbles and warps in glass: hurried backswing, too much right hand at impact, failure to finish high.

The pro strips off his glove. "Come over to the eighteenth green." I think we are going to practice chipping (a restricted but relaxed pendulum motion) for the fiftieth time, but he says, "Lie down."

The green is firm yet springy. The grounds crew has done a fine job watering this summer, through that long dry spell. Not since childhood have I lain this way, on sweet flat grass, looking up into a tree, branch above branch, each leaf distinct in its generic shape, as when, in elementary school, we used to press them between wax paper. The tree is a sugar maple. For all the times I have tried to hit around it, I never noticed its species before. In the fall, its dried-up leaves have to be brushed from the line of every putt. This spring, when the branches were tracery dusted with a golden budding, I punched a nine iron right through the crown and salvaged a double bogey.

Behind and above me, the pro's voice is mellower than I remember it, with a lulling grittiness, like undissolved sugar in tea. He says, "Mr. Wallace, tell me what you're thinking about when you freeze at the top of your backswing."

"I'm thinking about my shot. I see it sailing dead on the pin, hitting six feet short, taking a bite with lots of backspin, and dribbling into the cup. The crowd goes *ooh* and cheers."

"Who's in the crowd? Anybody you know personally?"

"No . . . wait. There is somebody. My mother. She has one of those cardboard periscope things and shouts out, 'Gorgeous, Billy!'"

"She calls you Billy."

"That's my name, Dave. William. Willy. Billy. Bill. Let's cut out this Mr. Wallace routine. You call me Bill. I'll call you Dave." He is much easier to talk to, the pro, without the sight of his powerful passionless gloom, his hands (one bare, one gloved) making a mockery of the club's weight.

"Anybody else you know? Wife? Kids?"

"No, my wife's had to take the baby-sitter home. Most of the kids are at camp."

"What else do you see up there at the top of the back-swing?"

"I see myself quitting lessons." It was out, *whiz,* before I had time to censor. Silence reigns in the leafy dome above me. A sparrow is hopping from branch to branch, like a pencil point going from number to number in those children's puzzles we all used to do.

At last the pro grunts, which, as we said, he never does. "The last time you were out, Mr. Wallace, what did you shoot?"

"You mean the last time I kept count?"

"Mm."

"A hundred eight. But that was with some lucky putts."

"Mm. Better stand up. Any prolonged pressure, the green may get a fungus. This bent grass is hell to maintain." When I stand, he studies me, chuckles, and says to an invisible attendant, "A hundred eight, with a hot putter yet, and he wants to quit lessons."

I beg, "Not quit forever—just for a vacation. Let me play a few different courses. You know, get out into the world. Maybe even try a public course. Hell, or go to a driving range and whack out a bucket of balls. You know, learn to live with the game I've got. Enjoy life."

His noble impassivity is invested with a shimmering, twinkling humorousness; his leathery face softens toward a smile, and the trace of a dimple is discovered in his cheek. "Golf is life," he says softly, and his green eyes expand, "and life is lessons," and the humps of his brown muscles merge with the hillocks and swales of the course, whose red flags prick the farthest horizon, and whose dimmest sand traps are indistinguishable from galaxies. I see that he is right, as always, absolutely; there is no life, no world, beyond the golf course—just an infinite and terrible falling-off. "If I don't give *you* lessons," he is going on, "how will I pay for *my* lessons?"

"You take lessons?"

"Sure. I hook under pressure. Like Palmer. I'm too strong. Any rough on the left, there I am. You don't have that problem, with your nice pushy slice."

"You mean there's a sense," I ask, scarcely daring, "in which *you* need *me?*"

He puts his hand on my shoulder, the hand pale from wearing the glove, and I become a feather at the touch, all air and ease. "Mr. Wallace," he says, "I've learned a lot from your sweet swing. I hate it when, like now, the half hour's up."

"Next Tuesday, eleven-thirty?"

Solemnly my pro nods. "We'll smooth out your chipping. Here in the shade."

THE
MOWER

·

JAMES KAPLAN

She ran every morning at six-twenty. At first I hardly noticed, but then it got so I'd look for her, and worry a little if she was late. She'd come out of the trees along the sixteenth fairway, run through the rough down the side, cut across the street, go down the seventeenth, then over the creek—there's a little wooden bridge—onto the third tee, and out of sight. I would never see her after that. If she finished where she started, though, she must have run four or five miles. Jesus. I couldn't run a mile if you paid me a million bucks. I never saw where she finished, because even though I was almost always on the fifteenth or sixteenth when she

199

started—you cut them alternate days, usually—as soon as she got out of sight I had to go down the hill and do the eleventh or the tenth, and then back into the garage before the four-somes started showing up at seven. Benito, the greenskeeper, had his own special little system; he completely flew off the handle if you did it any other way, and he was always around, in that yellow cart with the flag on it, to make sure you did it right. Benito was *everywhere.*

Practically as soon as I began seeing her I hoped two things: one, that Benito wouldn't catch her—he'd love that—and two, that she got off the course before the foursomes came on. There's something about four guys together that I don't espe-cially like. There's something about *golf* I don't like, as a matter of fact. But the course—that was different. Have you ever been on a golf course at six in the morning? It's very misty, kind of spooky; all the hills and bumps look like giant animals or some-thing. Then the sun comes up—if you're lucky and it's clear out. I saw the sun rise every clear morning for six years. Not many people can say that. I'll take a sunrise over a sunset every time. But even if it's raining, it's beautiful out there. Ask most people what color a rainy day is, and what do they say? Gray. Not on a golf course. Everything is green—but not the same green. There are about eighty-two different kinds of green out there. Blue green, gray green, yellow green, orange green, brown green, purple green, green green. You name it.

I'd show up at five-thirty, try and steer clear of Benito, and get on one of the machines. Usually I'd do roughs first—not much fun. Then I did around the greens—kind of finicky work; the edges are the worst. But my favorite was the fairways. The big eighteen-foot mower—you feel like a king, going right down the middle. You have to use a different machine for each length of grass. They don't adjust like your little Lawn-Boy. There were three of us; we did nine holes every morning, three apiece. Benito had this whole complicated system worked out so you could trade machines with another guy when you were through. It was all done by the clock. Six-ten was when I started the sixteenth fairway, and six-twenty was when she came out of the trees.

It was nice watching her. Most people look terrible running. Most women, especially, don't look very good running. They don't seem to be built for it, usually. The only people I've ever seen that look any good running are these really skinny guys who run cross-country for the Catholic school across the mountain. They practice every afternoon; I see them when I drive home. They always look like they're about to die, extremely thin guys with sweaty undershirts and bony chests, their mouths open and their eyes staring. And their eyes kind of go dead every time one of their feet hits the ground. But there they are, running, mile after mile—you can't imagine them doing anything else. And then you see one of these fat guys huffing along in sweat pants and fluorescent shoes. Or one of these housewives. (I should talk. I could stand to lose twenty myself. Beer.) But you should have seen *her*. Once, when I was in high school—it seems like about thirty years ago—my music-appreciation class went to the ballet, and all of my friends and I were getting off on how faggoty it was, which is the kind of thing you get off on in high school. Most of the time I was pretty bored, I have to admit, but there were a couple of things I really liked, like when the guys jumped. Those guys can *jump*. And when they picked the girls up. You can't be that much of a fag if you can pick up somebody who weighs about a hundred pounds and make it look easy. I also liked it when the girls ran off the stage. I loved watching the way their behinds moved when they ran off the stage. That's just the way she ran. Exactly the same. Down the sixteenth fairway and out of sight.

She waved to me three or four mornings after the first time I saw her. I almost fell off my mower. Came out of the trees and waved at me, and did I wave back? Schmuck. I was too startled. But the next morning she waved again anyway. This will sound dumb, I know, but she had the nicest wave I ever saw. Most people just put up their hand and shake it back and forth, but she did something different—how can I describe it? It was sort of a periscope wave, or maybe like a little sea monster. Her arm was up, but her hand was at right angles to it, the back of her hand was arched, and she fluttered her fingers, like a pianist or something. When I got home, I did that wave at myself in the mirror. I felt like my hand didn't belong to me.

At the end of the month, it rained, hard, for a solid week almost. Sometimes when it's raining just a little bit, a lot of these guys who are nuts about golf will put on their funny hats or bring out their cute umbrellas and play anyway, but this was *rain.* I mean, there were swimming pools on the greens. Nobody was playing golf, running, anything. Or maybe she did run. I don't know. I wasn't out there to see her. When it was like that out, all you could really do was sit around the garage, pretending to repair stuff. The club paid you anyway. Big deal. I'd rather be outside. The guys I really felt sorry for were the caddies. What the hell could they do? But the four of us, mostly we'd just sit around, smoking, shooting the breeze, even playing poker. The funny thing was, when the weather got like that Benito was the first one to break out the cards. He'd make this amazing change, from a little rat into a sweetheart. Then he'd always worry about the manager, Mr. Mahaffy. He'd talk real quiet while he dealt the cards, and look over his shoulder a lot. I loved it. I loved the way it smelled in the garage when it was raining out—sort of a combination of wet grass and gasoline and cigarette smoke. You could almost go into a trance with the rain coming down on the roof. It was like being high. Over on the wall, next to the fire extinguisher, somebody wrote in pencil: JULY 2, 1961. RAIN. I used to stare at it and wonder what the hell it was like on July 2, 1961. It seems like at least four hundred years ago. What day of the week was it? Who was cutting grass? What did they look like? Were they playing cards? Was the course still full of creeps then? Who was greenskeeper? (Benito's only been there since '67.) Kennedy was President. Probably everyone had crewcuts. Then I wondered where *she* was then. Probably not born yet. No, probably like three, four years old. I wondered if I ever saw her someplace—a supermarket, maybe.

The rain finally stopped after five days. One afternoon it just stopped, and the sun came out, and all of a sudden it was real hot, and we had to go out and cut. Benito made us stay late. There were still big puddles on the greens. Clouds of mosquitoes everywhere. Clumps of wet grass stuck to the blades. Usually we didn't cut in the afternoon, but Benito was panicking. Mahaffy was on his ass. So the next morning the regular schedule was all screwed up. I was way the hell on the other side of the course, and suddenly it hit me: I wasn't going to get to see her come out of the trees. And it was killing me. That's when I knew I was in trouble. I was cutting the seventh green, going around and around in circles, cursing and punching the steering wheel. Around and around. Christ, I hated greens. And then, bang, I see her, running down along the trees. And she waves, kind of nonchalant, like we're old friends, like it hasn't been raining for the past week, like we always meet this way on the seventh hole. But what could I do? Bawl her out? I waved back—not a big wave, just a little one. I was pretty mad. Then, on an impulse, I cut the engine and yelled to her. "Hey!" I said. She was on her way to the eighth tee. "Hey!" I yelled. But she just sort of half turned around and gave that wave of hers. Then she was gone. I got *really* wrecked that night.

You know how it is when you drink too much. It's pretty hard to sleep. Maybe I got four hours that night, I don't know, but I dreamed I was awake the whole time, and the room felt like I was riding that goddamned mower around and around the seventh green. I dreamed about her. When I woke up, in the dark, I made up my mind that I would *definitely* talk to her at six-twenty. Definitely.

The sun came up through the trees like a giant orange golf ball sitting in the rough, the birds were making a racket, and I was riding down the sixteenth fairway at six-fifteen, with a head that felt like a piano or something, not a head. I was just riding, not cutting. I was really supposed to be on the fifteenth—Johnny D. had already done the sixteenth the day before. So I had the blades up, and I was just riding along, watching the trees. Benito would've murdered me. Out she came, right on schedule, and she waved. I was not feeling too sharp. I couldn't have looked too sharp, either, but I just cruised up next to her, about as close as I could get with the blade arm sticking out, and I said, "Hi!" She waved again. I don't think she heard me. The engine was pretty loud. We went along together for a little bit, just smiling at each other. Then I got up my courage. "What's your name!" I yelled. She smiled and put her hand up to her ear. I forgot to say she had really nice ears. She wore her hair up, and there were those little wisps of blond hair coming down. "Your name!" I shouted. "What's your name?" Then she said something, but I couldn't hear. I cut the engine. Now she was out ahead of me. I asked again. She called something back over her shoulder. Juliana?

I really think that's what she said. Juliana. What the hell kind of name is that? Practically all the girls I ever meet are named Cathy. Sometimes I think half the girls I've ever *known* have been named Cathy. Their favorite song is always "Cherish."

There was no rain at all the next month. Zero. Plus, it was about a hundred out every day. The course almost fried. We were allowed to water the greens but not the fairways. Town ordinance. Benito would just stand there and stare at his precious grass shriveling up and look like he was about to pop a blood vessel. The weird thing was, every afternoon there were all these big black clouds, sometimes even some thunder and lightning—but no rain. There was always a lot of static on the radio. I wanted to say something to her about running on the fairways—Benito was at the point where he would've shot someone for taking a divot—but I was scared to talk to her. Can you believe it? The funny thing is, usually I'm never that way. Usually I'm just the opposite.

Then Benito put us back to just doing greens. My favorite. That's all that was growing. And he said if the weather didn't break he was going to have to let one of us go. He said we could draw straws. I should've told him what he could do with his straws. He assigned me to the first six, way the hell on the other side of the course from where she ran. I asked him if I could switch with somebody else, but he just gave me this look.

Then, next morning—it was *hot;* by six-thirty my shirt was soaked—I was coming over the hill to the fourth green when suddenly I just got goose bumps. I knew what was happening even before I knew, if you know what I mean. Way down the fairway, about three hundred and fifty yards out, I could see this yellow dot and this red dot. That was all. I knew right away what was going on. I don't know why, but it reminded me of November of seventh grade. We were playing football one Friday afternoon, and Mr. Finelli, my gym teacher, came running across the field with his hands in his pockets. I knew it was bad news. I just knew. Everybody else on my team kept running, and I stopped in my tracks and watched him coming across the field. It was the same way now. I should've started on the green, but I headed down the fairway. We were only supposed to drive on the service roads, because the course was so dried out, but I just went right on down the middle. She was standing there with her hands on her hips, sweating like crazy, and Benito was shaking his finger in her face. I could've killed the little bastard. But I couldn't *get* there. It was like a bad dream: the stupid mower would only go about ten miles an hour. I should've just hopped out and run, but I probably would've dropped dead, my heart was beating so hard. Then Benito heard the engine noise and turned around. He started

jumping up and down—I swear it, jumping up and down. You
should have seen it. I must have been trailing a dust cloud half
a mile wide. And then she just took off. Vanished into the
trees. I couldn't really blame her. I still can't. What was she
supposed to do—wait around till Benito got finished with me?

So now I'm looking for work. My brother-in-law has this
Arco station out on Route 17. Maybe I'll go there. Anything
but cutting grass. I mean, in a way this whole thing might have
been kind of lucky. Can you see me sitting on a mower when
I'm forty? Every once in a while I miss the course a little bit.
Not the job—the course. I liked the way the sky looked over it,
all the different kinds of clouds. The way the grass smelled.
The wind in the trees. You don't get that on Route 17. But I
won't miss Benito. I won't miss the golfers.

For a while I kept thinking I was seeing her places—in the
mall, walking down the street—but it was always someone else.
Once, this white 280-Z pulled up next to me at a light and my
heart almost stopped. She was at the wheel. I honked, but
when she turned around I saw it was another girl. She gave me
the finger. I gave it to her back.

MY
LIVELIHOOD

·

CHARLES DICKINSON

I lost my dairy job and was not troubled. One of my brothers-in-law said he could get me into the carpenters' union. He said he'd lend me the tools and instruct me in their use. I was tired of the dairy, all that whiteness every day, and the hairnets we had to wear. Hair in milk. Shows right up.

But I didn't want to be a carpenter, either. I wasn't looking for work. This bothered the hell out of my Stella, who was expecting our second child, hoping for a girl this time. She was six months' gone. Two-thirds there, her belly was nice and round. Her cheeks were fat. My Stel is tall and took it well. She is very close to being pretty. My son's name is Ray.

My Stella's father is a contractor of some renown. He told me I was lazy. Her brothers, seven carpenters, said the same thing. Ray even picked it up: Daddy's lazy. Stella's family makes me nervous. They are too hearty in their work, out all day driving nails. They have muscles and great tans. They told me I could be a carpenter too and called me lazy when I said no thanks. I was waiting, I told myself. I felt something happening.

I'm thirty-three years old. I've been out of work a number of times in my life. Never like this, though, Stel tells me. She's right. I must avoid panic. I mustn't get roped into the first thing that pays. That is the old me. I was raised to hate work but to do it. I always had to have a job. This time I'm going slow.

The dairy told me adios April fifteenth. My foreman called me into his office and said, "Kids ain't drinking the milk they used to." I didn't have the seniority to weather such a trend, but I liked the irony; Ray Boy drinks the stuff by the ton. Me and three other guys in hairnets went out the door. One guy started to cry and shake right there in the parking lot. A young guy, married, but no kids, he went right to pieces before my eyes. I shook hands all around, told the crying guy to grab hold. I got in my car and went straight home. Me for a sandwich and beer.

Along the way home I saw ads for things I couldn't afford anymore. On my dairy pay I couldn't afford most things, but there was always the chance; now, no way. The world was hung with ads, I noticed. All those deluxes beyond my reach.

I got out of my whites at home and threw them down the laundry chute. This was a small favorite with me, the boy in me coming out. I held on to the clothes until I could get my head in the chute to watch them fall; they got smaller falling, they stayed in flight longer than I expected. It was a cheap special effect and reminded me of science fiction.

Ray came home a little later and screamed when he saw me. I was out of place lying on the couch in the middle of the afternoon with a beer on my stomach. I gave him a hug. He said my arms smelled like cheese.

"Where's Mom?" I asked. He didn't know. I took him out back and we threw the Frisbee until Stella came home.

She brought an armload of old clothes with her. More Goodwill crap. Her face glowed with the pleasure of doing good for others. She dropped a black shoe when she came to the door to call Ray and saw me running after the flying saucer.

"Why are you home?" she asked.

"I lost my job."

My Stella wet her lips with her tongue. She carried the old clothes into the utility room and dropped them on the floor. I picked up the black shoe and followed her. She gave me a kiss. Wet salt taste. Her stomach bumping me. I felt a rising. When was the last time we'd done it in the afternoon? I was always working. Ray Boy. Something. See, I told myself, a positive thing already.

"It's not so bad," I told her. "Nothing to worry about."

I looked outside at Ray. He was talking to a kid on a bike and throwing the Frisbee up and catching it. I suggested to my Stella, "Let's go upstairs."

She stepped behind the pile of clothes. She wanted that crap between us, I guess. Her face had changed. I felt the moment getting away from me. My Stel wanted me to be afraid for our quality of life. She'd kissed me, sure, but she'd also bumped me with her hard belly. Number two, hello in there.

"Nothing to be worried about?" she said. She was tapping one of her feet, which are big.

"It'll be all right," I said.

She was not ready for this. My Stella is the baby of her family, though she is older than two of her brothers. Stella and her mother and her father and seven brothers. Her father paid for our house as a wedding present. Her brothers built it. I remember that as a hard time for me. Her brothers had something to do, they laughed at each other's jokes. I just sat on the lumber and watched. I fetched them beers to make myself useful.

Stella had been raised in a world that was a happy place. All lines were plumb, all nails were straight. Her grandfather was dead a year, flattened by a slipped ton of bricks, before Stel was told. She was not prepared for a husband out of work. I saw her start to cry. Her mother's tears. It was the lone soft spot in the men in Stella's family, and that spot was mush. Don't use it too often, I could hear Stella's mother coaching her, dry-eyed. Use it sparingly and it will hit home every time.

I took a step forward, kissed my wife, and smiled. I would not be bullied. If she kept it up, I'd go outside and play with Ray.

"Pretty soon . . . pretty soon," my Stella sobbed, bringing one of her big feet up through the pile of Goodwill crap, filling the air with it, "we'll be wearing this stuff ourselves."

I got into a poker game with some of the dairy guys, and though I won $122 I went home sad. All that dairy talk, it made me miss it. Tales of women on the routes. Stray things that dropped in the milk. A driver named Del was being sued for running over a champion Afghan. He laughed and said the dog looked like an old flame, and that was why he went after it, but still he was being sued. They let me play but I didn't belong. I imagined they were mad because I was ungrateful enough to win, too.

My Stella saw me sitting at home and decided I was sad and bored. She dragged me along on her Goodwill rounds. "It will do you good to get out of the house," she said. "It will lift your spirits until you find another job."

"My spirits aren't low."

"Yes, they are," she told me.

At every place we stopped she worked the fact of my unemployment into the conversation. I'd stand out by the car and she'd point at me, and I'd wave and smile. She might have asked for something in my size. She used me as an example of the type of person all those rags would help.

When I asked her not to tell everybody I'd lost my job, she answered with words that even made a little sense. "These people are very successful, and you never know who might offer you a job."

We stopped at the Blatt house. Mrs. Blatt was going to donate an old set of golf clubs to Goodwill. I offered to buy them from her for ten dollars.

"You'll do no such thing," my Stella protested.

"Here." I folded the bill in Mrs. Blatt's hand. I saw it in her eyes: charity was fine, but profit was holy. "You can get rid of the clubs," I told her, "and make a little money."

I slung that bag of jangling sticks over my shoulder. "People who need Goodwill don't have time to play golf," I told Stella. "They're too busy looking for firewood."

I took my clubs to the public course the next day. The new ball I teed up reminded me guiltily of an egg that should have been on Ray Boy's plate, and that reminded me of my joblessness. But then I hit the ball and it swooped out of sight. The feeling was solid in my hands. A motion down the fairway caught my eye. My ball landing. It hit and rolled, it might have gone forever but the ground was damp. I set off after it. I played thirty-six holes that day.

I never was an athlete. My father owned a grocery and I went to work for him when I was seven years old, cheap help, a roof over my head, and a dollar allowance a week making me, in my father's words, "rich enough." I worked in that store for an hour before school, then after school until we closed at seven, and all day on weekends. I was ringing sales on the cash register when I was nine years old and all the kids my age were outdoors hitting baseballs or shooting free throws. These kids came indoors in winter, red-faced, to buy gum or oatmeal cookies, skates hanging from their necks. Their taped sticks and black disks were exotic tools to me. I was a flop in gym. I once brained myself getting under a fly ball and probably survived only because we were playing softball.

One day, I was fifteen, I stopped to watch the golfers on my way to work. For more than two years they had been building the course and all that land hadn't meant much to me. I had seen the yellow graders and the scalloped dents filled with sand and the troops of Mexicans brought in to lay rolls of sod. It had meant nothing to me. I clerked in a grocery for my old man.

Then the golf course opened. I was passing by and saw a guy on the tee, and I watched him whip his club around and smack that ball a mile, though I couldn't see where it landed. The guy watched it and watched it, then he slid his club into a bag and covered it with a tasseled sock.

This was golf. It looked like something I might like. There were no moving balls to hit or control. I would not be required to be quick, or to do something instantly for the good of the team. But I didn't dare tell my father. I had a job; that was all I needed. Eighteen years would pass before I would tee it up.

I have two brothers, three sisters. I think that's part of why I fell in love with Stella; she understood the big-family life. All of us worked in the store. My mother, too. When my sister Diana got up the money and nerve to leave and was planning to move to Phoenix, my old man snuck into her room the night before she was to leave and cut up her bus ticket. Diana avenged this by upending every pyramid of cans in the store at the height of the Saturday rush. A terrific racket. We watched and cheered and refused to restack them. We never came closer to open revolt.

Why did we stay and work there so long? It was part of our training. All of us realize that now. My father hated that store.

He told us so often how he hated it that we hated it, too. Now none of us can stand the things we do for a living. To the old man, work was a curse. Now it is to us, too. We may like the money or maybe the people on the job, or the end of the day, but none of us get anything from the actual work. It makes me angry. My father had no right. This is one reason I'm not looking right now.

Diana finally got to Phoenix and became a cocktail waitress and hooker. I've seen pictures of her taken there. She's a pretty girl, though I don't recognize her as my sister. She says she hates her jobs. Rachel is a nurse and hates it. She writes me long letters from Boston, filled with complaint. She hates the old man's ghost for what he gave her. That ghost has driven us all away. Me here, Rachel in Boston, Diana in Arizona, Tim in Paris, of all places, Rosie in Vancouver. Vic owns a bait and tackle shop in the Upper Peninsula of Michigan, on the shore of Lake Superior, and hires kids to run it for him. He told me they rob him blind, but he accepts this as the price he has to pay to be able to stay away from the place.

My father died when I was twenty-one. My mother sold the store and split the proceeds evenly among herself and her children. It made a nice lump, and it is this, to some extent, that feeds my family now. Vic bought the bait shop with his share. Rachel put hers into nursing-school tuition.

My mother took her share and moved to New Orleans. I visited her once and she made me cry, she was so content. She lived in a large apartment that had a thousand plants, french doors, and a thin strip of balcony you could stand on and smell the Gulf of Mexico. She cooked a ton of shrimp for us. She played Bingo every night. She sat in that smoky room and inhaled deeply. She was good. She claimed to have increased her inheritance by a fourth. I liked that she had her groceries delivered by lanky black boys eager for the good tip she was known for. She's still there.

So my father's death and the store's being sold was my first taste of being out of work. I stashed my inheritance and pan-icked. I took the first job I could find, going to work in a factory that made gizmos for detecting police radar. I sat on a high stool under perfect light doing the same four steps over and over again. It was boring work and I kind of liked it the first three hours. But the business was on the rise, and automa-tion came along and did my job better. Last hired, I was first fired. That was only fair. A second time I was out of work.

I knocked around a few years. I worked odd jobs and tested my reactions to losing them. It was like giving myself increas-ing jolts of electricity to see how much I could stand. The longest I went without work, without looking for work, was three weeks. I started waking up depressed, bathed in sweat. I knew I had to find work right away. It was not lack of money that drove me, but something deeper. It was the values of my father, what he had nailed in me with all those hours in the store. Hating work was in my blood.

I'm a glib guy when I have to be. Getting a job has never been a problem. I come across as earnest, reliable, eager to do the job. I knew that once I started looking I'd find something right away. When I was twenty-five, I took a job working for the city at a recycling center, real moron's work that paid $7.70 an hour, a king's ransom. My job was to sort all the crap people brought in to have recycled, weigh the stuff, and throw it in the respective dumpsters to be hauled away. We took in only glass bottles, aluminum cans, and newspapers.

We paid twenty cents a pound for aluminum cans. A tall young lady with a kind of obsessed look on her face argued with me one day that our scales were off, that I was cheating her. I explained that the scales were accurate, that she'd have to trust me, but that if she wanted to complain, she could go up to the village hall and talk to them. She said she just might. I weighed her cans and wrote out her receipt. I watched her walk to her car, an emerald Lincoln Continental, and maneuver her body into it. She had large hips, breasts, and feet and was almost six feet tall. She didn't seem comfortable with all she had been given. It looked like too much for her to handle. I guessed she was twenty or twenty-one and would learn to be graceful later. Of course, this girl was my Stella.

She was back in a week with more cans, bags of them stuffed in the trunk and back seat of her Lincoln. I asked where she got them all.

"Along the highway," she said. "Everywhere you look. People can be such pigs."

I asked if that was how she paid for her car, smiling to let her know I was flirting.

"My daddy bought my car for me."

She kept returning with cans all that summer, and when I drove home I always was surprised to see any cans along the road, I was sure she had gotten them all. She had an anxious face. She was eager for something and late in July I began to have dreams that it was me. I asked her for a date the next time she was in. She agreed and volunteered to drive. We went miniature golfing and had a pizza on our first date. On other dates we necked in her wide back seat. She was clumsy with her size only until she got into my arms. Then her grace and invention were startling. She began driving me to and from work; on occasion, we scouted the highway together for cans, though I lacked her prospector's lust. The first time I took her clothes off I was amazed at all that was involved. My Stella, big, smooth-skinned riddle. We were married in a year. Ray Boy soon followed. I was making $10.11 an hour at the recycling center and hating it so much it had the feel of a career. Then about a year ago my Stella came home and told me her father knew someone at the dairy, that he could get me a job if I was interested.

I played 180 holes the first week of May. My Goodwill clubs were in sorry condition but I didn't mind. After I scraped the crud from their faces they worked fine. When I wasn't on the course, I was practicing in my yard with plastic golf balls.

The pro at the public course where I played told me my swing was "a natural" and that it could really be spruced up with a few lessons. I had no use for lessons. If I was taking a lesson, that would mean less time I'd be out on the course actually playing. I was afraid to take golf seriously. I was afraid I'd learn to hate the game.

The pro told me I was lazy. "You have to put some effort into it," he told me.

"Effort," I said, "implies resistance."

I hit the ball long and straight from the first. I didn't lust after scores like so many guys who were out to break a hundred, then ninety, then eighty. I was living on that fascination for the game planted eighteen years earlier when I'd seen that guy hitting his drive on my way to work. I was playing. It was a strange thing: work and play. Some days, if I was short or didn't feel like spending my money on a round, I worked it off in the pro shop washing balls, cleaning clubs, or filling driving-range buckets for Dave, who ran the place. When I did finally get out on the course, I wasn't ashamed of my clubs or my shoes (which I paid two dollars for at a garage sale; they fit perfectly but one was missing a heel cleat). I had a sport. And when my playing partners had to quit to go back to work, I could play all afternoon.

June came. The summer was dry and hot. I could feel the greens quickening by the moment. My Stella's face got fatter. I was in the front yard practicing my nine iron when one of my brothers-in-law appeared. This one was named Jack. He was about forty years old, with thick forearms, a tan, and a cigarillo in his mouth.

"How's she holding up?" he asked.

"Just fine."

"No leaks?"

"Stella?"

Jack broke off a laugh and walked up to the house he had helped build. He smacked the wall. "No, man! Our house. A damn fine job we did for you."

"The house is fine," I assured him. I had seven plastic balls lined up at my feet. One by one I would hit them down the yard. I looked forward to Jack leaving so I could get on with it.

"Stel tells us you're still out of work."

"Stel tells everybody that," I said. "I expect to see it on the news."

"Been a while, hasn't it?"

I swung smoothly through the first ball and it floated away with a faint *snick!* sound. I liked Jack best of that hopeless knot of carpenters I had married into. He was the oldest, and the only one to thank me for the beers I fetched while they built our house. Not much of a swap, I know, beers for a house, but I appreciate good manners wherever they occur.

"We'll be okay," I said. "Thanks for your concern."

"You got any prospects?"

"Prospects for a job? I haven't been looking too hard."

"You've got a pregnant wife in there, pal," Jack said.

"No. She's not home."

He grimaced. Me, the smart-ass. "What do you do with yourself all day?"

"I play a lot of golf. You play?"

"No. Look, how about being a carpenter? We can get you in the union."

"No, thanks."

"Dad said he can call in a few favors. It's good money. The work is seasonal, sure, but when you work, the money is damn good."

"I can't even hammer a nail, Jack." With the softest *tick!* I sent the next ball away down a sweet, high path.

Jack dismissed my ineptitude. "That can be taught. Any asshole can drive a nail. We'll lend you some tools until you can get your own. With a little pull from Dad we can even skip your apprenticeship. You'll start right off in the serious money."

"You've given us enough already," I told him. I settled myself over the next ball. Jack momentarily ceased to be. I hit it nicely. "This house," I said, "and I know your father gives Stella money. I can't take another job from you, too."

"Is that so terrible? Taking something from your family during hard times?"

"Yeah, Jack. It's gotten to that point."

"It's not easy getting into the union. The waiting list is a mile long."

"Let someone in who wants to be a carpenter."

"It's true, I guess, what Stel says."

"Probably," I agreed.

"She says you're lazy. She says you like being out of a job."

"My Stella speaks the truth."

My Stella gave us a daughter on a steamy August morning. Cecilia Joan was a big girl like her mother, coming in an ounce shy of ten pounds. I laid my hand on Stella's wet forehead and put my ear to her chest to listen to her heart. She had worked hard. The baby was red and creased. We took our mothers' first names, flipping a coin to determine the order.

The elevator dumped a load of carpenters. We heard them coming and Stella laughed. She rolled her tired eyes at me and hooked her lank hair behind her ears. She knew I'd be leaving soon.

Her father led them in. He carried a giant stuffed panda.

"So here's the numbnuts who's too good to be a carpenter," he said. "Too good to be helped out by his family that works up a sweat on the job."

"Daddy!" Stella protested.

They filled the room with the smell of pine. Shavings hung in their hair. Their pants were functionally adorned with loops and slots to hold the gizmos of their calling. They had brought fragile nightery and bluebird mobiles.

"Mr. Out-of-Work don't know what a sweet deal he blew," Stella's father pressed.

I kissed my pretty wife goodbye. Her forehead tasted of salt. Already her face looked not so fat.

"See you, boys," I said to the carpenters, and made my way through them to the door.

I met three strangers and we went out. I played my round to an eighty-nine. The others finished in the high nineties and low one hundreds. These men were quick to anger; they beat themselves. I counted a half dozen times when each of them could have made a run at me, but I knew they wouldn't. Over the summer I'd learned to read my opponents by the hunch of their shoulders or the smoke from their ears, and to know when another bad shot was about to emerge to compound their anguish. I waited for these moments and threw a bet their way just before they shot. They would straighten up, glare at me, and accept. They hated themselves for being less than perfect; now they had bet on it. A vein of cash ran from their brains to my wallet.

Toward the end of the day, I waited in the pro shop drinking lemonade.

"Didn't do much today," observed Dave.

"Too hot," I agreed.

"Too hot for anything."

"Hey, Dave! I'm a father!"

Dave smiled at me. "No shit?"

"Second time around," I said. "But undeniably no shit."

"That's great." He shook my hand. "You got any cigars?"

I patted my pockets: "Sorry."

"That's a screwy tradition anyhow," Dave said. "The father'll be paying out the nose all his life. He should be the one getting the see-gars."

"Amen," I said.

"So what can I give you, Dad?"

"New set of sticks."

"Be serious, Dad."

"A free round?"

"Play on, Dad."

I found a foursome. We moved over the course through a cooling dusk. Bugs swirled in the pro shop's lights. I was pushing up the fairway on my thirty-sixth hole of the day. I planned to shower, have a beer, then get Ray Boy and go visit his mother and sister. I felt pretty grand. I was on in three. Nobody could stop me from winning money on the round. And nobody said I couldn't win a little more.

My opponents had been at work and had come to catch the late-afternoon reduced fees. They played the front nine as though still in suits and ties. They bitched about their work between shots. They expected too much. Their anger increased and I skimmed it like cream.

On the eighteenth green I turned to one of them, a guy named Herb. He could not believe he trailed me by seven strokes. He was on in three, too.

"Ten to whoever gets down from here first?" I said.

"Yeah." He jumped at the chance.

I let him go first because I liked to savor any day's last putts. They always made me a little sad. What promise did I have I'd ever play again? Away from the game I was just another guy out of work.

Herb jerked his first putt eight feet past the cup. I easily rolled mine within a foot. I tapped in to get out of his way. No problem, he went wide. I swear his eyes were glowing.

They paid me my due in the twilight. Herb had to write me a check (he kept his checkbook in his bag, as though he sus-

PERFECT LIES

pected something about himself), and I accepted it gracefully. Another guy paid me in quarters.

All this money amazed me; my livelihood was seasonal, like carpentry.

A coin fell through my fingers while I was putting my earnings in my wallet. I left it there on the green for a fellow player to mark his ball.

An
Afternoon
with the
Old Man

·

Andre Dubus

Now Sunday was over, and Paul Clement lay in bed in his room and wished for Marshall, his one wish in all the world right now (and he was a boy with many wishes; "If wishes were horses beggars would ride," his mother said when people wished). But Marshall was in Baton Rouge; he had not seen her since the Clements moved from there to Lafayette after the second grade. Maybe he would never see her again. But he would. When he was old enough to drive a car, he would go to Baton Rouge and surprise her. She would squeal and hug him. He saw her, sixteen years old, running down her front steps and sidewalk to meet him; she had breasts and used lipstick and she wore a white dress. Paul knew that now, at ten, he was good-looking—his face was his only pride, it was why Marshall had been his girl—and when he was sixteen he would be even more handsome and bigger and stronger, too, because he had been praying every night and at mass for God to make him an athlete.

He met Marshall in the second grade, a brown-eyed tomboy; she hated dresses, she got dirty when she played, and she brought two cap pistols and a dump truck to the scrap-iron pile at school. ("We sold the Japs our scrap iron, and now they're using it against us," his father said.) Once at recess she drove away with rocks fat Warren, who was kicking dust at Paul. There was a girl named Penny, with long black hair; she sat behind him in class and handed him pictures she drew (he remembered one of her father lying in bed with a broken leg, the leg suspended and weights hanging from it). Penny was prettier than Marshall, but she sometimes irritated him because she always wanted to hold his hand while they waited in line to go into school, and when there was a movie at school she held him captive, pulling him down the auditorium aisle and into a seat beside her, and during the movie her head was warm on his shoulder, her long hair tickling his throat and damp where it pressed his cheek. So he loved Marshall more. His sisters, Amy and Barbara, and his mother knew about Marshall, but his father did not. When Paul told his mother, she said, "Aren't you going to tell Daddy you have a girlfriend?"

"No."

"You should talk more with Daddy. He loves y'all very much, but he doesn't know how to talk to children."

His mother said she would keep his secret. One warm afternoon after school he was to go to a birthday party at a girl's house. His mother asked if Marshall would be there, and he said yes. She smiled and combed his hair with her fingers. "Now don't you kiss her," she said in her tease voice.

At the party, they played hide-and-seek, and he and Marshall sat on a running board in the garage; the boy who was "It" passed by without looking in. The lawn and garage were quiet now; the game had passed them, and Marshall said, "Kiss me."

"No."

"Please." She had olive skin, her brown eyes were large, and a front tooth was missing.

"If you close your eyes," he said. She did, and he kissed her lips and tasted the line of sweat above her mouth.

After hide-and-seek, Marshall and Paul got on the swing hanging from an oak. Marshall wanted him to sit; she stood facing him, her feet squeezed between his hips and the ropes, her skirt moving against his face as she pumped them higher and higher till they swung up level with the branch where the ropes were tied, and she said, "I'd like to go *all* around, over the branch." Paul hoped she wouldn't try.

When he got home his mother asked if he kissed Marshall and he said yes. She smiled and hugged him.

Here in Lafayette he did not have a girl. He did not even know a girl his age, because he didn't go to a public school now; he went to Cathedral, a boys' school taught by Christian Brothers. At the school in Baton Rouge there had been recess, but no one told you what to play and usually he had been with Penny or Marshall, mostly Marshall. But at Cathedral there was physical education for an hour every day, and it was like being in Baton Rouge when his father still played with them, throwing a tennis ball in the backyard. If Barbara or Amy threw to Paul, he sometimes caught it and sometimes did not, but when his father threw it or even if his father was just watching, his muscles stiffened and his belly fluttered and he always missed. At Cathedral it was like that, like being watched by his father.

His father had not played golf in Baton Rouge, or for the first two years in Lafayette; then a priest named Father O'Gorman started coming over and eating supper with them. In summer before supper the men drank beer on the screen porch and listened to the six o'clock news. Father O'Gorman was a bulky man who always smelled like cigars; he liked to tousle Paul's hair. He told Paul's mother not to worry that her husband was an Episcopalian and didn't go to church. "Any man who kneels down and says his prayers every night the way your husband does is a good man." That is what Father O'Gorman told her; she told it to Paul, who had not worried about his father going to hell until the day his mother said the priest said he would not.

Father O'Gorman got Paul's father interested in golf. Soon he had clubs and a bag and shoes, and was taking lessons, playing every Saturday and Sunday, and practicing two or three times a week after work and sometimes on Saturday mornings. One night at supper Paul's mother said to Father O'Gorman, "If I run off with another man it'll be your fault, Father." She was smiling the way she did when she didn't see anything funny. "My husband and I used to be together every weekend, now I'm all by myself."

Paul had not liked those weekends very much. On many Sundays they had gone to New Iberia to visit his mother's family, the Kelleys, who had once had money and lived in a big brick house with Negro women working inside and Negro men working in a yard as big as a school ground, but later all the money was gone and the house, too, and the married aunts and uncles lived like the Clements in small white houses on quiet streets. Those drives to New Iberia were quiet; once there, though, his parents had drinks, and on the way home there was talking.

"I'm home every night," his father said. "She knows that."

"Well, sure you're home, when it's too dark to see the ball, and all your cronies and Betsy Robichaux have gone home, so there's nobody to drink your old beer with." She was smiling at Paul's father, and winking at Father O'Gorman.

Paul's father practiced on a school ground near their house, and he wanted Paul to shag balls for him. The pay was fifty cents, and it was an easy job to stand daydreaming with a canvas bag in his hand and watch his father's small faceless figure, the quick pencil-small flash of swinging golf club, and then spot the ball in the air and stay clear of it till it struck the ground. Easy enough, and he liked earning the money. But he did not like to shag balls, for it wasn't simply a job like raking leaves. He was supposed to like picking up balls that his father hit; afterward, in the car, he was supposed to be interested while his father explained the different irons and woods, and told why sometimes he sliced and sometimes hooked. And he was supposed to want to caddie, to spend all Sunday afternoon following his father around the golf course. "Maybe you'll want to caddie one of these Sundays," his father said as they drove home from the school ground. "I know you can't miss the Saturday picture show, but maybe Sundays—keeps the money in the family that way." Paul sat stiffly, looking through the windshield, smelling the leather golf bag and his father's sweat. "Maybe so," he said.

Now tonight if Marshall were here with him, and if for some reason his parents and Amy and Barbara left the house and went someplace, like visiting in New Iberia, he and Marshall would go to the kitchen and he would make peanut butter and blackberry preserve sandwiches. They would take them with glasses of cold milk to the living room, where the large lazy-sounding oscillating floor fan moved the curtain at one end of its arc, then rustled the Sunday paper on the couch as it swept back. He would sit beside her on the couch, and when they finished the sandwiches he would rest his head in her lap and look up at her bright eyes and tell her about today, how at Sunday dinner his father had said, "Want to come out today?" and he had chewed a large bite of chocolate cake, trying to think of a reason not to, and then swallowed and said, "Sure."

After dinner, his father got an extra pack of Luckies from the bedroom, and then it was time to go. His mother walked out on the screen porch with them; the wisteria climbing the screen was blooming lavender. "Keep an eye on him in this heat," she said to his father.

"I will."

She kissed them. As they walked to the car, she called, "Look at my two handsome men. Paul, be a good influence on your father, bring him home early."

In the car, they did not talk for six blocks or so. Then his father told him he ought to have a cap to keep the sun off his head, and Paul said he'd be O.K.

"That mama of yours, if I bring you home with a headache she'll say the golf course is the only place the sun shines."

Paul smiled. The rest of the way to the golf course they did not talk. Walking to the clubhouse, Paul trailed a step or two behind his father. Caddies stood near the sidewalk—tall boys with dirty bare feet or ragged sneakers and hard brown biceps. Several of them were smoking. ("It stunts the growth," his mother said.) They were the kind of boys Paul always yielded the sidewalk to when he walked to the cowboy show and serial in town on Saturdays. Paul looked out at the golf course, shielding his eyes with one hand, and studied the distant greens and fairways as he and his father passed the boys and their smell of cigarette smoke and sweat and sweet hair oil.

"Mr. Clement, you need a caddie?"

"No thanks, Tujack. I got my boy."

From under his shielding hand, Paul stared over the flat fairway at a tiny red flag, hanging limply over the heat shimmer. As he followed his father into the clubhouse, he felt their eyes on him; then, turning a corner around the showcase of clubs, he was out of their vision, and he followed his father's broad shoulders and brown hairy arms into the locker room. His father sat on a bench and put on his golf shoes.

"That Tujack's going to be a hell of a golfer."

"He plays?"

"They all play, these caddies."

Outside, in the hot dust behind the clubhouse, his father

strapped the golf bag onto a cart, and Paul pulled it behind him to the first tee. Tujack was there, a tall wiry boy of about sixteen, a golf bag slung over his shoulder. Paul shook hands with Mr. Blanchet, Mr. Voorhies, Mr. Peck. Each of them, as he shook hands, looked Paul up and down, as though to judge what sort of boy their friend had. Paul gave his father the driver and then pulled the cart away from the tee, stopping short of the three caddies, who stood under a sycamore. He was the only one using a cart, and he wished his father hadn't done that. I can carry it, he wanted to say.

The first hole had a long dogleg going to the left around a field of short brown weeds. His father shot first, driving two thirds of the way down the first leg; he came over and gave Paul the driver and stood between him and the caddies, closing the distance. "You'll be on in two, Mr. Clement," Tujack said.

"You could, Tujack. Not me."

They were quiet while the others shot, and then Paul walked beside his father, pulling the cart behind him. It seemed badly balanced, and he watched the ground ahead of him for those small rises that might tip the cart over on its side with a shamefaced clanking of clubs. After the first nine, they stopped at the clubhouse for a drink, and his father asked him how he was holding up. "Fine," Paul said. He was. He didn't tire on the second nine, either. It was a hot afternoon, but he liked to sweat, and there was not much need for talking. ("Good shot." "Well, let's see what I can do with the brassie.") Usually, between shots, he walked a little to the rear, and his father talked to one of the men.

When they finished playing, his father gave him a dollar and a quarter and told him he was a good caddie, then asked if he was tired or too hot and what did he want to drink, and took him into the clubhouse and up to the counter. "Give this boy a Grapette and some cheese crackers," his father said, his hand coming down on Paul's shoulder, staying there.

"That your boy?" the man behind the counter said.

2 2 8

"That's him," the hand on Paul's shoulder squeezing now, rocking him back and forth. Paul lowered his eyes and smiled and blushed, just as he did each time his father said, "I'd like you to meet my boy," his father smiling, mussing his hair, Paul shaking the large extended hand, squeezing it ("Always squeeze," his mother told him. "Don't give someone a dead fish"). "He's got a good grip," one man had said, and for a moment Paul had been proud.

Now his father was drinking beer with his friends—what Paul's mother called the nineteenth hole. Paul liked watching him have fun, pouring the good summer-smelling beer in his glass, laughing, talking about the game they just played and other games they had played. They talked about baseball, too; a team called the Dodgers was going to have a colored boy playing this year. Betsy Robichaux and another woman came to their table, and the four men and Paul stood up; Mr. Peck got two chairs from the next table. Paul squeezed the women's hands, too, but not quite as hard.

"He's got his daddy's looks," Betsy Robichaux said.

His father grinned and his blue eyes twinkled. She was not really pretty but she was nice-looking, Paul thought. She sat opposite him with her back to the window that ran the length of the clubhouse, so he watched her, caught himself staring at her now and then, but most of the time he remembered to pretend he was looking past her at the eighteenth green, where long-shadowed men leaned on putters. She was deeply tanned and slender. Her voice was husky, she laughed a lot, she said "hell" and "damn," and she was always smoking a Pall Mall, gesturing with it in her ringless left hand. Paul knew she was not a lady like his mother, but he liked watching women smoke, for a cigarette made them somehow different, like women in movies instead of mothers. She sat there talking golf with the men, and Paul knew his father liked talking golf with her better than with his mother, who only pretended she was interested (Paul could tell by her voice). But thinking about his mother made him feel guilty, as though he were betraying his father, as though he were his mother's spy, recording every time his father said, "Betsy." He decided to count the beers his father drank, so if his mother said something Paul could defend him.

His father drank five beers (Paul had two Grapettes and two packages of cheese crackers with peanut butter), and then it was dusk and they drove home, his father talking all the way in his drinking voice, relaxed, its tone without edges now, rounded by some quality that was almost tenderness, almost affection. He talked golf. Sometimes, when he paused, Paul said yes. As they approached the corner of their street, his father reached over and lightly slapped Paul's leg, then gave it a squeeze.

"Well," he said. "It's not so bad to spend an afternoon with the old man, is it?"

"Nope," Paul said, and knew at once how that sounded, how his father must have heard only their failure in that one little word, because how could his father possibly know, ever forever know, that even that one word had released so much that tears came to his eyes, and it was as if his soul wanted to talk and hug his father but his body could not, and all he could do was in silence love his father as though he were a memory, as the afternoon already was a memory.

His mother met them on the screen porch. "Did my two men have fun together?"

"Sure we did. He's a good caddie."

"Did you have fun?" she asked Paul.

He took a quick deep breath, closed his mouth tightly, pressed a finger under his nose, and pretended to hold back a sneeze as he walked past her.

Now in his bed he grew sleepy to the sound of the fan. He wondered if they would have a new car when he was a big boy. He saw the car as a blue one, and it smelled new inside. Now

Marshall came out in her white dress and kissed him in the evening sun right there on her front steps; she had the line of sweat over her lips and smelled of perfume. Holding hands, they walked to the car. Her head came to about his shoulder; just before he opened the car door, she put her hand on his bicep and squeezed it. Her face was lovely and sad for him. "I'm glad you're taking me," she said.

In the car, she slid close to him. Her arms were dark against the lap of her dress. He offered his pack of Luckies, and they lit them from the dashboard lighter. They drove out of town, then on a long road through woods. The road started climbing and they came out above the woods at trimmed bright grass and spreading live oaks, and in their shade old tombstones and crosses. They left the car and very quietly, holding hands, they walked in the oak shade to his father's grave. He made the sign of the cross, bowed his head, and prayed for his father's soul. When Marshall saw the tears in his eyes, she put her arm around his waist and hugged him tightly while he prayed.

PUTTING

&

GARDENING

·

WILLIAM F. VAN WERT

"Looks like rain," my father says with a mixed stare of genteel benevolence and childish malice. As with most things at his age, rain is a mixed blessing: good for the garden, bad for golf.

My father has been retired for twelve years, but he still eats his businessman's breakfast of poached egg and grapefruit at 7 A.M., then works on the house and the yard, then "clocks out" at two to play golf. He makes lists for himself the night before of things to do, then crosses them off with the gold Cross pen his employees gave him when he closed the appliance store. He changes lightbulbs, he fixes the toilet that won't flush, he makes wooden shelves for the shanty or devises yet another clothesline for my mother. His clotheslines have been looking more like Calder mobiles in recent years, but he takes no pride in them nor in any "indoors" work. For he is still a farmer in his heart.

He is a farmer who hasn't farmed since he was sixteen. His father died of a heart attack when my father was only thirteen and the last of six children left on the farm. My grandmother kept him on the brand-new Oliver my grandfather bought but never got to use. She watched him going up and down the rows of wheat and corn and beans until sunfall when they would eat together their simple Dutch supper of half meat and double starch. He would eat only half of his roast beef, saving the rest for his sandwich the next day at school. But he would eat double helpings of corn and mashed potatoes, something he still does. And he would drink a cold beer, before and after supper, falling asleep in his father's rocking chair promptly after the latter beer. And my grandmother would yell at him in Dutch to wake up and do his lessons and go to bed. She insisted on the lessons even then, knowing that she would sell the farm as soon as he graduated from high school. Perhaps she also knew that he would make his way from Bay City to Midland, selling tomatoes to passing cars.

"Let me check the garden and then we'll clock out fast, okay?" he says with a wink. He doesn't have to ask. I know it's my cue to get the golf bags from the shanty and put them in the trunk of the car.

"Make sure the tees aren't broken and pack a few practice balls for four and seven," he adds. Four and seven are the par-three holes at the Clare golf course, and they have water traps in front of them. You have to use a five iron or a three wood, you have to elevate your tee a little and you have to get the ball up in the air, pop-up fashion, or you go in the woods on the right, into another fairway on the left or into water front and back. I prefer the water, even though it costs my father a ball.

every time. I like to see the water jump like gunshot in the afternoon sun and hear the "plop" like frog-talk around the green.

My father still has a drink before and after supper, but now it's a manhattan before and a bourbon-and-soda after. And he promptly falls asleep, only now it's a black felt recliner instead of the old wooden rocker. And sometimes my mother blames it on the golf . . . and sometimes on the drinks.

"Jim . . . ?" my mother says, as though she were taking his pulse.

"Let him sleep, Mom," I coax, "he's had a long day."

I know I'm not exaggerating, for my feet are tired too after eighteen holes, front and back, plus four more, a practice four for me to straighten out my drives and for him to practice his putting. I suppress a yawn as I say this, knowing that I would never go to sleep at seven in the evening. My mother and all seven of her children were born night owls. My father is still a farmer. He can't keep his eyes open after ten o'clock.

"But he promised to make a bonfire tonight."

It's true. He likes to light up the sky on these summer evenings. He does it for his children and their children, the marshmallows half eaten, the cigarettes smoked to keep the mosquitoes away and then thrown into the fire, the last looks at the lake and its flat blue ripple like a worried forehead. And my father relaxes as he eases the logs into the pit and watches the flames dance up at him. His worried forehead cannot keep its frown, the money ledger in his mind, his Dutch farmer's respect for habit, the forty years he kept the books. His mouth goes slack with the breeze through the birches behind him. He looks off and surveys the lake with the look of a man about to drown. He eases the spring on his sadness, the firm jaws of silence and too tight control of a lifetime. And sometimes he laughs at nothing or tells a joke that's not funny or curses or swings an imaginary number one wood into the lake. But mostly he surveys the land, sometimes as an alien might. He doesn't swim or boat or sit on the dock. Sometimes he likes to fish at night when one of his sons will go along. Sometimes he makes one go along . . . to have a chat. But these are not flatlands of ploughed fertility, this is not God's soil for growing, and these white birches will never put food on the table.

"Nice night," he says softly, as much to himself as to me. We both have hands in pockets, and I realize that my gaze goes where his does, my body stretches when his does, involuntarily. Perhaps this is what is meant by being my father's son.

"Jim . . . ?" my mother says again, this time more insistently.

My father turns slightly in the recliner, still snoring and mumbling softly in his sleep.

"Damn . . ." he whispers, "I could have parred that baby."

"I'll par you one, you ole bloater," my mother says, mock-sternly.

It's not the sleep she minds. It's the snoring, the look of lax pleasure around the corners of his mouth, the jaws going gentle, his usual look of kind but unswerving purpose going to putty, the deep lifelines puffing out again, as though his face were up for grabs, an invitation to sculpt. My mother is tired at this time of night. It's too early to play cards and too soon after dishes to do much else but sit. The evening news is just finishing on TV. My mother likes the game shows in the morning, the soapers in the afternoon and the "family" shows at night, especially "Little House on the Prairie," "The Waltons" and "Eight Is Enough." This is the only time she doesn't watch TV, because she doesn't like the news. My father puts the news on at six and eleven. He wants to catch the weather, he wants to hear the sports and know what the next day will be like for the garden and the golf. But he often misses the weather on the six o'clock news, because he's asleep, and then he has to stay up for the eleven. If he gets the weather at six, he can go to bed at ten.

My mother has known these habits for forty-some years, and

still she objects every night. Yet even her objections are comfortable now, more by rote than by passion, familiar and perfected, a little like the way an Olivier recites his Shakespeare, having recited it a thousand times already.

"Well? What is it, dear?" my father asks finally, some ten minutes after my mother has stopped prodding and begun her sewing in the other room. During the day my parents both act as though I were their honored guest, someone to laugh with and cater to and look lovingly upon, one of their flesh grown up. But at night they revert, they can't help themselves; they act, I'm sure, the way they act when they are alone with no more children left in the nest.

And when there were no more children left, almost seven years ago now, my father did as so many men from Michigan have done: he bought a winter home in Florida. He was like a little peacock for the first few years. It was as though he had bought the entire state of Florida. He began to wear sunglasses and white belts and short-sleeved flower shirts with the top buttons undone, so that his chest hair peeked out like the tuft of a woman from an X-rated movie. He even grew a moustache for a time and looked Jewish and Italian at the same time. He announced that he would never shovel snow again.

"I never realized you hated Michigan winters so much," I told him. "Have you always felt this way?"

He just smiled and that was his answer. I never knew what he had felt all those years of supposed "White Christmas" and "Winter Wonderland." But he really retired with grace and for good when he bought up Florida. That's when he began to play golf and grow his gardens. The fruit trees brought forth at least twice a year in southern Florida. It reminded me of having read somewhere that women in and around the Amazon menstruate twice and sometimes three times a month, dying of "old age" at thirty. I wonder at that kind of climate where things grow in double time, while the people, those suede faces that look like immigrants or outpatients from the geriatric ward, the endless Midwestern Mayflower, those people come to retard the harvest of their own spoiled skin.

And my father thrived in that climate. He ate the grapefruit off his trees for breakfast, put on his gloves and went out to mow the lawn, spray the trees, spread mulch and prune the shrubs. He would lay the sticks around his tomatoes that looked so big and gaudy-bulbous, like the insides of watermelons. And he would fondle his limes, the good green smell of photosynthesis all about them, overbig and awkward on the branch, the size of avocados. He spent hours in his yard, chatting with the neighbors who were in their yards, all retired and all watering the lawn.

And my mother would wince at noon and take off her blouse, close the curtains and turn on the air conditioner. She would iron clothes and watch the afternoon soaps and never peek outside. She missed her children, she missed her sisters and brothers, she missed the Michigan friends who shared cups of coffee with her in the mornings. She adjusted, after a fashion. She baked brownies for the sick, and there were always the sick in their new trailer park. She joined a poker club and went to that every Tuesday night. She started quilting and putting the several hundred photographs of all of us as children into albums. She longed for summer and the cottage in Michigan. She did a lot of waiting, especially at times when her children couldn't get away from their jobs and come down for a visit. She stopped writing letters about this time. She said we were too old now and she was too lazy. She started taking naps in the afternoon, and she began to call us long-distance once or twice a week. And at the same time that she stopped going to church, she began to say "pray to God" in the middle of many of her sentences.

"I don't know," she would giggle, the prerequisite self-denial every time she was about to say something serious, "but I pray to God he don't die before I do. I mean, he loves it down here. He tends his trees and gets down on his knees and plays in dirt for hours. He makes his little visits to the neighbors, brings their mail to them, cuts their lawn for them. If it's finished in our yard, he looks for someone else's yard. And you should see the living dolls down here. Looks like someone erased their faces years ago, but they're still ready, and do they ever love your father. Pray to God I don't ever look like that, live long enough to look like that."

"And what about you, Mom?"

"Oh, I'm fine. It's okay. You know me, I like to complain a lot."

"Tell the truth. What about you?"

"I guess it would be okay, honest, if it weren't so stinking hot down here. I itch all the time. I go to scratch a mosquito and it's only heat. I hit myself all the time for nothing."

We both laugh and hang up. That's the way the calls have gone for seven years.

Then she got cancer.

My father called in January, the week after New Year's. Classes had just begun, I was teaching again. I was in the middle of a writing binge.

"Your mother went in for a test last week . . ."

I waited, even though I already knew the rest.

". . . and, well, they found something."

He choked up. He could barely finish his sentence.

"She didn't want to tell any of you, but I said to her, 'We have to tell the kids.' "

They found something. My poor father couldn't even name the thing, couldn't say that word, couldn't bear that thought. It was his way, this honesty so indirect that the listener had to fill in the blanks. When he told me the facts of life, he called it "intercourse" and "copulation." I was ten years old. I didn't understand a thing he said. I had heard about "screw" and "lay" and "go down" and "all the way," but I had never heard of copulation. He couldn't name the thing.

Something in his voice denied emotion while calling S.O.S.

in baby screams. I couldn't sleep, I couldn't think. I took the next plane to Florida and met the man without his mask. My mother was to be operated on the next day. He had just come back from twelve hours at the hospital.

He looked fit and trim in his blue panama suit. He looked ready for Mass, but his eyes were bloodshot and the drink in his hand showed only ice, for the third time in thirty minutes.

"How are you, Dad?"

He tried to say "Fine," he tried to hug me and play host and make me a drink, but he couldn't. He just collapsed in my arms, big bear-man of Dutch silence, his body too shrieked to control and his sad need to control, to fall back into fatherly silence, to hold it all in, the patterns I learned so well from him. I held his body in my arms, his chest expanse so big I could barely lock my fingers around his back. I held him and whispered to his cheek that he could let down now, and he never said a word about that, not then and not after. But he broke down and sobbed and our bodies, standing near the bourbon bottle, our bodies rocked back and forth, like slow dancers in the smoke of public places. How they look as though they've melted into each other, or maybe just holding each other up, still swaying to the music, even with the band on break.

And when he broke from my hug, he made himself another drink and cursed and cried for another hour. Trying to be sensible, philosophical, jovial, he kept begging that it be him instead of her. My sister, who had just arrived that afternoon, couldn't stand to see him that way. She kept telling him he had to be strong, and his eyes flashed dark sparks at her, but his head bobbed up and down in mute assent. He shut it up and said no more.

He told me in the car the next day that it did no good to pour forth. It made him weak and tired, so much so that he couldn't "hold his cheer" when he was with my mother. And so he had resolved to shelve the emotions and make the rest of her time some kind of circus of smiles and Crackerjacks, worry-free.

He let me sit alone with my mother in her hospital bed. We didn't look at each other much. We just held hands and talked about the weather in Philadelphia and, the few times our eyes met, we tried to laugh but it came out tears. She looked so old and shorn like a bald crow, hunched up like my grandmother and scared and proud, still too proud to complain for herself. I gave back the letter she had written me two years earlier, the one marked "personal" that scolded me for loss of faith, the one that reminded me that I was a "cradle Catholic." Her eyes filled up with wet thanks, but her throat caught, the bandaged throat where they took the lump, it squeaked, and it looked like she wanted to spit on me.

My father paced the floor of the hospital and he sat like a mannequin in the recliner at home. He felt guilty that he couldn't take it away from her and give it to himself. He felt guilty about not showing us a good time, but he felt guilty about going out.

"Let's go hit some golf balls," I urged.

He smiled and nodded no.

"Dad, let's go hit the balls," I commanded.

"I can't do that. What would anyone think, seeing me play golf while she's like that?"

"To hell with what they think. You need to get it out. You need to kill some balls."

He just got up and walked out the door and waited for me in the car. It was the only time that he didn't preach to me on the golf course. No lessons about keeping my left foot on a line with the tee, taking my practice swing, keeping my left arm stiff and not going any further than my shoulder with the arc. He dribbled his first few drives. He was still trying to play good golf.

"Dad, we aren't here to break forty today. I want you to wind up and cream that sucker. I want you to put all your anger into it and rip the cover off the damn ball. Pretend it's the lump they took out."

He wasn't used to such a reckless swing. He wound up high and far behind his neck like some Tarzan reaching overhead for a vine. The silver stick held for a moment behind his neck, looking like a brace for polio. And then he swung through, wild and Babe Ruth striking out. He missed it all and found himself on the seat of his pants. He just put his head into his hands, and I thought I ought to crouch and cradle him. But he came up laughing like a mystic, pray to God, cocked to the eyeballs with root anger and fear. And we just banged away all day, like terrorists. Some holes we didn't even bother to putt out. We just picked up our battered balls and went around the green to the next fairway to swing as hard as we could one more time. We lost about twenty balls between us that afternoon in water and woods and bunkers of quicksand. The balls were flopping like pigeon droppings in the air and skittering helter-skelter through the high grass. And then we went home and got sudden-drunk, so drunk we laughed through the evening news of hurricanes and hijackings, record interest rates and police brutality. After cancer, it was all a joke, a belly-buckle bottle-sucking mother lode of gold humor. It was good to hear that other people were dying.

I went to Florida to hold it in, like my father, to hold it all together and heal them both. To give back what they had given, wasn't that what a son was supposed to do? To make them laugh. Scold them. Take care of the essentials, like meals and laundry and groceries. I went down there to touch my mother, the untouchable one now, and to talk with my father, the silent master of mind control. But instead I ended up hugging my father and being with him in his silence. I ended up talking a lot with my mother and asking her to ask for herself.

"What's the lesson in all of this, Mom? What does it mean for you?"

"Hell if I know," she said casually, eyes off on the floor somewhere, biting her lip.

She had what was called the early superivenicaval syndrome, and what it meant was the choking off of blood, the puffed cheeks and collapsed right lung and vessels on her neck like bean sprouts. Before I left she had begun her cobalt of five thousand rads, a little Hiroshima at a time, in the squat aluminum hovel with the sign on the door: WARNING: DO NOT PLAY ON ROOF.

"Looks like rain," my father would say, driving to the treatments. It rained every afternoon in Fort Myers, and the rain whipped up the royal palms that usually looked like sculptures of cement, it whipped them up and made them look like helicopter blades, and then it all dried up just as predictably as the fast food huts and the endless excursions to Winn-Dixie for the "sales." Rain was not the enemy here. It came and went every day, and my father gardened before it and golfed after it. And in between, during the downpour, we would go for the treatments, the traffic bumper to bumper, slow-mo and excreting exhaust so thick the houses shimmered in the sun and the pampas grass looked like a cheap cowboy movie.

"Hot," my mother complained. "Hot as Dutch love."

We watched the other patients come in and go out, some bandaged and some burned, all of them making weak gestures of good luck to each other, the modern-day lepers. My mother got nauseous looking at them, the treatment more hideous than the disease, all those people with red-beet noses, wigs on and wobbly, their lips looking green and withered like the pulp of the lime.

I tried but I could not go gentle into that good night. I had the most pornographic dreams every night, as though the savage sexual mutilation of babies, the sweet surrender of my brother's wife, the hind-end humping with any and every woman I have ever known were the antidote, the only cure for cancer and this helpless hopeless feeling of standing still and watching my mother turn into a prune. It reminded me of the whores I used to see in Thailand, their imperious eyes of yellow peril and their sweet, noxious breath between pale-pink teeth from the betelnut juice, asking me the passerby:

"Hey, honey, you want fucking or sucking?"

And it was true now. I thought of every last one of them in my dreams, and it was true. That was all I wanted out of life.

We all went to Florida to be with my mother. Some brought their children, and there was no way to predict behavior, before or after. Two of my brothers went down and spent their days on the beach, unable to cope, to look at her without breaking down. My sister began to act like my mother, look like her, scolding my father for drinking and falling asleep and playing golf.

Where was the lesson in all of this?

I went down there again in March during our spring break. My mother had just finished the cobalt treatments and was about to begin chemotherapy, biting her nails and looking a little unkept, derelict, taking bird-bites of despair for breakfast and lunch, a piece of old toast and twenty cups of black coffee. The grapefruit on my father's trees were in their second bloom, fresh and plump and pink inside, somehow so sexual that this pink pulp be the first thing the tongue should touch in the morning. By contrast, my father's golf balls looked a little smaller, a little bruised from bad contact and off-center chipping.

My mother was still alive, even though the doctors said she might not last beyond April. Carcinoma and metastasis. Even the doctors couldn't name the thing, and my father felt so guilty because he couldn't understand them. He kept dropping by their office, kept calling on the phone, and he couldn't form a picture in his mind for the words they told him.

My mother stayed alive, because my little sister was still anything but little, unmarried and over two hundred fifty pounds. She stayed alive because the summer was coming, and that meant the cottage in Michigan. My father tried to suggest that maybe they should stay in Florida, not risk a long drive, stay with the doctors they already knew. My mother wouldn't hear a word of it. She wanted the cottage now more than she had ever wanted any of her seven children.

"I'm still alive, because you kids keep praying, that's what. I don't see how I can die with all that interference," she smiled.

And when I left, she winked at me, the silent sign that this would not be the last time. She still had not come to grips with the cancer. She just offered it up to God, merits for one of her children every time she threw up or went dizzy or got depressed and put her head under the pillow. My parents had buried my Aunt BaBa of cancer two years before. My mother had sworn then that she would never want to die of cancer. My father took out two cancer insurance policies.

They told me about the difficult visits with BaBa in the hospital, how she begged them to take her up to the cottage to die, how they washed their hands after every visit, because they still thought cancer could be caught like a common cold. They talked about wishing friends well who got cancer and about avoiding those people. Now my mother could separate her friends into distinct categories: the ones who called but didn't name the thing; the ones who sent cards with spiritual quotes or Rod McKuen poems; the ones who never got in touch with her and the very few who came in person right away and kissed her on the forehead.

"Ain't life cruel?" she said, with the tone of a blackjack dealer, as though you had to expect the unexpected.

My father kept stroking his chin and wondering if he had a lump of his own.

My father taught me how to gather the topmost grapefruit first, the ones that get the most sun. He taught me the time of the day when one could spray; how to tell the quality of an orange by the firmness and shadow at the umbilicus, the place where it was attached to the tree; how to crate tomatoes for best weight and least bruising, the smaller, unripe tomatoes on the bottom and the big red ripe ones on top, separated one from another by little cardboard cutouts.

He wiped the dew line of sweat from his bald head and smiled.

"Sometimes I wonder why I ever did anything else."

"Because you had seven kids . . ."

"Perhaps. But if you work the ground, I mean, if you really work it every day, my mother used to say you'd never get dizzy. You'd always know where you were."

"Is that why you do it?"

"Huh? Oh, not really."

"Why, then?"

"I don't know if there are words for that sort of thing."

"Come on, Dad. Why?"

"Well, it teaches me the love of the body. Especially at my age."

I didn't say anything.

"I told you there weren't any words."

And he went back to digging.

My mother's cancer had devoured everything: the worry, the attention, the prayers. My father was a forgotten man. Nobody asked how he was. He stopped getting on the phone when anyone called.

And when I left, she winked at me, her silent promise that this would not be the last time. And my father waited until the last minute, hugged me quickly, the usual fast feeling between grown father and son. But then he kissed me. He did it so quickly that I had to wonder on the plane going back if it had really happened. I cannot remember a single other time that my father has kissed me. I cried, and maybe the crying was somehow assurance that, yes, it actually happened.

"Looks like rain," my father says with his mixed stare of the green thumb and the imp. "We'll go anyway, huh?"

I nod and go to pack up the golf bags in the trunk of his car.

And then I walk down to the dock, while he tends his garden. I stare at the lake and wonder why it is that I can never get enough of this clean air and quiet lake. It's more than nostalgia, the remembrance of a good childhood, the carefree swims with my brothers and sisters, the only time my father ever got out his movie camera, some twenty years of cryptic film, from kindergarten to college, of kids that looked like any kids but got to look like him, doing belly-smackers off the end of the dock.

I take a mental snapshot this time, something to develop and return to the next time winter in Philadelphia oppresses me. I like this lake in the morning and at night, lit up or in shadow. I step on the dock and stare for miles, wondering as I walk across the boards why it is that people don't live in the place that speaks to their heart, that feeds their passion. There is no money to feel in my pockets, and of course I know the answer. But maybe the cottage offers me the chance to ask the really foolish questions. I wear my father's sweatshirts and baseball hats, I stop shaving and waste time, I actually take time to stare again. First foot on the dock and I become a character out of Dr. Seuss, a Zanzibar Buck Buck McFate fishing for Doubt-Trout in the cool pool of Nool. I compete with everyone and everything in the city, but here I talk back to crickets and wonder what else these big Dutch hands of mine were made for, besides driving a car and moving a typewriter.

I turn and look at my father, who is throwing up his hands at someone higher than these thunderclouds overhead. My father is two men, the man in Florida who can make anything grow, who can eat what he grows. Because his garden is always green down there, his golfing is a luxury, something he does as much for the companionship with other men from the park as for his own passion, something he does deliberately, with flair and style. Here in Michigan, there is only this lake and the beach sand that is as barren as it is beautiful. He has imported the grass, which goes bald each summer, the sand swallowing up the little blades of green. He plants no fruit or vegetables in

Michigan. Here it's flowers, flowers whose seeds he has bought in a store. He gives them dirt, he waters them and watches over them, even though he doesn't even know their names. The pine trees grow on either side of his flower boxes, the birches swing freely behind them, but the boxes are coffins. His flowers die as quickly as he can plant them.

"Damn," I hear him mutter, unaware that I'm that close, "woman's work . . ."

And he turns to me with that look I've noticed recently, the twisted look of the Feeble in his eyes, the look of drunk driving, delirium tremens. My stomach sinks to see that look of no-care in his eyes. The cancer policies have their limits. My mother is neither dead nor cured, and my father has taken to calculating the cost of the future. I look away at the flowers and understand his despair and their lesson: they bloom and die outside of anyone's control or calculations. Like children. The lesson here is something other than the love of the body, something beyond bad dirt and fallen petals, shriveled stems and bees that have to look elsewhere to drop their pollen. You can't eat the flowers.

So the golf is his business and passion. He goes alone or he goes with the neighbor, but he goes for the golf, not the camaraderie. I go for something else.

Not one of his five sons wanted his appliance business and neither of his two daughters wanted to learn how to type and be a secretary. Now nobody wants to golf with him. But I have consented, at first as a way to be with just my father, this man I have loved all my life and never known. My father goes through a complete personality change on the links. His old shoulders straighten up and he walks with a bounce again. He laughs and jokes, winking and whistling at the women golfers, exchanging quick repartees with the men, these other retirees with the hard knocks of their working days written all over their faces, including the eighty-five-year-old crustacean with the craggy cheeks and the twinkle in his eyes, who comes up to tell a joke as stale as the seat of his baggy pants.

"Hey, Jim, you hear the one about the geezer who passed gas in this public place? His friend says, 'Hey, Ed, not with a lady present,' and Ed, he says, 'I didn't know we was taking turns.'"

My father laughs, because respect is required on the golf course. It's a private world of old fools acting young again, and my father admires them because they play eight hours a day. I go along, because it's my only chance to see the boy in my father, and he's happy I've come with him to share his passion. He doesn't care if I lose the balls or if we have to wave the hard hitters through while we look for my errant drives. And when I really peg one, he watches it go its three hundred yards and stands transfixed, as though before a miracle.

"Gee, if I only had your power. You don't have to whack it hard, see? It just goes and goes."

I ask him what would have happened if he had discovered golf before he was sixty-two. He shrugs his shoulders in such a way that I know he's asked himself this same question a thousand times.

"I might have spent everything we had," he says with a mock-horrified look on his face.

"Would that have been so terrible?"

"I couldn't have bought in Florida," he says, and this time he's serious.

On my first drive I get to within a hundred yards of the green. The closer I get to the green, the worse I get. I takes me seven more shots to put the ball in the cup. My father, whose drives rarely go more than a hundred and fifty yards, has put it in with four shots. He comes close to par on every hole, usually missing with his bad putting.

"It's the chip shots and the putts that separate the men from the boys," he says from someone else's sermon. "Who takes the time to learn how to putt?"

He has taken to hacking the weeds around the cottage with his nine iron and putter, so that these clubs are as much an extension of his hand as the watch around his wrist. So far, it hasn't helped.

He teaches me the etiquette of golf, all the polite positions of where to stand while someone else swings, what happens if your ball hits someone else's ball, when to take a mulligan and when not, how you can't touch the sand on your practice swing in the sand traps. And we talk golf from the tee to the green. Only on the green and only after we've both put our balls in the cup do we talk about our personal lives. The time it takes to walk from the green to the tee-off mound for the next hole is the allotted time for any real talking.

I have come this time just to be there and be healed as much as to heal. In the nine months from January to August, my marriage has gone bankrupt. One brother and one sister have already left their marriages in these nine months. And, because my parents never talk about the cancer, they have taken on the burden of these marriages as their concern, their worry, their sorrow.

On the green for number three, after my father has put his putt in for par, he asks me:

"Are you compatible?"

"What do you mean?"

"You know. Are you sexually compatible?"

"I don't know how to answer that. I'm turned on all the time. She's turned on almost none of the time."

"But is it something that can be helped? In time? Or therapy?"

"I don't know, Dad. We used to think we saw it the same way."

"Do you need money?"

"Yes. But not from you, thanks."

By then we've reached the mound for teeing off on number

four and have to wait another four hundred fifty yards before we can talk about anything but golf again.

Something has shown up in my mother's blood test for the week. The new oncologist is afraid that it has spread to her liver.

"As long as it's not my brain," she jokes, for she is most afraid of someone irradiating her brain, of becoming a vegetable. But she's also worried about her liver, her lungs and all those organs she can't see and can only feel by the poison of the cytoxin in her chemotherapy.

"Can we say a rosary together?" I ask. It's something we haven't done as a family for at least twenty-five years. Mary insists that she has to do the dishes and Jo goes to the toilet, so the "family" consists of me and my parents. I can scarcely remember the sorrowful mysteries—the scourging at the pillar, the crowning of thorns, the carrying of the cross, the crucifixion—all those necessary steps toward the resurrection of the body. My father and I take turns saying the "Hail Mary" and my mother says the "Holy Mary."

I ask my mother to stop saying novenas for my marriage and to start praying for herself. I suggest that the "lesson" to her cancer can only come when she feels worthy enough to pray for herself.

"I'll think about it," she says.

I massage my father's feet as I have done every night of my visit. The knotted feet with corns and calluses and bulging veins, gnarled as a hunchback from so many years of steel arch supports, have actually straightened out and lost some of their "crystals," their pus and their stink. And because we have just said the rosary, I begin to feel a little like Christ doing Peter's feet. There are so many questions I want to ask this man, so many things he could tell me, but talk never comes easily. So I massage his feet and let that be enough.

When he has gone to bed, my mother and I talk. With her the talk comes freely, the jokes and sidelong glances as codified as traffic signs. We know when to start and stop. And I rub her aching shoulders, she who resists any kind of touching. I realize that I can give to them separately, but I am confused by them as a couple. I revert to stupor, to being their son, to letting them do for me. And I realize why I am a writer: verbose, like my mother, but on paper, preserving the silence of my father.

The next day we go to the hospital and she is proclaimed an N.E.D. (non-evaluative disease): clean scans, remission time. There's no overt joy or celebration that night at supper, only this sense of pause in the eye of the storm.

"The lesson," my mother confides that night when we're alone, "is that I have been too proud. I had seven children, they were all whole and healthy, and I bragged them up too much. God is punishing me for that."

It's not the answer I expected after nine months of living with this auto-cannibalism. But it was surely the only way that my mother could rationalize the Book of Job all around her, the only way she could hold the cancer and the broken marriages in the same perspective. One thing about prayer: you always get what you ask for and it never looks like you thought it would.

The next day, my last day at the cottage, my father pleads sheepishly to clock out early and take me golfing.

"Again?" my mother says, irate.

"Honey, what have you got in mind?"

"Not a thing, Jim. Go on, both of you."

We go with her cursed blessing. In the car, his hands so hard around the steering wheel that his knuckles look like polished piano keys, my father starts to sob, the Feeble dancing in his eyes, and he begs for himself.

"It's the only time I don't have my mind on it. I thought she understood that."

I don't say anything. I have no idea of the bargains and compromises they have struck to stick together for forty-two years. But I shudder, involuntarily, for the bare fog of what this body has been through in its lifetime passes over me, this body born on the farm before there was any pollution, this body now strapped in a Buick LeSabre on cruise control, and only the golf course is left to remind one of what the "natural" world must have been like.

"The bitch," he whispers.

I had to hear that whisper to know she was safe with him, to know that he still loved her after all these years.

The greens are separate from everything else on a golf course. They are alone their named color, green and carpet-soft. And my father has a special reverence for putting on these greens. I have watched him walk more softly when he approaches the greens. I have seen him tiptoe around a ball and measure the distance between him and the hole. I still swing too hard on my putts, and today, on this, the ninth hole, I have hit grass before ball, so that the ball skipped right over the cup like a stone thrown sideways across the surface of the lake: bump, bump and bump, without ever dropping. My father flicks the ball with his putter, so that it has topspin, and the ball backs its way into the hole. His ball says "caution" and mine "abandon," and I wonder if we wouldn't be better off, this beloved stranger and I, at our ages, to trade styles for the sake of those who live with us. What do they say? Rage is to age what truth is to youth?

I'm thinking these things when I realize that my father is not walking with me to the car. I turn to see him on hands and knees, lovingly replacing my divot on the magic carpet, this essence of green, the only garden that is left for him.

SUNDAY
UNDER PAR

·

WALKER PERCY

The first sign that something had gone wrong manifested itself while he was playing golf.

Or rather it was the first time he admitted to himself
that something might be wrong.

For some time he had been feeling depressed without knowing why. In fact, he didn't even realize he was depressed.
Rather was it the world and life around him that seemed to
grow more senseless and farcical with each passing day.

Then two odd incidents occurred on the golf course.

Once he fell down in a bunker. There was no discernible
reason for his falling. One moment he was standing in the

bunker with his sand iron appraising the lie of his ball. The next he was lying flat on the ground. Lying there, cheek pressed against the earth, he noticed that things looked different from this unaccustomed position. A strange bird flew past. A cumulus cloud went towering thousands of feet into the air. Ordinarily he would not have given the cloud a second glance. But as he gazed at it from the bunker, it seemed to turn purple and gold at the bottom while the top went boiling up higher and higher like the cloud over Hiroshima. Another time, he sliced out-of-bounds, something he seldom did. As he searched for the ball deep in the woods, another odd thing happened to him. He heard something and the sound reminded him of an event that had happened a long time ago. It was the most important event in his life, yet he had managed until that moment to forget it.

Shortly afterward, he became even more depressed. People seemed more farcical than ever. More than once he shook his head and, smiling ironically, said to himself: this is not for me.

Then it was that it occurred to him that he might shoot himself.

Next, it was an idea that he entertained ironically.

Finally, it was a course of action that he took seriously and decided to carry out.

The lives of other people seemed even more farcical than his own. It astonished him that as farcical as most people's lives were, they generally gave no sign of it. Why was it that it was he, not they, who had decided to shoot himself? How did they manage to deceive themselves and even appear to live normally, work as usual, play golf, tell jokes, argue politics? Was he crazy or was it rather the case that other people went to any length to disguise from themselves the fact that their lives were farcical? He couldn't decide.

What is one to make of such a person?

To begin with: though it was probably the case that he was ill and that it was his illness—depression—that made the world seem farcical, it is impossible to prove the case.

On the one hand he was depressed.

On the other hand the world is in fact farcical.

Or at least it is possible to make the case that, for some time now, life has seemed to become more senseless, even demented, with each passing year.

True, most people he knew seemed reasonably sane and happy. They played golf, kept busy, drank, talked, laughed, went to church, appeared to enjoy themselves, and in general were both successful and generous. Their talk made a sort of sense. They cracked jokes.

On the other hand, perhaps it is possible, especially in strange times such as these, for an entire people, or at least a majority, to deceive themselves into believing that things are going well when in fact they are not, when things are in fact farcical. Most Romans worked and played as usual while Rome fell about their ears.

But surely it is fair to say that when a man becomes depressed, falls down in a sand trap, and decides to shoot himself, something has gone wrong with the man, not the world.

If one person is depressed for every ninety-nine who are not or who say they are not, who is to say that the depressed person is right and the ninety-nine wrong, that they are deceiving themselves? Even if this were true, what good would it do to undeceive the ninety-nine who have diverted themselves with a busy round of work and play and so imagine themselves happy?

The argument is abstract and useless.

On the other hand, it is an undeniable fact that more people than ever are depressed nowadays. At last count, the symptom of depression outnumbered all other symptoms put together. What if the proportion of undepressed to depressed people changes from ninety-nine-to-one to fifty-fifty? Perhaps the argument will become less abstract.

At any rate and regardless of who was or was not demented, something odd did happen to him on the golf course.

It happened, in fact, on the day after he had received the local Rotary's man-of-the-year award for service to the community.

He and his partner, Dr. Vance Battle, were one down and two to go in the foursome. Number seventeen was a par-five medium-long dogleg with a good view of Sourwood Mountain, curving past a pond and a low ridge of red maples, which in the brilliant sunlight looked like a tongue of fire searing the cool green fairway. It was not a difficult hole. Par golf required only that you hit two fair woods to clear the point of the ridge for an easy straightaway pitch to the green. His drive was well hit and went high in a strong following wind. It carried a good three-hundred yards. His partner gave him a wink. The other players looked at each other. Though the ridge and the pond lay between him and the green, he decided to go for the flag. The instant he hit the ball with a three wood, he knew it was all right. It drew slightly, enough to give the distance and to grab and hold the sloping green. Without seeing the ball, he knew he had a putt for an eagle.

His partner, Dr. Vance Battle, who sat in the cart on the outside of the dogleg waiting for his third shot, was watching. Vance looked at the green, looked back at him, held his hands apart as if he were measuring a fish, cocked his head, winked again, and, though it could not be heard, gave a cluck: *tchk.*

He looked down at the glossy brown club head. We used to call this club a spoon, he thought, not a three wood. What do you think? he once asked an ancient black caddy at Sea Island. That's a *spoon* shot, the caddy said with a certain emphasis and a rising cadence and handed him the club with the complex but clear sense of what a *spoon* could do.

Now you choose a numbered club from the back of an electric cart.

2 5 6

It was at that moment that he paused for several seconds, wood still held in both hands, fingers overlapped, and seemed to listen for something. He gazed up at the round one-eyed mountain, which seemed to gaze back with an ironical expression.

Certain "quasi-sensory" symptoms, as one doctor explained later, began to manifest themselves. There was a slight, not unpleasant, twisting sensation in his head. A pied weed at the edge of the rough gave off a faint but acrid smell that rose in his nostrils. The bright October sunlight went as dark as an eclipse. The scene before his eyes seemed to change. It was not really a hallucination, he learned from another doctor, but an "association response" such as might be provoked by a lesion in the frontal lobe of the brain, the seat of memory.

The doctors did not agree on the nature of his illness or even if he had an illness.

Instead of the immaculate emerald fairway curving between the scarlet and gold hillsides of the Appalachians, he seemed to see something else. It was a scene from his youth, so insignificant a recollection that he had no reason to remember it then, let alone now, thirty years later. Yet he seemed to see every detail as clearly as if the scene lay before him. Again the explanation of the neurologist was altogether reasonable. The brain registers and records every sensation, sight and sound and smell, it has ever received. If the neurons where such information is stored happen to be stimulated, jostled, pressed upon, any memory can be recaptured.

Nothing is really forgotten.

The smell of chalk dust on the first day of school, the feel of hot corduroy on your legs, the shape of the scab on the back of your hand, is still there if you have the means of getting at it.

Instead of the brilliant autumn-postcard Carolina mountains, he seemed to see a weedy stretch of railroad right-of-way in a small Mississippi town. It wasn't even part of the right-of-way but no more than a wedge-shaped salient of weeds angling off between the railroad tracks and the backyards of Negro cabins. It was shaped like a bent triangle, the bend formed by the curve of tracks. Perhaps it was owned by the railroad or perhaps by the utility company, because in one corner there was a small fenced and locked enclosure that contained an even smaller metal hut. Or perhaps it was owned by the city, because at the end of this narrow vista of weeds rose the town water tower. Or perhaps it belonged to no one, not even the Negroes, a parcel of leftover land that the surveyors had not noticed on their maps.

Only once in his life had he ever set foot on this nondescript sector of earth. It was shortly after he had seen Ethel Rosenblum. As he took the shortcut home after school, walking the railroad tracks that ran behind the football field, he saw Ethel Rosenblum practicing her cheerleading. She was in uniform, brief blue skirt flared to show gold panties. She was short, her hair was kinky, her face a bit pocked. But as if to make up for these defects, nature had endowed her with such beauty and grace of body, a dark satinity of skin, a sweet firm curve and compaction of limb as not easily to be believed. She was smart in algebra and history and English. They competed for four years. She won. She was valedictorian and he salutatorian. She could factor out equations after the whole class was stumped, stand at the blackboard, hip hiked out, one fist perched cheerleaderwise on her pelvis, the other small quick hand squinched on the chalk, and cancel out great $a^2 - b^2$ complexes *zip zap slash,* coming out at the end with $a/a = 1$. $1 = 1$! Unity!

No matter how ungainly the equation, ugly and unbalanced, clotted with complexes, radicals, fractions, *zip zip* under Ethel Rosenblum's quick sure hand and they factored out and canceled and came down to unity, symmetry, beauty.

Would not life itself prove so?

No, as it turned out.

They knew each other, had sat in the same class for four years. Not twenty words had passed between them.

Once in his life had he set foot on this unnamed unclaimed untenanted patch of weeds, and that was when he saw Ethel Rosenblum and wanted her so bad he fell down. So keen was his sorrow at not having his arms around her, his fingers knotted in her kinked chalk-dusted hair, that he flung himself down in a litter of algebra books, ring-binders, *Literature and Life,* down into the Johnson grass and goldenrod, onto the earth smelling of creosote and rabbit tobacco.

Ah, *that* was the smell of the pied weed on the golf course, the acrid smell of rabbit tobacco!

Ethel, why is the world so designed that our very smartness and closeness keep us apart? Is it an unspoken pact? Is it an accursed shyness? Ethel, let's me and you homestead this leftover land here and now, this nonplace, this surveyor's interstice. Here's the place for us, the only place not Jew or Gentile, not black or white, not public or private.

Later a doctor raised the possibility of a small hemorrhage or arterial spasm near the brain's limbic system, seat of all desire, a location that would account for the sexual component of his disorder.

"What sexual component?" he asked. "Doc, that was Ethel Rosenblum and I was fifteen."

"Yeah, but you're talking about her now."

Now in the middle of this pretty Carolina fairway in the sweet high mountain air, as the sky darkened and the acrid smell of rabbit tobacco rose in his nostrils, he fell down again, but only for an instant. Or perhaps he only stumbled, for the next thing he knew, the electric cart hummed up behind him and there was Vance.

No, he did fall down, because he seemed to see and smell the multicolored granules of chemical fertilizer scattered in the bent Bermuda.

I wonder, he said to himself nose down in the bent Ber-

muda, what would my life have been like if I had had four
years of Ethel Rosenblum instead of four years of a dream of
Ethel Rosenblum—and the twenty words between us:

"How you doing, Ethel?"

"I'm doing fine, Will. How are you?"

"Fine. Did you have a good summer?"

"Fine. I didn't do a thing. Well—"

"Well, I'll see you, Ethel."

"Yeah, I'll see you, Will."

Ethel, give me your hand. I know a place.

On the other hand, how could his life have turned out better
if things had fallen out otherwise between him and Ethel Rosenblum, for had he not succeeded in his life in every way one
can imagine? The only sign of something wrong was that he
was thinking about a girl (and a place) he had known in high
school thirty years ago.

What if he and Ethel had followed their inclinations, assuming she was of like mind (and she might have been! On com-
mencement day after she had given her valedictory and he his
salutatory, he had taken her small hand in his and told her
goodbye. She had held his hand for a second and shaken her
head and said in a fond sorrowful exasperation: "Oh,
Will—!"), and fallen down together in the Johnson grass or
wherever, whenever—what then? Would he have been better
off? Would he have become more like the young people and
not so young he saw in town who lay about at their ease, good-
humored and content as cats but also somewhat slack-jawed
and bemused, who looked as if they could be doing the same
thing ten years from now and not discontent then either—
would he have been better off? Who knows?

At least he probably would not be falling down on golf
courses and recalling odd bits and pieces of the past.

Lately he remembered everything. His symptom, if it was a

symptom, was the opposite of amnesia, a condition as far as I know unnamed by medical science.

A whiff of rabbit tobacco in North Carolina reminded him of Ethel Rosenblum and a patch of weeds in Mississippi.

An odd-shaped cloud in the blue Carolina sky reminded him of a missing tile in the Columbus Circle subway station that marked the spot where he stood every morning to catch the Eighth Avenue express to work. The tile had been broken out except for a strip at the top that left a grayish concrete area shaped like Utah.

Yes, he must have fallen down in the fairway, for now Vance had him by the arm in some kind of expert doctor's double-grip that holds you erect without seeming to.

"That was quite a shot."

"Did you see the ball?"

"It's a gimme. I been meaning to talk to you."

"Okay. Talk."

"Not here. Come see me at my office."

"Why?"

"I think something is wrong with you."

"Why?"

"People don't fall down in the middle of the fairway."

"I was thinking of something."

"You thought of something and fell down."

"That's right."

"You been acting a little off your feed. You worried about anything?"

"No."

"Did those sleeping pills I gave you help?"

"Yes." No. I didn't take them.

"You haven't been with us for some time."

"Us?"

"Us. Your family, your friends."

"How's that?"

"You don't say anything. And what you say is strange."

"Such as?"

"You asked me if I remembered a movie actor named Ross Alexander. I said no. You let it go at that. Then you asked me if Groucho Marx was dead. Then you asked me if the tendency to suicide is inherited. Do you remember?"

"Yes. You didn't answer."

"I didn't know. Are you feeling depressed?"

"No."

"What were you thinking about a minute ago after you hit that three wood?"

"I was thinking about a girl I once knew."

"Then I'll stop worrying about you."

"Let's putt out."

"Okay."

"No, wait." And again he went into one of his spells, a "petty-mall trance," his doctor friend called them. They were sitting in the cart. He sat perfectly still for perhaps five seconds, which was long enough for the doctor to smile uneasily, then frown and lean over the seat to touch him.

"What is it, Will?"

"I just realized a strange thing."

"What's that?"

"There are no Jews up here."

"Jews?"

"I've been living here for two years and have never seen a Jew. Arabs, but no Jews. When I used to come here in the summer years ago, there used to be Jews here. Isn't that strange?"

"I hadn't thought about it. Hm." Dr. Battle knitted his brow and pretended to think, but his eyes never left the other's face. "Interesting! Maybe they've all gone to Washington, ha ha."

"Come to think of it, how many Jews are left in the state of North Carolina?"

"Left? Have they been leaving? I hadn't noticed. Hm."

2 6 2

Again Dr. Battle frowned and appeared to be searching his memory.

"Think about it. Weren't there Jews here earlier? You're a native."

"Well, there was Dr. Weiss and Dutch Mandelbaum in high school who played tackle."

"They're not here now?"

"No."

"You see."

"See what?"

"You know, my wife, who was very religious, believed that the Jews are a sign."

"A sign of what?"

"A sign of God's plan working out."

"Is that so?" Vance's eye strayed to his wristwatch. He pretended to brush off a fly.

"But what about the absence of Jews? The departure of Jews?" he asked, looking intently at the doctor until his eyes rose. "What is that a sign of?"

"I couldn't say." Vance looked thoughtful. "Hm."

It is not at all uncommon for persons suffering from certain psychoses and depressions of middle age to exhibit "ideas of reference," that is, all manner of odd and irrational notions about Jews, Bildebergers, gypsies, outer space, UFOs, international conspiracies, and whatnot. Needless to say, the Jews were and are not leaving North Carolina. In fact, the Jewish community in that state, though small, is flourishing. There were, at the last census, some twenty-five synagogues and temples, ten thousand Jews with a median income of $21,000 per family.

The foursome finished the round without further incident. He sank his putt, a ten-footer not a gimme, for an eagle three, won both the $50 Nassau and the press bet, some $200 in all, took much good-natured kidding from his friends while they drank and rolled poker dice in the locker room bar, a cheerful place smelling of sweat, bourbon whiskey, and hemp carpeting, and dominated by a photomural of Jack Nicklaus blasting out of a sand trap. In all respects he seemed quite himself, though a bit absentminded, but smiling and nodding as usual—so normal indeed that his doctor friend gave no further thought to his "petty-mall trances." After all, a golfer who cards a seventy-six can't be too sick.

Surely, though, all is not well with a man who falls down in the fairway, who thinks the Jews have left North Carolina, who finds himself overtaken by unaccountable memories, memories of extraordinary power and poignancy. But memories of what? Of the most insignificant events and places imaginable, of a patch of weeds in Mississippi, of a missing tile in a gloomy New York subway station, of a girl whom he had not thought of since leaving high school!

It was a fine Sunday morning. The foursome teed off early and finished before noon. He drove through town on Church Street. Churchgoers were emerging from the eleven o'clock service. As they stood blinking and smiling in the brilliant sunlight, they seemed without exception well-dressed and prosperous, healthy and happy. He passed the following churches, some on the left, some on the right: the Christian Church, Church of Christ, Church of God, Church of God in Christ, Church of Christ in God, Assembly of God, Bethel Baptist Church, Independent Presbyterian Church, United Methodist Church, and Immaculate Heart of Mary Catholic Church.

Two signs pointing down into the hollow read: AFRICAN METHODIST EPISCOPAL CHURCH, 4 BLOCKS; STARLIGHT BAPTIST CHURCH, 8 BLOCKS.

One sign pointing up to a pine grove on the ridge read: ST. JOHN O' THE WOODS EPISCOPAL CHURCH, 6 BLOCKS.

He lived in the most Christian nation in the world, the U.S.A., in the most Christian part of that nation, the South, in the most Christian state in the South, North Carolina, in the most Christian town in North Carolina.

Once again he found himself in the pretty reds and yellows of the countryside. As he drove along a gorge, he suffered another spell. Again the brilliant sunlight grew dim. Light seemed to rise from the gorge. He slowed, turned on the radio, and tried to tune in a nonreligious program. He could not find one. In the corner of his eye a dark bird flew through the woods keeping pace with him. He knew what to do.

Pulling off at an overlook, he took the Luger from the glove compartment of the Mercedes. As he stepped out, he caught sight of a shadowy stranger in the mirror fixed to the door. But he quickly saw that the stranger was himself. The reason the figure appeared strange was that it was reflected by two mirrors, one the rearview mirror, the other the dark window glass of the Mercedes door.

He smiled. Yes, that was it. With two mirrors it is possible to see oneself briefly as a man among men rather than a self sucking everything into itself—just as you can see the back of your head in a clothier's triple mirror.

He gazed down at the wrist of the hand holding the Luger. Light and air poured onto the wrist. It was neither thick nor thin. Who can see his own wrist? It was not a wrist but The Wrist, part of the hole into which everything was sucked and drained out.

He fired five times into the gorge. The sound racketed quickly back and forth between vertical cliffs of rock. Firing the Luger, he discovered, helped knock him out of his "spells." But it did not work as well as before. He shot again, holding the Luger closer and firing past his face. The sound was louder and flatter; a wave of hot air slapped his cheek. The gun bucked, hurting his bent wrist. He held the muzzle against his temple. Yes, that is possible, he thought, smiling, that is one way to cure the great suck of self, but then I wouldn't find out, would I? Find out what? Find out why things have come to such a pass and a man so sucked down into himself that it takes a gunshot to knock him out of the suck—or a glimpse in a double mirror. And I wouldn't find out about the Jews, why they came here in the first place and why they are leaving. Are the Jews a sign?

There at any rate stands Will Barrett on the edge of a gorge in old Carolina, a talented agreeable wealthy man living in as pleasant an environment as one can imagine and yet thinking of putting a bullet in his brain.

Fifteen minutes later finds him sitting in his Mercedes in a five-car garage, sniffing the Luger and watching a cat lying in a swatch of sunlight under the rear bumper of his wife's Rolls-Royce Silver Cloud three spaces away. During the six months after his wife's death, the Silver Cloud had occupied its usual space on the clean concrete, tires inflated, not dripping a single drop of oil. Not once had he been able to bring himself to think what to do with it.

Beyond the big Rolls, almost hidden, crouched his servant Yamaiuchi's little yellow Datsun.

Absently he held the barrel of the Luger to his nose, then to his temple, and turned his head to and fro against the cold metal of the gunsight.

Is it too much to wonder what he is doing there, this pleasant prosperous American, sitting in a $35,000 car and sniffing cordite from a Luger?

How, one might well ask, could Will Barrett have come to such a pass? Is it not a matter for astonishment that such a man, having succeeded in life and living in a lovely home with a lovely view, surrounded by good cheerful folk, family and friends, merry golfers, should now find himself on a beautiful Sunday morning sunk in fragrant German leather speculating about such things as the odd look of his wrist (his wrist was perfectly normal), the return of North Carolina Jews to the

Holy Land (there was no such return), and looking for himself in mirrors like Count Dracula?

At any rate, within the space of the next three minutes there occurred two extraordinary events that, better than ten thousand words, will reveal both Barrett's peculiar state of mind and the peculiar times we live in.

First, as he sat in the Mercedes, Luger in hand, gazing at the cat nodding in the sunlight, it came to him with the force of a revelation—the breakthrough he had been waiting for, the sudden vivid inkling of what had gone wrong, not just with himself but, as he saw it, with the whole modern age.

Then, as if this were not enough, there occurred two minutes later a wholly unexpected and shocking event that, however, far from jolting him out of his grandiose speculations about the "modern age," only served to confirm them. In a word, no sooner had he opened the Mercedes door and stepped out than a rifle shot was fired from the dense pine forest nearby, ricocheting with a hideous screech from the concrete floor at his foot to a *thunk* in the brick of the inner wall. A vicious buzzing bee stung his calf.

Later he remembered thinking, even as he dove for cover: Was not the shot expected after all? Is this not in fact the very nature of the times, a kind of penultimate quiet, a minatory ordinariness of midafternoon, a concealed dread and expectation that, only after the shot is fired, we knew had been there all along?

Are we afraid quiet afternoons will be interrupted by gunfire? Or do we hope they will?

Was there ever a truly uneventful time, years of long afternoons when nothing happened and people were glad of it?

But first his "revelation." As he sat gazing at the cat, he saw all at once what had gone wrong, wrong with people, with him, not with the cat—saw it with the same smiling certitude with which Einstein is said to have hit on his famous theory in the act of boarding a streetcar in Zurich.

There was the cat. Sitting there in the sun with its needs satisfied, for whom one place was the same as any other place as long as it was sunny—no nonsense about old haunted patches of weeds in Mississippi or a brand new life in a brand new place in Carolina—the cat was exactly 100 percent cat, no more, no less. As for Will Barrett, as for people nowadays—they were never 100 percent themselves. They occupied a place uneasily and more or less successfully. More likely they were 47 percent themselves, or rarely, as in the case of Einstein on the streetcar, 300 percent. All too often these days they were 2 percent themselves, specters who hardly occupied a place at all. How can the great suck of self ever hope to be a fat cat dozing in the sun?

There was his diagnosis, then. A person nowadays is 2 percent himself. And to arrive at a diagnosis is already to have anticipated the cure: how to restore the 98 percent.

Perhaps it is not necessary to say any more about Will Barrett's peculiar revelation except to note that if it applied to anyone it applied to him and not to the good folk of Linwood, North Carolina, who, sitting on their sunny patios, did in fact seem happy as cats on this beautiful October Sunday.

At any rate, as he absently climbed out of the Mercedes, Luger forgotten but still in hand, he was musing over his discovery of this strange shortfall of the human condition and had no sooner reached the middle of the garage on his way to the interior door when *whangEEEEE* the concrete erupted, spat, stung his calf. There followed not in succession but all at once, it seemed, the sound of the shot, a sharp sting, and the solid *thunk* in the brick.

Then—and now occurred the most remarkable part of this odd episode—in the next instant he was transformed. It was as if the sting in his calf had been the injection of a powerful drug. Quicker than any drug, in the instant, in fact, of hearing and recognizing the gunshot, he was, as he expressed it, miraculously restored to himself. The cat of course had jumped four feet straight up and fled in terror, as any sensible animal would, reduced instantly to zero percentile of its well-being. But Barrett? The missing 98 percent is magically restored! How? By the rifle shot! In the very same motion of lifting his stinging leg, he is diving for the floor, hitting the concrete in a roll, shoulder tucked, Luger cradled in his stomach. He rolls over at least three times, enough rolls anyhow to carry him under the high-slung 1956 Silver Cloud and against the far wall, where now he is feeling himself to be himself for the first time in years, flanked as he is by two adjoining walls, the Rolls above him as good as a pillbox affording a slot-shaped view of the sunny woods. And without his taking thought about it, the Luger is now held in both hands stretched out in front of him as steady as if it were propped on a sandbag.

Were terrorists after him? A knee-capping? Or just shooting up a rich man's house and Rolls? Or were they after his daughter Leslie upstairs?

None of the above, as it turned out. It is enough to report that in another minute he had caught sight of an oddly shaped peak of a red cap disappearing in the pines, not a deer-hunter's cap but a Texaco or Conoco (he forgot which) mechanic's cap; that he recognized the cap-wearer and knew who fired the shot and why. It was Ewell McBee, a covite from the valley below, once his wife's family's gardener, who poached deer on Barrett's ten thousand acres of mountainside.

No apocalyptic last-days irruption of terrorism, then, no more than the annual unpleasantness with McBee. No, maybe a bit more: wasn't McBee saying, in fact, Maybe you'd better let me poach so I won't make the mistake of shooting up your garage?

He sighed: he'd rather an Italian terrorist than the complex negotiations with McBee (Pay him a call? Let him poach? Call the sheriff? Buy him a drink? Shoot him?). At any rate, don't tell Leslie.

There he lay for some minutes, sighting down the Luger and speculating on the odd upsidedownness of the times, that on a beautiful Sunday in old Carolina, it takes a gunshot to restore a man to himself.

What man? How many men besides Will Barrett would have shared his feelings? How many men would have felt better for being shot at on a peaceful Sunday? Very few white folks and no niggers at all, as they say in old Carolina.

Even Barrett wondered. Why is it that I know perfectly well that it was Ewell McBee, that it was an accident, and that I am disappointed? How does it happen that this is what I do best and feel best doing, not hitting a three-wood on a green fairway but rolling away from gunfire and into a safe corner where I can look out without being seen and where I can't be enfiladed—all with a secret coolness and even taking a satisfaction in it? This is better than—than what?

Very well, here I am and here it is at last, let them come. What have I to do with this Luger? I don't know, something. Why do I feel myself most myself here and not hitting a three-wood for an eagle on the back nine? What does my ease with gunfire portend? How is it that I know with certainty that everything is going to be settled in the end with a gun, with this gun, either with them or with me, but with this gun?

How could I know such a thing? How do I know that somehow it is going to come down to this, should come down to this, down to me and a gun and an enemy, that otherwise this quiet Sunday makes no sense?

Ewell McBee, it would turn out, had not of course meant to harm him or his house. At least not consciously. He was in fact poaching, had been circling to get upwind from a deer, had lost his sense of direction and got off a shot that by the purest chance (surely) had gone ricocheting around the Barrett garage.

Strange to say, that made matters worse, to have to listen to

Ewell apologize for shooting up his house. If there is an enemy, it is better to know who he is.

Ewell McBee, he reflected as he lay prone under the Rolls, was another example of the demented and farcical times we live in. Did the growing madness have something to do with the Jews pulling out? Who said we could get along without the Jews? Watch the Jews, their mysterious comings and goings and stayings! The Jews are a sign! When the Jews pull out, the Gentiles begin to act like the crazy Jutes and Celts and Angles and redneck Saxons they are. They go back to the woods. Here we are, retired from the cities and living deep in the southern forests and growing nuttier by the hour. The Jews are gone, the blacks are leaving, and where are we? Deep in the woods, socking little balls around the mountains, rattling ice in Tanqueray, driving $35,000 German cars, watching Billy Graham and the Steelers and "M*A*S*H" on forty-five-inch Jap TV.

So said Will Barrett.

Ewell McBee was one of them, a new southerner and as nutty as a Jute. Ewell, who was exactly his own age, he had known as a boy when his father and mother spent the summers in Linwood. Ewell caddied for his father. A country boy who lived in a cove of the valley below, hence a covite, he went barefoot and shirtless and wore soft bib-overalls smelling of Octagon soap. He was overgrown and strong and a bully. They used to neck-rassle, stand sweating and grunting, elbows crooked around necks until Ewell threw him down and sat on him for an hour, grinning and daring him to get up, thighs squeezing him, a heavy incubus smelling of sweet boiled cotton, Octagon soap, and thick white winter-white skin.

From Ewell's mother they got fresh eggs and country butter and from his father liquor, not white lightning but charcoal-cured light-amber corn whiskey.

From Ewell he had first heard the word *pecker* and had seen an uncircumcised pecker that he took at first to be a peculiarity of country boys. To his even greater astonishment, Ewell showed him how to jerk off. A bully and a jerk-off Ewell was and remained.

Then Ewell had become the Peabody's head gardener. Then he moved to town and became a businessman. As an ex-employee he figured he had a proprietary right to an occasional buck deer.

So Ewell had changed and yet not changed. Now if he had a drink with Ewell in a bar booth, Ewell might make a show of not letting him out, actually stand in his way daring him to get past, half-joking, no, not even half-joking. "Boy, I want a piece of you. I could throw you down rat now."

"Well, I doubt if you could but right now let me out."

And Ewell would give way reluctantly, yielding to their middle-aged respectability and to Will Barrett's great Peabody wealth.

All that was left of the bullying was the poaching. "Hail fire, Will, I'm doing you a favor. You got so goddamn many deer in there they're chewing on the trees. Anyhow what you going to do about it?" I'm sitting astride your ten thousand-acre mountain like I sat on you, and how you going to get up?

When Ewell came up from the cove, he also came up in the world, operated a Texaco station, then owned a Conoco station, then five Exxon stations, then a movie theater. He shed bib-overalls for the Jaymar Sansabelt slacks and short-sleeved white shirt of small-town businessmen, joined the C of C, ate lunch with Rotary at the Holiday Inn. But Twin Cinema had gone bust and Exxon cut back on gas and so now Ewell needed money and had a new proposition. Ewell wanted him to put up some money for the home-entertainment videocassette business. He had a connection, a fellow in Miami who could supply him with any number of copies of any film at all, *Jaws I* and *II*, *Godfather I* and *II*, *Airport* of any year, you name it. More important, there was this whole new market for cassettes designed for motel and home bedroom viewing; but best of all he knew a young lady, a real professional, a recognized moviemaker, who made such movies right next door in Highlands, using as actors and actresses the college boys and girls who flock to resorts looking for summer jobs and are happy to work for minimum wage.

As if it weren't demented enough to go to Rotary lunch every Tuesday where there might be a guest speaker on Encounter and Enrichment in Marriage and hear Ewell tell him solemnly about the value of erotic movies in couples therapy—redneck Ewell come up out of the cove and talking about couples therapy! America is still on the move! A poor boy can still come up in the world. The South is rising again! As if this weren't enough, Ewell in the very act of making his pitch—"your hundred thou will buy you forty-nine percent; me and my potner, the little lady, got to keep fifty-one"—Ewell couldn't help coming at him again, shouldering him, hemming him up in a corner of the Holiday Inn Buccaneer Room! He didn't want to let him out! He wanted to neck-rassle! Thow him down! "You gon talk to my potner," said Ewell, eyeing him. "She'll fix you up with a little lady, her leading lady. We gon boogie at my villa tonight."

Lying under the Rolls, Luger still gripped in both hands, he gazed at an arc of sunlit pines. Was Ewell threatening him? Did he shoot up the garage as a warning: "Either you back my cassette business or—"? No, it was too simple. That would mean having a simple enemy. The world is crazier than that.

He smiled and nodded: I know why it is better to be shot at on a Sunday afternoon than not be shot at. Because it means maybe there *is* an enemy after all. If there is no enemy then I am either mad or living in a madhouse.

Peace is only better than war if peace is not hell, too. War being hell makes sense.

THE YEAR

OF

GETTING

TO

KNOW US

·

ETHAN CANIN

I told my father not to worry, that love is what matters, and that in the end, when he is loosed from his body, he can look back and say without blinking that he did all right by me, his son, and that I loved him.

And he said, "Don't talk about things you know nothing about."

We were in San Francisco, in a hospital room. IV tubes were plugged into my father's arms; little round Band-Aids were on his chest. Next to his bed was a table with a vase of yellow roses and a card that my wife, Anne, had brought him. On the front of the card was a photograph of a golf green. On the wall above my father's head an electric monitor traced his heart-beat. He was watching the news on a TV that stood in the corner next to his girlfriend, Lorraine. Lorraine was reading a magazine.

I was watching his heartbeat. It seemed all right to me: the blips made steady peaks and drops, moved across the screen, went out at one end and then came back at the other. It seemed that this was all a heart could do. I'm an English teacher, though, and I don't know much about it.

"It looks strong," I'd said to my mother that afternoon over the phone. She was in Pasadena. "It's going right across, pretty steady. Big bumps. Solid."

"Is he eating all right?"

"I think so."

"Is *she* there?"

"Is Lorraine here, you mean?"

She paused. "Yes, Lorraine."

"No," I said. "She's not."

"Your poor father," she whispered.

I'm an only child, and I grew up in a big wood-frame house on Huron Avenue in Pasadena, California. The house had three empty bedrooms and in the backyard a section of grass that had been stripped and leveled, and then seeded and mowed like a putting green. Twice a week a Mexican gardener came to trim it wearing special moccasins my father had bought him. They had soft hide soles that left no imprints.

My father was in love with golf. He played seven times every week and talked about the game as if it were a science that he was about to figure out. "Cut through the outer rim for a high iron," he used to say at dinner, looking out the window into the yard while my mother passed him the carved-wood salad bowl. Or "In hot weather hit a high-compression ball." When conversations paused, he made little putting motions with his hands. He was a top amateur and in another situation might have been a pro. When I was sixteen, the year I was arrested, he let me caddie for the first time. Before that all I knew about golf was his clubs—the Spalding made-to-measure woods and irons, Dynamiter sand wedge, St. Andrew's putter —which he kept in an Abercrombie & Fitch bag in the trunk of his Lincoln, and the white leather shoes with long tongues and screw-in spikes, which he stored upside down in the hall closet. When he wasn't playing, he covered the club heads with socks that had little yellow dingo balls on the ends.

He never taught me to play. I was a decent athlete—could run, catch, throw a perfect spiral—but he never took me to the golf course. In the summer he played every day. Sometimes my mother asked if he would take me along with him. "Why should I?" he answered. "Neither of us would like it."

Every afternoon after work he played nine holes; he played eighteen on Saturday, and nine again on Sunday morning. On Sunday afternoon, at four o'clock, he went for a drive by himself in his white Lincoln Continental. Nobody was allowed to come with him on the drives. He was usually gone for a couple of hours. "Today I drove in the country," he would say at dinner as he put out his cigarette. Or "This afternoon I looked at the ocean," and we were to take from this that he had driven north on the coastal highway. He almost never said more, and across our blue and white tablecloth, when I looked at him, my silent father, I imagined in his eyes a pure gaze with which he read the waves and currents of the sea. He had made a fortune in business and owed it to being able to see the truth in any situation. For this reason, he said, he liked to drive with all the windows down. When he returned from his trips his face was red from the wind and his thinning hair lay fitfully on his head. My mother baked on Sunday afternoons while he was gone, walnut pies or macaroons that she prepared on the kitchen counter, which looked out over his putting green.

276

I teach English in a high school now, and my wife, Anne, is a journalist. I've played golf a half dozen times in ten years and don't like it any more than most beginners, though the two or three times I've hit a drive that sails, that takes flight with its own power, I've felt something that I think must be unique to the game. These were the drives my father used to hit. Explosions off the tee, bird flights. But golf isn't my game, and it never has been, and I wouldn't think about it at all if not for my father.

Anne and I were visiting in California, first my mother, in Los Angeles, and then my father and Lorraine, north in Sausalito, and Anne suggested that I ask him to play nine holes one morning. She'd been wanting me to talk to him. It's part of the project we've started, part of her theory of what's wrong—although I don't think that much is. She had told me that twenty-five years changes things, and since we had the time, why not go out to California.

She said, "It's not too late to talk to him."

My best friend in high school was named Nickie Apple. Nickie had a thick chest and a voice that had been damaged somehow, made a little hoarse, and sometimes people thought he was twenty years old. He lived in a four-story house that had a separate floor for the kids. It was the top story, and his father, who was divorced and a lawyer, had agreed never to come up there. That was where we sat around after school. Because of the agreement, no parents were there, only kids. Nine or ten of us, usually. Some of them had slept the night on the big pillows that were scattered against the walls: friends of his older brothers', in Stetson hats and flannel shirts; girls I had never seen before.

Nickie and I went to Shrier Academy, where all the students carried around blue-and-gray notebooks embossed with the school's heraldic seal. *"Sumus Primi,"* the seal said. Our gray wool sweaters said it; our green exam books said it; the rear-window decal my mother brought home said it. My father wouldn't put the sticker on the Lincoln, so she pressed it onto the window above her kitchen sink instead. "*Summa Prima*," I read whenever I washed my hands. At Shrier we learned Latin in the eighth grade and art history in the ninth, and in the tenth I started getting into some trouble. Little things: cigarettes, graffiti. Mr. Goldman, the student counselor, called my mother in for a premonition visit. "I have a premonition about Leonard," he told her in the counseling office one afternoon in the warm October when I was sixteen. The office was full of plants and had five floor-to-ceiling windows that let in sun like a greenhouse. They looked over grassy, bushless knolls. "I just have a feeling about him."

That October he started talking to me about it. He called me in and asked me why I was friends with Nickie Apple, a boy going nowhere. I was looking out the big windows, opening and closing my fists beneath the desk top. He said, "Lenny, you're a bright kid—what are you trying to tell us?" And I said, "Nothing, I'm not trying to tell you anything."

Then we started stealing, Nickie and I. He did it first, and took things I didn't expect: steaks, expensive cuts that we cooked on a grill by the window in the top story of his house; garden machinery; luggage. We didn't sell it and we didn't use it, but every afternoon we went someplace new. In November he distracted a store clerk and I took a necklace that we thought was diamonds. In December we went for a ride in someone else's car, and over Christmas vacation, when only gardeners were on the school grounds, we threw ten rocks, one by one, as if we'd paid for them at a carnival stand, through the five windows in Mr. Goldman's office.

"You look like a train station," I said to my father as he lay in the hospital bed. "All those lines coming and going everywhere."

He looked at me. I put some things down, tried to make a

little bustle. I could see Anne standing in the hall just beyond the door.

"Are you comfortable, Dad?"

"What do you mean 'comfortable'? My heart's full of holes, leaking all over the place. Am I comfortable? No. I'm dying."

"You're not dying," I said, and I sat down next to him. "You'll be swinging the five iron in two weeks."

I touched one of the tubes in his arm. Where it entered the vein, the needle disappeared under a piece of tape. I hated the sight of this. I moved the bedsheets a little bit, tucked them in. Anne had wanted me to be alone with him. She was in the hall, waiting to head off Lorraine.

"What's the matter with her?" he asked, pointing at Anne.

"She thought we might want to talk."

"What's so urgent?"

Anne and I had discussed it the night before. "Tell him what you feel," she said. "Tell him you love him." We were eating dinner in a fish restaurant. "Or if you don't love him, tell him you don't."

"Look, Pop," I said now.

"What?"

I was forty-two years old. We were in a hospital and he had tubes in his arms. All kinds of everything: needles, air, tape. I said it again.

"Look, Pop."

Anne and I have seen a counselor, who told me that I had to learn to accept kindness from people. He saw Anne and me together, then Anne alone, then me. Children's toys were scattered on the floor of his office. "You sound as if you don't want to let people near you," he said. "Right?"

"I'm a reasonably happy man," I answered.

I hadn't wanted to see the counselor. Anne and I have been married seven years, and sometimes I think the history of marriage can be written like this: People Want Too Much. Anne and I have suffered no plague; we sleep late two mornings a week; we laugh at most of the same things; we have a decent house in a suburb of Boston, where, after the commuter traffic has eased, a quiet descends and the world is at peace. She writes for a newspaper, and I teach the children of lawyers and insurance men. At times I'm alone, and need to be alone; at times she does too. But I can always count on a moment, sometimes once in a day, sometimes more, when I see her patting down the sheets on the bed, or watering the front-window violets, and I am struck by the good fortune of my life.

Still, Anne says I don't feel things.

It comes up at dinner, outside in the yard, in airports as we wait for planes. You don't let yourself feel, she tells me; and I tell her that I think it's a crazy thing, all this talk about feeling. What do the African Bushmen say? They say, Will we eat tomorrow? Will there be rain?

When I was sixteen, sitting in the backseat of a squad car, the policeman stopped in front of our house on Huron Avenue, turned around against the headrest, and asked me if I was sure this was where I lived.

"Yes, sir," I said.

He spoke through a metal grate. "Your daddy owns this house?"

"Yes, sir."

"But for some reason you don't like windows."

He got out and opened my door, and we walked up the porch steps. The swirling lights on the squad car were making crazy patterns in the french panes of the living room bays. He knocked. "What's your daddy do?"

I heard lights snapping on, my mother moving through the house. "He's in business," I said. "But he won't be home now." The policeman wrote something on his notepad. I saw my mother's eye through the glass in the door, and then the locks were being unlatched, one by one, from the top.

PERFECT LIES

When Anne and I came to California to visit, we stayed at my mother's for three days. On her refrigerator door was a calendar with men's names marked on it—dinner dates, theater —and I knew this was done for our benefit. My mother has been alone for fifteen years. She's still thin, and her eyes still water, and I noticed that books were lying open all through the house. Thick paperbacks—*Dr. Zhivago, The Thorn Birds*—in the bathroom and the studio and the bedroom. We never mentioned my father, but at the end of our stay, when we had packed the car for our drive north along the coast, after she'd hugged us both and we'd backed out of the driveway, she came down off the lawn into the street, her arms crossed over her chest, leaned into the window, and said, "You might say hello to your father for me."

We made the drive north on Highway 1. We passed mission towns, fields of butter lettuce, long stretches of pumpkin farms south of San Francisco. It was the first time we were going to see my father with Lorraine. She was a hairdresser. He'd met her a few years after coming north, and one of the first things they'd done together was take a trip around the world. We got postcards from the Nile delta and Bangkok. When I was young, my father had never taken us out of California.

His house in Sausalito was on a cliff above a finger of San Francisco Bay. A new Lincoln stood in the carport. In his bedroom was a teak-framed king-size waterbed, and on the walls were bits of African artwork—opium pipes, metal figurines. Lorraine looked the same age as Anne. One wall of the living room was glass, and after the first night's dinner, while we sat on the leather sofa watching tankers and yachts move under the Golden Gate Bridge, my father put down his Scotch and water, touched his jaw, and said, "Lenny, call Dr. Farmer."

It was his second one. The first had been two years earlier, on the golf course in Monterey, where he'd had to kneel, then sit, then lie down on the fairway.

At dinner the night after I was arrested, my mother introduced her idea. "We're going to try something," she said. She had brought out a chicken casserole, and it was steaming in front of her. "That's what we're going to do. Max, are you listening? This next year, starting tonight, is going to be the year of getting to know us better." She stopped speaking and dished my father some chicken.

"What do you mean?" I asked.

"I mean it will be to a small extent a theme year. Nothing that's going to change every day of our lives, but in this next year I thought we'd all make an attempt to get to know each other better. Especially you, Leonard. Dad and I are going to make a better effort to know you."

"I'm not sure what you mean," my father said.

"All kinds of things, Max. We'll go to movies together, and Lenny can throw a party here at the house. And I personally would like to take a trip, all of us together, to the American Southwest."

"Sounds all right to me," I said.

"And Max," she said, "you can take Lenny with you to play golf. For example." She looked at my father.

"Neither of us would like it," he said.

"Lenny never sees you."

I looked out the window. The trees were turning, dropping their leaves onto the putting green. I didn't care what he said, one way or the other. My mother spooned a chicken thigh onto my plate and covered it with sauce. "All right," he said. "He can caddie."

"And as preparation for our trip," my mother said, "can you take him on your Sunday rides?"

My father took off his glasses. "The Southwest," he said, wiping the lenses with a napkin, "is exactly like any other part of the country."

Anne had an affair once with a man she met on an assignment. He was young, much younger than either of us—in his late twenties, I would say from the one time I saw him. I saw them because one day on the road home I passed Anne's car in the lot of a Denny's restaurant. I parked around the block and went in to surprise her. I took a table at the back, but from my seat in the corner I didn't realize for several minutes that the youngish-looking woman leaning forward and whispering to the man with a beard was my wife.

I didn't get up and pull the man out with me into the parking lot, or even join them at the table, as I have since thought might have been a good idea. Instead I sat and watched them. I could see that under the table they were holding hands. His back was to me, and I noticed that it was broad, as mine is not. I remember thinking that she probably liked this broadness. Other than that, though, I didn't feel very much. I ordered another cup of coffee just to hear myself talk, but my voice wasn't quavering or fearful. When the waitress left, I took out a napkin and wrote on it, "You are a forty-two-year-old man with no children and your wife is having an affair." Then I put some money on the table and left the restaurant.

"I think we should see somebody," Anne said to me a few weeks later. It was a Sunday morning, and we were eating breakfast on the porch.

"About what?" I asked.

On a Sunday afternoon when I was sixteen I went out to the garage with a plan my mother had given me. That morning my father had washed the Lincoln. He had detergent-scrubbed the finish and then sun-dried it on Huron Avenue, so that in the workshop light of the garage its highlights shone. The windshield molding, the grille, the chrome side markers, had been cloth-dried to erase water spots. The keys hung from their magnetic sling near the door to the kitchen. I took them out and opened the trunk. Then I hung them up again and sat on the rear quarter panel to consider what to do. It was almost four o'clock. The trunk of my father's car was large enough for a half dozen suitcases and had been upholstered in a gray medium-pile carpet that was cut to hug the wheel wells and the spare-tire berth. In one corner, fastened down by straps, was his toolbox, and along the back lay the golf bag. In the shadows the yellow dingos of the club socks looked like baby chicks. He was going to come out in a few minutes. I reached in, took off four of the club socks, and made a pillow for my head. Then I stepped into the trunk. The shocks bounced once and stopped. I lay down with my head propped on the quarter panel and my feet resting in the taillight berth, and then I reached up, slammed down the trunk, and was in the dark.

This didn't frighten me. When I was very young, I liked to sleep with the shades drawn and the door closed, so that no light entered my room. I used to hold my hand in front of my eyes and see if I could imagine its presence. It was too dark to see anything. I was blind then, lying in my bed, listening for every sound. I used to move my hand back and forth, close to my eyes, until I had the sensation that it was there but had in some way been amputated. I had heard of soldiers who had lost limbs but still felt them attached. Now I held my open hand before my eyes. It was dense black inside the trunk, colorless, without light.

When my father started the car, all the sounds were huge, magnified as if they were inside my own skull. The metal scratched, creaked, slammed when he got in; the bolt of the starter shook all the way through to the trunk; the idle rose and leveled; then the gears changed and the car lurched. I heard the garage door glide up. Then it curled into its housing, bumped once, began descending again. The seams of the trunk lid lightened in the sun. We were in the street now, heading downhill. I lay back and felt the road, listened to the gravel pocking in the wheel wells.

I followed our route in my mind. Left off Huron onto Telscher, where the car bottomed in the rain gulley as we turned, then up the hill to Santa Ana. As we waited for the light, the idle made its change, shifting down, so that below my head I heard the individual piston blasts in the exhaust pipe. Left on Santa Ana, counting the flat stretches where I felt my father tap the brakes, numbering the intersections as we headed west toward the ocean. I heard cars pull up next to us, accelerate, slow down, make turns. The blinkers echoed inside the quarter panels. I pulled off more club socks and enlarged my pillow. We slowed down, stopped, and then we accelerated, the soft piston explosions becoming a hiss as we turned onto the Pasadena freeway.

"Dad's rides," my mother had said to me the night before, as I lay in bed, "would be a good way for him to get to know you." It was the first week of the year of getting to know us better. She was sitting at my desk.

"But he won't let me go," I said.

"You're right." She moved some things around on a shelf. The room wasn't quite dark, and I could see the outline of her white blouse. "I talked to Mr. Goldman," she said.

"Mr. Goldman doesn't know me."

"He says you're angry." My mother stood up, and I watched her white blouse move to the window. She pulled back the shade until a triangle of light from the streetlamp fell on my sheets. "Are you angry?"

"I don't know," I said. "I don't think so."

"I don't think so either." She replaced the shade, came over and kissed me on the forehead, and then went out into the hall. In the dark I looked for my hand.

A few minutes later the door opened again. She put her head in. "If he won't let you come," she said, "sneak along."

On the freeway the thermal seams whizzed and popped in my ears. The ride had smoothed out now, as the shocks settled into the high speed, hardly dipping on curves, muffling everything as if we were under water. As far as I could tell, we were still driving west, toward the ocean. I sat halfway up and rested my back against the golf bag. I could see shapes now inside the trunk. When we slowed down and the blinker went on, I attempted bearings, but the sun was the same in all directions and the trunk lid was without shadow. We braked hard. I felt the car leave the freeway. We made turns. We went straight. Then more turns, and as we slowed down and I was stretching out, uncurling my body along the diagonal, we made a sharp right onto gravel and pulled over and stopped.

My father opened the door. The car dipped and rocked, shuddered. The engine clicked. Then the passenger door opened. I waited.

If I heard her voice today, twenty-six years later, I would recognize it.

"Angel," she said.

I heard the weight of their bodies sliding across the back seat, first hers, then his. They weren't three feet away. I curled up, crouched into the low space between the golf bag and the back of the passenger compartment. There were two firm points in the cushion where it was displaced. As I lay there, I went over the voice again in my head: it was nobody I knew. I heard a laugh from her, and then something low from him. I felt the shift of the trunk's false rear, and then, as I lay behind them, I heard the contact: the crinkle of clothing, arms wrapping, and the half-delicate, muscular sounds. It was like hearing a television in the next room. His voice once more, and then the rising of their breath, slow; a minute of this, maybe another; then shifting again, the friction of cloth on the leather seat and the car's soft rocking. "Dad," I whispered. Then rocking again; my father's sudden panting, harder and harder, his half words. The car shook violently. "Dad," I whispered. I shouted, "Dad!"

The door opened.

His steps kicked up gravel. I heard jingling metal, the sound of the key in the trunk lock. He was standing over me in an explosion of light.

He said, "Put back the club socks."

I did and got out of the car to stand next to him. He rubbed his hands down the front of his shirt.

"What the hell," he said.

"I was in the trunk."

"I know," he said. "What the goddamn."

The year I graduated from college, I found a job teaching junior high school in Boston. The school was a cement building with small windows well up from the street, and dark classrooms in which I spent a lot of time maintaining discipline. In the middle of an afternoon that first winter a boy knocked on my door to tell me I had a phone call. I knew who it was going to be.

"Dad's gone," my mother said.

He'd taken his things in the Lincoln, she told me, and driven away that morning before dawn. On the kitchen table he'd left a note and some cash. "A lot of cash," my mother added, lowering her voice. "Twenty thousand dollars."

I imagined the sheaf of bills on our breakfast table, held down by the ceramic butter dish, the bank notes ruffling in the breeze from the louvered windows that opened onto his green. In the note he said he had gone north and would call her when he'd settled. It was December. I told my mother that I would visit in a week, when school was out for Christmas. I told her to go to her sister's and stay there, and then I said that I was working and had to get back to my class. She didn't say anything on the other end of the line, and in the silence I imagined my father criss-crossing the state of California, driving north, stopping in Palm Springs and Carmel, the Lincoln riding low with the weight.

"Leonard," my mother said, "did you know anything like this was happening?"

During the spring of the year of getting to know us better I caddied for him a few times. On Saturdays he played early in the morning, when the course was mostly empty and the grass was still wet from the night. I learned to fetch the higher irons as the sun rose over the back nine and the ball, on drying ground, rolled farther. He hit skybound approach shots with backspin, chips that bit into the green and stopped. He played in a foursome with three other men, and in the locker room, as they changed their shoes, they told jokes and poked one another in the belly. The lockers were shiny green metal, the floor clean white tiles that clicked under the shoe spikes. Beneath the mirrors were jars of combs in green disinfectant. When I combed my hair with them it stayed in place and smelled like limes.

We were on the course at dawn. At the first fairway the other men dug in their spikes, shifted their weight from leg to leg, and dummy-swung at an empty tee while my father lit a cigarette and looked out over the hole. "The big gun," he said to me, or, if it was a par three, "the lady." He stepped on his cigarette. I wiped the head with the club sock before I handed it to him. When he took the club, he felt its balance point, rested it on one finger, and then, in slow motion, he gripped the shaft. Left hand first, then right, the fingers wrapping pinkie to index. Then he leaned down over the ball. On a perfect drive the tee flew straight up in the air and landed in front of his feet.

Over the weekend his heart lost its rhythm for a few seconds. It happened Saturday night when Anne and I were at the house in Sausalito and we didn't hear about it until Sunday. "Ventricular fibrillation," the intern said. "Circus movements." The condition was always a danger after a heart attack. He had been given a shock and his heartbeat had returned to normal.

"But I'll be honest with you," the intern said. We were in the hall. He looked down, touched his stethoscope. "It isn't a good sign."

The heart gets bigger as it dies, he told me. Soon it spreads across the X ray. He brought me with him to a room and showed me strips of paper with the electric tracings: certain formations. The muscle was dying in patches, he said. He said things might get better, they might not.

My mother called that afternoon. "Should I come up?"

"He was a bastard to you," I said.

When Lorraine and Anne were eating dinner, I found the intern again. "I want to know," I said. "Tell me the truth." The intern was tall and thin, sick-looking himself. So were the other doctors I had seen around the place. Everything in that hospital was pale—the walls, the coats, the skin.

He said, "What truth?"

I told him that I'd been reading about heart disease. I'd read about EKGs, knew about the medicines—lidocaine, propranolol. I knew that the lungs filled up with water, that heart failure was death by drowning. I said, "The truth about my father."

The afternoon I had hidden in the trunk, we came home while my mother was cooking dinner. I walked up the path from the garage behind my father, watching the pearls of sweat on his neck. He was whistling a tune. At the door he kissed my mother's cheek. He touched the small of her back. She was cooking vegetables, and the steam had fogged up the kitchen windows and dampened her hair. My father sat down in the chair by the window and opened the newspaper. I thought of the way the trunk rear had shifted when he and the woman had moved into the back of the Lincoln. My mother was smiling.

"Well?" she said.

"What's for dinner?" I asked.

"Well?" she said again.

"It's chicken," I said. "Isn't it?"

"Max, aren't you going to tell me if anything unusual happened today?"

My father didn't look up from the newspaper. "Did anything unusual happen today?" he said. He turned the page, folded it back smartly. "Why don't you ask Lenny?"

She smiled at me.

"I surprised him," I said. Then I turned and looked out the window.

"I have something to tell you," Anne said to me one Sunday morning in the fifth year of our marriage. We were lying in bed. I knew what was coming.

"I already know," I said.

"What do you already know?"

"I know about your lover."

She didn't say anything.

"It's all right," I said.

It was winter. The sky was gray, and although the sun had risen only a few hours earlier, it seemed like late afternoon. I waited for Anne to say something more. We were silent for several minutes. Then she said, "I wanted to hurt you." She got out of bed and began straightening out the bureau. She pulled my sweaters from the drawer and refolded them. She returned all our shoes to the closet. Then she came back to the bed, sat down, and began to cry. Her back was toward me. It shook with her gasps, and I put my hand out and touched her. "It's all right," I said.

"We only saw each other a few times," she answered. "I'd take it back if I could. I'd make it never happen."

"I know you would."

"For some reason I thought I couldn't really hurt you."

She had stopped crying. I looked out the window at the tree branches hung low with snow. It didn't seem I had to say anything.

"I don't know why I thought I couldn't hurt you," she said. "Of course I can hurt you."

"I forgive you."

Her back was still toward me. Outside, a few snowflakes drifted up in the air.

"You shouldn't forgive me."

"Why not?"

"Or not so fast, at least. You should hate me."

"I don't hate you," I said. "It's something you did. It's like running over an animal. It's passed."

The night he died, Anne stayed awake with me in bed. "Tell me about him," she said.

"What about?"

"Stories. Tell me what it was like growing up, things you did together."

"We didn't do that much," I said. "I caddied for him. He taught me things about golf."

That night I never went to sleep. Lorraine was at a friend's apartment and we were alone in my father's empty house, but we pulled out the sheets anyway, and the two wool blankets, and we lay on the fold-out sofa in the den. I told stories about my father until I couldn't think of any more, and then I talked about my mother until Anne fell asleep.

In the middle of the night I got up and went into the living room. Through the glass I could see lights across the water, the bridges, Belvedere and San Francisco, ships. It was clear outside, and when I walked out to the cement carport the sky was lit with stars. The breeze moved inside my nightclothes. Next to the garage the Lincoln stood half lit in the porch floodlight. I opened the door and got in. The seats were red leather and smelled of limes and cigarettes. I rolled down the window and took the key from the glove compartment. I thought of writing a note for Anne, but didn't. Instead I coasted down the driveway in neutral and didn't close the door or turn on the lights until the bottom of the hill, or start the engine until I had swung around the corner, so that the house was out of sight and the brine smell of the marina was coming through the open windows of the car. The pistons were almost silent.

I felt urgent, though I had no route in mind. I ran one stop sign, then one red light, and when I reached the ramp onto Highway 101, I squeezed the accelerator and felt the surge of the fuel-injected, computer-sparked V-8. The dash lights glowed. I drove south and crossed over the Golden Gate Bridge at seventy miles an hour, its suspension cables swaying in the wind and the span rocking slowly, ocean to bay. The lanes were narrow. Reflectors zinged when the wheels strayed. If Anne woke, she might come out to the living room and then check for me outside. A light rain began to fall. Drops wet my knees, splattered my cheek. I kept the window open and turned on the radio; the car filled up with wind and music. Brass sounds. Trumpets. Sounds that filled my heart.

The Lincoln drove like a dream. South of San Francisco the road opened up, and in the gulley of a shallow hill I took it up over a hundred. The arrow nosed rightward in the dash. Shapes flattened out. "Dad," I said. The wind sounds changed pitch. I said, "The year of getting to know us." Signposts and power poles were flying by. Only a few cars were on the road, and most moved over before I arrived. In the mirror I could see the faces as I passed. I went through San Mateo, Pacifica, Redwood City, until, underneath a concrete overpass, the radio began pulling in static and I realized that I might die at this speed. I slowed down. At seventy drizzle wandered in the windows again. At fifty-five the scenery stopped moving. In Menlo Park I got off the freeway.

It was dark still, and off the interstate I found myself on a road without streetlights. It entered the center of town and then left again, curving up into shallow hills. The houses were large on either side. They were spaced far apart, three and four stories tall, with white shutters or ornament work that shone in the perimeter of the Lincoln's headlamps. The yards were large, dotted with eucalyptus and laurel. Here and there a light was on. Sometimes I saw faces: someone on an upstairs balcony; a man inside the breakfast room, awake at this hour, peering through the glass to see what car could be passing. I drove slowly, and when I came to a high school with its low buildings and long athletic field I pulled over and stopped.

The drizzle had become mist. I left the headlights on and got out and stood on the grass. I thought, "This is the night your father has passed." I looked up at the lightening sky. I said it, "This is the night your father has passed," but I didn't feel what I thought I would. Just the wind on my throat, the chill of the morning. A pickup drove by and flashed its lights at me on the lawn. Then I went to the trunk of the Lincoln, because this was what my father would have done, and I got out the golf bag. It was heavier than I remembered, and the leather was stiff in the cool air. On the damp sod I set up: dimpled white ball, yellow tee. My father would have swung, would have hit drives the length of the football field, high irons that disappeared into the gray sky, but as I stood there I didn't even take the clubs out of the bag. Instead I imagined his stance. I pictured the even weight, the deliberate grip, and after I had stood there for a few moments, I picked up the ball and tee, replaced them in the bag, and drove home to my wife.

The year I was sixteen we never made it to the American Southwest. My mother bought maps anyway, and planned our trip, talking to me about it at night in the dark, taking us in her mind across the Colorado River at the California border, where the water was opal green, into Arizona and along the stretch of desert highway to New Mexico. There, she said, the canyons were a mile deep. The road was lined with sagebrush and a type of cactus, jumping cholla, that launched its spines. Above the desert, where a man could die of dehydration in an afternoon and a morning, the peaks of the Rocky Mountains turned blue with sun and ice.

We didn't ever go. Every weekend my father played golf, and at last, in August, my parents agreed to a compromise. One Sunday morning, before I started the eleventh grade, we drove north in the Lincoln to a state park along the ocean. Above the shore the cliffs were planted with ice plant to resist erosion. Pelicans soared in the thermal currents. My mother had made chicken sandwiches, which we ate on the beach, and after lunch, while I looked at the crabs and swaying fronds in the tide pools, my parents walked to the base of the cliffs. I watched their progress on the shallow dunes. Once when I looked, my father was holding her in his arms and they were kissing.

She bent backward in his hands. I looked into the tide pool where, on the surface, the blue sky, the clouds, the reddish cliffs, were shining. Below them rock crabs scurried between submerged stones. The afternoon my father found me in the trunk, he introduced me to the woman in the backseat. Her name was Christine. She smelled of perfume. The gravel drive where we had parked was behind a warehouse, and after we shook hands through the open window of the car, she got out and went inside. It was low and long, and the metal door slammed behind her. On the drive home, wind blowing all around us in the car, my father and I didn't say much. I watched his hands on the steering wheel. They were big and red-knuckled, the hands of a butcher or a carpenter, and I tried to imagine them on the bend of Christine's back.

Later that afternoon on the beach, while my mother walked along the shore, my father and I climbed a steep trail up the cliffs. From above, where we stood in the carpet of ice plant, we could see the hue of the Pacific change to a more translucent blue—the drop-off and the outline of the shoal where the breakers rose. I tried to see what my father was seeing as he gazed out over the water. He picked up a rock and tossed it over the cliff. "You know," he said without looking at me, "you could be all right on the course." We approached the edge of the palisade, where the ice plant thinned into eroded cuts of sand. "Listen," he said. "We're here on this trip so we can get to know each other a little bit." A hundred yards below us waves broke on the rocks. He lowered his voice. "But I'm not sure about that. Anyway, you don't *have* to get to know me. You know why?"

"Why?" I asked.

"You don't have to get to know me," he said, "because one day you're going to grow up and then you're going to *be* me." He looked at me and then out over the water. "So what I'm going to do is teach you how to hit." He picked up a long stick and put it in my hand. Then he showed me the backswing. "You've got to know one thing to drive a golf ball," he told me, "and that's that the club is part of you." He stood behind me and showed me how to keep the left arm still. "The club is your hand," he said. "It's your bone. It's your whole arm and your skeleton and your heart." Below us on the beach I could see my mother walking the waterline. We took cut after cut, and he taught me to visualize the impact, to sense it. He told me to whittle down the point of energy so that the ball would fly. When I swung he held my head in position. "Don't just watch," he said. *"See."* I looked. The ice plant was watery-looking and fat, and at the edge of my vision I could see the tips of my father's shoes. I was sixteen years old and waiting for the next thing he would tell me.

THE
VALLEY
OF
SIN

·

LEE K. ABBOTT

Neither Deming's best golfer, nor its worst, Mr. Dillon Ripley was, as the six thousand of us in these deserts now realize, its most ardent, having taken to the sport as those in the big world we read about have taken to drink or narcotics. Almost daily, you'd see him on the practice tee—elbows, knees and rump in riot—his fat man's swing a torment of expectation and gloom. With him would be Ivy Martin, our resident professional, and together—hip to hip, faces shaded against the fierce sunlight we're famous for, hair flying in the breezes—they'd stare down the fairway, as if out there, waiting as destiny is said to wait, stood not riches or happiness, but Ripley himself, slender and tanned and strong as iron—a hero wise and blessed as those from Homer himself.

On the weekends, noon to dusk, he'd be accompanied by his wife, Jimmie. He had bought her the spiked shoes and loose cardigans of the linkster, and he tried teaching her, as he was being taught, how to grip the club, what "break" was, and what enchantments came to mind when the ball soared, as it ought, or plopped into the cup on its last revolution. Golf, he told her, was bliss and bane. Holding her by the shoulders, as earnest about this as others are about religion, he would say that golf was like love itself. He used language like *passion* and *weal.* He mentioned old terms for the equipment: mashie, niblick, spoon. He knew everything about the game, its lore and minutia, and his weekday playing partners—Watts Gunn, Phinizy Spalding and Poot Taylor—had often heard him remark that one day now, when he'd squared his affairs at the Farmers and Merchants Bank, where he was a vice president (loan dept.), he, Jimmie and the four children would vacation in Scotland, specifically near the Old Course at St. Andrews, home of the Royal and Ancient Golf Club. He imagined himself, he told them, among the ridges and hillocks, cheerful at the sight of meadow grasses and sheltered dunes, knolls and hollows and whins as dear to him as money is to some. So profound was his affection for the spot that once, at the fourteenth tee, already set over his ball, scarcely any traffic at all on the gravel service road which paralleled the fairway, he announced—a week before Jimmie ran off with Ivy Martin—that he knew what best tested the kind we are: it was not death or travail or such woe as you find in newspapers; it was the hazards of unmown fescue and bent grass, or a sand wedge misplayed from a bunker known as The Valley of Sin.

It happened in May, the Sunday before Armed Forces Day. We suspect that Dillon was too involved in his forthcoming round to notice that Jimmie—erect as a hat model, brighter in the eye and cheek, leggier—seemed nervous or rather too beautiful that morning. Dressed in his so-called Cuban outfit (red NuTonics, pink slacks, black polka-dot shirt), he felt superior. Eating as if starved, he told his oldest boy, the teenager Brad, that today was an anniversary of sorts: On this day in 508 (A.D.), Dillon claimed, King Clovis had established Paris, formerly Lutetia, as the Frankish capital, following his vanquishing of the Visigoths. "So what?" the boy grumbled. There was evidence—Dillon had the boy by the ears now, smiling like a clown—that golf (which may have been suggested by the Dutch game *kolven)* was already being played in Scotland. "Oh," the boy said, "great." To the youngest girl, Marcia, Dillon described the ancient burns and thickets that were extant when our forebears—smaller, hairier, ruder—ruled a world flat as a cookie sheet. "Jeez, Dad," she said, shaking her head, "You know some awful dumb stuff."

Looking as if he'd slept for a century, Dillon arrived at the first tee before noon. He did not use a cart, instead hiring as his caddy Tommy Steward, a Wildcat football player thought to be the most wayward AA right tackle in Luna County, New Mexico; and through the front nine, which he played well if not stylishly, Mr. Dillon Ripley had the stride of a general, as well as the amused expression of a citizen worth seventy thousand dollars a year. "I feel young," he told Phinizy Spalding. He recounted an anecdote about his Lambda Chi days at SMU, a boozy, melancholy escapade about women embarrassing enough to be true; then, at lunch in the clubhouse, he revealed that this July he and the family would be visiting the British Open. He mentioned Watson, Nicklaus and Trevino, plus such legends as Old Tom Morris and the vaunted Harry Vardon. He mentioned Strath Bunker and Hill Bunker—the Scylla and Charybdis of the 172-yard par-three eleventh. And, after buying them all (including Tommy Steward) a Bloody Mary, he marched his foursome to the tenth hole, quoting Sir Guy Campbell on "the thick, close-growing, hard-wearing sward that is such a feature of true links turf wherever it is found."

Hard for us it is to know our fate—or Grace or, for that matter, our Doom—when it appears. For some, it has a hue; for others, a sound. For Dillon Ripley, as for most, it had a face and a name and it swept by him—on the fourteenth fairway, of course—at upwards of forty miles per hour, a silver '79 Volvo sedan. "Hey," Tommy Steward said, waving his chunky tackle's fist, "ain't that Ivy?" Yonder, gaining speed, its horn whining, the car flew toward them, dust boiling up in the wake. Dillon, his wood balanced against his leg, was washing his Maxfli, watching the Volvo swerve. Light glinted from the windshield like sparks. It looked as if, though you couldn't be sure, there were two people inside, the passenger lifeless as sculpture, the other thrashing to and fro as if overcome with ecstasy. For a time, Dillon's foursome had a single organ of understanding: they looked and shrugged and opened their hands to say that, well, what'd you expect? This was old Ivy Martin, Mr. Cut-up. Tommy said, "Is he drunk or what?" Poot Taylor recalls he had no thoughts at all, just the notion, felt as ice in the heart, that something—our planet, its moon, the hithermost stars—was awry. Watts Gunn believed he smelled rain in the west, where clouds had built into a pavilion high as heaven, and he wondered if the windows in his Monte Carlo were closed. Next to Dillon, Phinizy Spalding, a fast driver himself, was thinking of chaos and a question came to mind regarding babble and sloth. He saw, as well, a pall falling between him and the future. And then, as the Volvo came abreast, horn blaring, throwing up road filth behind, Tommy Steward hollered, "Hey, Mr. Ripley, ain't that your—?" Zooming past, looking headlong, was Jimmie, indifferent as truth, her shoulders pearly, luminous and bare. "Lordy," Tommy said, aghast, "she's naked!" There was a noise, choked but awful as thunder, and when our linksters turned around, stricken Dillon was in collapse, his lips a disheartening shade of blue.

After three weeks in the Mimbres Valley Hospital, his heart

mended with diet and drugs, Dillon Ripley returned home. His instructions from Dr. Weems said to avoid difficult physical activity. No lifting, for example. Walking was fine. But no golf. Not yet. A housekeeper, Mrs. Fernandez, who lived on Iron Street, had been hired to tend to the children; and, though few saw him, the rumor was that Mr. Ripley was well, reading his chief diversion, not mournful. Many spouses, we were learning, had been abandoned by their mates and Mr. Ripley was being as stalwart about his condition as, say, the fish is about its. Life was a jungle, it was said in the clubhouse, and we, its upright creatures, were no more noble or charmed than thinking worm or sentient mud. Hereabouts, in fact, heartache was compared to history; both had to do with time and inevitable sadness. Many people, moreover, accepted the view offered by Dr. Tippit at St. Luke's Presbyterian—a view which held that ours was a fallen orb, burdensome indeed, but bound to improve, to yield itself to the wish of an enlightened master. Yesterday, it was argued, man was only an ape; today he was more upstanding, to be sure, but hardly far enough from the trees he'd sprung from.

That winter, Dillon Ripley attended the Christmas and New Year's parties at the club, turning a cha-cha-cha with Millie Gunn and doing a modified Twist with Grace Spalding. He looked pale, thinner by thirty-five pounds, and everyone wondered when we'd again see him at the practice tee, his spine stiff as a sentry's, his powerful and collected gaze fixed on the horizon. "Soon, soon," he'd answer. Though no one said as much, people were still keenly interested in Jimmie and Ivy. Poot Taylor, for example, had heard they lived in Florida, Ivy trying to qualify for his A card so he could compete on the satellite tour. Dr. Weems understood they were in Honduras, Ivy in a field which included all manner of felon and vagabond duffer. Watts Gunn thought they had fled to Cincinnati, as Jimmie supposedly had a younger sister there. If Dillon knew, he wasn't saying. Instead, he danced—the Cleveland Chicken, the rhumba, a naughty knee-knocking mambo Jackie Gleason would have envied—and proposed a champagne toast to what his daddy had called fortune: "Which, as I understand it," he began, smiling at us whom he had known all his life, "is part pluck, part guile and part sense of humor. Happy New Year!"

In February, the month Dillon put his house on the market, Tito Garza, who handled the night watering at the club, found the flagsticks on the tenth and eleventh holes twisted into impossible shapes—one, it was said, an idea of horror made steel, the other a loop a drunk might make falling down—the nylon flags themselves scorched. We had the sense, felt like an icy current of air, that something parlous—of claw and cold blood, perhaps—had invaded our course, its vast mind consumed by a single thought of rage.

Three weeks later, we Sunday linksters began finding notecards stuffed in the cups on several holes on the backside. Each card was margin to margin with handwriting so fine and peculiar it looked like an arrangement of human bones or like the crewelwork practiced by a lost race of tiny, nearly invisible people. Under the magnifying glass Mr. R. L. Crum kept in the men's locker, you could tell the writing was either complex as knowledge itself or witless as mumbo-jumbo. THE WORLD IS ALMOST ROTTEN, read one. Another: WE ARE A BREED IN NEED OF FASTING AND PRAYER. On a third: PORPOZEC CIEBIE NIE PROSZE DORZANIN. His face blotchy with passion, Abel Alwoody, who'd been to Vietnam, insisted it was all gook to him and called forth for us a vision composed of fire and ash. Judge Sanders suggested it was a prank, probably from the Motley brothers, whose shed adjacent to the twelfth hole he had recently condemned. "Hold on a second," Garland Steeples said. The air in that locker was close, heavy as wool. Steeples was the high school counselor and it was clear he was bringing to our mystery his professional training in the human arts of hope and fear. He pointed to several words—*want, venery, vice*—and a phrase, *the downward arc of time.* His face, particularly around the eyes, was dark as winter. It was a moment to which the word ruin might apply. "What I see is this," he began. He was speaking of misrule and bolsheviks when we began edging away.

Through April and May—a season glorious in our arid clime —there were no disturbances, other than several late night calls to Yogi Jones, the new pro, who felt he was listening either to a ghost or to a very arch infant. Then, the first week of summer, near midnight one Wednesday, when he was necking with Eve Spalding, Phinizy's daughter, on the fourteenth green, Tommy Steward, fuzzy-minded on red-dirt marijuana, thought he spied a figure, possibly human, darting amid the cottonwood trees. There was a new moon, pouring light down like milk, and the high wispy clouds that mean a wind is up from Mexico. While he held Eve, he spotted it again—loping like a low beast but wearing the togs of a sportsman—and his heart shot to his throat like a squirrel, all claws and climbing. Words came to mind: flank, cranium, haunch. "Eeeeeffff," he groaned. "Aaarrgghh." Even from a distance, the thing appeared murderous, a creature of carnage and outrage like those scale-heavy, horned, thick-shouldered figures he knew about from nightmare. In an instant, tumbling Eve aside, he was dashing in a dozen directions at once, shirttails flapping. "What's the matter?" Eve was saying, almost frightened herself. She had her blouse open, her breasts—like Jimmie's, months earlier—firm and white. Tommy sputtered: "Naaaaaa, naaaaa." His arms, as if jointless, whipped the air. He felt he was breathing sand. A thousand ideas came to him, none concerning humans. And then, in a way more swift than flight itself, the thing, wretched as a savage, leaped in front of him, not ten giant steps away. It was in skins, yes, and dirty as orphans you see in French movies. One fist was shaking overhead and in the other, like a cudgel, hung a golf club heavy with sod. "Goddamn," Tommy was yelling, "Jesus H. Christ!"

There was noise everywhere—roars wrathful and morbid, both. The ground had begun to tilt and Tommy, dry-mouthed and trembling as if frozen, felt he was staring at the hindmost of our nature, its blind pink eyes, its teeth wet as a dog's. Then, dragging and pushing and carrying Eve, Tommy was gone, running elsewhere—anywhere!—in a fury, too addled to scream.

That month, until too bored to continue, Poot Taylor and Watts Gunn, riding in an electric golf cart, patroled the Country Club at night, each armed with a .22. The night the lookout ended, someone sneaked onto the ninth green and, using a shovel (later found in a mesquite bush), dug several pits, the deepest in that spot from which the great Billy Newell had once sunk a chip for the Invitational championship. In the morning, signs were discovered. They had themes of heartwork and dealt with such concepts as travesty and blight. PRAY AND YOUR LIFE WILL BE BETTER, one read. WE ARE BASE, another said, AND NOTHING CAN BE DONE.

In August, Dillon Ripley sold his house and moved his family twenty miles farther south in the desert, to Hatchia, where, as we understand it, there is no sport at all save hunting and where the winds, infernal and constant, blow as if from a land whose lord is dark and always angry.

CADDIES'
DAY

·

JEANNE SCHINTO

The bottle is sticky around the spout. Do not pick it up by its spout. Keep your hands far away from the spout. A caddy's mouth has germs.

Two brown ants run around the rim of it. The caddy who threw it left a sip. Maybe the golfer was calling him to come on along. So he flung it beyond the caddy path, and it would have broken if he hit a rock. Behind those rocks caddies hide their bicycles. Caddies steal from one another.

I don't often walk along this path during the day. I come out here after supper. The golf course is empty of everyone then, but not sounds: the sprinklers tick around. And I take the flag out of its hole and march and sing. Sometimes I drop the flag and run because the darkness falls so soon. I run and climb the chain-link fence behind our house without cutting open my hand. My sneaker toes fit into the fence holes exactly. In a year or two they'll be too big. I do not tear open my hand, because I'm careful.

My mother thinks I am walking home the other way. On the road. I usually do. But today I have dirty paw prints down the front of my new dress, and I'm sneaking. I'd like to sneak into the house the cellar way so my mother won't see me and scream. Maybe I can take my dress off outside and bury it under the leaf pile in the corner of the backyard. If my mother says why don't you wear that little party dress Aunt Rhoda gave you anymore, I'll say I will next time, next time. And then I'll think of it rotting. And if she looks for it in my bedroom closet and doesn't find it and asks me where it is, I will say I don't know, it's not in there? It's not? And I'll start to look for it too.

The path is dusty, the color of a dog. The dust rises up. Over the bunker, on the green, the grass is short. Short as hair. As short as the milkman's. He told my mother: I don't even have to comb it when I get out of bed in the morning. Lucky duck! Sometimes the milkman pinches my cheek. It hurts. I give him a look. Then my mother gives me a slap. What'sa matter? He's saying he likes you.

On the green, a golfer is down on his knees, with his cheek to the grass. He's looking to see which way it's growing. My father said. He doesn't play golf, but he knows the greens-keeper, Mike, and Mike knows plenty. He runs the machines and he's very tall and dark, with a smile like an open tractor shovel. He talks to policemen all the time, and in summer, he has a crew of boys working for him. Members' sons, my father says, and this makes him shake his head and look sorry.

Change falls from the golfer's pocket. Nobody sees it but

me. Not the golfer and not the other three with him. If the golfers had caddies, the caddies would see, but they have carts instead. And after they are going up the fairway, I scramble over the bunker. I pick up the coins—there are three—quarters, so big and round and silver. They looked funny lying on the grass. After the coins are in my pocket, the men look back and see me and wag their fingers. These are the two of them who are walking. The other two have driven the carts far up the fairway. And they say no, you better not play here, little girl. A ball could come and knock you on the head. Dangerous. Someone will hurt you, little girl. And don't be walking on that green.

Back on the path, I think, that's what they always say, and a ball hasn't hit me yet. I'd like to see them try and hit me with such a tiny ball. I'd go up on the fairway and stand. And I'd bet them, and I'd win. If I saw the ball coming close, I would duck, and they wouldn't see me. They would be too far away. And God would forgive me. He wouldn't want me to be killed. He loves me and watches out for me and knows the number of hairs on my head. He sees everything. And if I pulled one out by the roots? He'd see, even if he was busy. Even if he was busy saving someone from drowning. I would not be killed. Heaven is scary.

I see the caddy shed. From here it looks like a shoebox. And I hear the caddies' voices. They are swearing, but do not be afraid.

I'm not afraid, but I stop to read each tree. They are carved deep with initials, names, and hearts with arrows through them. My mother says that will kill the poor trees, gouging out bark with knives, and where do those boys get knives anyway? My father says the letters will grow, stretch right along with the bark. I'd like to see that. And I'd like to carve my initials here, but I don't have a knife. Some night after supper, I'll take one from the drawer in the kitchen.

The caddies' voices get louder as I walk along. It sounds like they are having a fight. Maybe they won't see me, and I'll sneak past them like a ghost. They'll be too busy spitting, shouting, shoving each other. On Caddies' Day they play golf themselves, and I hide behind the bunker and watch. They have fights, spit their words, raise their clubs. In the fall the bunkers burn. I used to think the caddies did it, and I cried. Our house would be burned. Then I saw Mike, the greens-keeper, with his torch. Fires burn black right to the path.

Not all of the caddies are young. Some of them are men my father's age, but they do not look like him. They look like his friends, the ones my mother says are vulgar. I do not see them yet. They are on the other side of the caddy shed, but I can hear them and I can picture them. They sit on two long wooden benches, their backs up against the shed. Unless they are playing cards, and then the benches face each other. Their shirts have wet marks under the arms. Hair curls around their ears. They smoke, hold their cigarettes between their teeth when they have to throw a card down. Sometimes they take the cigarettes from their mouths and call out to me. Comeer, little girlie. Sit on my lap, little girl. Other times they don't see me at all, and I walk the rest of the way home with my heart beating right out through my shirt.

And today? I think I will be safe! I will crawl past them unseen! They are all standing, shaking their fists, shouting, pointing to the benches. Both of the benches have been dragged out from their places up against the shed. One of the benches has been kicked over, legs up. Yes, I think, I will be safe! And I stride along. But then something happens.

A boy holding a card between his fingers swaggers to the center of the crowd. He wears a black T-shirt and his pants are too short and a curl of hair hangs in his eyes. He holds the card up, shows it, each side, as if it's a moth he's caught. He flicks it, watches it flutter down, turns and walks away.

Half of the caddies follow him, walking backward and swearing at the others, who stay behind. Passing the fallen bench, they lift it high onto their shoulders. They walk with it to the carved trees and are about to set it down. But then the boy in the black T-shirt sees me.

He nudges the others, lifts his chin, looks behind him, smiles. I smile, too, a little. Then he takes the bench up himself, lifts it over his head, walks to the path with it, and sets it down across it.

The fence runs the length of the path. It runs all around the golf course. I could climb it right here and then walk home on the road. I would go in the kitchen doorway, and my mother would see my dirty dress, and I don't care. But the caddies all are watching me. They would watch me climb. They would see my underpants. They would see if I fell. And if I cut my hand on the twists of wire at the top of the fence? I wouldn't want to run to them and ask them to make it stop bleeding.

Besides, on the road there are dogs I'm afraid of. They are not like the dog at the party. One of them bit me, a tiny dog, no bigger than a cat. But its teeth were like a rat's. It was a Chihuahua. My mother told me a dog can smell fear, and I must have had the smell on me that day. My father said next time give it a good kick in the teeth. Should I? A dog that small. God wouldn't like it. One of his creatures. They all have their purpose. What should I do?

I could go around them on the other side, on the golf course grass. The golfers would scream, but I would explain. They would give me time. Then they would come back to the caddy shed and scream at the caddies. I've seen them scream at them before. Men with red faces, red pants, red shirts, potbellies like they're expecting. White belts around them, white shoes, little hats. My father calls them fairies. I ask him what do you mean? He laughs. My mother makes a smirk. Sometimes the golfers hit the caddies. Well, I saw that once. And when it rains, a storm, golfers don't share their umbrellas with the caddies. The golfer takes the bag and walks ahead and the caddy walks behind—or runs. Or stands under a tree. My father says that's one way to get his hair curled but good when the lightning strikes him. I watch them shivering under the trees. No wonder caddies are so mean.

One of them comes up to me. His shirt is striped, his pants cuffs drag, he is holding a bottle. His palm is flat to the bottom of it, one finger stops up the spout, and he tips the bottle sideways and watches the bright red soda slosh. I watch it too, and then I see there is something else inside. It is filled with tiny brown ants riding on the surface of the red. They make a ship inside the bottle, inch-high, climbing over one another. Below, some have sunken into the red and are drowning.

I look up into the caddy's sweaty face. He is as tall as a tree and smiling. One of his front teeth is chipped. All of his teeth are yellow and must have germs, but you can't see them. Germs are invisible. He says, "Hey, girlie, you gotta pay the toll," and he turns and points his chin back over his shoulder at the other caddies on the bench across the path. The one in the black T-shirt gets up and starts coming toward me. "Don't walk backwards," he says to me. "You might trip over something. A tree root. See those roots behind you?" He laughs and the one with the ants in the bottle laughs too.

And then I laugh. I cannot help it. I cannot stop the laugh. I try to make my eyes look mad, but they are laughing too. Sometimes when my father's friends tell a joke my mother tries to frown, but I can see her smiling, laughing behind her frown. Once, I was kissing my doll and I could not stop it either.

I feel a tickle. The caddy in the black T-shirt is tickling my neck. Then he tries to brush the dirt from the front of my dress. And he straightens my bow. If he were my father or my mother or my aunt, he would tell me to twirl and show him how far the skirt goes out. Well, that was when I was smaller. But he doesn't ask me to twirl. He is talking, like the other one did, about the pay toll ahead.

3 0 9

He asks me if I have any money while the other caddies from the bench gather around. I tell him no with a shrug. I shrug and shrug to each question he asks, because that eases the tickle. His hand is still tickling my neck.

He asks me, "What are you doing walking down the caddy path anyway? This is for caddies only. Didn't you know that? And nobody should leave the house without at least a couple pieces of change. Didn't your mother even give you a dime for a phone call in case you got lost? And how'd you get your dress front all dirty?"

Sweat.

I sweat from my upper lip, from my forehead, my chest. I like to feel the first sweat of summer. It happened in the schoolyard this year. I was playing jump rope: high-water, low. A girl everyone hates was holding the rope, and she tripped me, and everyone sneered at that girl and came to see if I was all right. With all of them standing around me in a circle, I started to cry. I was not hurt very badly, no blood, but I knew they wanted me to cry. I knew. They wanted to see me hurt good enough to cry so they could make the other girl scared, feel bad, worry that we would tell the teacher. And we did. And I cried some more when she came over. I wonder if I should cry now. Wonder if that is what the caddies want me to do.

"Hey, girlie, how 'bout a little kiss?"

I do not look into their faces. I look at their knees spread wide. One of them has his hands out.

After supper my father puts his hand palm up on the table, and I'm supposed to put my hand inside it. And I do. This is an old game. I'm too old now. But he makes me play. And I do. And he says, "How much do you love me?" And I say, "Five hundred." "How much?" He squeezes my hand. "A thousand." "How much?" "Ten thousand!" "How much?" "A million!" "That's better," he says. Then he lets go.

One of them puts a hand on my shoulder. It is heavy as an iron. I used to not be able to pick up my mother's iron. She used to tell me to stay away from the board when she was ironing. Once, I was playing underneath it. That was my house. I was hiding. She was on the phone. When she walked back into the room and found me, she screamed.

They are whispering among themselves. Maybe I can walk away. My feet in my shoes are sweaty—they will squeak. But if my feet were bare they would make little footprints in the dust. And then the caddies would follow them right to the cellar door and up to my room.

Their voices are like low rumbles of thunder. I look up and watch the Adam's apple of the one with the bottle of ants. It looks as if it will soon burst through. It looks as if it hurts him. The hand on my shoulder is squeezing hard. It's the hand of the black T-shirt boy. Then it's lazy—resting, not holding. I start to walk away. Then I run. And a shout goes up. And everything changes.

My ankles hurt me. My nose hits their knees. I am upside down. They hold me by the ankles and laugh, thumbs pressed into my bones. Then money drops. Coins on the ground. They are dropping their money? No. It's the money I found on the green. I forgot about it.

"No money for the toll, huh? What's this? What's this?"

Someone picks up the coins. Snaps my underpants. I try to cover them with my dress. Someone takes my hands.

Sometimes I walk around my room with a mirror under my eyes. Everything is upside down. And I walk in the world upside down. I like to do this best when my room is messy and my mother says clean it up, it's a pigsty, clean it up now! And I take the mirror and instantly it's clean! The ceiling-floor so white and neat makes my room instantly picked up! I want my mother to look into the mirror with me, but she won't. I know without asking. Besides, there's only room for one pair of eyes at a time.

I want to cry. Will my mother hear me? I don't want my father to see. He would come and kill them with steak knives from the kitchen drawer. I would stand behind him and plead: they don't mean any harm. Passing me from one to the other. It's a game. They are laughing. Hear them laugh! My ankles hurt, and my nose. But they don't know it. They think I like it. I am laughing, too. Sometimes when you squeeze my hand, it hurts, and I say nothing. I laugh. And you, mother, nod, and say that's a good girl, and you laugh. Look at their faces! What do you think? Maybe they're saying they like me.

Then they put me down.

My feet feel funny on the ground. I'm dizzy and do not walk away. They are waiting, watching me to see what I will do next. They look a little afraid. That is funny, too. I think they think I'm going to do something back to them. What could it be?

The boy in the black T-shirt whispers something to the one with the ants in the bottle and gives him a smack on the shoulder to send him on his way. The ant boy throws his bottle down—it doesn't break; it rolls—and he goes back to the caddy shed, hands in his pockets, head down. The rest of the caddies are all around me, watching and waiting still. There is an opening in the circle. I could walk out of it, but I don't—even though I know that they wouldn't stop me if I tried.

When the ant boy returns, he has a new bottle of soda. He hands it to the black T-shirt boy, who hands it to me. It's orange. My favorite. How did he know? The bottle is icy and clean. I want to put it to my cheek, but they are waiting for me to take a sip.

I take a small one. The black T-shirt boy says, "You're okay, right, girlie? Right?" And he's frowning, and I'm scared again, but I know what to do. I nod. And all of the caddies smile. And I smile, too, and sip again.

Two of the caddies sit down on the bench and start to deal the cards. A couple more go get sodas of their own and bring them back to the path and drink them. I am getting full, but I keep drinking, even when a golfer comes over. "Who's this? Who's this?" he asks. "What is going on?" But all of us keep drinking our sodas. We are celebrating something.

HUSTLE

·

LES STANDIFORD

Berto Garza shaded his eyes with his hand and peered into the brutal desert sun, striking a pose familiar to millions of golf fans around the world. He wasn't thinking about his image, though. He was trying to find a fairway out there in the mess that was supposed to be a golf course. Instead of a rolling expanse of green, all he saw was a shimmering expanse of sand and shallow arroyos, speckled with mesquite, spiny ocotillo, and greasewood. There was a hawk cruising a late-afternoon updraft, or maybe it was a buzzard. There was a city somewhere around, but they were miles outside it.

"Over there, man!" It was the urgent whisper of Horace at his ear. His massive longtime caddy steered him a quarter turn away from the sun and pointed at a thin ribbon of grass that curled between a dry stream bed falling away on one side, a sheer red bluff rising up on the other. They stood on an elevated tee. It was a two-hundred-yard carry over the intervening barranca.

"Shoo," Berto shook his head. "Where do the members play from, Juarez?"

There was a weak chuckle from the smallish gallery. His playing partners, three other aging pros, nodded impatiently, ready for him to hit. Garza's agent had convinced him to sign on for this gig, some bullshit promotion for a new development. A morning clinic for the members, an afternoon match. Five thousand apiece and a five thousand bonus for the medalist, if the winning score was under par. That's how far he'd slid, playing for what used to be pocket change, and the money already spent.

Furthermore, he could forget the bonus check. They all could, except for Sorry Williams, who'd held it to one under this far.

Even though it was December, the temperature was over ninety. A tall, gaunt man with papery skin stretched tight over his cheekbones called out from the gallery: "We like a true test of golf here, Mr. Garza."

Garza took his stance. "Yeah? Well, the last time I covered ground like this, the Immigration Man was chasing me." He went on talking right through his backswing. "I'm glad this is eighteen. I had just about all the fun I can stand." He felt his hips cutting in late, didn't have to look to know where the shot was headed.

"Fucking A," Horace grumbled.

Berto glanced up at the ball, which caromed off the hard tongue of fairway, slicing into some scrub up against the cliff. The caddy stalked off, down the torturous incline of the tee.

The gallery had scurried on, filtering through the badlands like a herd of rabbits.

"Don't worry about it, hoss," Berto said, catching up with him. "We're playin' for pay today."

"Ain't worried," Horace said. "Except about rattlesnakes." He glanced balefully at the rocky landscape surrounding them.

Garza nodded. "You been wondering who'd ever come live in a place like this?"

Horace shook his head. "Have to be weird, that's all. Just take me to New Orleans."

"*Mañana,* hoss. *Mañana.*"

They'd crossed the narrow fairway and were kicking through the dusty brush, looking for his ball. Finally, Horace took his arm and pointed. Garza stared in disbelief. They'd found it, all right, impaled on a spiky cactus thorn.

"You wanta drop?" Horace asked.

"Get out of the way," Garza told him, and yanked a five iron from his bag.

Garza finished with a seventy-nine. His putt on eighteen lurched like a drunken frog toward the cup, a stub of cactus thorn digging into the grain with every revolution. Three to get on, three putts. The perfect ending to his day. Sorry Williams wasn't very happy either. His approach shot had flown the green and nailed the gaunt man who'd been heckling Garza right between the eyes. The guy was alive, but there'd been a lot of blood on the ball. Sorry, pale and shaking, gunched his chip and had forty feet of downhill, sidehill left, for par. Sayonara, five grand.

Garza was killing time in the deserted locker room, sucking on a Carta Blanca at a card table, waiting for the parking lot to clear. Sorry and the others had already cut out, Garza waving them on. It was one narrow road in and out of the place, twenty miles of twisting two-lane. He wasn't anxious to join that line of traffic. He wondered how long it'd take the ambulance to get the death's-head heckler to the hospital. Well, he'd gotten his "test of golf," that was for sure.

There was the sound of someone clearing his throat, which in this case was more like a load of gravel being dumped down a metal chute. Garza looked up as Horace shambled down a row of lockers toward him, flashing a bill between his massive thumb and forefinger. He'd changed into his "casual" clothes, a black satin shirt with red amoebalike designs crawling over it, a pair of red polyester pants.

"You look good, Horace," Garza said.

Horace took it as a compliment, and nodded at the bill. "Man gave me fifty scoots, wants to talk to you," Horace said.

Garza stared at him. "What man? A reporter? I told them no reporters." The guy wanted to know about his divorce, about the falling out he'd had with the sporting goods company, about the jerk he'd punched out at the La-La Land Open. He sure didn't want to discuss his standing on the money list. Or maybe he did. It was his worst finish since he'd joined the tour, twenty-four years ago.

"Ain't no reporter," Horace said.

"How do you know?"

Horace shook his head. He'd left off explaining himself a long time ago. "You want to go out the other way?"

"Then you'd have to give this guy his money back."

"Shee-it," Horace said.

"Mr. Garza?" A voice carried down the row of lockers. Garza tried to get a look around Horace's bulk. Someone was coming toward them. Horace glanced over his shoulder.

"I told you, wait outside," the caddy rumbled.

Garza could see him now, a wiry, dark-skinned man in chinos and a faded polo shirt. He looked in his late twenties, but it was hard to be sure. Horace had been right about one thing, however. This was no reporter.

317

"It's okay, hoss. Man gave you some money, didn't he? Show him in." Horace looked unhappy but moved aside.

"What can we do for you, pardner?"

The man flashed Garza an appreciative smile. He approached the card table, turning a gimmee cap in his hand. *A trucker?*

Garza waved at a chair.

"Want me to sign your cap for you? What's your name?"

The man glanced down at his cap, then back at Garza, smiling again, but differently. He was amused.

"My name is Fly," he said, his voice surprising in its assurance. "I was thinking we might play some golf."

Horace bellowed. It sounded like someone had goosed a donkey. Garza shot his caddy a glance. This was an earnest kid. They didn't need to embarrass him.

"Hey, pardner, the clinic was this morning . . ." he began, but the kid cut him off.

"No, I don't need no clinic," he said. He reached into his pocket and tossed a wad of bills onto the table. There was a hundred on the top. Who could be sure about the rest?

"I read what you said about the tour, you know, about how nobody plays for their own money any more. About how real pressure's when you feel your own empty wallet in your pocket and you're putting eighteen with a triple press working." The kid shrugged. "So I thought I'd see if you really meant it."

"Look, asshole . . ." Horace was moving toward the kid.

"Leave him alone," Garza said. Horace gave him a disgusted look, but stopped.

Garza stared at the kid, who stared back, waiting. Garza knew the piece he was talking about. He'd been pissed after missing the cut at the Greater Hartford and mouthed off to a reporter who'd been trailing him around. GARZA BLASTS COLLEGE BOY SYNDROME, the resulting headline read. Made him a *lot* of friends. And brought him this one. "Fly." *Mosca.* A bro' from the barrio. Garza grinned. It was the sort of thing he might have done, twenty-five years ago.

"So you want to shoot some golf, huh? When did you have in mind?"

The kid juked his head toward the high windows of the locker room where the last sun still burned golden. "There's nine out there you didn't see. We could work in three of them, easy."

"Nine I didn't see?" Garza glanced at Horace, who shrugged. "They as much fun as the eighteen I did?"

The kid dismissed the question with a little twist of his lips, and nodded at the wad of bills. "Five hundred a hole. All right with you?"

Garza laughed then. "Only if Horace will fade me," he said, and stood up from the table.

The kid had a battered maintenance cart drawn up by the back entrance. "You take it," he said to Garza, hefting a tiny carry bag from the shallow bed which normally carried hoses, fertilizer, canisters of insecticide.

Garza looked at Horace, whose red pants were blinding in the setting sun. "We'll walk," Horace growled.

They followed the kid down a path that twisted through one of the million arroyos that crisscrossed this desert landscape. It looked as if it would need a lot of work before they'd be sending the members this way. There were potholes in the macadam, Johnson grass way out of control along the berm, no signs pointing the way.

"Can't wait to see *this*," Horace grumped. There were already twin patches of wet below his breastbone. "We ought to be on the way out of here."

"I know, hoss," Garza told him. "But what the hell, we ain't had a whole lot of fun lately."

"Um-hmm," Horace said, laboring up the far slope of the arroyo. The macadam had broken up entirely now and they followed the clatter of gravel the kid kicked up just ahead. "And furthermore, you don't even *have* five hundred dollars in your pocket."

"Why, Horace," Garza laughed. "I thought you were listening. That is the very point."

They came out of the brush-choked arroyo then and Horace stopped short. "Well, kiss my big fanny," he breathed. Garza stepped up behind him and saw what it was about. They had emerged onto a meticulously groomed tee box. It arrowed toward a rich swath of green fairway curling through the dusky hills below. There was a broad landing area about two hundred and thirty yards out with a slight dogleg back to the right. The green was a big one, slightly elevated, framed by huge white traps. Shadows fell across most of the green, but the flagstick still glittered silver in the sun.

"Made for my game," Garza said.

"Who built *this* part the course?" Horace asked rhetorically.

"It was part of Mexico, once," the kid told them. "Before the Rio shifted its banks." He pointed to a distant ribbon of water, miles to the south. "Old bottomland. It likes the grass."

Garza nodded. "It surely does." He glanced at the kid. Outside, with the sun lending relief to his features, he looked older. " 'Fly,' huh. You work here, or what?"

The kid shook his head. "A friend of mine knows the greenskeeper. He told me they'd been working this side up."

Horace grunted. "What you mean, working it up?"

"It was a country club when this was Mexico. Everything laid-out. All they had to do was irrigate, reseed. Now look."

"Way out here?" Horace marveled.

"It's pretty," Garza said, "but we're running out of light."

The kid nodded then and motioned Garza to the tee. Garza shrugged, took a three wood from Horace and faded a perfect shot to the neck of the landing area. The ball hopped once and sat up, twinkling like a white flower in the shadows far below.

Horace grunted his approval. "Not bad," the kid said. He

dropped an orange ball onto the carpet and pulled a battered iron from his bag. Garza glanced at Horace, who rolled his eyes. The kid took what seemed like an awkward, three-quarters backswing and moved down on the ball. There was an explosive sound, like a watermelon being broadsided with a baseball bat, and a blur of orange shot out from the tee. The ball soared high over the desert to the right of the fairway, then drew back left, still climbing as it cut the corner of the dogleg. It hit the upslope of the fairway, bounced right and came to rest no more than fifty yards from the pin.

"Used to be I could do that," Garza said, whistling softly.

"When?" Horace grunted.

Garza gave him a look. "Maybe you're getting tired of this line of work."

Horace shrugged. "I was looking for a job when I found this one." He hoisted Garza's bag and started down the slope toward the fairway.

Fly waited for Horace to pass, then fell in beside Garza. Garza gave him a nod in recognition of the shot and stole a glance at the clubs in the tiny bag: it was a mismatched set, full of nicks and dents.

"I hate to let go of a club, once I get to like it, know what I mean?"

Garza nodded. He'd put together a similar set once, when he was caddying, learning the game. One of the maintenance men at the municipal course in Brownsville had let him dive the irrigation canals, searching for clubs that had been deep-sixed in anger. That's where he found the putter he had used all the way through his first year on tour. It was a classic bull's-eye which he'd last seen when he was cleaning out the garage after Winnie split.

"Plenty of shots left in those sticks," Garza told him. Fly smiled his thanks. He seemed about to say something, when there was a crash just ahead.

Garza looked up to find Horace and his golf bag rolling

PERFECT LIES

down the steep incline between the tee box and the fairway. Clubs flew from the maw of the bag, bounding end over end down the hillside like they'd been give life. Horace yelped, cursed and finally dragged himself to a stop. By the time they reached him, he had risen to a sitting position and was holding one of his feet gingerly in his lap. He looked up at Garza and shook his head. "Turned it bad," he said. "Goddamn rattlesnake hole."

Garza glanced back up the slope. It seemed unblemished from where he was. "Let me see," Garza told him. He pulled down Horace's sock and grimaced involuntarily. The ankle was already swollen double its normal size.

"Well, that's that," he said, glancing up at Fly, who pursed his lips when he saw the knot on Horace's ankle.

"Yeah," the boy nodded. "Hell of a way to lose a bet, though."

Garza stared at him. "Wait a minute . . ."

"We said three holes, five hundred a hole. You want to quit now, it's okay with me, but you owe me fifteen hundred dollars."

Garza laughed. "You're dreaming, son."

Fly looked at him scornfully. "I never figured you for a chiseler."

Garza took a breath, measuring the kid. He was about his own size, not impressively built, but he *had* creamed that golf ball. The heckler he'd punched in L.A. had gone down like the drunk pig he was, but something told Garza it wouldn't be the case with Fly.

"I'm going to let that pass," he said finally. "My caddy's hurt himself and he needs help. You better take you and your golf game on down the road."

"Kick his ass," Horace muttered. Garza glanced down at his caddy. "Go on, play him," Horace said, glowering. "I'm all right. I'll wait right here for you."

Garza shook his head. "We don't need his money."

"The hell with his money," Horace said. "Ever was a guy needed his clock cleaned, it's this one."

Garza hesitated.

"Number three green's just the other side of that hill," Fly volunteered. "We'll finish up inside a half hour, come right back here. Your man'll be fine," he added. "If that's what you're really worried about."

Garza studied him for a moment, then turned back to Horace. "See what I mean," his caddy said.

Garza drew a deep breath, forcing himself to calm as he stood up. Fly took a step back, watching him carefully.

"Let's play golf," Garza said, and picked up his clubs.

Sorry Williams wouldn't have bothered. That's what Garza was thinking as he stood over his approach shot. In fact, no one he knew would be doing what he was doing right now, settling a dumb-ass score on the golf course. He had to be crazy. He ought to drop this and go after that maintenance cart, get him and Horace back to their rented car and move it on down the road. Tell Fly to go to small-claims court if he didn't like it.

He glanced up. The wiry kid was standing sixty yards on up the fairway by his own ball, waiting for Garza to swing. Garza had no doubts about the outcome of the match. He'd played them all: hustlers, fellow pros, businessmen with handicaps great and small. He'd played one-handed, on his knees, with one club, left-handed. In the dark. In the snow. With money in his pocket and without. The only constant was the outcome: he won.

He always won. Maybe it was on the last hole, on the press, or maybe it was knocking chip shots into a wastebasket off the asphalt of the parking lot, but always, he found a way to win. And he would beat this small-time hustler who wanted to say he'd played the great Berto Garza for his own money. Still, he didn't like the way it'd shaped up: it was mean-spirited, now, all the fun gone, and he cursed the whim that had moved him to go along with the kid's challenge in the first place.

He drew his club back, then, and swung. The ball flew low, as he intended it, and struck the front edge of the putting surface. It took one hop toward the flagstick, then checked up abruptly. Instead of bounding on toward the hole, it spun backward, trickling nearly to the apron of the green before it stopped. Garza cursed softly. The first green all day long to hold a shot.

He tossed his club back in the bag and looked back, just as Fly lofted a half-wedge shot toward the green. The shot was on line, but far too strong. *Drive for show, pitch and putt for dough,* Garza was thinking . . . when Fly's ball struck the flag. The ball caught in the fabric and whipped about the flagstick. It hung for a moment like a walnut shrouded in nylon, then dropped straight down into the cup.

Fly turned to see if he had witnessed it. Garza shook his head. "I guess you're one down," the kid called.

"I guess you're right," Garza said, and went to get his ball.

The second hole was a par three, with another elevated tee that looked down onto a small green surrounded by water. To a weekend golfer the sight would be dramatic as well as intimidating. To Garza, it was merely the place where he would set things even.

Fly motioned Garza to the tee, but he shook his head. "Your honor," he said.

He watched the kid toss a few wisps of dry grass into the air to test for wind. Winnie wouldn't find this strange, not at all. She always complained his lived his entire life on the golf course, and she was right. He really couldn't blame her for leaving. And he couldn't say he was altogether sorry she had gone. His schedule was certainly simplified.

Fly had selected a club and stood addressing his shot. He launched into his awkward swing and struck the ball just as a little gust of evening breeze swept over them. The ball rose up high against the blue shadow of the distant mountains and Garza saw with satisfaction that the shot would be well short, possibly in the water. He was already pulling his club from the bag, ready to put this hole to bed, when Fly's ball came down, striking one of the thick wooden pilings that surrounded the green with a loud crack.

The ball sprung high into the air, and for a moment, Garza lost perspective in the fading light. He thought the shot was going into the water, but instead it landed on the green, and began rolling toward the cup.

"*Go,* sweetheart!" Fly called. As if it heard him, the ball curled hard against the incline of the green, bore down on the cup, and came to rest against the stick. When the flag wavered in another gust of wind, the ball dropped out of sight.

"I don't believe it," Garza said.

"You owe me a thousand dollars," Fly said evenly.

Garza glanced back toward the flagstick where the ball had fallen, then back at the figure in khaki beside him. At this angle, his opponent was only a dark shadow against the evening sky. Garza felt eyes upon him, however, and a chill prickled his flesh as he remembered a tale of his youth about a devil who roamed the badlands in the shape of a man.

"Some luck," Garza said finally, his mouth dry.

"My mother, she said you make your own luck," Fly answered.

Garza turned to pull a club from his bag. "I still got my shot," he said.

"Be my guest," Fly said and stepped back to watch him pound it far past the pin.

It was nearly dark as they reached the tee box for the third hole. There was a hand-carved sign that bore a map of the par-five hole in mild relief: Garza ran his hand over the polished surface, feeling the undulations of the low hills, the traps, the smooth plane of the distant green. Unlike many such renderings he'd seen, this map bore no colors—it was more like sculpture than a golfer's aid.

"It's old!" came Fly's voice from the shadows behind him. "They found it in storage. There must have been one for every hole, but this is the only one that's left."

Garza ran his finger along a deep fissure that cut through the fairway.

"The Rio," Fly said. "It used to cut right through here. Can you imagine that?"

Garza glanced out over the landscape. The sky was purple over the distant mountains. Far to the east was a glow cast up from the city and a silver speck of light above it, probably an airliner setting down. He tried to imagine a river cutting the dusty landscape out there, but it was difficult. It would be the same river he had played in as a child, a muddy, shallow ribbon robbed of its force by a network of irrigation canals, useful mostly to slow down the illegals on their steady stream north.

"It was a wild river, then," Fly added, as if he'd read Garza's thoughts. "Played hell with this country."

Garza heard something strange in his voice and gave him a look. Fly shrugged. "So they tell me," he added, and bent to tee his ball.

This time Fly drew his club back in a smooth arc and swung effortlessly. The ball rose from the club with an explosive sound, low at first, then climbing abruptly as if a booster rocket had kicked in. For a moment, Garza would have sworn it was glowing as it raced across the dark sky.

He paused before he teed his own ball. "Maybe you're better than you look," he said. Fly turned and gave him a hint of a smile. Garza gave him a smile back. "So why don't we play this last hole for two thousand?"

Fly's smile broadened. "You're up," he said, nodding assent, and motioned Garza to the tee.

Garza struck his ball well, favoring the right side of the fairway. He would be thirty yards short of the kid's drive, but he was used to that. He'd never been a long hitter. He had relied on accuracy, a consistent putting stroke, and uncanny iron play to make his way. Where other players might be undone by weather or varying course conditions, Garza was unfazed. Rain or cold, knee-high rough or parched hard-pan, he played his steady game.

To Garza it was no mystery: as a boy, the only time he could get on the course was when the members were huddled in the clubhouse. And he loved the game. He had always loved it. How on earth could you complain about anything, especially the golf course, when you were out playing golf? Of course, his obsession had given Winnie plenty to complain about, but, as he had told her many times, she should have known what she was getting into. Besides, golf had bought her a lot of pretty dresses.

And still was, he thought, as he approached his ball. That was the hell of it. While he'd been struggling to keep his game together, she'd gone out and gotten herself a good lawyer. Instead of fighting her, he'd tried to squeeze more out of the sporting goods company when his endorsements contract came up for renewal. They'd stood fast, citing his recent, lackluster record.

Then some asshole had made the mistake of heckling him about the divorce as he strode to the eighteenth tee at Riviera. He was six over, sure to miss the cut, and well on the other side of the normalcy line. He took out two of the guy's teeth and put a major hurt on his happy-go-lucky image. The resulting lawsuit was still pending.

He was still trying to calculate what it was all costing him every month when he saw what had happened to his drive: the divot could have been carved from the turf with a pickaxe. The ball was nestled in this miniature canyon, resting against an inch-thick lip of turf. He'd be lucky to move it a hundred yards, if he could hit it at all.

He glanced across the fairway. Fly was still moving toward

his ball, which sat up on the pristine turf, glittering like an egg. He was positioned to reach the green in two. Garza was looking at three shots, minimum. He looked down at his ball, considering. One little flick of his toe, the old foot-mashie shot, and he'd be out of trouble. Hackers had run it on him, plenty of times. He'd never called them on it, because it didn't matter. They could throw it up the fairway if they wanted. But he'd never done anything like that himself. He'd never had to.

He drew a wood from his bag and edged his foot closer to the ball, keeping his eye on Fly, who still had his back turned. He could feel the broken edge of the turf at his toe. He felt himself moving forward, the tip of his shoe about to lever down, scoop the ball . . . and then he heard the voice.

"Olla!"

Garza whirled, jerking his foot away from the divot as if there were a snake coiled there. A dark-skinned boy, maybe ten, wearing jeans and the kind of striped T-shirt K-mart had been selling since it was Kresge's, stood in the nearby rough, watching him cautiously.

"Where'd you come from?" Garza said, his heart still pounding.

The boy turned and pointed out over the scrubby landscape. Garza thought he saw the tin roof of a shanty up a far-off draw. Maybe there was a thin column of smoke rising from a chimney. He couldn't be sure.

"I know who you are," the boy said softly.

"Yeah?" Garza said.

"Sure," the boy answered. "Everybody does."

Garza nodded. "That's TV for you."

"No," the boy said. "We don't have TV."

Garza paused. Another strange one. "How come you're out here in the dark, *muchacho?*"

"I pull up the Creeping Charley around the greens," the boy said, pointing to a plastic bucket in the weeds beside him. "I fill that up, and I get a dollar from the man in the place." He pointed back up the fairway. "And I get to play sometimes."

Garza nodded. "You want to be a golfer, huh?"

The boy grinned. "Sure." He glanced across the fairway where Fly stood in the near-darkness, waiting for Garza's shot. "You got a bet, huh?"

Garza looked at him. "How do you know?"

"That's why *you're* out here so late."

Garza nodded. You'd have to grow up quick, he thought, glancing up the shallow canyon. Or you wouldn't grow up at all. He reached in his pocket and found his walking-around money. Minus the tips he'd spread around earlier, there might have been twenty dollars left.

"Take the rest of the day off, pardner," he said, and clapped the money into the boy's hand.

The boy stared down at the bills. It was hard to see what his expression was, but Garza could guess. He tossed the wood back in the bag, pulled out a five iron and skidded his second shot out of the divot, a hundred yards up the fairway.

As Garza started after his shot, followed by the boy with his bucket, Fly bent over his ball and swung his effortless swing once more. He'd used a wood, possibly even a driver, and the ball shot forward, driving toward the hole like a comet. Garza didn't have to watch. He knew it was going onto the green.

He strode forward, up a slight rise that hid his ball from sight, calculating his own chances. He'd have two hundred yards, at least, into the green, but if he got it close and Fly two-putted, he'd at least halve the hole. That would leave only the problem of the thousand he was down. Maybe blindfolded putting, double or nothing. He'd think of something.

He came over the rise and found Fly waiting for him. Garza was about to give him a grudging compliment on his shot when he stopped short, his mouth falling open. There, before them, where he expected to find a shelf of grass with his ball nestled on it, was a broad swath of water cutting across the fairway.

Garza shook his head. A river. A goddamn, go-to-hell river slicing through the fairway. He turned to Fly.

"You said the river *used* to run through here."

Fly shrugged, giving the young boy the once-over. "I said the *Rio* used to come through here. This is something the development dug, for irrigation." He looked mildly at Garza. "Two in, three out. You're hitting four."

"And you're full of shit," Garza said. "You want my money, you'll have to take it."

Fly looked at him and shook his head. "I thought you'd have it figured out by now." His face seemed much older. "Some matches you just can't win."

"Any game that's fair, I'll take my chances," Garza told him evenly.

Fly laughed. "No game is fair, Mr. Garza."

Garza saw something in his eyes and felt the chill return to him. This was a lunatic. He might have a gun or a knife. He might do anything . . .

Abruptly, he saw a flash of red light whisk across Fly's face and a startled look appear there. Garza turned toward the distant green where a cloud of dust boiled behind a pair of carryall vans, their flashers whirling as they charged along a service road through the desert. *La Migra,* he thought, reflexively. The Immigration Man.

He turned back to Fly, who was shouldering his bag, backing away. He glanced over at Garza, a wry smile on his face. "You're in luck, *compadre.* I can't go up there."

"Wait a minute . . ." Garza said, but Fly was already hurrying away into the shadows.

"You don't forget what I told you," he called. In seconds, he had disappeared.

Garza turned back as the vans skidded to a halt on the far side of the water. When the doors flew open, Garza saw the unmistakable orb that was Horace emerge with the others. He stood facing them across the swath of roiling, angry water.

"Where is he, boss?" Horace called.

Garza hesitated. He thought he heard a distant scuffling in the arroyo, but it could have been a rabbit, a lost spirit, anything. He glanced at the young boy standing there behind him, his bucket in hand, watching.

Garza turned back to the others, who milled about the water's edge in frustration. "He's gone," he called to Horace. "He went two down and cut out before he had to pay."

Garza turned to the boy. "There a way across this?" he asked, pointing at the water.

The boy smiled. "Use the footbridge," he said, pointing at a place on the far side of the fairway. "But be careful going across."

Garza gave him a nod. "You bet, pardner," he said. "You be careful too."

There wasn't any conversation until they had turned off the development road onto the highway that cut through the desert into town. Once Horace had set the cruise control and rearranged his bulk behind the wheel, he turned to regard Garza, who was leaning back in his seat, his fingers drumming on the armrest.

Horace cleared his throat, filling the car with the sound of gears being shaken in a huge steel bucket. "You are lucky," he said finally.

Garza nodded. "How's your ankle?"

Horace shook his head. "It quit hurting a few minutes after you two left. How you think I got up to the clubhouse and called the police?"

Garza shrugged. "Kind of strange, don't you think?"

"Kind of strange that nut case didn't blow you away, or something. You should of heard them members when I said who you were out there with. Dude's been lurking around the place, weirdin' everybody out . . . *Mmmm-mmm.* You're lucky, that's all."

3 3 1

He paused, and stared back down the road. His thick fingers gripped and regripped the wheel. "Maybe you'll get lucky in New Orleans this week, too."

A rabbit cut across the highway suddenly, followed by a huge, swooping shape that flashed in the lights momentarily and was gone.

"Holy shit," Horace breathed, when he had brought the car back off the shoulder. "What was that?"

Garza seemed not to have noticed. He was staring out the side window of the car. South lay the Rio and beyond that, a vast plain where no lights burned. He turned back to Horace finally and lay his hand on his caddy's massive shoulder.

"Pardner," he said, "I think I'm going to sit a few out."

Horace looked over at him. "Give me a break."

"I mean it," Garza said. "We need a little rest."

Horace looked back down the road, his gruffness fading into uncertainty. Possibly, he'd been expecting this. "You ain't quittin' on me, are you? Just because things been tough?"

Garza shrugged. "I got some things to see about back home, that's all." He gave Horace's big shoulder a reassuring squeeze. "Like you said, maybe I'll get lucky." He turned to gaze out into the darkness, Fly's warning an echo in his mind. He wondered how he would begin, and if he might beat time, after all.

ZEN
GOLF

·

GORDON WEAVER

*Zen: a Chinese and Japanese school of Mayhayana Bud-
dhism that asserts that enlightenment can be attained through
meditation, self-contemplation, and intuition.*

*Golf: a game played on a large outdoor obstacle course having
a series of nine or eighteen holes spaced far apart, the object
being to propel a small ball with the use of a club into each
hole with as few strokes as possible.*

*And the wind shall say: "Here were decent godless people:
Their only monument the asphalt road
And a thousand lost golf balls."*
— *T.S. Eliot*

*The Zen golfer is he who comes to the game in search of a
clarity of vision and an exactitude of execution denied him in
the mundane world.*

Clancy, a middle-management executive with Unitron,
Inc., felt himself on the brink of collapse; his family, his
job, and whatever space in his life not filled by either
seemed doomed—when he wasn't botching his domes-
tic life, he was screwing up on the job, and when he was en-

333

gaged in neither, all he could think about was how utterly hopeless both were.

To his wife, Clancy said, "I'm forty-three years old. We've been married nineteen years, and the only time you talk to me is when you complain I'm not making enough money or I don't pick up after myself around the house."

She said, "That's silly." And "By the way, are you hearing any rumors about your promotion to bonus row at Unitron?" And "How many times do I have to ask you to please throw your towel in the hamper when you finish in the bathroom?"

Clancy said, "I have two children. I joined the country club just so my daughter could have her debut dance there, and she hasn't even said thanks. My son wants to cut his hair in a Mohawk and dye it orange and wear a safety pin in his ear; I don't think he's spoken to me for a year except to say I'm hassling him when I ask him to please turn down his hi-fi when I go to bed."

His wife said, "You know how kids are, Clancy." And "Is that or is that not your yesterday's shirt lying on the bedroom floor?" And "I asked you a question: Are there any rumors down at Unitron about your making it up to bonus row this year, or are we still scrimping in limbo for another year?" And "When you take off your socks at night, Clancy, I'd appreciate it if you'd turn them inside out for washing, okay?" And "Why don't you take up a hobby, get interested in something to take your mind off yourself, Clancy?"

"Like what, for example?" Clancy asked.

"Stamp collecting," his wife said. "Bird watching. Woodworking. Lapidary. Current events," she said. "You could read a good book once in a while."

"I watch television," Clancy said.

"You do," she said, "and leave dirty ashtrays and half-full cups and glasses and dishes from your snacks. I have to clean up after you every time."

334

PERFECT LIES

The Zen golfer is he who seeks the fulfillment of satisfaction in the realm of sport when all other paths to inner peace present only the prospect of failure.

At Unitron, Inc., the rumor was that Clancy would not be promoted to bonus row. Clancy discussed it with Southard, his middle-management peer, who was rumored to be a cinch for promotion to bonus row this year.

"I don't understand it," Clancy said. "I'm diligent, I'm loyal, I'm dependable, I give as much of my time as anyone, even you."

Southard said, "True, true enough, Clancy. But you're not keen, you're not sharp. You seem distracted, detached."

"Be specific," Clancy said.

"Your necktie knot's off-center," Southard said. "Even now your shoes could stand buffing, you get your haircuts a week too late all the time—you bite your fingernails, you smoke unfiltered cigarettes, and once I saw you picking your nose at a staff conference. Don't deny it, Clancy, you turned your head away to hide it, but everyone saw!"

"I have a lot on my mind, my wife and kids—" Clancy began to explain.

"No excuse!" Southard said, "We all have problems, Clancy. Everyone has a wife who nags or spends money like water or drinks too much and flirts at parties, right? Who doesn't have kids failing in school or into dope or going off in cars to attend rock concerts or getting married too young under the gun? No excuse, Clancy!" Southard said.

"You too?" Clancy said.

"Me in spades!" Southard said. "My wife's gone wacko active in women's rights organizations, my son's one step away from ward-of-the-court status for vandalism and truancy, and the twins, I won't even tell you the mess the two of them together got into with some guy about thirty who rides a motorcycle."

"How do you do it? How do you manage to cope?" Clancy asked.

"Do what?"

"Stay keen. Sharp. On the ball. You're going up to bonus row this year, everyone says so," Clancy said.

"You're damn tooting!" Southard said. "My secret is I have an escape. I get away from it all when it feels like it's crushing me. Two afternoons a week and twice on weekends. I golf," he said.

"Golf?"

"Golf. You should try it, Clancy," he said. "Golf. Handball. Raquetball. Anything. You belong to the country club now, don't you?"

"We joined so my daughter could have her debut dance there," Clancy said. "My wife insisted."

"I figured," Southard said. "So golf. Members get a reduced greens fee."

"I don't know the first thing about the game," he said.

"So get yourself a book on it and read up. What's the use of education and affluence if you can't learn something, Clancy?" Southard said.

> *The Zen golfer prepares himself before commencing his game; by diligent study, he progresses from a condition of the innocence of skills to one of sophistication, and by this knowledge attains to the innocence of vision requisite to satisfaction.*

Clancy, no ready cash to spare, bought books with his Visa card. First he read E. P. Walkiewicz's classic *Historical Origins of Golf;* after skimming Bobby Jones's anecdotal *Grand Slam: How I Did It* and *Our Legendary Matches,* coauthored by Walter Hagen and Gene Sarazen, he completed his background studies by reading Hogan's *Adversity Made My Game Stronger.*

"Clancy," his wife said, "Clancy, I'm talking to you!"

"What?" he said, "Sorry, I was reading."

"Your nose is always in a book," she said, "but at least it's better than you doddering around the house leaving messes for me to clean," she said. "What do you hear about your odds for promotion to bonus row lately? Clancy!" she shrieked when, his nose in a book, he failed to answer.

"What? Oh, sorry!" he said, "No, nothing tangible, dear." He then read a series of modern and contemporary tomes written by acknowledged masters, a sampling of manuals devoted to the game's techniques. In order, Clancy read: Arnold Palmer's *How to Sustain the Charge on the Back-Nine,* Nicklaus's *Baby Beef Speaks: Tips from the All-Time Money Winner,* Gary Player's *Golf Methods Know No Race, Creed, or Ethnic Origin,* and the indispensable anthology, *Birdies and Bogies: An Alphabetical Compendium on Techniques Secured in Personal Interviews with PGA Tourney Champs.*

"Clancy," Southard said to him one afternoon in Unitron's executive cafeteria, "what is it with you lately?"

"Do I seem different?" he said.

"Sort of," Southard said, "I'm not sure. Yeah! Maybe. Yeah, you seem more composed, sort of. You still act like you don't know which way's up half the time, but it's like you're more relaxed about it."

"I've been reading a lot," Clancy said.

"Do tell," said Southard. "The pro at the country club said you were out there yesterday afternoon when you were supposed to be at that production control meeting. But you didn't play. He said you just asked if you could walk the course. Is that true, Clancy?"

"I feel the need," Clancy said, "to get the lay of the land."

"Come out this weekend with my foursome, shoot a round with us," Southard said.

"I'm not ready for that yet," Clancy said.

"Suit yourself," Southard said. "Oh hey, Clancy, did I tell you the personnel board's meeting next month to finalize this year's promotions to bonus row?"

"Do tell," said Clancy, "I guess I should be sweating it out like you, but somehow I don't seem to take it as seriously as I know I should."

The Zen golfer utilizes only the finest equipment, full knowing the game cannot be well played, the visionary goal realized, no worthy end attained, if the tools employed are not suitable.

Having reached his Visa card's credit limit, Clancy purchased his clubs and accessories with his Master-Card. He bought custom-length-shaft top-of-the-line irons (two through nine with sand and pitching wedges), a precision machine-balanced Klemp putter, and space-age metal alloy woods (one through five) endorsed by the legendary Geoff Walker. To carry them, he bought a buffed cowhide Rorgelberger bag with tube-slots, imported knitted wood covers, Naugahyde face-savers for his irons, a striped umbrella with a fixture that attached to the handle of his portable pull-cart. He stored his gear in a rented locker at the country club, along with a gross of best-quality maxidistance Lucke balls, his new pair of Italian-made Sciori mini-spike shoes, and three complete outfits—caps, pullover jerseys, knickers, and long argyle-pattern socks.

"I got a phone call from the credit bureau today, Clancy," his wife said, "asking if we needed our credit limit expanded, and also a notice from American Express approving our application. Clancy, are you listening to me?"

"Sorry," he said, "I was thinking."

"That's an improvement," she said. "Do you know anything about this?"

"Must be a computer glitch of some kind. Don't hold supper for me, I'll be back as soon as I can," he said.

"Where are you going, Clancy?" she said. "Do you know your daughter's debut is in three short weeks and all the invitations still need to be mailed and your son swears he won't even come to the dance unless we hire a punk-rock band and let him wear one of his crazy get-ups instead of a tuxedo?''

"Right," Clancy said as he went out the door of their split-level. "That's where I'm headed, to the country club to check on things. Don't expect me back soon."

"Why?" she said, "What's going to take so long?"

"I need to use all the light that's left until sundown," Clancy said, and was gone before she could speak again.

> *The Zen golfer understands, beforehand, that the path to ultimate satisfaction will be strewn with frustrations, yet he persists in the face of all obstacles, confident that his triumph is ordained if he but endures in the proper state of spiritual and emotional equilibrium.*

Playing late in the afternoon and at dawn's first light, Clancy managed to avoid being joined by the tee starters with long-established foursomes and fivesomes. His game was wretched.

Off the tee, he whiffed often, resorting to Mulligans that he more often than not squibbed left and right, seldom carrying farther than the ladies' tee box marked with red blocks. When he did make contact, he sliced deeply into the rough, even into the parallel fairway, or hooked left, or skyed, high as a mortar shell or a softball pop-up. But he felt a rush of joy when he drew his driver from the bag, marveled at the high-gloss enamel of the club's head that caught highlights from the sun; when he managed to loft the ball, his heart rose with it, and his eyes flashed as he tracked its brief flight through the crisp air.

"You're never home, Clancy," his wife said. "If I didn't know you better, I'd think you were carrying on with someone."

He lost balls by the score to the roughs and water hazards, but felt an unexpected ease as he tramped in search of them, eyes fixed on the ground, slashing casually at the long grasses with an iron; once he discovered a nest of baby field mice, once an unbroken robin's egg, once thrilled at the sudden chill that swept his bones as a harmless snake slithered across his shoes. On the fairways, his lone irons were a disaster. He skulled the ball, skewed it off the shaft and toe of the club face, dug deep divots without even making contact. But the morning sun warmed him, painted a brilliant wash of colors on cloudbanks when it set, and breezes splashed his cheeks like the soft caress of a mistress's hand on the open fairways.

"I saw your name on the sign-in sheet at the clubhouse, Clancy," Southard said. "You must be becoming some kind of a fanatic. You sure you wouldn't like to join my foursome this weekend? Clancy?"

"I'm sorry," Clancy said, "I guess I was miles away."

"So I noticed," Southard said.

Around the greens Clancy was pathetic. He dubbed his attempts to pitch and run, or else swung too hard and shot over the green; he rarely avoided bunkers, had to swing again and again to get up and out, churning up sand like fountain water. He could not read the breaks on the greens, and his putting stroke was as graceless as a hesitant slap at the ball. But he loved the barbered grass that was a shade lighter than its surroundings, and the sandtraps reminded him of ocean beaches he knew as a boy, and when he hunched over the ball to putt, there was a sudden still in the air, a total quiet impervious even to the shrill twanging of bluejays.

"Mom," his daughter said, "I asked Daddy three times if he called the country club about the catering, and he just kept looking at me like I wasn't there!"

"Where's Dad?" his son asked his mother. "I want to tell him I'm getting my hair cut the way I want and that's final, but I can't find him. You think he'll really hassle me about it?"

"Your father," Clancy's wife said, "rarely talks to me these days, so don't expect any answers from me!"

The Zen golfer confronts obstacles, but sees only opportunities; the Zen golfer wastes no anguish on what is past, no anxiety on what is to come; the Zen golfer, ever-conscious of the oneness of all things, exists with tranquility in a never-ending present.

Clancy's play never improved, but his delight in the game increased. When his lie was impossible, the ball against a tree trunk, mired in ooze at the edge of the creek, wedged in a crack in hard-pan dirt, he felt blessed by the cool shade, the slow trickle of water, the packed solidity of the earth beneath his feet. His approach shot to a green blocked by a clump of graceful willows, their leaves trembling in the breeze, he saw only the narrow window of space between them he tried for, and the hard *thunk* his ball made when it rebounded back toward him sounded like the snap of a lock opening. When his drives were held up in the winds he failed to compensate for, he experienced a sense of magic, as if he had a momentary power to suspend gravity. When he hit into water, the loss of his ball and the penalty stroke were as nothing against the liquid sound it made as it broke the surface, nothing against the concentric circles that radiated like a natural geometry.

He found a wholeness emerging in the small acts of replacing divots, repairing ball marks on the greens, raking sandtraps smooth, the tiny bubbles of detergent that clung to his cleaned ball when he took it from the ball washer. Slaking his thirst at the fountains situated at every other tee box was like drinking chilled wine, and cleaning his spikes on the metal bristles set in the sidewalk outside the pro shop felt like sloughing off the woes of the world. He breathed deep sighs of pleasant exhaustion when he shouldered his bag at the end of the eighteen holes, the sun-warmed odor of fine leather like dusky incense.

From the seventh tee, the highest elevation on the course, he paused before setting his stance to swing, looked out at the emerald symmetry of the course, fairways lined with trees and rough, dotted with ponds and sandtraps, crossed and recrossed by the casually meandering creek. Lifting his eyes, he could see the pro shop and clubhouse, the country club's pool and tennis courts and parking lot, the bar and restaurant where his daughter's debut would be celebrated, only a week away now. Squinting to pierce the distances, he saw the whole of the great city stretching away to infinity, the towers of Unitron, Inc., on the horizon.

"Well!" said Clancy. "Oh my!" And he experienced a tiny epiphany of knowing that the sum of things was greater than its parts, and that he, Clancy, might claim to be the center of it all.

"Are you losing some weight, Clancy?" Southard asked him.

"Not that I'm aware," he said. "Maybe it's just your tan," Southard said, "you look like you just came off a Florida vacation."

"I quit smoking," Clancy said. "I didn't do anything special, I just found I wasn't even thinking about it after a while."

"Lucky you," Southard said, "I also notice you broke yourself of biting your nails to the quick. What are you, Clancy, on some self-improvement kick?"

"Did I?" Clancy said. "I guess I did at that. So how's it going with you, Southard?" he asked.

"Murder," he said. "The wife, kids. I did hear the personnel board won't announce this year's promotions for a few days. I can't sleep nights worrying, and my golf's gone into the dumper."

"You're a cinch," Clancy said, "I'm almost just as glad knowing I don't stand a chance."

"Nothing's certain," Southard said. "Hey, got your invite! I'm looking forward to your daughter's bash at the club. By the

way, what's your handicap these days if you don't mind my
asking?"

"I never keep score," Clancy told him.

*For the Zen golfer, there is no failure, no success; for the Zen
golfer, there is only Being, the changeless law of change, the
union of cycles and seasons that form the constant inconstancy
of existence; for the Zen golfer, the ultimate vision is the marriage of means and ends.*

Clancy was startled to realize that, despite the boundless ineptitude of his game, he executed every possible shot to perfection
at least once in every eighteen-hole round.

At least once, his swing on the tee was fluid, effortless, and
he struck the ball with the club head's sweet spot, drove long
and straight and high, rolling to a stop in the exact center of
the fairway. At least once in each eighteen holes he played he
picked the ball up cleanly off the fairway with his number three
wood, or lifted it out of long grass with an iron, watched it
streak toward the green as if fired from a gun. At least once he
pitched and ran to the lip of the cup, avoiding water and sand
like anathema; at least once he one-putted from thirty or forty
feet across swales on the green, downhill, as if he had calcu-
lated distance and break with a minicomputer. Twice he shot
pars on the back nine, once a birdie on a tricky par three, and
held out with his wedge from the deep bunker that half-circled
the fourteenth green.

He found his wife huddled at her vanity table, crying.
"What's wrong, what is it?" Clancy asked.

"Everything's terrible!" she said through her tears. She hic-
cuped, sniffed, dried her eyes. "The debut's going to be a
nightmare. Our friends from Unitron won't know what to
make of that crazy band your son made me hire, and I'm going
to have to hide him somewhere if we don't want him dis-
gracing us with that haircut and what he swears he's going to

wear, and our daughter's going to hate the memory of this for the rest of her life, and we'll embarrass ourselves in front of all the bonus row people from Unitron I've invited, and lord knows you're no help always out golfing, and I've plucked so many white hairs out of my head my scalp burns!" she said, and began to cry again.

"It will be okay," Clancy said as he patted her on the back, "I know it will."

"What do you know!" she said. "What have you got to smile about, Clancy?" and, "Are you dieting or is it just that tan from golfing?" and, "Have you seen how I look in my dress I'm going to wear to this humiliation?"

> *The Zen golfer is all things unto himself, yet is as nothing. Certain of his uncertainty, the Zen golfer weighs all things in the balance, yet neither accepts nor rejects. The Zen golfer knows, and knows he knows, and knows the sufficiency that lies therein.*

Clancy's daughter's debut was a debacle. The sneering caterer blamed the country club's surly waiters for the cold, bland dinner served. The bar was popular, but the drinks tasted watered and were inhospitably poured. The orchestra's lifeless dance music could not compete with the electronic frenzy of the amateur punk-rock band. Clancy's wife looked overdressed in her new gown, and the color rinse in her hair looked garish against her complexion. Their son, clad in a sequined caftan, his hair a harlequin of orange, grape, and sea-blue stripes, his earlobes crusted with pins and studs, his face painted grotesquely, caused guests to point, whisper, giggle, and shake their heads sadly. When Clancy danced the first dance with his daughter, she muttered in his ear, "Stop stepping on my instep." And "This is the worst moment in my entire life." And "I hate myself, and I hate you, and I hate everything forever!" The ritual applause of the bored guests was scattered and faint.

Southard, flushed and grinning, said to him, "When you get a minute, Clancy, I've got something to tell you. Don't forget to talk to me before I leave, okay?"

When it approached midnight, and the musicians began to yawn as they played, and only confirmed alcoholics still patronized the free bar, and Clancy's wife had taken their daughter to the ladies' lounge to calm her, and his son had disappeared, Clancy went to the clubhouse locker room, took off his tuxedo jacket, untied his bow tie, and changed his patent leather pumps for his spiked Scioris, hoisted his bag, and walked out into the night, stumbling in the dark to the first tee.

The end of Zen golf is not playing the game, but The Game itself; the vision of the Zen golfer is not a means by which to see Life, but the identification of seeing with seen, seen with he who sees—the Zen golfer's vision is of himself as Vision.

"Clancy?" his wife called as she searched for him. "Clancy, I need you! Your daughter's incoherent and your son's gone and gotten himself caught smoking those funny cigarettes in the men's! Clancy, if you don't answer me I'll never talk to you again. I'm warning!"

"Clancy?" He heard the voice of Southard in the darkness near the pro shop. "I saw you come out here, Clancy, where are you? I've got great news, man! I made it, Clancy! I talked with a person in the know, I made it! Old Southard's wife may be wacko and his kids are a mess, but he's on bonus row, Clancy!"

In the total dark at the number one tee box, Clancy teed up his ball, groping in the blackness. Placing the club head behind the ball, feeling his way like a blind man, he stepped back, set his stance, and found his grip on the shaft. He breathed deeply, once, twice, three times to relax.

Then the voices of Southard and his wife still calling his name out to the empty night, the warring music of the orchestra and the punk-rock band playing their final sets, wafting up to the star-studded vault of the universe, Clancy drew his club back slowly, then swept it forward.

Clancy swung, oblivious to voices and music, to industry and civilization, to night and nature, yet in and of them. In the heart of his vision, himself the vision, he swung, anticipating the crack he was sure he would hear when the sweet spot made contact with the dim white orb that seemed almost to pulse and glow in the black night.

A
PERFECT
DAY FOR
GOLF

·

TOBY OLSEN

All day the Chair had been thinking about the way things were going at Seaview Links, and by early afternoon he had cooked himself up into a significant and frustrated rage. It was Monday, and it was raining. He'd soon have to call and cancel the evening's mosquito league play, and it would be another five days before the next tournament. He'd bitten his wife's nose off when she had asked him why so glum, and she'd stayed clear of him after that. He'd gone down into the basement to fuss with his clubs and bag.

As recently appointed Chairman of the Golf Commission, he had responsibilities, and one of them was to ensure that golf was taken seriously and played in a dignified manner. He'd tried in his brief tenure to impart this to the men, but with Sammy in his beard and cutoffs as counter man and pro and the druggie Chip as groundskeeper, it seemed impossible for him to set proper standards. Everyone just acted as if he were joking, and even the weekly tournaments remained a rag-tag affair.

He rapped his five-iron head against the workbench, then quickly checked it for damage. Maybe shopping will help, he thought, and he went back upstairs, managed to speak a few civil words to his wife, then headed for the mall. He found what he was after, and he only lay awake for an hour or more when he went to bed that night.

When he woke in the morning he was still angry, but when he looked out the window he saw that the rain was gone. It was a perfect day for golf, and this soothed him. He'd drive out to Seaview in the afternoon, work at the handicap cards, maybe even play a little. He was feeling better, and he headed back to the bedroom to try his new clothing on.

The Chair had purchased a pair of white cotton pants with little boats on them. The boats were set a good three inches apart, so there was no mistaking that the pants were white. They had no cuffs and were double-stitched with kelly-green thread down the outer seams. On the wide belt loops, fragments of the little boats could be made out. The boats were toylike, and each of them floated on a curl of wave that was equal to their length and about a quarter-inch deep. The waves were a few thin lines of green and blue, with the white of the background showing through. The boats seemed not to be located in any clear pattern; some were at right angles with the leg, but some were set askew, and a couple were almost upside down. Their hulls were dark green, and they had bright red masts that were topped with orange sails. They did not seem seaworthy. Each one had a small porthole with crosshatched lines in its side, and each had a little pink rudder and a pink point at its prow.

At five places on the legs there were five little whales. They were the same size as the boats, and they too floated on little waves. They were pink in color, with curvy tales, and they each spouted a curl of water from their blowholes. Each had a little eye and little green lines for smiles. Near the slit of both front pockets, but not printed in a symmetrical way, there were two dolphins. These were the same size and general shape as the whales, and only their color (they were blue) seemed to distinguish them. But at a closer look, which the Chair had taken before buying the pants, one could see that the dolphins, though they sat on similar waves, had no blowholes or curls of spout, and they were not, like the whales, riding the waves but were arched in mid-dive, halfway between the exit from one wave and the entrance into another. They didn't seem to have any pupils in their happy eyes.

Alongside the pants on the bed was the Chair's shirt, a knit pullover, kelly-green in color with white stitching around the edge of the collar and pocket. A canvas cap and a belt were beside it. The cap was red and had a white-and-green emblem, a golf tee with a ball beside it, and the words SEAVIEW LINKS stitched in the front of its crown. The belt was white and made of plastic, its edges stitched with black thread. It had a black, plastic-covered buckle. On the floor below the garments were the Chair's socks and shoes, the socks lying neatly over the shoes, not touching the floor. The shoes were two-toned, green-and-white Foot-Joys, with scalloped dust tongues (devices the manufacturer called "shawls") covering the laces. They had been brightly shined. The socks were new, green-and-black argyles.

The Chair stood in his boxer shorts and undershirt in front of the full-length mirror on the closet door to the side of the bed. He turned in a slow circle, keeping his eyes on the mirror, checking himself out. He reached up into the legs of the boxer shorts to the tails of his undershirt, pulling it down until there were no wrinkles where the elastic waistband met the shirt. He sucked in his stomach and adjusted the straps at his shoulders. Then he sat down on the bed beside his clothing. He ran a hand along the leg of his pants, and then he reached down and lifted the socks from the shoes, rolled each one down to the toe and adjusted them on his feet, unrolling the tops until they were straight and tight to his lower calves. He twisted the left one to get the ribs and diamonds in line.

When his socks were in order, he got up and lifted his pants, shook them slightly, then lowered them and stepped in. Pulling them up, he danced a little to get them to hang properly in the leg. He noted the way the little boats fell. He turned and took his putting stance in full view in the mirror. With his left leg extended, the right back and firm, the little whale on the inside of his thigh could be seen. He smiled at himself. Then he picked up the belt and slipped it carefully through the loops. He left it unbuckled and lifted the shirt up and shook it out. He slipped it on, and rather than pull at the fabric, he did another little jig so that it fell down around his body until he could see himself in the mirror again. He adjusted the collar, unzipped the pants, and squatted with legs apart to hold them up while he tucked his shirt over his boxer shorts, smoothing out wrinkles around his body. When the shirt was secure, he gripped the pants, stood up and pulled them over the shirt. He zipped them and fastened his belt, adjusting the buckle over his fly. He checked the pants fold to make sure the zipper was covered.

He went to the closet and opened the mirrored door and took out a piece of rug, which he brought back to the side of the bed, and placed his shoes on it, taking the spikes off the floor. Then he sat down and put the shoes on it, lifted the scalloped shawls and laced them. When this was done, he picked up the cap, smoothed back his hair and put it on, pulling the peak down firmly. Then he stood up on the piece of carpet and looked at himself in the mirror.

At first he stood straight, then he slouched a little, casually, putting his weight on one leg, the way he would stand while one of his partners was putting or teeing off. Then he took his putting stance again, checking the inseam of his trousers and the placement of the whales, the place where his pants met his socks, the protrusion of his anklebone with a diamond directly over it, and the arc of the side of his shoes and the way the first two scallops of the shawls angled along them. One of the tips of the laces was protruding from under the shawl, and he reached down and opened the bow a bit and then took his stance again and nodded. He checked his right leg to see that the pants came to the tops of his shoes. Then he took another casual stance, the one with his left hand on his hip, his right arm hanging loosely, bent at the elbow, his hand in his pocket with thumb protruding along the fabric. This is the way he would stand in the clubhouse before they went out, talking jovially and authoritatively with the men.

Then he took various stances and went through various motions. There was the motion of pulling the peak of his cap down with conviction, snugging it as he prepared to address his ball for a long iron shot only after he had studied the distance and other issues perceptively. There was the motion of picking and throwing bits of grass in the air, watching their speed and direction as they fell, checking the variations in wind conditions before he teed off. There was the stance of disapproval when someone moved while another was putting. There was the stance and look of condescending approval at a shot well made. Once he let his left arm rise up and fall in mild philosophical despair at the behavior of Sammy and Chip. Once he put his hand on his head, looking to the heavens in disbelief. Once he smiled warmly, very loose in his body, his clothing showing brilliantly, suggesting obviously desired friendship.

Near the end, he went to a drawer in the dresser at the foot of the bed and from among carefully stacked packages of golf balls, tees, markers, and hats—his winnings over the years in the tournaments—got out a new glove from a pile of them. The glove was dark green with a white flap of Velcro on its underside to secure it, and in the middle of the flap was an emblem, a spherical figure in the middle of which was a small green club head. At the tip of the flap was a pearl button that could be removed and used as a ball marker. He slipped the tight glove over his hand, securing the Velcro. He went back to the mirror and stood before it. He lifted the gloved hand in front of his body at a level with his chest, the back of the glove facing away from him, the sphere and the pearl button clearly visible in the mirror, in a position where all would be able to see it. He formed a loose fist with the hand, his index finger extended and pointing. He was about to speak, and they all were listening attentively and with much anticipation for what he was about to say.

Sometimes in the early evenings, on days when it was slow, Sammy and Chip liked to get out and play a little Hit and Throw Ball, one of the games they had invented, Chip giving the names. On this particular day, one following four days of heavy rain, the sky was bell-clear, the temperature warm and dry, and most everyone on the Cape had headed for the beaches, staying there for hours, a little glassy-eyed in wonder at the weather. In the later afternoon, as if by some plan, a lightly cool breeze had come up, very soft and just a little bracing, and most of the beachgoers, in sweet wonder exhaustion, had headed home for drinks and evening cook-outs. A couple of foursomes, husbands and wives, had started out around four o'clock, but when they got to the sixth tee and saw the ocean from the high dune cliff they could not help themselves. The second foursome joined the first one when they got there. They left their clubs standing like a strange committee in their hand carts around the tee and went through the brush to the sea perch and sat down, talking in low tones about the weather and the sea, counting the buoys on the lobster pots, making friends with each other.

For close to a month now, ever since the French Canadian campers, the weekenders, and the other summer tourists had been coming to Seaview Links in some numbers, Sammy had THE LIST out and ready behind the counter. Sammy and Chip had started keeping THE LIST two summers before, writing down the most interesting questions the tourist-players asked, once they were out of sight. THE LIST got longer, and only a few of the questions were the fake ones that Chip added, appending his name after them in parenthesis in his small clear hand.

THE LIST
1. Is this the golf course?
2. Are you open?
3. Where did you buy the rest room signs?
4. How do I stand?
5. Are you cutting the grass?
6. Do you sell charcoals here?
7. Do you sell fishhooks?
8. Do you believe me when I speak? (Chip)
9. Is the Coke good?
10. Is this the old building?
11. Is this the clubhouse?
12. Is this the right place?
13. If it rains, will I get wet? (Chip)
14. Do you rent balls?
15. Is that the ocean?
16. Can my friend walk with me? Can she hit my balls?
17. Are you a French Canadian too? *Sacrebleu!* (Chip)
18. Are you a native?

19. Are these the score cards?
20. Is that the foghorn?
21. Are there any places to eat?
22. How deep is the ocean? (Chip)
23. Is it going to rain?
24. How high is the sky? (Chip)
25. Can I wear golf shoes?
26. Does it get cold when it snows?
27. I'm from an elite club in Philadelphia. Can I play here?
28. Did anybody turn in a ball?
29. Are those wooden clubs old?
30. Do you remember anybody? (Chip)
31. Is this the bus stop?
32. What do you do when you play nine holes?
33. What are winter gloves?
34. Is this where you play golf?
35. Will you read this lighthouse? [The Chipper hands over a copy of JW tract to listener] (Chip)
36. Is the wind blowing?
37. Is it raining up here?
38. Do you have buffets?
39. Where is the ocean beach?
40. Who did that wonderful job on the aprons? (Chip)
41. Can we play in one bag?
42. Do you have little sticks to hit the ball off?
43. What do you do in the winter?
44. What kind of white bread is in the sandwiches?
45. Who is the best chipper on the course? (Chip)
46. Can I get married on the cliff?
47. Who makes the grass grow? (Chip)
48. Do you have to take a test to play?
49. What happens when it rains?
50. What happens when the fog comes in? (Chip)

51. Is that the lighthouse?
52. Am I right- or left-handed?

In Hit and Throw Ball, one made every other shot by chucking the ball in the general direction of the green. If one was on the green when a throw shot came up, one simply bowled the ball at the cup. Sammy and Chip also played Cross Golf, Over and Under, Change, Back Ball, and other invented variations. Chip was waiting on the second tee, practicing his windup, when Sammy drove up in a power cart. Ordinarily, on a day as slow as this, Sammy would put his sign out on the door, but on this day the Chair had come in to work at the handicap cards and said he would watch things while Sammy went out to play. He was wearing bright new clothes, but his disposition wasn't up to them. He was gruff, making it quite clear that he judged Sammy's leaving the clubhouse as inappropriate. Nothing unusual in this, Sammy thought. It's a beautiful afternoon, so out I go.

Bob Days, an electrician at the Air Force Station, was doing a little volunteer wiring at the clubhouse and said he'd watch out for things too.

Sammy and Chip teed off, both electing to hit their first shots, and when it came to the second, Chip winged his off into the rough to the right of the fairway so that he could get to where the blueberries were. After Sammy had thrown his and they had had a friendly, joshing argument about whether Chip had thrown his ball out of bounds, they both got their balls to the green. Chip was one shot behind Sammy when they got there, so while Sammy had a bowl, Chip had a putt. Sammy missed his bowl, complaining that the green had not been well cut and that that had thrown his ball off. Then they argued about the quality of Chip's work on and around the green, joking and trading insults. Chip said that nobody who dressed as bad as Sammy did had any right to complain about anything that had to do with quality or taste. Sammy retorted as how

Chip might do a better job once he got out of Cape Tech and became an adult. Things went on this way until they, like the others before them, reached the sixth tee and saw the ocean. They could not help themselves either, and they went to the edge of the cliff, said hello to the husbands and wives, and sat and looked.

The beach was crowded, but those on it were as still and awestruck as the ones sitting on the cliff above them. The only movement came from the curling at the edges of beach umbrellas in the breeze and the few children who played in quiet ways in the edge of surf. People sat in beach chairs looking out. Some stood, together or alone, facing the sea. It was so clear, the horizon at such a distance and yet a sharp clear line, that the sea seemed a contained massiveness, and as such dwarfed even the crowded beach, making it seem half empty. In the places between the colorful spread-out blankets and towels with the brown-and-white bodies lying on them, the sand was a clean tan, and where it joined the surf, it darkened and opened, untouched and running as far as they could see to the left, until it hit against the escarpment that moved up to the promontory where the hard white lighthouse stood. Gentle and foamy whitecaps kept the children back, and beyond them the water turned blue, and as it went out and deepened it became emerald green. About two hundred yards out there was a finger of seaweed rising and shifting and lowering in the swell, and beyond the weed, where the water was blue again, long lines of variously colored lobster-pot buoys were bobbing.

The whales' river appeared so gradually that the watchers on the beach took no notice of it. Those on the cliff saw it coming, a broad white line of gentle turbulence snaking from beyond the promontory on which the lighthouse stood and stretching a good two miles before them, well to the other side of the pots. Then they saw the backs, the dark islands rising, lingering in slow movement along the coast, and sinking again. There was a glittering line in the air above the whales' river: gulls and terns riding the currents, diving occasionally in the whales' wake, lifting the bait fish that were stirred to the surface. The two lines, of whales and birds, continued far out, moving parallel to shore, and after they had passed a mile off to the right they turned and headed seaward in the direction of Europe. When the drama was over the watchers leaned back on the cliff's edge, realizing they had been tensed by the sight. The sea continued as if nothing at all had happened. Below where the whales had been were the shipwrecked hulls the comers to the New World had left. On a day like this, they might have risen to the surface and moved leisurely in to the shore. Today, there was a Japanese factory boat in the far distance, working the water with its indiscriminate nets. Two boats steamed around the lighthouse point and began pulling the lobster pots. There were no pleasure crafts on the sea, and this seemed right. Everything was serious, unconcerned, and real.

Back at the clubhouse, the Chair finished up with the handicap cards, got a cup of coffee, and went into the pro shop to see if there was anything he could use his holdover winnings from last season to buy. Bob Days was there, working on a bad connection, and while the Chair checked out the shirts with the alligators on them and the various versions of the golf cap, they chatted about nothing in particular, and both of them greeted Barney Packett, another enlisted man, when he came in with four cases of beer he had gotten at the P.X. and fed the refrigerator in the small snack-bar area. The Chair disapproved of drinking at the course. Not only was it dangerous, inviting golf injury, it was evidence of a slackness in administration. Both Bob and Barney laughed when they saw the look on his face, and he turned away from them and went to the window.

In the middle of the eighth fairway, across from the short ninth and the clubhouse, seven Canada geese were moving around and pecking in the grass. They had drifted in at three in the afternoon. The adults were fat and sleek, and the young kept close to them. A few terns and a crane in from the edge of the sea moved inland lightly at times, the crane dropping down for a few moments to find food, then lifting away and sailing. From where the Chair stood, he could see the whole of the short ninth fairway, from the tee to the two-tiered green only a few yards from the clubhouse to his right. The fairway was shaded a little by the building and the three pines standing back near the park bench that overlooked it. John Reuss and Tony Worthington were lazily practicing on the ninth in the crisp air, and the Chair watched them. They would each hit a few balls from the tee, then stroll up and chip the ones that had landed around the green. When all the balls were on the green, they would putt the longest ones, joking and laughing lightly when a difficult one fell in the hole or came close. The two were in their early eighties. They had fine, casual, almost second-nature chip shots. Their game was very relaxed and very sure. They drove the short green not with conventional wedges but with low straight pitch-and-run shots, trickling their balls up through the fringe, rolling them into good positions on the green. Their clubs were old and well used. They fit their hands like good and familiar tools.

While the Chair was watching, Eddie Costa came into vision from the parking area and greeted the two players and joined them. Eddie was wearing baggy work pants and a bright red shirt. John and Tony joked about his shirt, smiling and nodding to one another. The three laughed, and Eddie dropped a couple of balls on the green and putted them.

By the time Chip and Sammy were back to the path across the road from the clubhouse, five others had joined the three in their practice on the ninth hole, and the Chair was getting ready to go out there himself. The sun was moving away, but it was still very pleasant and dry, and the light breeze had shifted to the bay side, toned down a bit, and became warmer. Bob Days had finished his electrical work and had gone out to sit on the park bench and watch the casual players. Some of them were not playing at all but were standing around, joshing the others occasionally and talking, their putters and irons hanging along their sides, an occasional can of beer in hand.

As Sammy and Chip got to the road, a large silver Cadillac with Texas plates drove slowly in front of them, heading up to the parking area at the lighthouse. A man and a woman were in the front seat, both wearing cowboy hats.

"Hey! That was Roy Rogers in that car!" Chip sang out, grabbing Sammy by the arm and pointing after it.

"Texas plates, a Cadillac, and those hats," Sammy said, "but that was *not* Roy Rogers."

"Yes it was!" Chip said, "Yes it was! Old Roy and Dale on the move! Rhythm away from the range! Good old Roy and Dale for sure!" And he dropped Sammy's arm and trotted off up the road after the car.

"Roy Rogers, my ass," Sammy said to himself, shaking his head and smiling, watching Chip trot up the road, slapping his thighs in little-boy horse-riding-play fashion. Then he crossed the road and went into the clubhouse, where he saw the Chair taking a seven-iron and a putter out of the club rack in the pro shop.

"What's up, Chair?" he said, still smiling.

"Going out back to hit a few," the Chair answered, "no business while you were gone."

He spoke a little sheepishly, avoiding Sammy's look. Ordinarily he would be royally pissed at these goings on. It's the weather, Sammy thought. Not even the Chairman can withstand it.

"Okay, Chair. Hey, see you out there in a minute."

Sammy went into the pro shop as the Chair left it, and by the time he got to the window and saw the crew gathered out on the ninth, the Chair had come around the side of the building and was already greeting this one and that one, asking about wives, children, putts and iron shots, complimenting and judging. Sammy went back to the cash register, checked the day's receipts and locked it. Then he got a beer from the refrigerator and headed out the door himself. Before he could go around the building, the Texas Cadillac pulled up in one of the parking places next to the clubhouse and Chip hopped out of the back door. He was grinning and winking; he opened the door on the driver's side, and a rather short and broad Texan got out.

"Sammy, this here is Bobby Lee Bando," Chip said, "and this here is Melda Bando." He indicated the rather squat woman in the squaw dress who got out of the other door. Sammy noticed the woman did look a little like Dale Evans, but he could see nothing of Roy Rogers in the man.

"Hi," he said, and the man extended his hand.

"How you be?" the man said. "Nice spread you got here. Course looks good. Is it on the pro tour?" His wife smiled and looked around, nodding in agreement with her husband's comment. Sammy glanced at Chip. They both figured they would have to get that pro tour question on THE LIST. Chip was a little off to the side and behind the Texans. Sammy could see him bobbing and winking, making furtive gestures.

"No, not on the tour yet," Sammy said. "Come a long way?"

"All the way from Texas," Bobby Lee Bando answered. "All right to look around a spell? Maybe hit a few?"

"Just closing," Sammy said, "but you're welcome to come out back and chip a bit."

Chip jumped a little when he heard Sammy's offer, and he stepped up and took the man and the woman by the arm, putting himself between them, and led them behind the clubhouse to where the others were gathered. Sammy was watching Chip introduce the two around when he heard a loud sputtering motor. He turned to the road and saw Manny Corea pull his old pickup into a parking place beside the Caddy.

"Hey, Manny!" he said as he went to the truck. Manny indicated the truck bed with his head, and when Sammy looked he saw four good-sized buckets, two of mussels and two of quahogs in the back.

"Can you use these?" Manny asked him.

"Hell yes!" Sammy said, "let's take 'em around back," and the two lifted the cans out of the truck bed and carried them over to the park bench where Bob Days was sitting.

The day was beginning to fade away, and the shadows of the three pines were extending over the fairway and touching the edges of the green. The Canada geese were still pecking over on the eighth, but they were hard put to find patches of sunlight in which to shine. Though some of the men still pitched and putted, most were by this time standing in small groups and talking. A few came over to see what was in the buckets. Chip was herding the two Texans from group to group, and when the shellfish appeared, he brought them over to the park bench. They had not seen quahogs before, and Melda Bando wondered if they were good to eat. The men standing around the buckets assured her that they were better than that even, and Manny Corea suggested that they steam them up in the clubhouse.

"Anybody for mussels and chokers?" Sammy yelled out to the crew on the fairway and green, and he was answered with assenting calls. Bob Days said he would fix some lights, and he went to his truck. Bobby Lee Bando said he had some music, one hell of a stereo tapedeck in his Caddy, and while Bob Days hooked up some spots and floods and fixed them to the trees, Bobby Lee went to his car to select tapes. Chip and Sammy went in and put two of the buckets up to steam on the small stove in the snack-bar area. When they got inside and were alone, Chip let his agitation go.

"That's him! Old Roy!" he said, "That's him! That's him!"

"Hell, look at how short and fat he is," Sammy said, "that's not him."

"He's in *disguise!*" Chip said. "Traveling *in*cognito! But pretty old Dale can't hide her cowgirl charms and beauty! That's *her,* did'ya see her?!"

"Looks like her," Sammy said, "but, hell, that's not her."

"Old Roy and Dale. Who-ha!" said Chip.

"You're nuts," Sammy said, getting the buckets of shellfish going over the flame.

"Come here!" said Chip. "Watch this!" and he pulled the mildly protesting Sammy over to the door of the clubhouse, stuck his head out and yelled.

"Trigger!"

Bobby Lee Bando was on the front seat of the Caddy with the door standing open, going through the tapes. When he heard the sharp yell, his head jerked up. Chip ducked back into the clubhouse, dancing around.

"See that! See that! Sound of the old hoss name! *Dear* old Trigger! Those little pistolas along his snout, stuffed and waiting for *re*-incarnation! My, oh my! Old Roy and Dale at Seaview!"

"Okay," Sammy said, "I give up."

They fixed the mussels and quahogs, adding some white wine to the broth and a few herbs that somebody managed to come up with. Bob Days got the lights up and on and carefully adjusted so that they lit the bench, the green, and a part of the fairway. Earl came in from his mowing, got his gallon jug of iced tea out, and joined the group. Bobby Lee Bando put a quiet Neil Hefti tape in the deck, with a Frank Sinatra backup. Chip was surprised at Roy's choice of music, but figured him for a low profile. The cases of beer were brought out to the park bench. A few of the men's wives, wondering why they had not come home, showed up and joined in. Chip and Melda Bando were the first to dance. They did a slow foxtrot, very gracefully and with considerable skill around the flagstick on the lighted green. Eddie Costa grabbed his wife and joined the couple, but he kept just below the apron on the fringe, not wanting to spoil the green's integrity. They ate the shellfish and drank the beer. A small cluster of men, with the Chair at its center, practiced and talked about various short-chip techniques in the middle of the fairway, at the edge of the lighted place. Bobby Lee Bando showed them a Texas grip he knew.

It got darker, and the lights created a kind of lawn party atmosphere, a lighted space with the slight mystery of the encroaching darkness held back. The tapedeck floated Frank Sinatra's "Nancy" over the various grasses and the trees. The geese, what few were left, quietly honked in response to Frank's singing. The owner of the nearby Exxon station and his wife, who took a lighthouse drive each evening, saw the activity and stopped and joined in. They were excellent dancers, and their turns on the green were admired by all.

There was a chipping contest. Sammy talked about the whales and saving them and handed out a few bumper-stickers. Chip talked to a few men about various green-maintenance techniques that he had learned in school. Melda Bando talked to the women about Texas chili. Manny Corea told the story of the mussel find. The Chair's poses and gestures were subtle and abbreviated and unobtrusive. He couldn't find a way to get his ire up. It's the weather, he thought, a perfect day for golf, and what the hell. His wife came, and he danced with her. They did a simple two-step. Eddie Costa sang an old Portuguese fishing song. They all loved hearing it, but he refused to translate it, saying that that would not do at all. The women gave Melda Bando recipes for kale soup.

It was a clear night, and the lighthouse was dark and silent; no warnings were necessary. Out beyond its softened whiteness, the lights of a few boats glimmered on the sea a mile away. The surf washed almost inaudibly on the sand, sparks of phosphorous in its gentle wake. The last of the day retired, and the stars came out. Frank Sinatra sang his songs again into the night. The people moved in loose and changing clusters, talking, laughing softly, and listening. The party continued, sweetly, until after twelve. Sammy took the last dance with Melda Bando. The two drifted formally across the green. Everyone became silent and watched them. When the song ended, a light applause rose up. The dancers bowed and smiled. When the party ended, they all went home knowing they would sleep peacefully when they got there. Chip was the last to leave. He stored his mower and his fine, oiled tools in his little shed by starlight, and as he biked away he turned the brim of his golf cap like a baseball catcher. A light mist developed out over the sea, and the lighthouse began its sweep, its beam touching the tops of the trees and the roof caps of the clubhouse. The air was perfectly still. The course, under the warning beam, was safe in darkness. And it was quiet at Seaview Links, there on the edge of America.